CONVERS

BOOK TWO OF SUBVERSION TRILOGY

RUHI PARIKH

This is for those who fear change and what terrors it might bring.
Just remember to hold on tight and never let go.
Even if life gets tough.

CON·VER·SION

the process of converting something from one thing to another

1

BEGINNING

BLAIRE

THE SUN IS BLINDING me.

I squint, shielding my eyes from the overwhelmingly bright rays. It's quite amusing that the heat index skyrockets right when I lounge by the tall beds of grass that protect the insides of the city from the uproarious river.

The icy waters around my feet finally diffuse the overbearing heat, sending waves of relief through me. From where I sit, I can see the lands ahead—barren yet endearing. They possess an ambiguous nature from this distance, smothered in the pervasive fog, and my curiosity reaches out like a bird's wing, beckoning toward the unknown.

"Decide to go out for a tanning session?"

I smile when I hear Vienna Powers's voice. I turn around, noticing all sixty-nine inches, spiteful agility, and gracious demeanor she holds. Seven months I have known this woman—this vivacious and selectively irreverent woman—and every moment with her has been priceless.

"I sure did." I beam, gesturing for Vi to take a seat beside me, which she does. Her recently cut and dyed dark hair curls around the back of her neck, with a small number of strands also dyed a bright red color. That's her only significant change, though; her tattooed and pierced body is still the same. It kind of reminds me of the haircut I had gotten weeks ago—which was nothing but a well-needed trim. Now, it almost touches my shoulders, daring to inch past them.

"Did you just meet the person you're taking care of today?" I ask her.

"Yeah," Vi says. "It's this old man named Samuel. He told me his wife passed away from the heat here. It was sad, the way he talked about her. He also told me he didn't want to live anymore. Said that there was no point, since the love of his life is gone."

"That's terrible," I mumble.

"I guess so."

I frown at her. "Are you not the slightest bit worried for him?"

"I *am* worried," she emphasizes. "But not too worried because he will live. He's not the only one that's lost someone."

"I understand that, but the least you can do is be somewhat sympathetic toward him."

"What's sympathy gonna do?" She cocks her head at me. "Believe it or not, people don't wanna hear empty promises anymore. They wanna hear the cold, hard truth. That's just how our world has evolved."

"Well, I can't bring myself to do that. God, how can *you* even do that? How can you detach your emotions from society so easily?" I sulk where I sit, craning my neck toward her. "I care about people way too much to tell them the brutal truth. Detroit, as amazing as it may be, is nearing an environmental collapse. The temperatures here are *unbearable*, Vi. There's no way this place was this hot several years ago."

"It wasn't," Vi says. "We may not know the reason why, but I do know it's because of our ancestors and the dumb mistakes they've made. It's sad, but it's true. And people must be informed of it.

"And I don't know how I do it," she continues. "All I know is we are just tiny humans roaming on a huge earth that's floating in a dark and empty universe, and nothing really matters. That's all."

I purse my lips, letting her words echo in my mind.

As the waters rush in and out between my toes, the hot beating sun radiates on my face, and I leer my eyes away, scrunching my eyebrows together. I am immediately reminded of how I went to the park the other day with Em, and Nico would've come too, but he had to go meet up with Jeremiah and Layla for an "adult" conversation. I know it had to do with the heat wave and the water drought that may or may not happen, but I don't see why he doesn't include me, Vi, Mal, or even Jax, since we all are adults too.

My throat swells up at the mere thought of Jax. The last time we talked was a couple of days ago, when Layla told us to keep watch on a couple of refugees. It's as if a block remains between us, and we both are struggling to remove it, but just looking at the other person puts us in a weird place. I can barely look at Jax without turning bright red, and that's only at the *thought* of us kissing when we left D.C. seven months ago.

Is it bad to want to kiss him again? Because it's all I can think about.

I decide to brush away all distracting thoughts as I realize that it may be my time to go to the refuge. And as I glance over at my electronic watch, 5:50 p.m. stares back at me. I jump to my feet, spitting at Vi, "Shit! I need to go before Layla yells at me. My shift starts at six."

"You're right." She jumps up to her feet. "I'll come with you. Something tells me I need to pay Samuel a visit."

3

And with that said, we turn around, our eyes immediately glued upon the overwhelming beauty known as Detroit.

Skyscrapers point to the sky like upright and jagged needles. Vehicles travel to and fro, ranging in all shapes and sizes. And—overall—the entire city is buzzing with energy. Whenever I find myself drowning in the haunting memories of D.C., I remind myself that I am in a different and much better city. Even as we fight for a place here amongst the unrelenting heat, no attack from any unwanted members has happened here since the War. Everyone is equal—no person is better than the other.

Charlotte Levine may be an exception, though. She is the leader of this beautiful city, yet she is nothing like Tobias Remington. And because of her, noteworthy festivals are held at every change of the season, since she believes they mark a new beginning. One such festival is the Summer Solstice Festival, which occurs tomorrow. Every single citizen of Detroit will gather at the beautiful bank near the waters surrounding it—where Vi and I sat—and celebrate the beginning of summer. My first summer here.

Vi nudges my shoulder. "You ready?"

I nod, feeling the sun beat at my neck. "Yeah. I am."

Something wanders into my mind. It's the flashback of when my mother was mentally preparing me to go to the Inauguration in D.C., when I was unwilling to leave my home. I wanted nothing to do with the Rich. I'm glad they're gone. I'm glad their decaying bodies are buried underneath the withered ruins of D.C., and I'm glad the Poor escaped to Detroit.

But what I can't seem to swallow is that there are no Rich and Poor anymore. We are all united now. We are deemed as worthy individuals now. We can carve our own paths now.

And we can develop our well-awaited beginnings now.

2

HATRED

JAX

I CRUMPLE UP THE paper in my hand when I see an overly affectionate family to my right. It's a little boy and his parents, stuffing his face with thousands of kisses. He squeals under their arms and giggles uproariously, his cheeks turning bright red. His parents continue to drown him in affection, carrying him in their arms and repeating how much they love him. While this boy has loving and caring parents, all mine have ever brought me was pain, pain, and even more pain.

Sometimes, all I want to do is punch a wall until my knuckles bleed, scream until my lungs ache, and then slide down that same wall, drowning my sorrows away by either booze or my tears. Maybe even both.

The notorious Tobias Remington may have been a caring father, husband, and president on the outside, but he was only a narcissistic asshole on the inside. In all honesty, he ruined it all —not just for this country . . . but for me, too.

Now that I think about it, I never really knew what love felt like either. Shit, ten-year-old me *thought* love was going to rallies with my father as he praised himself, brainwashing his fellow fans of how *special* he is and what *greatness* he'll bring to this broken country and how we *need* someone to lift our spirits from the depths of hell.

I'm lit with envy. If only my parents were normal, loving, and didn't care about their reputation.

Then I wouldn't have had to kill my father and leave my dying mother behind in the rubbles of D.C.

"Sir? Are you okay?"

I am snapped out of my thoughts, heat creeping up my neck. "What?"

The man in front of me chuckles, numerous wrinkles appearing on his face. "There's a line forming behind you, so I would appreciate it if you'd decide what you want already."

"Want *what?*" I mumble, but before the man can answer my supposed stupid question, I realize that the paper is a bill I am holding in my hand—

In order to buy something from the markets.

I frown, turning around and seeing that there *are* many people behind me. And their expressions indicate that they are not too pleased with my slow ass. *How did I forget that I was in line to buy something from the markets? What the hell is wrong with me?*

Plastering an embarrassed smile on my face, I say, "I'm so sorry, uh"—I take a quick glance at the man's name tag—"Winston. My apologies." I lean in closer to him, suddenly remembering *just* what I came to buy. "Can I have item number 3A?"

Winston's tired eyes rake over the designated item. He looks at me in surprise, his face flushing red. And I don't even think it's because of the stupendously hot weather outside.

"Are you sure, sir? This item is quite expensive. Once you buy it, you cannot return it."

"Oh, yes. I know." I smile. "I want it more than anything."

He hesitates, yet the notion of someone buying quite an

expensive item from him overtakes all. Winston eventually nods. He tells me the price, to which I immediately wince to myself. It's going to be worth it, though.

Because this is for her.

I hand him the money as he hands me the item wrapped in delicate material and placed into a small brown bag. The object feels light underneath my palm, allowing the overwhelming feeling of gratitude to outrank it. It's going to be worth it, it's going to be worth it, it's going to be—

"Jax? What are you doing here?"

As I am just starting to walk away from the stall, I see Mallory standing in front of me, her blue eyes wide. Blonde bangs fall barely over her eyebrows, unruly and messy. I'm still getting used to this change, as she cut her legendary long hair only yesterday, which I honestly saw coming because she was complaining about how her hair was bothering her for a while.

I have to physically crane my neck down to make eye contact with her. Sometimes, I'd joke with Mallory on how "vertically challenged" she is, which results in a funny death glare from her. But then I remember how Mallory slapped me quite vigorously and honestly bruised my ego when I was kidnapped by the Subversives, so I always get my shit together in the end and hope history doesn't repeat itself.

"Hey, Mallory," I say, beginning to walk with her. "I just went and bought something from the markets. There's a huge sale going on because of the Summer Solstice Festival tomorrow, so I decided to make good use of the opportunity."

"Oh, really?" she asks. "I was wondering where you were, actually."

"Why?"

"Uh . . . you have things to do at the refuge? The little girl you're helping recover after she lost her parents in the fire?"

"Oh, shit!" I curse, clutching the item tighter. "What time is it?"

7

Mallory takes a quick glance at her electronic watch—the same one we were all assigned to by Layla. "Well, luckily for you, we have a good ten minutes before you're supposed to clock in. If it weren't for me, then you would've just been wandering around like a headless deer."

"Thanks." I grin. "You're a lifesaver, Mallory."

"Why, thank you, Jax. That is exactly what I expect to hear from you."

I let out a snort. Mallory laughs afterwards.

As we stroll through the beating heart of Detroit—otherwise known as the markets and the transportation facilities—I ironically find the weight my soul has been lugging around for twenty-one years gradually increasing. It was a long and extensive battle that we had to deal with in D.C., yet still I get awful nightmares—especially about my father. Just when I thought I was rid of him, he still lingers behind me, and every act and notion of his is somehow linked to me.

But I guess I can't get fully rid of him. Because his blood is still on my hands.

And I am going to have to deal with that for the rest of my life.

"Okay, something is going on here, and if you don't spill, then this is not going to be a very easy conversation for you."

I snap out of my thoughts once again. Embarrassment clings to my back as Mallory impatiently arches her eyebrow at me.

"Okay." I take a deep breath, clenching my jaw. "I've just been really . . . tense lately."

Her pace slows, and at the same speed, a concerned look creeps onto her face. "Why is that?"

"I don't know." I shrug, pushing my hands into the pockets of my cargo shorts. "I think it's because I'm not really over my father's death yet. Even though it's been seven months. And *I* killed him."

Mallory gestures toward the train station, and we make our

way over there. As we do, she says, "That's perfectly normal to feel, Jax. And just because you were the reason for his death doesn't mean that you're not allowed to feel even slightly disturbed about it. Besides, you did something that was *well-needed*. Tobias was bound to die either way. You were just the one that was destined to get the job done." She looks over at me while we begin to board the train, leaving for the outskirts of Detroit. "We escaped D.C. because of *you*."

I scoff, feeling oddly warm. "That's not true."

"It *is*," she emphasizes, clearly not in the mood for a back-and-forth argument with me. "Your bravery and passion got the job done for *us*. You were courageous enough to kill your father. While I do not glorify murder, I feel as if in this situation it was necessary, and that's all that matters."

We board the train onto a cart overwhelmed with passengers. "You're right, Mallory. I just need to take life one step at a time."

"Exactly." She beams, gesturing to the view outside. "And look at where we are now—*Detroit*. This is the place to be. So let's enjoy our time here. And let's especially enjoy the Summer Solstice Festival tomorrow."

"Yes," I murmur, my insides lifting with joy. "You're right. Thank you."

"Ah, it's no problem. What are friends for?" Mallory nudges my shoulder. The grin on my face is suddenly wiped away as her face contorts into a humorous expression. "But anyway, I want to talk to you about your awkward encounter with Blaire the other day."

I frown at her, hoping my reddened cheeks are not too obvious. "What do you mean by that? It's not awkward between us."

"Yes, it *is*," she emphasizes. "It's been like this between you guys ever since we left D.C."

Because whenever I look into her green eyes, I feel the burning desire to kiss her again. "Nothing is awkward between us," I manage to say. "We're just friends, like we always have been."

"You need to ask her out," Mallory blurts out. I swivel my head, suddenly speechless. *There's no way she just said that.* She scoffs, pushing me a bit too harshly. "Gosh, you men are so stupid. You do know that she likes you, right?"

My mouth dries. "Did she tell you that?"

"No, but it's pretty obvious, and it's pretty obvious that you do too." She looks at me pointedly. "So what are you waiting for?"

I shake my head. "I don't know, Mallory. I'll figure it out."

She sighs and turns to the window, holding onto the railing above us. "You better."

The edge to her tone makes me realize that I *need* to do something about me and Blaire. I mean, ever since our first kiss when leaving D.C.—which I think about *every single day*—we *have* been awkward. Sure, we have conversations here and there and laugh a bit too, but there's this aching and yearning between us that we just don't know what to do about. So we just prance past it and act like everything's completely normal between us. As if that kiss was just a kiss, and nothing will happen beyond that.

But I don't want that anymore. To be honest, I *never* wanted that. I just went along with it because I thought that's what she genuinely wanted.

Not one day goes by where I don't think about her. Her soft hands that I dream to hold onto every single day. Her luscious short hair that I dream of raking my fingers through every single day. Her calming voice that I can listen to every single day. Her gracious smile that makes me melt into a puddle every single day. And her radiating green eyes that makes my heart always skip a beat—

Every single day.

I don't know how to tell her my feelings, though. I guess that's why I bought *this*.

As the train begins to move, accelerating at every second, I notice the beautiful atmosphere beyond the windows. The sky is wisped with a gradient of a blood red to a gleaming orange. The sunrays dance and bounce off the buildings, casting entrancing shadows on the formations. And the birds in the distance hum their daily melodies, flapping their wings as they soar into the unknown.

The unknown.

Past the aquatic border around Detroit is a lone piece of land that we still have yet to roam. It's drenched in fog, hovering over the place ominously. I've always wondered what was there, beyond the Detroitian borders. I know in the opposite direction is the rest of Michigan—completely deserted—leading into the Canadian borders. But this piece of land looks open for all, since nothing or no one is present there. And I am automatically intrigued.

The train is filled to the brim, people of all shapes and sizes huddling around us. They look at us in intrigue, which is not surprising because the reputation of us being Subversives, or the people that took down D.C., is still reigning. We aren't overwhelmingly popular, that's for sure; but we are generally well-known. And people applaud us for having the bravery to stand up to a dangerous individual such as my father. Honestly, I was worried that people wouldn't accept me into Detroit, even though they are known for being accepting of all people. And while people were seemingly reluctant to include me in their society, the Subversives vouched for me, saying that what I did was needed. It took a while, but I was finally accepted. I was finally able to roam the streets without glances and murmurs here and there. I was finally *normal.* But there is only one thing I felt then and even now.

I feel *proud* of myself.

Because I am finally independent. While my father's ghost

may haunt me forever, I know, at least physically, that I am free. That I am not a Remington anymore; I am just Jax. The man that I was destined to be.

And as the blurring trees and buildings pass by, almost like streaks of paint on a canvas, I take a relaxing breath in as the sprawling building known as the refuge appears majestically. With large tan walls adorning off-white windows, the magnificent modern structure makes my jaw unhinge.

And filled with hundreds of people that need *our* help. The former Subversives' help.

I clutch the prestigious object in my hand even tighter, but not too tight, and I suddenly feel a rush of excitement that travels up and down my bones. My past doesn't define me anymore. Instead, my future choices do, and I am determined to make the right ones.

Especially with her.

3

WELFARE

BLAIRE

VI AND I ENTER the bustling and rambunctious building where hundreds of people walk around, involved with their own assignments. However, this was nothing compared to when we first arrived at the refuge months ago, alongside many Poor people in great need. Everyone, young and old, boasted bruises and scars from the battle in D.C. We, as in the Subversives and the five hundred volunteers from Detroit, were required to make sure no one died from those injuries as *soon* as we arrived.

About four hundred died.

It was a despondent time, and I still think of those horrific days, when we would travel out into rural Detroit and bury those bodies, our souls and hearts in pain. They were so close to living better lives, not undergoing the same atrocities as a Poor person would in D.C., but due to there not being more of us than them, we were unfortunately unable to take care of everyone.

Now, approximately six hundred Poor people remain in this

city, in contrast to the abundant thousand that used to be there. And that is why Layla pledges to make sure that never happens again, that we recruit as many volunteers as possible and ensure every sick and injured person is tended to. This is not just a refuge anymore; it's a hospital. It's not just meant to take care of the Poor escapees anymore; it is for *everyone.*

I scan my surroundings, feeling the cool AC rush around me. Where we stand now is the reception desk, where the receptionist sits, preparing to call in Layla when she sees us. People can recognize a Subversive a mile away, since we are sort of *known* here. The citizens of Detroit claim that if it weren't for us, then they would've continued to feel isolated, since they believed it was the only city remaining in America—just like D.C. They learned afterwards that there *are* other cities around, which the Detroitian military plans to explore in a couple of months, or at least when they resolve the possible water shortage.

Because our number one goal right now is to heal.

Moments later, Layla comes into the front wing of the refuge, where we currently stand. Her eyes lighten up when she sees us, her dark and voluminous curly hair bouncing up and down as she runs to us. "Blaire! Vi! So glad to see you guys here." She rushes to us and gives us a group hug.

I smile into her shoulder as I say, "Just doing our job, ma'am."

"Blaire, we established this months ago." Layla glares at me as she releases us. "Call me *Layla*, not *ma'am*. Makes it seem like I'm your headmaster or something."

"No problem . . ." I smirk. "Ma'am."

"Blaire!" Layla hisses playfully. We all start laughing.

Once our laughter dies down, Layla's expression quickly sobers as she grabs us by the shoulders and leads us into the corner of the entrance, all of us huddled into a tight circle. My heart plunges to the bottom of my stomach when I see her saddened features.

14

"There have been a lot of patients lately," Layla whispers, looking up at us.

"Why is that?" My hands begin to shake, thinking of the daunting times in December and the many dead bodies increasing every ruthless second.

"I don't know. I think it's the heat and the tightening of the water supply. Word is that the Detroitian military is going to reform and go on a search for more water because if this continues . . . God, I don't want to think about it." Layla shakes her head.

"It's gonna be okay," Vi says. "I'm pretty sure they'll figure it out. Right now, our main objective is to save as many people as we can."

"Yes, you're right," Layla says, her voice trembling. "The actual reason I called you guys over is because I have assigned you guys to different patients. They are going to be a bit difficult to handle, so after reviewing their profiles, confirm with me if this is what you want."

"What about Samuel?" Vi asks.

"Don't worry, I'm with him. I just need you guys to take care of the others to the best of your abilities."

"All right, Layla." I smile. "We won't let you down."

"Wonderful." She beams, crossing her arms over her orange shirt that compliments her dark skin perfectly. "I'm going to go spend some time with Jeremiah and Tamia, since I've been doing nothing but work for the past few hours."

"No worries, Layla, go ahead." I grin.

As Layla frantically waves us goodbye, Vi shouts, "Tell your husband that I said hi, since he's apparently way too busy with you!" Once she disappears down one of the many hallways, after blushing profusely, I let out a snort as Vi claps my back. "Let's go take care of some people, eh?"

As we start to go pick up their profiles from the reception

desk, I feel my throat drying as I see two familiar figures step into the building.

First is the beautiful and kind-hearted Mallory Reaves, shimmering with the same energy as a Greek goddess and a royal figure. She walks in so majestically, almost as if the ground were her servants and she was a glistening block of gold —but in the most down-to-earth way possible. And her petite frame looks even more miniscule beside Jax, who towers over her.

Jax.

His gray eyes glaze over the refuge, smiling as dimples crease the skin around his mouth. His tan skin is glistening with sweat, taut and formed muscles bathed in glory and masculinity; his scar has faded now, but it still clings to him. His dark hair is gloriously disheveled, gloriously beautiful. His tight black tank top and his cargo shorts stick to all the right parts of his body, his hard and strong body. And his quiet, yet lethal presence continues to poison anyone in a mere five-foot radius.

Just like he's poisoned me with his alluring presence.

I feel my heart stop at the exact moment his eyes meet mine. They soften temporarily before lighting up with energy. My feet are glued to the ground, and I scream to myself that I should move, that I shouldn't stand here, breathless, like an idiot.

But, to my surprise, he comes to me instead.

The way he walks, the way he smiles like a king, and the way that one strand of hair falls onto his eyes is enough to make my limbs weaken. I don't know what spell he's put on me lately. I really don't know.

He opens his mouth to speak, standing dangerously close to me. "Hey, Blaire." *I'm still not used to him saying my name.* "I didn't realize we had the same shift today."

"Uh, me neither," I murmur, failing to look him in the eyes because whenever I do, troubling thoughts begin to lurk into my mind.

He chuckles. "Are you excited for the Festival tomorrow?"

After much debate with myself, I lock eyes with him. "Of course I am. Are you?"

"Absolutely." He grins.

Nothing is said for a while. Instead, our eyes communicate, pupils dilating and opening to all the thoughts and emotions we feel for each other . . . almost like opening a book to reveal the wondrous story. Jax knows my story, and I know his. Sometimes, our eyes say so much more than our words. And beneath the beautiful pits of his pupils, I see a man who's become more brazen, witty, and determined—not the indecisive, unwilling, and brash Jax I knew before. He's on our side now, and I know he's especially on *my* side too.

Oh, the look in his eyes is really not appeasing my extreme desire for him.

"Um, Mal? You want to come check this plant out with me?"

Mal jumps at the opportunity a bit too enthusiastically, as I notice from the corner of my eye. "Yes, of course, Vi!"

And they leave.

Jax and I suddenly break from our trance, as he lets out a low chuckle. "I think we should get going. I need to go check up on the girl I'm assigned to."

"Yeah, me too," I say, almost too breathlessly.

He grins brilliantly, says bye to me, and treads over to the end of the hallway where the elevators are.

Suddenly, something dawns upon me.

I have parents who love each other with every breath they take, even after years of marriage. I've known Jeremiah for months, and I've observed the way his eyes light up and his chest rises whenever Layla is in the vicinity. I may not be aware of desire personally, but I know how to recognize it. And amongst all our cumbersome and wary moments where I've had no choice but to look deep into Jax's serene silver eyes . . . I've realized one thing.

I have feelings for him.

———

The man I am taking care of is Henry Lee, an eighty-year-old patient who just suffered a heat stroke. His entire family, including his grandkids, are nowhere to be found, and he's been roaming the rural side of Detroit—alone—desperate to find his family. When the refugee seekers found Henry convulsing on the side of the road, they quickly brought him over just this afternoon and Layla sought for me to take care of him.

And hell, I will take care of him.

His face is like a cracked vase due to ancient scars and bruises that tell heartbreaking stories of their own. His skin's pallid and drained, and his almost soulless blue eyes are wavering, eyelids closing periodically. I press my hand into the nook of his chest, desperate to feel a heartbeat. When I hear a faint and dying beat, panic begins to filter through me. It hangs on for dear life, his body willing to fight for him, but Henry is slowly losing his grip.

"Hey, you're going to be okay," I whisper. "Hang on tight for me, Mr. Lee. We are going to take great care of you."

The hospital bed he is set on has him attached to the IV, so when I go over to the computer monitor to check his vitals, I see him almost flatlining. I was informed in the profile too that he recovered miraculously after his stroke and now he is just recovering in bed and needs someone to take care of him. I don't know how to save people medically, though. I only know how to speak to and soothe others. That's all.

My little sister, to my surprise, yanks the door open and rushes in, basically pushing me to the side. "I got this, B," she murmurs.

As an older sister, I would disapprove of Em's sudden confidence to take care of an old man recovering from a stroke, but the way her eyes dart back and forth as she effortlessly picks up tools around the room makes me realize that maybe I should just sit back and relax on this one. Ever since we settled in Detroit, she has grown an interest in taking care of people and all things medical, so she began to sneak into hospital rooms to help doctors and nurses to the best of her ability. Soon enough, she became slightly knowledgeable in the field and is now a part-time volunteer. Honestly, I'm not surprised by her interest in taking care of people; she's been like this ever since she was a toddler, always willing to get the first-aid kit out whenever I got a paper-cut or Nico got a random cut or bruise.

She mutters unknown medical terminology to herself and frantically rushes over to me, saying, "Get some nurses for me and tell them we need a bunch of ice and cold water. Something tells me this is not going to be a one-man job."

I nod, running toward the door. But before I can twist the door handle open, I take a quick look toward Em, who looks deep in thought, murmuring soothing words to him.

"I'm proud of you, Em." I grin.

She looks up at me for a quick moment, smiles to herself, and whispers, "Thanks, B. I love you."

Beneath her deep and gracious brown eyes, I see a girl who is slowly but surely maturing. I remember in D.C. she was struggling with English—and not just English—but complicated human emotions as well. Her brain just wasn't at the same level as a normal twelve-year-old, and it was highly concerning. My parents and I worried about that daily.

But ever since we moved to Detroit, she has grown quite considerably—physically and mentally. Her face is forming into her legitimate adult shape, her features sharpening and her eyes less naïve. She stands more firmly now, rather than her normal cowering and timid shape. And not just that, but she's begun to understand the complexities of our situation now and lends out a helpful hand whenever she can. It has made me realize just how much our work paid off for guiding Em through our complicated world and understanding it through our eyes too. And, with her being a teenager now, I can also talk to her about my boy problems.

Which I honestly regret because she desperately wants Jax and I to date.

Once I escape the room, I enter the general floor, where the neediest of patients are placed. Nurses and doctors are running to and fro identical doors, speeding past others and mumbling incoherent words to each other. I am just a volunteer here—I have no clue what they're saying.

I tap on a passing-by nurse's shoulder. "Excuse me? There's a patient who is suffering from Alzheimer's in there that needs an entire team's help. My little sister Emilia is taking care of him right now."

The nurse's eyebrows knit together, her expression suddenly very serious, and she says to me, "Thanks for letting me know. I'll be bringing a team very shortly."

I nod thankfully as I let her go through the door. Then, I take a deep breath and oversee my entire surroundings.

The large floor is drowning with people, either dying or helping. I've grown used to these surroundings, though, because I spend most of my time here. It's only when darkness hits that I go home near the outskirts of Detroit and spend well-needed time with my family and especially my brother—I still haven't gotten used to him being alive.

Sometimes Nico visits here, willing to help with the refuge's operations, but most of the time he works on larger projects with Jeremiah to improve Detroit, and once they do, they present those ideas to Charlotte Levine. Tomorrow we will meet her at summer's commencement, and we will fully involve ourselves in the vivacious and warming community that we have learned to conform to. And we will enjoy as much time as we can here, no matter how many problems arise, because we have been through it all.

Nothing can be as disruptive and traumatizing as the time we spent in D.C., which means anything ahead of us is either going to be child's play or an unforeseen calamity.

And I certainly hope it's the former.

4

REVERE

JAX

I WALK THROUGH THE spacious field, noticing the lovely line of flowers welcoming me into the outdoor Festival. People surround me, dressed in colorful clothing and engaged in great conversations. Since I'm so used to living in a cold and isolated mansion with emotionally detached parents who couldn't give two shits about me, I'm still getting acquainted with the lively atmosphere around me. Now there are many supportive people that look past my unfortunate family and are willing to accept me as a changed man.

The marking of each seasonal festival, as stated by Charlotte Levine, is the beginning of each chapter in the year. The Summer Solstice Festival, on June twenty-first, celebrates the great nourishment we get from the sun, which arises from the frozen depths in the winter and allows its rays to replenish the parched Earth. So today, we will be feasting on delicious food, dancing wildly, and ending our festival with an enlightening speech from Charlotte and Renata Levine, her daughter.

I rock back and forth on my heels, pushing my hands into

the pockets of my dress pants. I am so unbelievably scared to approach anyone, only because I've been feared and hated for so long. No one dared to approach me during the D.C. days because they *knew* I was associated with my father—especially the Poor. I hated being in a position like that.

Sometimes, I wonder, what took me so long to kill him?

I should've just snatched the knife from his hands as he tried to gouge me, before he had a chance to scar me—I should've just gutted him. I should never have let him carve that line into my face. It's slowly fading, but every time I see myself in the mirror, anger boils my blood, and I'm overcome with the desire to scratch it away.

I want to scratch my past away.

The wind blows as I take a deep breath, admiring the river stretching out ahead of us, since the Festival takes place on the banks of the Detroit river. I need to forget about my past. I *want* to forget it all.

When I see everyone huddled around the center of the Festival, I slowly smile. I make my way past the large crowds, whilst astounded by the beautiful modern architecture and design, and meet everyone.

First, I meet Jeremiah and his family. Jeremiah is someone I will forever be intimidated by, which is something I will never admit aloud. He is formed of nothing but steel, his body rigid with muscles. If he were a stranger to me, then I would fear him for my entire life. But his looks are completely misleading of his personality, since he is nothing but kind.

I've grown quite close to him because we were the only men in the Subversives—excluding the traitor Zachary Everett—and sometimes, I join him and Nico at the outskirts of Detroit to discuss the large projects they're working on, regarding improving the city. The Detroitian government has been working hand-in-hand with the refuge, so we gather with them sometimes to discuss ways to relieve the drought and the heatwave. This place is developing at every second, so major changes still must be implemented: such as the military, which hasn't been used or needed in a very long time. The location of the military is secret, what they do or did is secret, and who can be recruited is an absolute secret too.

I personally hope they won't have to be needed any time soon.

Next, I greet Layla and Tamia. Layla is an outspoken woman, in great contrast to her husband who is more to himself, and I guess her personality is just what we need as for the leader of the refuge. When we all came to Detroit, she was incredibly helpful in guiding us to adjust to the strange atmosphere. Honestly, it is all because of her and Nicolas that we are here.

When we all gather, I see Mallory, Vi, Nicolas, and Blaire approach us. They all look rather elegant and poised in their Festival attire, but who I am interested in looking at the most is Blaire, extremely ravishing in her dark green dress that perfectly accentuates her eyes. It's just the way she walks, leaving behind everlasting remnants of gracefulness, and the way her eyes light up when she sees us all that makes my knees weaken. Never has a woman ever occupied my mind this much.

I adjust my tie, suddenly conscious of my looks.

As we make our way to each other, my eyes continue to glaze across Blaire, who wrings her hands together as she makes her way between Vi and Nicolas. Her short dark hair is wrapped into a low bun, some strands escaping and framing her truly beautiful face. I want to spend my time studying her, as if she's art, and explore the intricacies of the curves of her smile and her body. I want to explore it all.

I let out a low breath, overwhelmed at the mere thought of her. I need to control myself. God, I don't even know how she even feels after our kiss in D.C. We haven't talked about our feelings much since then because we were just so *busy* with the refuge and adjusting to Detroit and meetings and moving on from the horrors of D.C. itself and—

We just haven't had time to escape the madness.

Once we meet up with everyone, we spend the remainder of the night dancing along to the music, eating quite substantially, and laughing until our stomachs ache. However, the entire time I am constantly thinking of ways to approach her. I've never struggled with something like this before. Why and how is she so capable of making me feel like this?

I feel someone nudge my shoulder. "All right in there?"

I jump back to reality and look to where I felt the nudging beside me. *Mallory.*

"Yep, I'm doing all right." I clear my throat, adamant to compose myself.

"Uh-huh." Mallory, unfortunately, is thousands of steps ahead of me and looks at Blaire for a split second. She leans into me and whispers, "You know, now is the time."

"For what?"

"For, you know . . ." She makes an incoherent sound.

"What?"

"Oh my God," she mutters underneath her breath and pulls on my arm in a rather cruel way. I wince as she growls into my ear, "Ask her out, you *idiot.*"

I pull away from her, my heart thumping. "Right now?"

"Not exactly right now. Just do it whenever you guys are alone. I'll make sure you are."

"Oh." My muscles stiffen. "You really think I should do this?"

"Uh, yes." Her eyebrows raise. "You know I'm not going to let you back down from this opportunity, right? It's either now or never."

When Mallory's words seep into my mind, I realize that she's right. I mean, I don't think I can handle much more of staring at Blaire helplessly. I need to make my move. I need to make my intentions known.

That I don't want our situation to be just a kiss many months ago. I want it to be *much* more.

"Okay, you're right," I say, my insides both relieving and tightening. "I'm going to do this."

"Good." She smiles. "I'm going to bring everyone to the bar so you can be alone with her. Got it?"

"Okay." I nod. "Got it."

Mallory, still smiling, pats my shoulder and as she's about to call the others over the bar, I grab her shoulder and whisper to her, "Wait, Mallory?"

She looks up at me, startled. "Yes, Jax?"

"Why . . . why are you doing this for me?"

Mallory sighs, her eyes softening. Beneath those eyes, I see the woman I've known since forever. The woman I went to in my darkest of times. The woman I was reunited with, after years of searching for her. *My childhood best friend.*

"Because," she starts off, "I can tell you genuinely like her, and I don't want you to throw away your only shot at happiness. You deserve to be happy."

When she tells me this, I grin.

She smiles too, patting my shoulder and turning around to say to the others:

"Hey, Vi and Nicolas! Let's go to the bar!"

Mallory turns to Blaire, who still stands in between them, and says to her, "You don't mind giving Jax some company, do you?"

She is clearly speechless, and moments later, she stammers, "No. I don't mind."

Pushing her blonde hair to the side, Mallory grins and weaves her way past Blaire, once she thanks her, while Vi and Nicolas follow her. She turns around for a split second, mouths *you got this* to me, and turns back around while they walk over to the bar.

Leaving me alone with Blaire.

My feet are molded to the ground, becoming one with the roots that reach out like claws. I don't know how to move, I don't know how to speak, and frankly, I don't know how to breathe either.

How can I, when I am faced with the woman I can't stop thinking about?

Her dark green eyes rake over me, and her posture straightens, feeling the fabric of her dress reluctantly with her shaking hands. "Hey, Jax. Happy Summer Solstice to you."

Why is my throat swelling up suddenly? "You too, Blaire."

I was so confident with women before. They all came to me and begged for my attention, so all I had to do was flirt with them in order to receive even more of their undying attention. It was a piece of cake back then, mainly because I wanted nothing to do with them. I just liked the attention to a certain extent. It sort of made up for the very little I received in my own house.

But with Blaire in front of me? It's as if all previous knowledge of English has left my mind. How is she so capable of squeezing out all the oxygen in my system and leaving me panting for air, enamored in her presence?

Suddenly, I hear a change of music occurring in the background. Most people on the outside floor exclaim and partner up with their loved one, slow dancing to the low and romantic music resonating through the calm air.

I look at the DJ by the far corner of the stage. *Thank you, DJ, for saving my ass.*

Before what I'm doing can even register in my mind, I thrust my hand out to Blaire, feeling sweat beads dance on my forehead. *No, now is not the time to sweat profusely like a goddamn idiot. Keep it together, Jax!*

"Come have a dance with me," I say, adamant to keep my voice poised and leveled.

Moments later, I see her eyes widen slightly, her mouth

opening and closing. I start to think she's going to reject me, but when I notice her cheeks flush red and her eyes gently fall to the ground, I feel a smile tickling at my lips. Is she . . . nervous?

"Sure," she murmurs, looking at my hand. I can tell she's also frustrated with her behavior, how she thins her lips and refuses to make eye contact with me.

All air leaves my lungs when she grabs my hand, attaching our palms together. Her fingers curl at the top of my knuckles, barely able to caress them all because of our varying hand sizes. I think it's adorable, really, how her hand is engulfed in mine. But, nevertheless, it feels comforting and just *right* that our hands are connected, almost like two ends of a bridge that were meant to be connected. Almost as if they were custom-made for each other.

Her grip on my hand tightens as I lead her onto the dance floor, veering past the swaying and grinning couples. Decorations anchored above us adorn the Festival floor, caked in tens and thousands of people. The entire Detroit population has gathered here this lovely evening, so of course the entire outdoor grounds will be drenched in people. *Way* too many people.

Once we've planted ourselves by the middle of the stage, I turn around to her, flashing her a bright and brazen smile. Her cheeks tinge a bright red color again while she lowers her eyes to her feet.

But I'm not going to allow that for the rest of the night.

I don't know what strange substance enters my body and defuses all my nerves, but I find my hand leaving hers and gently landing on her chin, feeling her soft skin that grazes against the pad of my thumb. And then, I tilt her chin up, unwilling to let her hide her sight from me. She's never done that before in D.C. Hell, all she ever did back then was hate my guts and every fiber of my being. So why is she acting nice with me now? This is not the Blaire I know.

Look at me, I think to myself.

Immediately, her eyes snap up to me, and I am startled, *perplexed* as to how she heard me. She can't read my mind, right? I don't even think she'd want to. My thoughts run wild when she's in my presence.

The forest that is her eyes gaze into me, and at this moment, I truly study every movement of her pupils. When we kissed, I didn't focus too much on her expressions—I honestly just wanted to kiss her. But at this moment that seems to have come out of my dreams? I want to use up every minute and second and *millisecond* in this world just to look at her. Study her. *Be* with her.

Her dark green eyes—so obscure and so endearing—are seeping into my mind, and I just know that every time I go to sleep, I will have a vivid memory of her radiating eyes, how they glisten amongst the beating sun. They seem so animated, so *unreal*—I have to lean in closer just to make sure she's a human. No way a woman like her is human.

Surprisingly, one side of her lips curl up, spreading into an eventual smile. "So, what is the plan for tonight? Are we just going to keep on staring at each other like this?"

I can't help but smile. Yep, she's *definitely* a mind-reader.

"Didn't I say that to you once?"

"You did," she clarifies. "Remember when we first kidnapped you and I had to watch you in the underground room?"

"And we hated each other's actual guts?" I sigh. "Yeah. Good times."

"Definitely." She laughs.

Shit, please don't laugh. Otherwise, my knees are going to give in on me.

In all honesty, I don't even know how I'm talking to her right now. I've struggled tremendously in initiating a conversation with her over the course of these seven months because, well, first, it took forever to adjust to this new environment, second, we were all drowning in tasks involving the refuge, and lastly, I lost all previous knowledge of talking to a woman, especially Blaire. Obviously, the odds were not working out in my favor.

But right now, I have the perfect opportunity to achieve the one thing I've been meaning to ever since our lips combined on that one December evening. And I'm sure as hell not going to lose my grasp of it.

"Shall we begin?" I ask, grabbing ahold of her hand again. When she nods, I wrap my unoccupied hand around the curve of her waist, my fingers dancing around her exposed back. Her expression visibly wavers, once again quite wonderfully affected by my touch. And then, our fingers lace together, connected by our touching palms. I pull her close to me, our torsos grazing each other's.

I hold my breath just for this moment. Just so I can take it all in.

And for the next few minutes, we cascade against the hard floor, the sun bright and merry and the music soothing and calm. Our movements are synchronized, and thank God I am somewhat trained in classical dancing because, of course, all Rich people were required to know. Blaire catches onto my movements perfectly after stumbling around at first.

Everything around me seems to fade out, all other noises submerged in water, allowing just me and Blaire to have our moment for once—this one perfect moment. I've yearned for this ever since we stepped foot in Detroit.

But this is still not enough.

Once the mesmerizing music changes to an upbeat track, we stop simultaneously, her face so terrifyingly close to mine. I just want to kiss her right here and right now. Let everyone know that she is mine, not theirs.

I can't do that now, though. There are too many people around.

I need to initiate the plan *now*.

From the corner of my eye, I notice Mallory and everyone else gathered by the bar still, laughing and talking wildly. Miraculously, she looks in my direction, smirks, and mouths, *Go for it already!*

I fight off a smile. Just barely.

"Everything okay?"

Startled, I murmur, "Uh, yes. I'm okay."

She arches an eyebrow.

"Okay, uh. Maybe not so much." I curse to myself. "Shit, all right. Here goes nothing."

"What are you talking about?" Her arms limpen in my presence.

I clench my jaw. "I want to talk to you in private."

"About what?" *God, I almost forgot that she's an insistent questioner.*

"You'll find out shortly," I say. "We just have to talk about this in private."

Moments later, she replies, "Uh, okay? Sure, why not?" She looks hurriedly to her family and the others, all gathered at the bar. "They shouldn't know, right?"

I bite the inside of my cheek. "It's probably best if they don't."

"Okay, that's fine." She nods once. "Where are we going?"

"Well—" I frantically look around the expanse, but there are just too many people around. *C'mon, I need a private and somewhat romantic place!* Luckily, seconds later, my eyes land on a small deck by the clearing of the ocean, leading to the strange island adjacent to the banks of Detroit.

Perfect.

I look over at Blaire, my insides a rampaging maelstrom. "Let's go over there."

5

CONFESSIONS

BLAIRE

JAX AND I SIT by the bank, stretching our feet out against the grass, very close to each other. The sun has begun to redden and dip against the horizon, the entire sky an amalgam of a raging fire—hues of blood-red and a lurid tangerine prominent. I want to dive into the calming sky, live amongst the wispy clouds, and feel the cool rush of wind brush my cheeks.

The air is still, ceasing its movements so all I can hear is my heavy breathing.

Just a few feet away from us, the water rushes in and out of the bank, almost touching our toes. I've heard from many Detroitian residents that the water looks the most beautiful in the summer, when the winters aren't brutal and raging with ice. The seasons have definitely been more extreme too; I thought that the winters were inhumane in D.C., when in reality, they are incomparable to the ones in Detroit. My bones almost shattered when we first arrived here. The limited heaters and generators were barely doing us much justice, so we instead had to relish in the body heat of others.

Thankfully, the winter transformed into a beautiful and blossoming spring, which then formed into an unbearably hot summer. The temperatures must be hitting the nineties every day, if not edging near the hundreds. And summer *just* started today . . . I can't even imagine how August is going to be.

I jump back to reality, reminding myself that Jax is next to me—possibly the closest we have gotten ever since we arrived in Detroit many months ago. We haven't had time lately to discuss anything in private, especially with adjusting to our life here and meeting new people and forgetting about the clinging horrors of D.C. Obviously, there hasn't been much time to think about our personal lives.

But now is the time, isn't it?

Jax sighs, leaning back on the grass. "It's been a while since me and you were alone."

I speak moments later. "Yeah. It really has been."

I turn to him, my body still angled at the waters but my eyes now latched onto his calm expression. "So much has changed," he says. "*You* have changed, too."

"Really?" I ask, intrigued. "In what way?"

"Well, for starters, I've noticed you're not really angry anymore."

"Angry?"

"Yeah. Back in D.C. you were always upset, always up in your head about something. You're calmer now, though. Your head is in a much better place."

"I think you're right about that one," I murmur.

"Of course I am." He scoffs, sitting up and shoulder-to-shoulder to me now. "You probably hate to hear this, but I know you. I can read you like a book at this point."

"Oh, really?" I cock my head. "Then read me."

My heart stutters as his mesmerizing gray eyes, nothing but dark storm clouds, rake over my figure and land on my face, his jaw visibly hardening and his lips forming into a lopsided smile.

It takes every part of me to not blush furiously, which is quite impossible considering there's a man terrifyingly close to me, looking at me as if I was the most dazzling star in the entire sky.

"You don't have hatred buried inside of you anymore," he says. "I think it's because you are glad you left D.C. behind and you're reunited with your entire family. You open up to others more often because you couldn't care less about being closed off to the world, now that you accomplished your dreams. And speaking of your dreams . . . well, you really did accomplish them. I notice you're more relaxed—you're not frustrated easily and you just go with the flow. And"—he sighs—"you smile more often. You really do, I've noticed. And it's something you should do more often. You could probably solve all the problems in the world with that smile."

"Jax," I whisper, my entire body burning hot.

"It's true," he cuts me off, inching closer to me. "You don't realize it but I do. I've always realized it. That you're just . . . so amazing. And the fact that you don't realize you are amazing is what kills me. How can a woman like you not know that?"

My mouth is agape. My body melts into a puddle. I physically cannot breathe.

Without a word, Jax gets up to his feet and looks down at me, his features ambiguous. "I've been waiting for this moment for so long, Blaire."

I get up to my feet too, wordless as well.

He walks over to me, his hands pushed into his pockets and seeming to be rummaging around for something. My heart pounds almost uncontrollably.

"Look at me," he urges.

My eyes snap to him.

He's suddenly so close to me, our torsos only a finger-length away. Maybe more or less—I don't know. But it's enough space to touch him, just to make sure he is real. He certainly can't be with those flawless features and body of his.

"From the moment we left for Detroit," he says, "I couldn't stop thinking about you. Your presence always seemed to be around, as if our kiss never truly ended. No matter how much I tried to stop thinking about you, you still were *always* there. But I'm not complaining because . . . shit, can't you tell? I like you so much. I've been wracking my mind, trying to find ways to confess this to you, but this world is just so cruel, you know? Because now that I found someone who actually cares about me, this world is just doing whatever it takes to pull us apart.

"But I'm not letting that happen." He shakes his head. "Oh, hell, as if I would ever let that happen. Because you're just . . . a special woman. I've never met someone like you. You're so kind, genuine, and—no, wait, what am I saying? You're neither one of those things." Jax's fingers meticulously carve itself onto my wrist, running them over my open palm. "Instead, you're upfront. You're passionate. And you're *certainly* not kind. But I like that," his tone drops, deep and resounding. "I like that because it's *you*. And I like *you*."

Before I can react, he pushes his free hand into his pocket, his palm curling around something delicate. I try to look over at what he could possibly be holding, but he releases his hand from my palm and immediately brings it up to my chin, angling my face so all I can see is his face, and absolutely nothing else.

"Not yet," he says, his tone teasing.

I feel my cheeks tinge with a red hot feeling as his eyes never leave mine, weighing the unknown object in his hand in *such* a tantalizing way.

"Not only are you upfront, passionate, and *certainly* not kind, but you are strong, too. Shit, you're the strongest and most badass woman I know. So that's why I wanted to give this to you."

In the blink of an eye, he releases his hand from me and holds up, with both of his hands, a gleaming necklace.

I can't believe my eyes. I can't believe much, really.

A gorgeous olive-green stone hangs from a smooth leather cord, its facets glimmering against the blood-red sun. From the looks of it, it can easily fit on the pad of my thumb, almost like a baby cocooning on its sheltered bed. This particular stone seems to be a rare kind, especially considering how it twinkles against the overcoming night.

I bring both of my hands to my mouth in shock, at a loss for words.

Jax, still dangling it in his hands, moves his pointer finger in a rotational motion. "Turn around."

Wordlessly, I turn, tears forming in my eyes—but heat grows on my veins as I feel his soft fingers brushing against the skin of the back of my neck, his breath tickling my ear. I dare to hold my breath, feeling his cautious hands wrap the cord around my neck and attach the two ends in the back. The green stone lands just above the top of my dress, its coolness seeping into my bones.

It's beautiful.

He speaks, his hands tracing the curve of my shoulders. "This is a peridot birthstone necklace, and it symbolizes strength and it will prevent any harm coming to you. Something I don't want near you at all."

My fingers gently reach up to the green texture. "This is the August birthstone, right?"

Seconds pass. "Right."

I take a deep breath in. "Jax, you didn't have to—"

"I wanted to," he says, his voice obdurate. "I did this simply because I wanted to. And I know your birthday is a little less than two months away, but I couldn't wait anymore. I *can't* wait anymore."

My breaths are low and ragged, and I silently turn around, my hand still grasping the breathtaking peridot stone. The greatest gift I've ever received.

His eyes are fervent, looking down at me as his hand curls

around mine, reassuringly squeezing it. "I don't want to be in this gray area with you anymore, Blaire. I want to try this out. I promise I'll treat you right. I know I can be annoying, but I promise I'll try my best to not be so annoying—even though that's my entire personality. But hey?" He chuckles nervously. "I would do anything for you."

My heart is running a marathon right now, heaving and pounding with every delayed breath.

Moments later, he squeezes my hand again, his eyebrows pushed together worrisomely. "Say something."

I shake my head, almost in disbelief. "I . . ." God, nothing seems to come out.

I look at him, studying his beautiful face. Carved with the utmost delicacy and precision, it's safe to say this man was artificially built—maybe from a laboratory. No way those sparkling gray eyes and rigid facial structure can be from a real-life man. He has to be a figment of my imagination.

But his fingers scaling over my knuckles, caressing them and soothing my nerves, makes me realize that maybe he is real. And maybe I'm just irredeemably lucky.

Somehow, I find my voice.

"I . . ." My hand continues to cling onto his. "I like you too, Jax."

His eyes sparkle just a bit more. "Really?"

I nod. "Yes, really."

"Oh." He sighs, chuckling lowly. "Oh, thank God. This . . . this is the best thing I've heard in my entire life." Both of his hands now run up to my wrist, his light touch driving me crazy. "You . . . you made my day, Blaire. My entire week, month, year, *life*—you name it. I swear this is something from my dreams. There is no way this must be real. You can't be real. This—"

"Stop."

His hold on my wrists loosen, his eyes pained. "What?"

A smile tickles my lips as I wrap my hand around the black

tie resting idly against his firm chest, gripping it tightly and pulling him to me, so close I can feel our hearts pounding together.

Words suddenly leave my mouth like a flowing river, breathless and rushed. "Just shut up and kiss me already, you talkative idiot."

He leans in, laughing quietly into my mouth—low and deep.

But then, his expression becomes dangerous and he places his hand on the underside of my jaw, his fingers curving around the side of my neck.

And we kiss.

I don't know who leans in first; honestly, I don't think it matters much. What really seems to matter is our lips tasting the familiar, what we've yearned to taste for months on end. How we're desperate, *so much more* desperate than the kiss in D.C. Now, we're hungry. And we find each other unbearably ravishing.

My hand, still grabbing his tie, pulls him to me roughly, giving him no choice but to put both his hands on my waist to steady himself. His hand runs up my exposed back, delicious shivers jamming through my spine, and we cling onto each other—our breaths clipped and panting.

Our lips still not leaving one another, I wrap my arms around his neck, my fingers grabbing his hair and just endlessly *desperate* for him. This entire moment itself I'm not able to get enough of—because I want *more.*

We release eventually, my lips swollen from his and my mind restless from his enticing presence. His nose grazes mine, his eyelashes tickling my cheek, and he presses a soft kiss at the edge of my lips. A zoo unleashes at the pit of my stomach. How is this man able to make my limbs weaken just from a mere touch of his?

His hand cups my cheek, his eyes studying me—scanning

over me as if I was the most precious person in the world to him. "I never want this moment to end."

My mouth twitches into a small smile. "Me neither."

Jax's eyes soften, trailing his hand over the stray strand of hair framing the side of my face. "God, how can you be so beautiful? You seem so unreal, Blaire."

My knees begin to buckle. *This man will be the death of me.*

"You're being too kind," I murmur into his hand.

His eyes widen, leaning back in shock. "What the hell are you talking about? I mean it. You're absolutely beautiful." He shakes his head, a humorless chuckle leaving his mouth. "Now that you're mine, I will make sure to tell you just how beautiful you are. And if that isn't enough, then I will show you instead."

Heat creeps up my neck, almost like a shadow forming against the night. This time, no words come out of me. How can I, when Jax keeps saying these sweet nothings to me? Mesmerizing my heart and casting a soothing melody onto my beaten soul? I don't deserve this at all.

His hold on my cheek tightens suddenly, his entire expression intense and unwilling. *You* do *deserve this,* he seems to say with his eyes. *More than you can ever know.*

I sigh to myself. And he can read my mind too? This must be a joke.

Suddenly, something interrupts us as a low sound screeches into the air.

"Welcome to the Summer Solstice Festival! In just a few minutes, Charlotte Levine and her daughter Renata Levine will arrive on stage to deliver their speeches. This will mark the commencement of the Summer Solstice Festival, where you all can then feast on today's delicious meals and enjoy the astonishing view! By then, I request all of you to gather by the stage and give your undivided attention to the Levines. Thank you."

Jax lets go of my cheek and brings his hand down to mine,

his finger grazing over my knuckles in an endearing way. "Shall we go, beautiful?" he whispers, his lips curling into a smirk.

Without any hesitation, I nod, allowing our fingers to intertwine, our hands clasping together. "We shall," I say, grinning.

As we leave, hand-in-hand and grinning ear-to-ear, I lug behind him, my movements slowing down. He turns around, confusion etched on his features. "Is everything all right, Blaire?"

I look at him, studying him again just to make sure this moment is actually real, and take a deep breath. This is my life now. I am . . . Jax's girlfriend. And as troubling as it feels to think that, it also feels so good.

So damn good.

I nod, reassuring him by squeezing his hand. "Yes. Everything is more than all right."

6

DREAD

JAX

WHAT THE HELL JUST happened?

Right now, I have Blaire Cohen's hand wrapped around mine, and I am leading her toward the dance floor, where we will watch Charlotte and Renata Levine appear on the stage and speak to us all. And Blaire and I will be together.

As a goddamn couple.

My lips dry as I rethink our unforgettable encounter. I must say, seeing her in that green necklace I've dreamt about giving to her for the *longest time* was the most satisfying sight on earth. That peridot stone fit so snugly against her skin, as if it was customized just for her. And honestly—I spent forever searching for that stone. I enquired so many jewelers across the city for weeks, dragging on like a discombobulated creature as I basically scoured through every corner of this place for what seemed like forever.

That was until I saw the gleaming peridot stone leaning against the satin cloth in the enclosed glass showcase—right in the middle of the Detroit markets. Since that day, my eyes never left that stone—even though the price on it was quite eye-widening. I worked my ass off in the refuge, garnered some money, and finally had enough to get that for Blaire.

How else was I supposed to show her that I couldn't stop thinking about her?

And now, as I feel her hand curling around my bicep, her hips inching to mine as we continue to walk across the grass licking at my feet, I can't help but smile to myself. Because all of my hard work paid off.

We squeeze our way through the crowds and make our way over to Mallory and the others. When she sees me, she beckons me over, also smirking mischievously at the sight of Blaire adorning my arm.

Finally, we've stood ourselves in the heat of the crowd, mounds of people growing at an increasing second as the lights dim by the stage. I feel Mallory nudge my shoulder. I look over at her with a perplexed glance.

"So, are you not going to tell me how it went?" She murmurs, her lips barely moving.

I sigh, still gleaming with pride as Blaire is *still* holding onto my bicep. "I think you can see just *perfectly* how it went."

Mallory grins, poking my ribs playfully. I wince as she laughs.

As we stand in the crowd, I notice everyone gives us curious glances, and a fresh wave of heat creeps up my neck. I definitely did not weigh in the fact that we will catch the attention from our friends and family, but in the end, I decide that it is well worth it, and they can stare all they want. Even though her parents and brother are basically death glaring at me. Emilia, on the other hand, bats her eyelashes at us and giggles to herself. Not to mention the priceless look on Vi as well. I would say our quasi-friendship has been pretty stagnant so far, which basically consists of me annoying Vi and her ignoring me for days on end. But I know, deep down, she doesn't mind me as much.

Or maybe she does mind me. Who knows?

Suddenly, the speakers around us hum with energy. "Everybody, please put your hands together for our wonderful leader Charlotte Levine, and her daughter, Renata!"

Roars of applause drown the area around us, as if I wasn't drowning with the overwhelming groups of people around me either. But then again, this isn't too bad, considering how I have *Blaire* pressed up against me.

Damn, I'm really obsessed with her.

Before I can drown in my thoughts any further, two women appear on the bright and glorious stage, their presences effervescent and sizzling like the sun blood-red against the horizon. The first I see is Charlotte herself, wearing a flowing white dress that matches the color of her pin-point hair, curling at her jaw. Her features are mature and sullen, but her smile is anything but. It reminds me of the smile Emilia and Tamia would have—innocent and joyous.

On the other hand, the woman beside her is definitely not innocent and spiteful. Her red hair falling against her back and inching past her hips tells me that this woman is the complete antithesis of her mother—completely vibrant and challenging. Her green eyes shine from here, the same shade as the grass tickling my ankles. The skin-tight red dress flaring to the ground perfectly embodies the fire in her eyes. And the broad smile on her face, dimples creasing onto her cheeks, is enough to send every man in this expanse into a frenzy.

Everyone except me, of course.

I sigh, thinking of how much younger Jax would have burned up in the sight of Renata. I have to admit, I was very . . . *indecisive* when it came to women, since I had no sense of commitment or feelings back then. I went from woman to woman like how squirrels go from tree to tree, never truly settling down and never truly understanding my own feelings. Younger Jax, when seeing Renata, would immediately introduce himself to her, spend the entire night with her, and then leave her the next morning as I would embark to my next woman.

But now? Just the mere thought of it makes me sick to my stomach. I couldn't and wouldn't now. Not when I have this beautiful woman by my side.

"Welcome to the annual Summer Solstice Festival!" Charlotte's voice interrupts me out of my thoughts, booming into the speakers. "I am Charlotte Levine, and this is my daughter, Renata. We are here to, of course, welcome you to this wonderful event and celebrate our thriving city." Charlotte clutches the microphone in her hands, her light blue eyes dazzling from here. We're not too far away from them, but they are not in an arm's reach either.

"I have to say, our city has remained prosperous for several years and counting." Charlotte sighs, looking around the area. "Of course, Detroit was one of the most advanced cities in America before the Dark Ages. And even after, we managed to thrive and avoid any further complications with the remaining cities, which I'm sure there are many out there. It is, quite frankly, *very* difficult to move on after the treacherous events many years ago. I'm sure many of you remember that—how much we suffered and struggled to endure those bleak moments. But in the end, we prevailed. We survived. And we *endured.*

"Most importantly, we are all one big family. No one is higher than another—even me, because I'm only appointed to lead our city through these complicated times." Charlotte takes a sharp breath in. "I'm sure the word has spread around that we are nearing a water shortage, but there is no need to fear because our environmentalists and water conservationists are determined to bring us back on track. It was inevitable that we would face problems such as these, considering we are running solely on generators and numerous supplies, but all we can do is make the best out of this situation and be grateful for being simply alive.

"As long as we stick together," Charlotte continues, "and face our problems like the one big family that we are, then we will easily overcome them. And with the help of many brave people, such as the Subversives who brought their remaining population here for our help and Layla Morgan, we will one day be united as not just the sole city of Detroit, but the entire America too. Thank you."

When the word *Subversives* slips from her mouth, I immediately get looks by all the people around us, murmuring and sending us intermittent smiles. I can't help but cower for a bit, overwhelmed by the sudden attention, but then I remember that this attention is the *positive* type of attention. Not the type I would usually receive from my parents—cinched with irritation and rage. With that thought in mind, I relax, giving everyone a bright smile.

"Now my daughter Renata would like to share some words too," Charlotte says, handing the mic over to her.

When Renata steps on stage, everyone immediately snaps out of their trances and glues their eyes onto her.

"Hello, everyone. I am Renata Levine, and I would like to welcome you all to the Summer Solstice Festival." I notice the faint Russian accent dragging from her tender tone. "Me and my mother are delighted to see each and everyone of you gathered here, dedicated to commemorate and celebrate our gorgeous city. Even though I may not have lived here my entire life, I still feel as if this is my long-lost home."

Her mouth curls up in contemplation. I remember when we found out from Layla, weeks after settling in Detroit, that she wasn't exactly Charlotte's biological child—which makes sense, considering their polar opposite physical features and Renata's foreign accent. All we really know about her is that she was an orphaned sixteen-year-old barely scraping by on the streets of

Russia when Charlotte took her in her care. No one knows how or why she adopted her, what happened to her parents, or anything of that sort. I don't think anyone knows—besides themselves, at least.

"Just like my mother had said, we are undergoing some issues," Renata continues, "but we can easily avoid them by banding together and protecting our city from these brutalities. It is imperative that we do." She brushes her flowing fire-like hair to the side, possibly for the tenth time since she's been speaking. "Once again, I am glad to see you all. Let's party, let's eat, and let's enjoy the night! Thank you."

Another batch of uproarious applause unleashes in the air, possibly more lethal than the ones I'd hear at the Center. I remember when I used to be on a stage just like the one I'm seeing right now—beside my mother and father. I would fight every urge of mine to not run off the stage and pack my bags and embark for a journey away from D.C. It took *every* urge from me not to.

Blaire's hand, which was curled around my bicep the entire time, releases itself and joins in on the applause too. When I turn to her, I notice she is grinning, her eyes speckled with contentment. My insides turn to mush at her beautiful smile that can probably light up the world just like the sun itself—maybe even more.

I join in on the massive cheering, the wind causing the sheer fabric of my suit to bristle against my skin. The sky is now a wondrous mixture, embellishing hues of dark blue and an ominous red. Everything in the background seems to fade, even the simultaneous clapping that has fused into a sharp sound—multiple knives slashing into shards of glass. I study the enigmatic engravings of the sky, almost as if it was communicating with us all through different brushstrokes and shades throughout the day. And, as the applause continues, I feel the incredible desire to blend into the sky itself. A place I've always dreamed of escaping to, especially when living with my emotionally estranged parents.

But a *bang* soon rings into the air, shaking the entire earth.

It all happens too fast.

The bullet travels faster than lightning itself, piercing into the most beloved woman on stage. The blood spreads on her in a frightening way, trickling down her legs and dripping onto the floor. Her knees give out, trembling and convulsing to the stage ground, and she lets out something in the mixture of a screech and a wail—a sound so horrifying it seems as if it has come from my worst nightmares. And then, with an abrupt tightening of my heart, I feel pregnant silence weigh in on all 50,000 of us. Choking us. Leaving us panting and out of breath.

And that's when the scream erupts.

The low-guttural and animalistic wail leaves Renata's mouth, piercing through the speakers and shattering our ears and our hearts and leaving them in the dust. Her eyes crinkle tightly, like a runaway plastic bag crunched by a passerby, and she falls to her knees, grasping her mother's bloody torso and letting out another earth-shattering scream that can possibly be heard from the deepest depths of an ocean.

7

CHAOS

BLAIRE

RED. THAT IS WHAT I see.

Red hot blood seeping past the edge of the stage, dripping onto the pointy tips of the blades of grass. Red hair falling past Renata's shoulders and dabbling the gaping wound. Red spreading like bacteria on the center of Charlotte's dress.

Red, red, red . . . *everywhere.*

I am suddenly submerged in water, my surroundings nothing but warped and warbled. My eyes have hundred-pound weights attached to them. I try to open my mouth to scream, just like the others are, but it is glued shut. Sealed tight.

A deep, masculine voice pierces through the air.

"Blaire, c'mon! Follow me!"

I gasp, my throat dry, hot, thick. I don't know how much time has passed now because I see people falling to the ground like dead flies, blood mixed with the tears of their mourning friends and families. The one bullet that seared into Charlotte's chest has become many, now entering many poor civilians. Piercing into them.

My vision blurs. No. No, no—this *cannot* be happening. This must be a figment of my worst nightmare.

The voice urges me again. "Please, Blaire! We have to run —*now!*"

My chest constricts as I share a desperate look with Jax, his gray eyes widened, his chest trembling. The look in his eyes terrifies me, and I want to cower to the ground like a child. I refuse to believe that the place I've considered my safe and comfortable home is now, unbelievably, under attack.

The hell I've escaped for so long has reappeared like a goddamn shadow that just won't leave my side.

And I run. I don't know when I do, but I do as soon as the thought has appeared in my mind. The last time I ran was with Em and Nico, just barely under a week ago when we were chasing a flock of geese by the markets. And I remember just how giddy we were—our breaths frantic and our intentions nothing but childish as we ran just like impish children.

Now, I run with desperation, my legs nothing but popsicle sticks on a hot summer day as I feel my knees convulsing and shaking and giving up. But I force myself to carry on, my hand squeezing the life out of Jax's bicep as he grabs Mal, Vi, my entire family, and Jeremiah and his entire family, and we desperately seek shelter before these rampaging bullets can find their way inside of us.

There is a large bar, right where everyone was when Jax and I shared our moment by the waters. I clutch the peridot necklace with my shaking hand as I shout to Jax, "There! That bar!"

He mumbles an incoherent sound to me and gestures for everyone to follow him. He speeds past everyone, me clinging by his side, and I wordlessly turn to the others, desperate for them to stay close. Em is cradled in Nico's arm, his jaw tighter than ever as our parents crowd around him, running alongside him. Vi and Mal are sprinting side by side, their faces marked with determination. And Jeremiah holds his wailing daughter in his large hands, Layla running beside him as tears sift down her cheeks.

Eventually, we crowd under the bar, making our way past shards of glass and puddles of alcohol. Em and Tamia hide under the corner of the vertically expansive island, Tamia still wailing and Em silently sobbing, hugging her knees as her long brown hair covers her fearful features. Once the children are secured, we all situate ourselves by them, hoping this island will be enough to cover us.

Everyone except Vi.

Her feline eyes narrow as she pushes herself up, grunting as she veers her head over the island. Jeremiah hisses to her, "What the hell are you doing, Vi? Sit down!"

She pushes herself back down, slowly shaking her head. "We need to be there right now. We need to save as many people as we can."

"No, we *don't.*" Mal's voice is trembling. "We need to save ourselves."

"We're the Subversives!" Vi growls. "We *have* to be there. It's our job."

"Yeah, in D.C. it was." Jeremiah traces the wedding band encircled around his ring finger. "We left those roles long ago. Besides"—he frantically looks at Layla and Tamia—"I have a family to protect."

"No." Jax shakes his head. "Vi is right."

"*What?*"

"These people look up to us. Hell, we're their saviors. We shouldn't be selfish. And we may have left those roles long ago, but we have no choice but to reprise them." Jax looks at me, his face inches away from me. "What do you think, Blaire?"

"I . . ." I gulp. "I think we should protect the others."

"Me too," Nico says, his eyes latching onto me.

"No." My mama's voice is rigid and unwilling. "You and your sister are not going anywhere."

"Please, Mama," I plead.

"Blaire and Nicolas, don't even think about it," my papa says, pointing an accusing finger at us.

"With all due respect, Mr. and Mrs. Cohen," Vi interrupts, "they have to do this as well. You see, your kids were both part of the Subversives. They know how to handle this sort of situation. They will be safe, don't worry."

"Vienna, *no.*" My mama shakes her head, her tone obdurate. "Don't even think about it."

Vi grumbles to herself, clenches her jaw, and pushes herself up, possibly eyeing the insanity occurring out there. She brings herself down to us again, her eyes raging with fire. "Besides Renata, who fled through the back of the stage, many people are either dead or injured. Ambulances should be coming shortly, but as of now, there is no support from anyone." Her black and red hair drapes her sharp face. "They *need* us. People are dying—"

Sharp bullets suddenly thump close to our heads, barely protected by the thick exterior of the island.

Layla grasps the back of Tamia's head, who screams into her collarbone. "This place isn't safe," she says hurriedly.

"Where else can we go?" Jax asks.

"We can go where Renata went," Mal says.

Vi presses her lips together, peering past the island and then coming to us seconds later. "It's risky, but definitely worth a shot." She hurriedly gestures us over, indifferent to the continuous noises of bullets slamming into both people and glass. "Follow me."

We all go out in a single file line, holding onto one another. Behind Vi is Mal, then Jeremiah and his family, my family, me, and Jax at the very back, his breath colliding with the back of my neck as he urges me forward.

And then we all run again.

Bullets fall around us in a shower, the large *booms* shaking my insides. I haven't heard these horrifying sounds since D.C., when we were constantly on the run. And my worst nightmare of all has come true. Because the last thing I imagined to be doing is now occurring.

Running for my goddamn life with death chasing after me.

Far up ahead, I hear a shriek and a strangled cry—someone from my line. A scream escapes my throat as my hand flies up to my mouth, hot and salty tears blurring my vision. *Who was it? Are they okay? Are they alive?* Hurried questions enter my mind, endless and relentless, bombarding my soul.

But my feet never stop, pitter-pattering against the wet grass speckled in pools of blood. Dead bodies are everywhere, and my heart wrenches at the sight of them. What is up with this sudden attack? Who can possibly do this out of nowhere? When everything was going so well?

My hands tremble when I hear an ominous voice erupt in the air like a volcano dying to spew its contents after years of quietude.

"Stop."

The bullets that first rampaged and spiraled around us seemed to have stopped. The air is stiff, with only the smells of blood and death.

And then, heavy footsteps come near us. *Many* heavy footsteps.

Our curiosity takes the best of us as we all slowly turn around, shocked at the overwhelming sight of soldiers dressed in black armor head-to-toe, their faces covered in black masks. The familiarity of the uniform reminds me of the Guards, but this uniform is so different. It's heavier. Bulkier. *More dangerous.*

When we all turn, huddled together and trembling at the sight of these foreign figures, I see a blonde head fall to the ground, soft and shaky breaths leaving their mouth in an erratic form.

"Mallory!" Jax yells, running to her side.

We all run to her, kneeling by her side and consoling her. I cry in shock as I see blood pooling out of her thigh at such an alarming rate. She grits her teeth as she sobs, her hand stained with blood as she grasps her gaping skin. Jax rubs her shoulder, whispering to her that it'll be okay, *everything will be okay.*

No, it won't, I can't help but refute in my mind.

Nico, who is the only one not kneeling by her side, looks at the crowd of soldiers enclosing us like a thick and heavy fog. A long dark strand of hair falls onto his eye, and his lips curl into a frown as his eyebrows squeeze together.

"Who are you people?" he whispers, his voice barely audible.

And that is when we turn to the soldiers pointing their rifles at us, cocked and ready to fire.

I am frozen, my limbs melting to the ground as Em runs up to me and buries herself in my arms, leering her head away from the terrifying figures. I wish I could console her, but I can't. Because I myself have no comfort left in me. Not after seeing *this.*

And that one stray soldier coming out of the suffocating bubble.

They amble toward us, their figure less tall and muscular than the other soldiers. Their strides are long, but also contented, their stagger nothing but collected. I clench my jaw tight, my heart bursting from the growing anticipation. Jax, a moment later, holds my hand. But even that is not enough to console me.

The lone soldier overlooking us takes their coal black mask off.

Long, pale blonde hair flows down their back, ending by their hip bone. Blue eyes the color of ice stare back at us, drilling and searing holes. Their figure is small, tiny, and skinny —but absurdly frightening. Their skin and lips are deathly pallid too, and I begin to question whether they are human. Whether they are *alive.*

Those lifeless lips move.

"I've been dying to meet you all," she says, her eyes never leaving us.

At the sound of her voice, I feel Mal's knee jerk beside me. I look at her in alarm, thinking her injury has gotten the best of her, but it is anything but that. She instead has pushed herself up to her knees, digging her fingers into her wound as she gasps, stumbling and staggering. I look at Jax, desperate to know what's going on, but he is a statue. It doesn't even seem as if he's breathing right now. All he is doing is staring at the lifeless woman or *creature* in front of us. Completely astounded.

Mal grits her teeth, waves of blonde hair falling on the curves of her shoulder. She struggles to say something, her chest convulsing as she drags her way past us and near to the figure in front of us. I begin to panic, about to stop her, but what she says next has my heart exploding altogether.

"Mom?"

8

NOSTALGIA

JAX

MALLORY'S MOTHER HAS ALWAYS scared the shit out of me.

My fear for her had really started to develop when, one day, Mallory and I were walking home from school, complaining about the chemistry exam we just took. It was nice that we were only a grade apart, mainly because the other children only talked to me solely because I was the president's son. I heard stories about the past presidents' children homeschooling to avoid the public, or rather eager children. Sometimes I wish that were the case for me, not because I wanted to be a self-centered asshole, but only because the constant attention from strangers made my stomach feel queasy.

That is why I felt rather relieved when Mallory would often assist me from those overwhelming moments. She would bring me aside from the crowds and distract me with an endearing story of hers, no matter how random they would be. I didn't really care, as long as they distracted me.

So, when Mallory and I were trekking along the snow-ridden grounds, nearing her modern mansion with the frigid air biting at our faces, I felt somebody's eyes burning at the side of my face—almost as if they were drilling into me. With an abrupt gulp, I looked over to the right, where I felt the drilling from.

It was Mallory's mother—*Veronica*—standing by the large double doors of their not-so humble abode. She was only a few feet away from me but I felt as if she were terrifyingly close, especially with her ice-like eyes staring into my soul. They never left my face. They were simply glued onto my figure, analyzing my every movement.

Mallory and I became friends when our parents did—which was sometime at the beginning of grade school. I was always fond of her father because, well, he honestly treated me as if I was his own son. Better than my parents had, obviously. Her mother, on the other hand? Well, she was kind and all, but hostile to a certain extent too. Then again, she was like that with everybody. Even to her goddamn husband.

I knew I always feared her, but the day I caught her studying me as if I was her prey . . . my mind went into a frenzy. And from there on out, Mallory's mother was my biggest fear. With those narrowed pale eyes—almost like glass—and skin so ghostly and cracked I would almost wince at the sight of her . . . well, I was bound to fear her. Of *course* I was.

So that is why, when we all left for Detroit, I felt a bit relieved knowing that not only was I released from my parents' wrath, but I was released from Veronica's too. I was *finally* released.

Or so I thought.

Because here she is, standing in front of us all, eyeing her shaky daughter cowering to the ground, her lips curled into a sneer.

"What a lovely surprise." Her raspy voice is like a slithering snake, inching through the core of the earth in swift-like motion. "It is truly an honor to meet you all."

"What the hell is this?" Vi blurts her voice filled with accusation and hidden traces of trepidation. "We thought you were—"

"—Dead?" Veronica finishes off, her throat rumbling out a laugh that honestly sounds like more of a strangled grunt. "Oh, Vienna. I thought so too. I thought I would die by the hands of some rebels that, unseemingly so, found our society a bit too bleak for their liking. I thought the explosions and the dead bodies around me would suffocate me. I really thought that."

She motions for half of the soldiers to disperse. "Take care of the others." Immediately, they all cock their guns and make way for the dying and mourning figures at the other end of the field, their boots sloshing against the bloodied grounds.

Bullets are heard in the distance, springing past the enigmatic soldiers' guns, almost like the ones Guards had. When they strike into the innocent citizens at the other end of the field, we let out protests but are silenced by Veronica swiftly taking a pistol out of her pocket and shooting in our direction, the bullet terrifyingly close to Layla's head and lodging itself into the island behind us. The island, then, crumbles to the ground, leaving nothing but a heap of wood and marble.

"I suggest you all keep quiet and listen." Veronica's voice irks me. "Otherwise, your daughter will be the first to come into my grasp." Her bony finger points at Layla, who cradles Tamia tightly. Tamia still hasn't stopped weeping.

Veronica, at that, pushes the gun into her pocket and gestures to the remaining soldiers around her to cave in on us. They encircle us, their heavy armor creating rhythmic noises of leather slapping against skin. Their guns now point at us, safeties off and ready to blow us to smithereens if we were to look at them the wrong way.

Beside me, Mallory whimpers, her hands drenched in her blood that spills out of her thigh. I rush to her side, attempting to soothe her with my words, but they only come out in shaky breaths. My heart threatens to leap out of my throat, running at a hundred miles right now. I can't breathe. *Shit.*

Fortunately, Blaire comes to my rescue. She kneels beside me, ripping a stray fabric from one of the topmost layers of her dress and desperately places it on Mallory's wound. Her dark and *beautiful* green eyes are widened in desperation as she murmurs over and over again, "You will be okay, Mal. Breathe. Just *breathe.*"

However, Veronica pays no heed to her dying daughter and hisses, "She will live." She tuts and waves impatiently at us. "I don't have much time to waste. So listen closely because I will say this once. *Only* once." She speaks again moments later, her voice raspy and ominous, inhabiting the darkest parts of my soul. "What you see in front of you is the Elite Regiment of the United States of America, or the ERUSA. We consist of multiple cities after much scavenging and we are determined to make you rebels *pay* for leaving us Rich folks in the dust back in D.C. I am the leader of the ERUSA, and it is my goal to make your life here a living hell, beginning at dawn."

My mouth dries, my breathing slowing with thought. *What the hell is going on? Mallory's mother is alive* and *the leader of some organization hellbent on revenge? This is bullshit.*

"This is bullshit," Vi voices out my thoughts, marching over to Veronica. All of the soldiers cock their guns at her, but Veronica raises her hand at them. They stop in their tracks.

Right when Vi raises her clenched fist at her, Veronica brings her hand back and strikes it against Vi's cheek. Her head snaps to the side, a harsh *smack* hissing into the air. Vi, as weirdly strong as she is, doesn't say a word and presses her lips together, her eyes fuming from what I can see from here.

Did I just see someone hit Vi for the first time? And they weren't killed by her shortly afterwards?

"You stay away from me, Ms. Powers." Veronica raises an

accusing finger at her. "You should be damn lucky I didn't strike you with a gun instead."

Vi's mouth curls down, her almond eyes narrowed at the lanky woman. She moves too fast for us to calculate her movements as she lets out a cry and charges at Veronica. Her fist collides with her jaw, her long blonde hair whipping to the side as she falls back, groans leaving her mouth. Vi hovers over her, gritting her teeth as she prepares to kick her in the abdomen, but Nico grabs her arm and lugs her back. "That's enough!"

As she cries out a protest, Veronica lets out another groan as she croaks out to her soldiers, "Go after them."

An alarm sets off inside of me as we share panicked looks with each other.

Suddenly, Nico bellows, "Run!"

Layla retreats first, holding on to a sobbing Tamia tightly. Blaire's parents and Em go next, followed by Mallory, who holds onto Blaire. It is just me, Jeremiah, Vi, and Nico left behind to fend after the soldiers and Veronica.

As the soldiers raise their guns at us, Nico growls and fights a soldier near him, kicking the back of his leg and catching the rifle falling from the soldier's hand as he plummets to the ground. He cocks the weapon and shoots the man square in the head. Meanwhile, Jeremiah and Vi have managed to overtake a couple of other soldiers, and a couple others seem to corner me.

Shit.

I catch a glance toward Blaire, who is still running with Mallory and helping her escape. She makes eye contact with me, her mouth hanging open as she shouts from the distance, "Behind you, Jax!"

I feel rough hands encircling my throat behind me with the air slowly leaving my lungs. The environment around me is hazy, and I gasp, clawing at the person's gloved hands squeezing the life out of me. *I have to get out of here.* We *have to get out of here.* Suddenly, I overpower them by kicking them in the shin, and their hands loosen around me. Behind me I feel them fall to the ground, and I turn around swiftly, kicking them in the ribs. The soldier yells, raising his gun at me. When the bullet leaves the weapon and hurtles toward me, I twist my shoulder to the side and swing to the right, my heart beating at my throat. As the soldier struggles to shoot me again, gritting their teeth in pain, a bullet lodges at the speed of lightning into the back of their head, blood splattering onto my dress shoes.

I look up and see Vi pointing the gun at him. As I go to thank her, she yells, "Guys, let's make a run for it!"

Jeremiah, Nico, Vi, and I—without a second thought—dash to the others, leaving the injured soldiers and Veronica at the ground. We eventually catch up to the others and manage to escape the vicinity, mangled bodies of innocent victims bringing fear into my veins. *I never wanted this to happen. Why did this have to happen?*

"Layla's called emergency backup and they're waiting for us," Nico gasps as we continue to sprint to the main roads, leaving the Festival grounds behind. I see ambulance trucks gathered at the side of the roads, and paramedics rush us onto the vehicles, some also running into the chaos to bring other victims. As we climb into the trucks, Mallory whimpers as she claws at her injury.

"It'll be okay, Mal," Jeremiah whispers.

"No, it won't," she cries. "It hurts so much."

Blaire's eyes slightly widen as she kneels in front of her. "Who shot you?"

Her lip wobbles, tears frantically falling down her cheeks. Then, she squeezes her eyes shut and says, "My mom. My mom shot me."

9

CONVERT

BLAIRE

A SLIVER OF LIGHT from the outside peers into the dim room, casting a translucent shadow on the mahogany table where we are all seated. Distant sirens can be heard in the background as ambulances cruise through the streets. I bite on my nails, squeezing my eyes shut every time I hear the heartwrenching wails of dying men, women, and especially children.

It has not even been five minutes since we've been sitting here, and Nico and Vi are standing at the front of the discussion room, currently in the midst of a heated argument.

"We should've just stayed behind," she mumbles to herself. "We should be back there helping everyone instead of retreating. We look like freaking *cowards*." Vi grumbles and scowls at Nico. "You of all people should've stayed back. Aren't you the leader anyway?"

"Please, Vi," Nico grumbles into his hands. His loose locks fall on his shoulders, clearly agitated being held up in a tight ponytail for the entire night. "I understand you're upset, and I understand we should've stayed back there. But we have family with us, so there's no way we could do so. We had to do what we had to do."

"Bullshit. This is just some sorry ass excuse, isn't it? People are *dying* back there, for Christ's sake."

"That is for the paramedics to worry about. Not us. Now please, Vi. It is eleven at night, and I cannot deal with your bickering right now."

"My *bickering?*" She lets out a low laugh and turns to me. "Blaire, please knock some sense into your stupid brother."

"Leave her out of this," Nico says. "The last thing she, let alone *anyone,* needs right now is fuel added to our idiotic argument. Can we just move past this and discuss what the hell we are going to do now?"

Vi grumbles to herself, sighs afterwards, and throws up her hands in defeat. "Fine. But we will definitely pick up on this conversation in private."

Nico sends her an irritated glance. "Anyway . . . we are all gathered here to discuss what happened just over three hours ago. Veronica Reaves came back from the ruins of D.C. and vowed to do something to us that I have no idea about. She also mentioned that she brought together leaders of other remaining cities and persuaded them into joining this 'ERUSA' league."

"And now," Vi says, "they have basically taken over our city, and apparently we will know exactly what they plan to do to us when the sun rises." She lets out a long breath, propping her feet on top of the table. "God, someone please pass me a cigarette."

Jax, who is sitting beside me, points to a no-smoking sign plastered on the large mahogany door. "Sorry, no can do."

She scowls at him.

Layla clears her throat to speak. "I don't know if it's obvious to you all, but we need the Subversives to come together."

Jax raises his eyebrows. "I appreciate your faith in us, but in what way can five people defeat multiple combined militaries that would rather walk through fire than have us defeat them *again* in any sort of way?"

"Uh, it's actually six now," Nico pipes in.

"Still five, though," Vi grumbles. Everyone looks at her, confused, and she looks at the ceiling pointedly. "Mal is shot, and she's been resting in the infirmary ever since we got here. Something tells me she will have no interest in fighting again, let alone against her own mother."

"I can't even imagine how she's feeling right now," I whisper. Once we all escaped the Festival grounds, we went to the refuge while some paramedics stayed back to bring the civilians here. We are well-aware not everyone will make it alive, but it was still worth a shot to gather as many people as we could. And hopefully Mal will be okay too. She *must* be okay.

Once everybody settled in, I told my parents and Em to rest in one of the other rooms in the refuge. The place we live, which is a homely condo situated not too far away from the refuge, seemed to not be the most ideal location to resort to merely because Veronica and her militia were headed there. I pray we can go back to our home now.

And ever since then, Jax, Vi, Nico, Layla, and I have been here in the discussion room. Jeremiah would've been here too, but Tamia's bedtime had long passed, so he took her to a room here in the refuge. It seems as if he has fallen asleep as well, which I don't exactly blame him for . . . it *has* been a tiring night.

But Mal. I can't even imagine the hell she must be going through right now.

Jax leans back in his seat, his hard jaw clenched. "She barely said a word to us when we were coming back. That just made my hatred for Veronica grow even more."

"Even more?" Vi asks, a hint of curiosity tracing in her tone.

"Yeah." He sighs. "I never liked that woman. Creeped me the hell out, if I'm being one-hundred percent honest. And she just never treated Mallory right. She always came after the way she talked, acted, *and looked* even." Jax shakes his head in disgust. "The woman had issues, I'll tell you that."

"No kidding," Vi mutters underneath her breath.

"I just don't get it." Nico laughs humorlessly. "Why now? Why during the Summer Solstice Festival? Why couldn't it be any other time?"

"And where did she even come from?" Jax asks. "Why is she even here to begin with? I mean, yeah, she's upset about being left behind while we escaped from D.C., but there has to be something deeper behind this. Like a motive she might have."

"I don't know," I say. "I just want to find some way out of this. I mean, we were so successful in escaping that terrible place—just to find out our actions led to bad outcomes."

"Gosh, this is a disaster," Layla whispers, her unruly thick curls framing her heart-shaped face as she stares at the table despondently.

"So . . . what should we do?" Vi gestures to us. "Besides the fact that us Subversives should come together, which, in all honesty, one group won't be enough to take down the ERUSA."

"Honestly," Layla says, "there's no other option. We only have ourselves as of now."

"Well, that's just lovely." Jax rolls his neck.

Seconds later, Vi gets up from her seat and says, "Then there was honestly no point in this meeting, right? Since we came up with absolutely nothing."

Nico sends Vi yet another exasperated glance. "That's not true. Brainstorming itself provided plenty of weight to our meeting. Besides, why don't *you* come up with ideas then, if you feel that way? Especially if you're just going to ridicule all of the ones we've suggested so far."

"Okay, you two"—Layla sends them a disdainful look—"*need* to cool off."

"But—"

"No buts."

"Fine," Vi says, walking toward the large mahogany door and turning to us. "I guess I'll just go to sleep then. Since I'm clearly not needed here." She salutes us, right before an overly exhausted look, and leaves the room.

Nico sighs. "I think we all should sleep on this too. It's the best decision to make as of now."

"I agree." Jax yawns, his arms outstretched and landing on the back of my chair. His hand pulls his chair toward mine, an unreadable expression plastered on his beautiful face. "You should get some sleep too."

I wring my fingers together when I notice his smoldering gray eyes on me. How the hell am I supposed to respond in a coherent sentence with *that* look on his face?

From the corner of my eye, I notice Nico and Layla have their eyes on us, one grinning ear-to-ear and the other crossing their arms with a scowl drawn onto their mouth. Heat rises up my neck, and that's when I realize I'm going to have to deal with a lengthy lecture from Nico sometime soon. I'm pretty sure he's put the pieces together and realized mine and Jax's relationship that started not too long ago.

I sigh. That conversation sure is going to be awkward.

Layla gets up from her seat and gestures for me, Jax, and Nico to get up as well. "We'll sleep on this now, and depending on the situation in the morning, we will meet up again and discuss what we should do next." She stands by the door, propping her foot by the inner corner of it. "Let's try to think positively. I'm sure we can fix this issue in no time."

I want to believe her reassuring words . . . but I just can't.

Eventually, we leave the discussion room and watch Layla disappear down the hall, where her husband and daughter are resting in one of the other rooms. Nico stands with us awkwardly, running his eyes over us.

"I've noticed that you guys have been, uh, sort of close tonight." He scratches the back of his neck, exchanging a glance with Jax. "You are a man, I believe, who'll treat Blaire the way she deserves to be treated, so I will support your . . . *companionship*. Just, uh, I have one request."

I narrow my eyes. "Yes?"

Nico winces, pushing his hands into his pockets. "I want Blaire to sleep with her family for a bit. Just to make sure she's being responsible."

"Oh, my God. Please leave. *Now.*"

Jax laughs in the background, seeming a bit too amused with this conversation.

"I'm just looking out for you, Bumble Bee. That's all."

"Okay, thanks," I say hurriedly, pushing Nico away. "I appreciate your concern. Now please leave. Thank you."

"Okay, okay. Leaving now." Before he disappears down the hallway, though, he gives Jax a threatening look and points a finger at him, saying, "If you break her heart or hurt her in *any sort of way*, then I will make you wish you never came out of your mother's womb. Got it?"

Jax, still laughing, throws his hands up in surrender. "Don't worry, Nicolas. I won't."

"Good." Nico nods—

And then finally leaves.

I release a long breath, and then I turn to Jax, mocking his amused expression. "Ha ha. Laugh all you want."

His laughter finally comes to an end, but then he surprises me when he grabs my hand and lurches me to him, our torsos clashing. While I hold my breath, I feel the hard muscles of his torso digging into my stomach as he intertwines our fingers, eyeing our combined hands. Finally, he looks at me, his lip tugged up with satisfaction.

"We're finally alone," he whispers, his mesmerizing eyes never leaving my lips.

"I know," I say, my stomach churning at how close we are.

He grins, but it quickly fades as his eyes stray away from me, landing on the ground. Confused, I plant my hand on his hard jaw, gesturing for him to look at me again. "What's wrong?" I whisper.

He doesn't answer for a long time. "Nothing, really. It's just the fact that . . . I finally confessed my feelings to you after so long, and because of that, this universe decides to make our lives like hell again. Just *barely* after we decided to give this a shot." Jax finally looks at me then. "I just find that a bit unfair."

"Hey." I run my thumb across his delicate scar and place it at the curve of his lip, my hand cupping his chin. "I know just how you feel, Jax. I find our situation to be a bit unfair too. But we will get through this. And I promise that I will be by your side."

My thumb slightly moves as his lips curl into a smile. "You do?"

I nod, but then I grin playfully afterwards. "And do *you* promise that you will be by *my* side?"

Something twinkles in the depths of his gray eyes. "Blaire," he says, "even if the devil himself was dragging me to hell, I would still find a way to be by your side."

Oh, goodness gracious.

Moments later, his hand grasps my waist and pulls me even closer, giving me no choice but to bring our lips together. It's only for a second—maybe even two—but it feels like an eternity either way. It is enough to mend our broken and helpless souls through only a shared interaction—*this* sole interaction consisting of lips *aching* for one another.

And then, we just hold each other. His arms hold me tight, pressing my face into the center of his hard chest where I can feel his heart beating boldly and wildly. Our souls are mended into one, consoling each other of our buried fears and past troubles. His troubles with his family and his identity. My troubles with fighting for a place in a world that cast me aside.

But, in some way, our troubles were similar.

We both struggled to belong. No matter if we were born into completely different worlds.

Seconds later, Jax releases me, placing my hand on his heart. It thumps like a wild drum beneath my shaky hand, each movement causing my limbs to weaken.

After he eyes my peridot stone necklace, he whispers into my ear, "This is what you do to me. You make me feel like I'm running a goddamn marathon."

Sunlight peers into the gaping window.

The bedsheets strewn on me are thrown to the side as I study my surroundings. Em's hand is draped across mine, soft snores erupting out of her. When I make the slightest movement, she turns to a sleeping Nico on the other side, resting her head against his shoulder.

My parents are on the other bed, sleeping peacefully as well. It is just me, eyeing everyone's behavior as I am clearly awakened by the intense light. However, the size of this room does not affect me, merely because I've lived in the worst places. Well, only *one* other place.

Minutes later, a screeching sound erupts outside.

That wakes everyone up.

"What's going on?" Em murmurs sleepily.

"I don't know," I whisper, anxiety clawing at my insides. I immediately pull her close to me, and she snuggles into my arms, whimpering under her breath.

The screeching sound soon converts into a ghost-like voice I have unfortunately become acquainted with. And it filters into every remnant of this room—possibly into every crevice in Detroit as well.

"Good morning, everyone. My name is Veronica Reaves, and due to Charlotte Levine's death last night, I will be taking over her position. For those of you who are not aware of this conversion, I will be reviewing the new rules of this society that is now under my control and the syndicate I am in control of as well. I am part of the ERUSA, or the Elite Regiment of the United States of America. The ERUSA is a group of appointed militia determined to monitor the behavior of the Impure, which are all of the Detroitian citizens. We believe the Poor are the reason for our downfall because of the attacks that occurred last winter in Washington, D.C. In order to show the Poor that us well-intended individuals are not to be messed with, I've dedicated my entire ruling as a leader here to control the behaviors of everyone. These are just a few of the many rules that will be appointed.

"Curfew is eight in the morning to eight at night for all Impure. Parties and social gatherings are restricted. Clothing should not be raunchy; they should be befitting. Any insults or attempted brawls against ERUSA soldiers will result in immediate execution. Any derogatory remarks toward Detroitian and ERUSA leader Veronica Reaves will result in immediate execution too. Electronic devices are prohibited in external usages except direct communication from the ERUSA. Everyone must sing the ERUSA Pledge at eight in the morning sharp, which is as follows:

"*Dear Great Members of Society, it is hereby declared that I will adhere to the ERUSA, by the ERUSA, and for the ERUSA. All Pure Bloods are United, while all of Impure will be Separated. Beautiful America will be Cleansed of all Impure, of all non-ERUSA. Failure to Adhere to the ERUSA will result in the Shedding of Blood and Skin. Therefore, I will Adhere, I will Pledge, and I will Obey. Amen.*

"And the refuge must be rescinded, for all tending to the Impure is illegal. If these rules are not adhered to, then there will be consequences. This is purely for the furtherance of our beautiful America, who has suffered enough. Thank you."

RECONVENE

JAX

"THE SUBVERSIVES HAVE TO come back together."

Nicolas raises his eyebrows in confusion. "I thought we decided as a group that the Subversives alone are not going to be of much help, Layla."

"I know." She sighs, wringing her hands together. "But we have no other choice. These Detroitians need some sort of hope, and I can't even imagine how they're feeling right now. They've successfully avoided any attacks from other organizations for so many years, and all of a sudden this aggressive woman comes waltzing out of nowhere and vows to treat anyone of 'Impure' blood like hell."

I scowl. "What the hell does she even mean by 'Impure'? How can she even tell someone's an Impure?"

"Well, she already knows who *we* are," Blaire says, who sits beside me. "The people we brought from D.C. have their Tags to out them to the ERUSA. And the original Detroitian citizens can easily be identified now because Veronica has access to all their records, since she has hijacked Charlotte's position."

"So, in conclusion, we're screwed," I murmur, pinching the bridge of my nose.

"Actually, we may not be screwed if we listen to what Layla says and bring the Subversives together," Nicolas says. "It's definitely worth a shot."

"I don't know about this, Nicolas." Jeremiah speaks for the first time today. His hand has been encircled around Layla's the past ten minutes we've been sitting here, and he doesn't seem willing to let go either. "I do not mind if we do reconvene, but it's gonna be extremely risky. I have a wife and a little girl and—"

"Baby." Layla places a reassuring hand on Jeremiah's broad shoulder. "You do not have to worry about me and Tamia. We will be fine."

"But I don't want to lose you guys again." His brown eyes are deep and tear at the painful memories buried into his soul. "I lost you and our baby girl for three damn years. I'm not going to lose you again."

"And you *won't*," she emphasizes. "I'll make sure of it."

"She's right," Nicolas says. "I know how it feels to lose my family too." He looks at Blaire for a split second. "But that is why I will make sure with all of my heart that everyone is safe and alive. Now that I am here, I will make sure of that. No one is dying on my watch."

"Well, I'm in then." I blurt out.

"Really?" Layla looks pleased.

"Of course." I lean back in my chair, stretching my legs out. "I mean, my father treated the Poor like shit, and I felt so helpless because I wanted to do so much to help them, but I just didn't have the guts to do anything about it. Finally, I cleared my mind and killed my father, which, in my opinion, I was dying to do anyway, and now I am determined to make up for the mistakes I made back then. So, of course, I'm willing to be a part of this again."

And it is true. I really do wish I could go back in time and redo all of my mistakes. I wish I had stood up to my father beforehand. I wish I had saved those innocent Poor people from his wrath because maybe they would still be alive to this day. Thousands of wishes unfurl into my mind, but merely wishing isn't enough anymore. As much as I want to go back to the past and better myself back then, I can't. What's done is done. So the least I can do is learn from my mistakes and better myself *now*. What other choice do I have?

"If Jax is joining, then I will too," my *girlfriend* says. I look at Blaire expectantly, and she grins at me. "I will do anything to bring Detroit out of this hell."

The delirious look she sends me has blood rushing to my body. I straighten myself, hoping no one's noticed my cheeks flaring. Those green eyes on me, let's just say, have *definitely* woken me up.

I think of our encounter last night, when Blaire and I kissed and she told me that no matter what, she will be by my side. It was definitely reassuring because I was pissed at the fact that right when we were *finally* together, the female form of Hell shows up out of nowhere and vows imminent doom on those who have indirectly or directly wronged her.

I was seriously thinking of suggesting for her to get therapy instead, but it seemed a bit too inappropriate at that time.

Her forest-like eyes leave my face, one corner of her full lips tugging in satisfaction. Shit, am I still blushing?

Thankfully, no one except Blaire has noticed the over-whelming rush of pink tinging into my cheeks because they are in the midst of their own conversation right now.

"What about you, Jeremiah?" Nicolas asks, tying his medium-length dark locks into a low ponytail. "Have you made your decision yet?"

Jeremiah immediately looks to his wife, but all she does is

grin and push his shoulder playfully. "Tamia and I will be fine. Just say yes, you idiot!"

He smiles seconds later, shaking his head and rubbing his forehead. "Yes. I'm in."

"Yes!" Layla cheers, kissing his cheek. "You have absolutely nothing to worry about."

"I better not." He smirks, kissing her lips.

Next, we have Vi, who aggressively pushes a few strands of red and black hair behind her ear. Her light brown eyes are radiating from here as she studies each and everyone of us. "Well, if everyone's joining, then I might as well jump on the bandwagon."

"Wonderful!" Nicolas grins, but his grin is wiped off his face and he turns to the other side of the room—

And faces Mallory.

She's been sitting in this room the entire time, and sometimes I felt as if she wasn't even here because of how *quiet* she's been. Her injured leg is propped against another chair, layers of gauze wrapped around the entire section of her bloodied thigh. Her back is rigid, her head strewn to the side as she takes leveled breaths in, and then out. Her lips are broken fragments of a vase—cracked. Heavy eyebags are located beneath her once bright blue eyes, but now they are nothing but dull.

I don't blame her. She's been through hell and back in the past twelve hours.

"What about you, Mal?" Blaire asks, her voice low and poised. "Do you want to be a part of this?"

Ten uneasy seconds of silence goes by before she straightens herself up, slowly but surely. Her lips open and close like a dying fish would, as if she's desperate to breathe again. Desperate to find happiness and an urgency to *live* again.

She's not the optimistic and upbeat Mallory anymore—not the girl who cheered me up whenever my father verbally attacked me or the girl whose smile made my frown disappear within seconds.

She is the Mallory that makes me fear my own damn life.

Moments later, she finally speaks.

"When I saw my mom standing in front of me, I felt my heart explode." Her voice is cracking, barely able to compose herself. "I've always felt so weak and vulnerable in her presence, but at that moment, I don't think I've ever felt weaker. Especially when *she shot me.*" She pauses. "That's when I decided that I don't want to feel like a piece of trash in front of her anymore. I'm tired of her running over me over and over and over again. I want to show her that I am not to be messed with either. That she does not have that control over me.

"So, of course I want to join the Subversives again." She nods with determination—just once. "But I want to fight too. Man, I *really* want to fight because I'm tired of being undermined. And honestly, I just don't care anymore."

And then, she stops speaking.

Her words weigh in on me, and I watch her as she readjusts herself and closes her eyes, leering her head away from the blinding early morning sunlight.

"All right," Vi murmurs. "It is decided. The Subversives are officially a thing again. But now what?"

"Now I think we just hold hands and sing nursery rhymes to each other." I snort.

Blaire nudges my arm a bit too harshly, looking at me as if I was a disobedient child.

I send her a wounded look. "That was *sarcasm.*"

A few moments later, Jeremiah awkwardly clears his throat. "I'm wondering that too. What *do* we do now?" He points to the large windows in front of us, where a view of the city is shown to us. "I'm already hearing gunshots and explosions in the distance. Before we know it, Veronica and the ERUSA will be making their way to the heart of the city, and we've already heard of her stupid rules this morning. And judging by the screams of innocent people I've been hearing all morning long, I'm pretty sure she's sticking to the consequences."

He is right. When I heard the shocking announcements this morning, I spent the subsequent ten minutes in my room pacing back and forth, refusing to accept the fact that this is the society we are all a part of. Even if we've made a plan to escape, one of the ERUSA soldiers will find us and shoot us right then and there—in the middle of the damn streets.

And I made a huge mistake when I peered out the window. The view itself was stunning—the sun was bright red as it raised into the sky. Birds flew past skyscrapers and buildings that made everything beneath look like ants.

But the *people.*

Every ten minutes I heard a gunshot or a scream. Blood was splattered on the streets, and the ERUSA's heavy military trucks came rushing by, cleaned up the blood, and left like nothing happened. And because of this great change in our society, few people are roaming the streets. But they know damn well Veronica and the ERUSA will hunt them down and eradicate them simply for being Impure.

This shit makes me sick to my stomach.

Layla brings me out of my thoughts as she suddenly says, "Wait . . . I have an idea."

"What is it?" Vi asks desperately as Layla pushes herself out of her seat and makes her way across the room and to the door.

She stops in her tracks and turns to us. "I wanted to tell you guys this when you all were formed into the Subversives. And now that you are . . . I think it's safe to say this now."

"Say *what,* baby?" Jeremiah's voice is filled with confusion.

Layla's big brown eyes land at the large windows, where yet another gunshot screeches past the glass. I wince to myself, but not before she says, "Have you ever wondered what's on the other side of Detroit?"

11

MYSTIFYING

BLAIRE

THE JEEP TRAILS AND hums across the smooth roads, and I veer my head toward the open window, the light breeze flapping against my cheeks as I observe the animated movements around me. People come in and out of office buildings, clutching briefcases and loose paperwork in their hands. Birds perched atop buildings and tall trees caw into the sky, initiating the start of the day. And the sky gleams, allowing imminent light to peer on us.

It is a normal day in Detroit . . . except the fact that a totalitarian group of people have taken over our city and have been executing anyone who does not abide by their rules. Every minute, it seems, I hear a gunshot rumble into the atmosphere. And then, immediately after, I hear gut-wrenching cries from those who have failed to save their friend or family member.

Jax squeezes my hand when he sees me shaking. I turn and look at him, and his gray eyes searing into me reassures me of all my troubles. He nods once, as if he is saying, *I am here for you.*

I release a breath and hold onto his hand as if my damn life depended on it.

As the refuge behind us vanishes into the engulfing surroundings, I recall the last rule Veronica spoke of just this morning: *"And the refuge must be rescinded, for all tending to the Impure is illegal."* I lurch up in my seat, confused as to why Layla had not brought this up before. Did she forget Veronica mentioned this?

"Hey, Layla?" My voice is wavering.

Seconds later, she turns around in the passenger seat and faces me. "Yes, Blaire? Is everything okay?"

"Uh, yes. Everything's fine. I was just wondering . . . Veronica brought up as the very last rule that the refuge must be rescinded because she believes all tending to the Impure is illegal. Does that mean we have to get rid of the refuge? Or shelter the refugees elsewhere?"

Layla sighs and says, "I was wondering that too, but I figured as soon as we get there I will see what everyone says. The volunteers are at the refuge, so the refugees should be okay."

"But what if the ERUSA marches into the refuge all of a sudden and kills all of the refugees *and* our volunteers?" I voice out. "Tamia and my family are there too. Aren't they making their way up from Dearborn as well? Before we know it, they'll be reaching the refuge, which is at the tip of Detroit."

"They will be fine," Vi says, sitting on the other side of Jax who is in the middle. "This trip to Windsor shouldn't last us more than two hours, right?"

We nod.

"Exactly. Then there's absolutely nothing to worry about."

"Yeah, there's absolutely nothing to worry about," Mal sarcastically whispers behind us. "My mother just killing innocent people throughout the country for not following her unreasonable laws is absolutely okay, right?"

Vi turns around to the third row of the jeep and says to Mal,

"Look, I didn't mean that—"

"Yes, you did. You did mean that, Vi. You can't just say there's nothing to worry about when, in fact, there's a *lot* to worry about. Our city is not free anymore, innocent people are dying, our refuge is at risk of being destroyed, and my mother is the reason behind all of this. Is that clear?"

Vi's eyebrows are raised as she turns back around, crosses her legs and her arms simultaneously, and murmurs to herself, "Yes, that's clear."

Five seconds of awkward silence goes by.

Jax scratches his jaw. "And that is why we don't irritate people who are under the influence of pain meds."

From the corner of my eye, I notice Vi slowly turning her head to Jax and jabbing her elbow into his hard chest. He winces and curses to himself.

For the remainder of the trip, we traverse through the windy roads as the Detroit river reveals itself to us. The waters blind us, due to the sun casting its rays and forming a translucent and shimmering vision. The bank and the large grassy expanse is exactly where the Summer Solstice Festival was and exactly where chaos ensued.

Horrifying recollections of Charlotte tumbling to the stage ground and convulsing as blood poured from her wound and stained her white dress flash into my mind. I will do *anything* to change the course of that day. Instead of Jax and I running to the bank, confessing our feelings for each other, and kissing shortly afterward, we could've been on the lookout for suspicious activity and easily avoided what came upon us during Charlotte and Renata's speech.

But I think that, maybe, weirdly enough, this was bound to happen. Maybe Jax and I running to the bank, confessing our feelings for each other, and kissing shortly afterward was written in our destiny. And the gunshots that rampaged later on were written in our destiny too.

I've heard that happiness is short-lived, and I never really believed it—only because I hadn't experienced true happiness until the moment we left for Detroit. But I do believe it now because the unregrettable moment I shared with Jax led to turmoil. Maybe happiness does come with consequences—or terms and conditions no one really is aware of and don't even bother to consider in the first place.

We drive over the Ambassador Bridge, the elevation slowly increasing as the waters gleam beneath us. Windsor, as Layla told us, is Canada's territory. During the Dark Ages, Canada and America got into a little tussle about who should have the control over Windsor. America believed that they should have the control because Windsor was in close proximity to Detroit. On the other hand, Canada wanted to keep it in their territory because it *was* theirs.

In the end, not one country prevailed because Windsor's population was dwindling due to the nationwide food shortage. What occurred in America also carried into the southernmost parts of Canada, which affected their situations greatly too. Windsor slowly became isolated and, when the war concluded, it was completely deserted. Neither Canada nor America interfered with what occurred in Windsor.

Until Detroit, many years later, took the situation into their own hands and made the westernmost tip of Windsor a Detroitian military base. By that time, the remaining cities were isolated from each other and refused to partake in another civil war. So, Detroit built a military base on the opposing side of the city in order to avoid surprise attacks or coups from anyone.

However, due to very few threats, the Detroitian military disappeared and was never heard of again, since many Detroitian leaders thought of them as unnecessary. Of course there were police officers in the city itself, but they never felt as if a military was required. So, they let them be.

Or so we thought.

Before we left for Windsor, Layla explained that the Detroitian military has been living underground and hasn't really vanished or dispersed. The citizens are aware they exist, but the government, Charlotte and her daughter, and Layla are the only ones aware of their location because it is extremely confidential. And that is why she wanted to tell us this when the Subversives were reformed because she never saw this attack coming a mile away and felt as if, in that moment, it was necessary.

However, because of the ERUSA capturing Detroit just this very morning, the leader of the Detroitian military contacted Layla and told her to bring us over to discuss ways to go about this situation.

When Layla told us of that when we were preparing to leave for Windsor, I couldn't believe or stomach a single word she was saying. But as I sit here with the wind slapping my face and roaring into my ears, it finally sits in my mind, and I can finally assess it.

Once we cross the Ambassador Bridge, we've finally entered Windsor territory.

And let's just say it's not as . . . *lively* in comparison to Detroit.

The grounds are murky and sullen, dead trees swaying against the humming breeze. The roads are cracked and barren, the body of the car groaning and moaning. A thick fog smothers the atmosphere like a virus that has taken over a human's system. And a lone sign leers into the road, bright words plastered that say: **WELCOME TO WINDSOR, ONTARIO, CANADA.**

Suddenly, a dirt path connects to the fissured roads, and Layla rapidly points to it. "Turn there."

Nico swerves the jeep and we all tumble to the right side as he turns onto the dirt path. My hip is pressed up against Jax's, and he looks down at me, his eyebrows raised and a smirk on his face. "Blaire, while I do like you pressed up against me, you have to realize that we aren't alone."

Heat sifts into my cheeks as I playfully swat his arm. From the right of Jax, I swear I can hear Vi fake barfing.

Gravel crunches against the tires as I look ahead and see a wide clearing with nothing but large trees surrounding it. When we approach the clearing, the crunching noises shift into silent treading, the tires rolling across the soft grass. This reminds me of when Vi and Jeremiah kidnapped me and took me to the underground bunker and I was astonished to see the large clearing that stretched on for miles.

Except this clearing stretches on for *acres.* Innumerable and uninterpretable acres.

"When do I stop?" Nico asks Layla.

"We're not stopping," she says.

"What?"

"Just keep going. Trust me."

Nico sighs and continues to drive the jeep forward, treading across the grassy plains.

Eventually, we see land where grass cuts off at a certain point and is intercepted by a gray material—the same color as Jax's eyes. Gleaming lights are drilled into the grounds, illuminating the road the car drives across. We feel a steep decline, and we are temporarily met with darkness.

Suddenly, dim lights are embedded into the spacious gray ceilings, the walls around us gray as well. Basically, *everything* is gray. The place we've stopped at showcases the largest of planes, helicopters, and many other technologically advanced vehicles. People dressed in black and blue armor walk to and from these towering vehicles. When they see our jeep in the center of the large showcase, they stop and gaze at us, and their eyes are immediately met with recognition.

Layla breaks the silence by saying, "Welcome to the Detroitian military's underground base."

After the intensive security check and walking through many long and narrow hallways, we have reached another large room, except this time it is not filled with state-of-the-art vehicles.

Instead, it is filled with people. *Many* people.

First I notice multiple black stairs originating from multiple points and ending at another location. Some stairs or even ladders are hung in the air, and people walk across it with no care in the world. Doors are lined at the ends of the walls, and more people enter and exit them, either talking to others or keeping to themselves. All of these individuals are dressed in the same blue and black armor I saw before, except, since I see them closely now, I notice a large white symbol engraved across their breastbone, seeming to be a decorative and cursive form of the letter "D."

As we walk through the wide and bustling area that might as well be known as a square, we hear a deep and demanding voice behind us.

"Layla Morgan, is that you?"

Layla, who is walking ahead of us, turns around and gasps at the sight she sees. "Yes, that's me! You're Commander Thatcher, right?"

Immediately, we all turn and I expect it to be a man like Jeremiah—tall, brooding, and overwhelmingly muscular—and the person in front of me *is* all of those things. Except they aren't a man.

They're instead a woman.

Short and cropped caramel hair tops her head, framing her sharp and rigid features. Her skin is beautifully tan, but gashed with cuts and bruises too. Muscles and veins line her skin like the vehicles showcased when we first entered—displayed proudly. Tattoos, just like Vi's, are imprinted on her gleaming tan skin, except they are carved literally *everywhere*. Even narrowing my eyes isn't enough to study all of them. The only place where there aren't tattoos is on her scrutinizing face, where her lips are set into a straight line and her protruding hazel eyes land on each and every one of us.

I gulp, suddenly conscious of how I look. All I've shown up in here is just a flimsy tank top and black shorts, and in comparison to this intimidating woman in front of me . . . all I want to do right now is conform into these stone walls.

"Yes, that's me," the woman says, clearing her throat. "Are these the Subversives?"

"Um, yes." Layla seems to be nervous too. "Do you want me to introduce them to you?"

The woman, or Commander Thatcher, nods. Her bored expression hasn't changed once. "Sure. Why not?"

I've noticed that the entire time she's been standing here in front of us, everyone has sent her prideful looks and relished in her seemingly godly presence. Judging by her title, I'm assuming she's an important figure here.

"Okay," Layla stammers. She turns to us as we all stand in a straight line. Mallory, who has brought crutches with her, stands at the end with Jax next to her, then me, then Vi, Jeremiah, and Nico. She points to Nico first. "This is Nicolas Cohen, the leader of the Subversives. Next to him is Jeremiah Morgan, my husband and the man who had assisted Nicolas in the making of this organization. Then we have Vienna Powers, and she has assisted the two men plenty too. Next to her is Nicolas Cohen's little sister Blaire Cohen, and she is the youngest of the Subversives. Then we have Jax Remington, the son of Tobias Remington—the president while we were in D.C. And lastly is Mallory Reaves, the daughter of Veronica Reaves, the leader of the ERUSA."

She clenches her jaw, her eyes landing on me a bit too long. "I can work with this."

"Great!" Layla claps her hands together. "Is there anything you would like to say to them? Particularly about the military?"

She stuffs her hands into the pockets of her military jeans—extraordinarily different from everyone else who is wearing a black and blue uniform. "Well, there's not much else to say except for the fact that we're preparing to defend our land from the ERUSA and that pretentious bitch." Commander Thatcher steals a glance at Mal. "No offense."

Mal sighs, clinging onto her crutches that dig into her shoulders. "None taken."

She looks back at us, cocking her head. "I will give you a rundown of this place, though, because if you Subversives want to become a part of us, then you must follow our rules and undergo training before you can even think of being out there with us. Is that clear?"

We nod.

Commander Thatcher chuckles lowly. "That doesn't sound clear to me."

"Yes," we all say, sharing uncertain looks with each other.

"There. That's more like it." She huffs and gestures around her. "This is, of course, the underground base for our military. I was informed Mrs. Morgan over here already gave you a history lesson of this place, so I don't see why I should waste my breath on that. The citizens are aware of our presence, but we haven't been needed in years; so we've been training for a long time for a surprise coup like this. No matter how peaceful everything seems, you must always remain cautious.

"I have been Commander for five years, and I value my soldiers' performances highly. I do not condone laziness or procrastination here. If I see you slacking during training, then I will rescind you from the program. I don't give a shit if you're a damn Subversive. That was all child's play—what you went through in D.C. This is the goddamn military you're a part of now. Your life rides on this.

"Once you meet our top soldiers, further information on your training will be provided and you will be required to start

84

your intensive program bright and early tomorrow morning. Timeliness is key; if you are tardy, then I won't be very happy." Commander Thatcher clenches her jaw. "You and your families have been re-appointed to reside by the outskirts of Detroit instead to ensure their safety. You are important figures in this city, especially because you have brought refugees too, so we will treat you as you wish. As long as you respect me and my soldiers, we will have no issues.

"Lastly, our military itself is called the Reformers. Not only is it our goal to get rid of the ERUSA and reclaim our land, but we also want to bring all of the estranged cities together and hopefully live harmoniously. But that last part can only be accomplished if we take care of our biggest and burning problem of all. This is possible solely if you Subversives join us."

When she finishes speaking, Layla turns to us and looks at us expectantly. "Well, what do you say? Do you accept her offer?"

When her question amalgamates into the air, we look at each other, confusion drawn on our expressions. This was a lot of information Commander Thatcher dumped on us, and honestly, even if I wanted to refuse this offer, I'd have no valid reason because I'm still trying to understand whatever this woman just said.

Eventually, we all nod. Mal seems the most adamant of all.

"Good." Commander Thatcher crosses her arms over her broad chest. "Any questions?"

"Yes, actually," Nico says. "What do we do about the refuge? Since Veronica said she will get rid of it in some way?"

"We can house a couple hundred of the refugees here," she says. "But there's no guarantee all of them can be brought here because of the capacity issues."

"Is there no way to house all of them?" Layla asks.

"No. I would if I could, but there is not enough space here for all refugees."

Layla sighs, her expression dejected. "Okay. At least most of them are safe."

"They will be." Commander Thatcher nods. "Any other questions?"

We all shake our heads.

"Good. Now let me introduce my top soldiers to you."

She reaches into her pocket and pulls out a slick black walkie-talkie. She raises her mouth to it and says, "Peterson, bring the top five ranks over to the commonplace ASAP."

Just barely a minute after she says that, five soldiers, so it seems, come marching over. They're all wearing the same blue and black uniforms as everyone else, except three gold lines are carved into the right side of their hip. Only one of them has four.

The five of them stand in a straight line, facing us.

"Our fifth rank is Joshua Brady. Brady, go and shake their hands."

He comes and shakes our hands.

"Next is our fourth rank, Tricia Reynolds. Reynolds, go and shake their hands."

After the fourth and even third ranks shake our hands, she gestures for the three of them to retreat, leaving just the last two.

"These two individuals are the most productive and skilled soldiers I have. They have been extremely loyal and dedicated from the start, which is why I have appointed them to lead you during your training program."

Commander Thatcher steps in front of a tall, brown-skinned woman with gleaming hazel eyes that are almost yellow. Her full lips are curved into a beam, her welcoming eyes lightened like the rays of the sun. She has jet black hair the same length as mine, but bangs the same as Mal's. This woman is . . . *extremely* beautiful. Ethereal and otherworldly.

"This is Annie Iyer, our second-best soldier. Go and shake their hands, please."

Annie comes up to us and shakes our hands, and every time she does, she says an abrupt, "Nice to meet you." I felt quite intimidated by the other soldiers, but Annie seems to have an aura around us that beckons her to me. Maybe conforming to this new environment won't be as difficult if she's going to lead us.

She goes back to where the other soldier stands, and Commander Thatcher now gestures to the person standing beside Annie, four golden lines drawn on their uniform. "Lastly, we have AJ Iyer, Annie's twin brother and the best soldier in the compound. Please go and shake their hands."

When AJ walks up to us, I notice the movement of his broad shoulders and the tightening of his muscles. Just like his sister, he has glossy brown skin and hazel eyes with golden and gleaming flecks. Tufts of jet-black hair are draped lazily on his head, and his face is chiseled like the cuts and edges of a mountain. He is just an inch or two taller than his sister, and is the same height as Vi, as I notice when he shakes her hand. A line of tattoos trail down the sleeve of his right arm, and his tattoos are readable, as opposed to Commander Thatcher's.

As I read his tattoos, he makes his way to me and my veins pound as his golden eyes trail over me, studying me a bit too intensely. His stiff features sear into my bones, and as he thrusts his hand out, he drawls, "Nice to meet you."

"Nice to meet you too, AJ," I say while shaking his firm and rough hand. "I'm Blaire."

At that, the corner of his lip tugs up as his eyes continue to drag over me. "Pretty name you have."

I raise my eyebrows. "Thank you."

He nods once and gently lets go of my hand.

Seconds later, Jax clears his throat.

AJ looks at him expectantly and chuckles. "Oh, sorry for the holdup."

I look over at Jax and notice how his eyebrows are raised at him, his posture seemingly defensive and restricted.

When AJ and Jax shake hands, AJ winces a little and reels his hand back. "Damn, strong grip you got there."

Jax frowns. "Sorry about that."

However, the fiery look engraved in Jax's eyes tells me he's anything *but* sorry.

Once he shakes Mal's hand, he stands beside his sister, but the entire time, he's looking at me. I bring my eyes down, my cheeks burning. *Why does he keep looking at me like that?*

To my avail, Commander Thatcher speaks. "Now that you have met our top soldiers, you will go on a guided tour with the other three that you have met. Once the tour concludes, then you will be informed of what your intensive training program will entail. And remember, during your entire time here, you must call me Commander Thatcher and nothing else. Is all that clear to you Subversives?"

As soon as she says those words though, a trail of men clad in black suits and black sunglasses march over to us with a female figure lugging in the back. Their shiny dress shoes pound against the concrete flooring, their mouths taut and their postures strict. At this, Commander Thatcher frowns and yells to them, "What the hell is this? Who the hell are you people?"

The men stop in their places and make way for the female figure to walk through.

Collective gasps grow through the commonplace as a red-haired and curvy-bodied figure garbed in the tightest and revealing of clothing walks to us, her green eyes latched onto Commander Thatcher in desperation. Her red lips are curled into a frown, and she places her hands at her sides, straightening herself and taking a deep breath in.

And then she speaks.

"Hello, Commander Thatcher. I am Renata Levine, and I want to join the Reformers too."

12

ARDOR

JAX

OUR TIME AT THE military base that was meant to be only two hours had lasted the entire day instead.

The tour lasted an hour because it just took *so long* weaving through the unnecessarily long hallways and innumerous rooms. After that, the *scary* Commander Thatcher explained our training program to us, which, in all honesty, isn't even that bad. Or maybe it's just something that's easier said than done. Who knows?

Once our *orientation* ended, we all met the other soldiers and talked to them about our lives in D.C. and how it was like to be a part of such a notorious organization. Apparently, all of the remaining cities are well aware of us because we did kill the President of the United States—or rather *I* did. Now there is no president. Just individual cities going about on their own.

While Detroit is obviously under attack by a crazy she-devil.

And then we just stayed there for the time being because Commander Thatcher sent a bunch of her soldiers to secretly bring as many refugees as they could to the base—of course in staggered times and when the ERUSA wasn't in the heart of Detroit yet. They had just gone past Dearborn, the city neighboring Detroit, to scour for runaways because of course people will make attempts to make a goddamn run for it. Finally, in the evening, they reached Detroit and their move there has slowed down because of the multiple "Impures" they have tracked there.

Of course, this was all seen through the Reformers' advanced technology.

Another thing that pops into my mind is when Renata Levine showed up out of nowhere—literally, *nowhere*—and requested to be a part of the Reformers too. She obviously wasn't as disheveled and shaken as she was when her adopted mother *died* in her own arms, but there were prominent eye bags wedged under her eyes and dry makeup smeared sporadically around her face.

She hurriedly said to Commander Thatcher she wanted to join in order to bring justice to Charlotte, not only for what she brought to this city, but the warmth and love she brought to Renata too. Although she had zero combat experience, she was still willing to learn. Just for her mother.

That is when Commander Thatcher dragged her away to talk in private and she never came back. Renata is obviously much higher than Commander Thatcher—on a social spectrum, at least—so she couldn't have ridiculed or offended Renata much. So I do wonder what she said to her.

Our relocated home stands in front of us, glowering beneath the city. Distant ambulance sirens and wails of gunshots can be heard in the background, and all I want to do is clap my hands over my ears and tune out the egregious sounds. It gets sickening hearing the same depressing sounds repeatedly, especially when you're trying to make yourself forget the fact that, well, life might just be shitty again.

But hey, at least I have a girlfriend, right?

In front is a security gate, which Vi opens through the access code Commander Thatcher gave her, and she gestures for us to follow her.

When we trek past the front yard, which has nothing but uncut grass and wilted flowers planted at the edge of the lawn, I notice the place where we will be staying until this unfortunate storm passes over. It seems to be nothing more than just an apartment complex with frayed walls and squeaky windows that slam into the pane every time the wind howls. The pillars holding the front entrance up are off-white and have dark lines running across them like caterpillars palming through grass. And the eerie glow reverberating from the home sends shivers down my spine.

"Are you sure Commander Thatcher didn't send us to a haunted house instead?" I scowl.

"Shut up, Jax," Vi deadpans as she paves her way to the front door.

Dejected by her response, Blaire links her hand around my bicep and gestures for me to move forward. When I look at her, admiring her radiating eyes and *such* kissable lips, my attention accidentally wavers to her family, who all have quite interesting expressions on them. Nicolas, Marianna, and David, for example, look like they are fuming out of their minds seeing their daughter and little sister with a man—*God forbid.* Emilia, on the other hand, is gushing out of her mind and squealing to herself.

Don't get me wrong, I love Blaire's family. But sometimes, a little privacy with my girlfriend wouldn't be so bad every now and then.

When Vi springs the door open, trails of dust linger out the door as if they were ghosts themselves. *This house is* definitely *haunted.* She stands behind the door and motions for everyone to go inside. Mallory goes in first, anchoring both her normal and injured legs into the door while still clinging onto the crutches. Then it is the rest of us piling inside like ants swarming into their colonies, eager to know just what this place will entail.

I remember when I was kidnapped by the Subversives and was expected to live with everyone in an underground bunker. Sleeping with the men wasn't all that bad—it was just the fact that I was stuck in an underground bunker with everyone that hated my living guts. Honestly, I don't even know who hated me the most.

Obviously, now they don't hate my living guts anymore— even though Vi makes me question our semi-friendship some- times. Sure, she doesn't seem to mind my presence as much anymore, but even to this day she rolls her eyes at some things I say. God, I do wonder what must've happened in her life that has made her act like she has a stick up her ass—which, of course, everyone seems to know except *me*.

But one day I will pry it out of her. I *will*.

When we all pile inside, Vi comes in last and slams the ratty door shut, leaving the walls around to shake as if an earthquake was approaching. She sighs, digging her hands into her thighs and allowing her unruly short hair to curl around her. "What is this place?"

Layla looks around, studying the multiple doors and the two identical staircases leading to the second floor. "It seems to be an apartment complex of some sort."

"Does that mean we get separate rooms?" Emilia squeals.

"I think so, Em," Blaire says.

"Well, there's about four doors," Nico says, counting two of them on the first floor and the last two on the second. "Com- mander Thatcher mentioned each apartment has two bedrooms. So I guess the Morgan's and Mallory and Vi can take the first floor, and my family and Jax can take the second."

Once we come to a consensus about the floorplans, we all go in our own directions. I follow Blaire and her family up the second floor, the stairs creaking beneath us. When we reach the second floor, Blaire and her family go to the room on the left while I go to the right. I turn around, hoping to make eye contact with Blaire because this may be the last time we see each other tonight.

But it turns out she has already gone inside.

Couple of hours after I fall asleep, I hear a light knock on the door.

I get up out of bed, the mattress beneath me releasing my body. Since I always fall asleep shirtless, I tug on the gray shirt strewn on the floor, yawning as I trudge out of the room.

I wonder who could be here at this time of night.

The narrow hallway from the door of the one other bedroom in this apartment leads me to the actual front door—painted in a dark blue. Next to me is a tiny living room with a decent-sized television and grainy couch. On the other side is a small dining table with plastic chairs and a kitchen that can fit five people at most. But in all honesty, this is more than enough for me. At least we're alive.

I tug open the door, astonished when I see Blaire in front of me.

As I'm about to open my mouth and speak, she runs inside my apartment and clamps her hand against my mouth, attempting to stifle a laugh. She closes the door behind her and grasps my shirt, smashing our lips together. Her sighs and the taste of her lips end up in my mouth as she tip-toes to me and wraps her arms around my neck, running her fingers through my hair.

God, I am completely enamored by this woman.

We pull away seconds later, and I stare at her in shock. "I have so many questions."

She laughs. "Did you really think I wasn't going to sneak out for you?"

"Well, yeah. Have you *met* your family?"

Blaire rolls her eyes. "It took me so long to tip-toe past them. Thank God they're all heavy sleepers, though."

"That's true." I sigh, grabbing both of her arms and pulling her to me, our noses grazing each other. "What time is it?"

She smiles, her teeth glinting against the dim lights. "Should be midnight."

"Works for me," I whisper into her mouth.

I slowly inch my mouth to her and trace the curve of her lips with my thumb. Her eyes peer into the window of my soul, aching for me to let her in. To embed and engrave herself in me.

And so, I do.

Our lips connect, followed by our frantic breaths. My fingers curl around the back of her head, running through her soft hair and unwilling to let go of her. Her nails dig into the back of my shirt, clawing through the fabric and leaning into me as if she depended on me—like I was her oxygen. My tongue enters her mouth, and she crumbles underneath my arms, mumbling softly.

I push her against the wall, grasping her waist with both of my hands, desperate to unravel and read her as if she was a book and I was a curious reader determined to dig through the pages and memorize every word. Figure her out as if she was a puzzle and I was just an eager solver. For *months* I had wanted to figure her out —the intricacies of the woman I could not stop thinking about.

And now I can finally call her mine. We can finally be each other's.

My lips escape from hers and I drag them down her jaw and onto her neck, marking my territory abruptly and desperately. A satisfying groan escapes from her as she clings onto me, gasping every time I run my lips over her soft skin—worshiping and praising her. Idolizing her.

The moment my mouth lands on her jaw, she grabs hold of my burning hot face and smashes our lips again, her back crashing against the wall for the second time. I laugh into her mouth, planting a searing hot kiss shortly afterwards. "The wall might just come crashing down on you if we keep this up, beautiful."

Her dangerous eyes are enraged with flames. "Honestly, I couldn't care less if the wall crashes on me, let alone the whole damn world."

My heart skips a beat. *This woman is* definitely *the reason my entire body's on fire right now.*

And for an hour straight, we kiss each other, murmur sweet nothings, and kiss again. It's a loop filled with burning and aching urges—a loop I have no intentions falling out of. And I mark that into the deepest pits of my soul. I engrave it into the veins pulsating through my throbbing heart.

We fall back onto my bed—exhausted and out of breath.

I pull Blaire in my arms, crushing her body against mine as she drapes her leg over mine. She sighs into my chest, her soft hair tickling my neck. "That was amazing."

"Tell me about it." I grin, placing a kiss on the top of her head.

Her chest moves in and out with her heaving breaths, and I feel my breathing adjusting to hers—rising and falling simultaneously. Our hearts sync together too, the separate beats colliding into one.

"Hey, Jax?" she murmurs moments later.

I answer after three heartbeats of ours. "Yes, beautiful?"

Blaire snuggles into my chest even more. "Why *do* you call me beautiful?"

I laugh. "Because you're beautiful. I thought that was pretty self-explanatory."

"I mean, I don't know. I guess so. But it just feels so weird . . .

I spent my entire life dealing with horrible insults from the Guards or Rich people themselves. Hearing you call me that just makes me feel unsettled. Don't get me wrong, I *love* it when you call me that. It's just gonna take a while for me to get used to it."

"And this is what I meant before about me finding ways to tell you you are beautiful—if not just showing you instead. Because you really are."

I feel her lips curving into a smile against my chest. "Damn, you really know how to get my heart racing."

I chuckle, and my arms are empty as she suddenly releases herself from me, but only to level our faces so we are eye-to-eye. Her unruly short hair falls across her flawless features, where my eyes graze across her wide green eyes and full pink lips and her small perky nose with skin that radiates against the dim lights. But not only is she physically appealing, she is on the inside too. She's passionate about what she believes in. She's protective over her family. She is not afraid to stand up for others. She just wants everyone to be treated equally.

And I admire her for that.

"Can I also ask you something else?" she ponders.

"Shoot." I inch to her until our faces are only a finger length apart.

Blaire thinks to herself for a moment. "You haven't really talked to me about what happened before we left in D.C. When you killed your father, I mean."

"Oh." I leer my eyes away, setting my lips into a straight line.

"It's okay," she says hurriedly. "I didn't mean to pry at you like that. I was just curious and wanted to give you some advice or some comfort because, well, I *am* your girlfriend. I just want to be here for you."

I shake my head, her words suddenly weighing into my mind. "No, you're right, Blaire. I need to step up and share my feelings with you. I shouldn't keep them buried inside of me."

Sighing, I turn onto my back and stare at the ceiling. I feel

Blaire lay her head down on my shoulder and draping her arm over my heaving chest, her breaths hitting the side of my neck as she lazily runs her finger across my shaven jaw.

And I speak.

"You know how horribly my father treated me. He never took my feelings into account and simply yelled at me anytime I opposed him or his viewpoints. Being in his presence literally and figuratively suffocated me, and I searched for ways to escape him. I was *dying* to, yet I had no idea how to. Until one day, of course, when I was presented with the perfect opportunity to get rid of him once and for all. He was just laying there on the stage, completely vulnerable and finally in my hands for once.

"So, of course I grabbed the knife and showed him no mercy. I was running on pure anger—a feeling that was buried deep inside of me the moment he started to treat me like shit. I was ten years old, Blaire, when he first laid his hand on me. And it was six years later when he gave me this scar. I want to remove it. I've *been* wanting to remove it—but I don't know how. So, I figured that getting rid of him once and for all would be the best way to get rid of this horrible marking on me."

A shaky breath escapes me. "I lost all sorts of control as I drove that knife into him so many times. I was like a madman— a mad man fueled by uncontrollable rage. And once my anger somewhat left, it was immediately replaced with regret and sorrow. I wondered at that moment whether I had done the right thing. Would the universe punish me, now that I had blood on my hands? Blood that led to my father? I was scared out of my mind.

"Those same thoughts revolved around me even when we arrived in Detroit. We couldn't talk much at that time, so I felt no desire in opening up to anyone else. I was considering opening up to Mallory because she is my childhood best friend and knows my father in greater detail, but she seemed too busy with her own issues. I didn't want to bombard anyone with mine. So I swallowed my problems and forced them down."

I turn my head to her, noticing her indecipherable eyes latched onto me. "Even to this day, Blaire, I think about that moment. The moment when I hovered over him and let my heart control my mind. My mind was thinking that I should stop, that I should control myself, that I was making a huge mistake. But meanwhile . . . my heart urged me to stab him even more. Like those multiple times weren't enough. In the end, I listened to my heart, but I can't help but wonder if, just maybe, my mind was right. Maybe I should've stopped, maybe I should've controlled myself, and maybe I did make a huge mistake. Because everywhere I go, every corner I pass and every breath I take . . . *he* shows up in the back of my mind and sometimes in my nightmares. It's as if these are the consequences of my actions—like no matter how much I sacrificed for myself just to get rid of him . . . he is still here. And I don't like that."

When those words seep into the air and eventually into Blaire's mind, I feel great relief yet also great regret. I know I can trust Blaire with anything, but I can't help but worry if she's going to think differently of me now. Maybe she'll be disgusted with my true thoughts and decide that, maybe, I'm not the fit for her. She deserves a guy who isn't screwed up. Who doesn't have his past lingering around him like an unwanted shadow and ghost coalesced into one esoteric substance.

But instead, she does the opposite.

She lifts herself off my shoulder and hovers over me, her torso digging into mine. Her soft hands cup my cheeks, angling it in a way where I *have* to look at her. She shakes her head just once, her magnificent and alluring eyes exuding into my wounded soul.

"You are the strongest man I know, Jax. I can't even imagine how that must've felt—the emotions you dealt with in that moment. God, I really can't. But what I can say is . . . you shouldn't regret something that your heart has always wanted. You know, my mama has always told me that no matter what we should always follow our hearts because they know our greatest wants and desires over everything. Happiness always outweighs logic, Jax. And in this case, you sided with happiness. Obviously, this happiness does not occur as soon as you follow your heart. You're first going to have to heal, to grow, to prosper, and *then* you will be happy. It can take three days, or maybe even three years for this process to conclude. Who knows? But if you stay dedicated and ignore your negative thoughts and memories, you won't have this problem anymore. I can promise you that."

Her words enter my soul like a flood of light. How the hell was she able to lift my sorrows just like that? How did she know just what to say? I am utterly speechless.

"Damn," I whisper. "That really helped me."

"Seriously?"

"*Yes.* That was probably the best advice I've ever gotten. Honestly."

She beams. "I'm happy to hear that, Jax."

I smile back at her, tucking a few strands of stray hair behind her ear. "Now, enough about me. How are *you* feeling?"

Blaire sighs, lowering herself on me. "To be completely honest with you, I haven't been doing great with this whole ERUSA situation. I don't think anyone has been. But it hit me so hard when I saw Veronica—I couldn't understand why she was there or what she wanted to do with us. But the moment she brought up that she was going to kill anyone who disagreed with her . . . I knew at that moment that my short-lived happiness was over. I finally got to spend the time with my family that I missed out on for so many years, and suddenly, this woman comes out of nowhere and disrupts our lives. To make matters worse, we're thrown into this whirlwind of joining the military and training from the crack of dawn to dusk and I am *so worried* that, one day, Veronica will decide to kill my family and—"

"Hey, hey, hey," I shush her, grasping her chin. "Don't say that, beautiful. It's gonna work out. Trust me."

"But what if it *doesn't?*" She frowns. "What if we're being optimistic for nothing?"

"We won't know that until we try. Everything will work out. I promise."

"God, I sure hope so," she says. "I'm tired of this shit already and it's only been a day."

I laugh a sad laugh. "Me too."

She smiles at me pitifully. "At least we're in this together, right?"

"Yeah." I sigh, kissing her knuckles. "At least we are."

Silence overcomes us, but it's not the uncomfortable and heavy silence I've dreaded for so many years. It's a silence I wouldn't mind living in, especially with the woman who just knows me *so well.* While we dwell in the chaos, we also dwell in the calm. And sometimes, quietude is needed to prosper in the chaos.

Blaire continues to lay on top of me, her breathing evening out and her arms wrapped around mine so tight I feel my blood circulation slowly cut off. But I don't care. My entire body could be drained of blood and I'd still let her squeeze the life out of me.

Minutes pass by until I break the silence.

"Also, I hate that AJ guy."

She laughs into my shoulder. I can't help but laugh too.

I stir awake in my sleep because of my never ending thoughts.

Blaire is not on top of me anymore; instead, she's beside me, her arm draped around me. Soft and quite adorable snores erupt out of her, her mouth slightly agape and her chest rising in and out. I smile, admiring her natural beauty. How does one even look good while sleeping? That honestly must be a talent itself.

I stare at the ceiling, placing my hands on my chest and releasing a low and leveled breath. Just in a day itself so much shit has happened. Shit I can't put a finger on either. Our city Detroit is under attack right now, as I can interpret from the distant flickering of flames and crashing noises. Veronica must've reached the city by now. She must've destroyed the refuge and everyone inside it by now. The Reformers tried to get as many refugees as they could, but there were still some left over.

My heart cracks for them.

This mayhem we've managed to escape has caught up to us like karma sneaking up when you least expect it. Is this my karma? For driving a knife inside my father *multiple* times? Maybe I should've listened to my mind instead of my heart. Maybe life would've been easier then.

But when I turn my head to the side and see Blaire sound asleep, her eyelashes framing and adorning her jaw-dropping features, I realize that me following my heart led me to Blaire. Sometimes I can't believe we both hated each other when I was kidnapped. She irked the shit out of me in numerous ways. But, somehow, we were drawn toward each other despite our hatred. We pushed our differences aside and stripped ourselves until we were vulnerable and unguarded in front of each other.

And here I am now, sleeping beside her. Memorizing her soft breaths and the unsteady beating of her heart. Closing my eyes and taking in this rare moment. Feeling my heart thud like a rampant drum. *Thud, thud, thud.*

I open my eyes.

Thud, thud, thud.

Once I realize that sound isn't coming from my heart and

instead from the living room, I realize that someone is knocking at the door.

Who the hell is here at this time of night?

Taking an uneasy look at Blaire's arm draped around me, I lightly move her arm off me and wince when she stirs but turns to the other side instead.

Thank God she's a heavy sleeper too.

I sweep the blanket off me and feel a rush of cool air as I step down onto the hardwood floor. I dig my hands into the pockets of my black sweatpants and amble over to the door. My heart is wedged at the edge of my throat as I approach the rapid knocking noises. Maybe it's Nicolas and he woke up and saw his sister was gone, so he assumed she would be here. God, that would be so awkward since he already laid down the rules of our relationship—one being that we *cannot* sleep together.

But when I open the door, it's not Nicolas.

It's instead a person clad in jet-black armor with a large rifle pointed at me. A gruff voice erupts out of them as I stare at them wide-eyed.

"Follow me, and don't make a single sound."

13

ORDEAL

BLAIRE

I can't see or feel anything.

What I can feel, though, is the burdensome beating of my heart—thrusting against my chest and pounding through my veins. My breathing is shallow, and every breath I take is ragged and difficult. It's as if I'm breathing contaminated air that infiltrates my lungs and pervades my body.

My toes dip into cool water that seems to be originating from nowhere—just pools at the tips of my toes and wherever I step. A rush of cool wind sifts past my ears in a movement I can't interpret. Besides that, though, I can't hear anything either. My senses are extracted from me, as it seems.

I decide to go out on a limb and take a step forward. Cool water splashes against my ankle, and I hiss as I retract my foot. Shivers trail down my spine like an invisible caterpillar, inching through my bones and trickling in my veins. I shake my head, my breathing uneven, and I dare to step back where I was before. I can't stand here forever. I must move forward. I must explore this unfathomable environment.

With gritted teeth, I take a step forth. And another. More and more until the glacial liquid trails up my calves with the more intensity I seek forward. I am determined to find my way out of here. Whatever the hell this place is.

My surroundings are terrifyingly dark, so dark I begin to see my reflection—but I eventually realize it's not because of the hounding tenebrosity. It's because of a slender mirror in front of me, seeming to appear out of thin air. It hovers against the wet grounds, seducing me to step forth once more and glide my fingers across the thin and sleek glass.

Which I do.

With two shivering steps forward, my fingers are like boas slithering across a grassy plain as I feel the hardness of the structure. The smoothness of it. And, endearingly enough, my reflection stares back at me. Except it seems to be a younger me adorned with longer dark hair, demuring eyes, and parted lips. She stares back at me, and any normal person would be frightened at this younger version of them staring back at them—drilling their laser-like eyes into the alcoves of their soul. They would step back reluctantly and run away, terrified at what they've regarded.

But I don't. Actually, the sight of a younger me intrigues me.

I stare back at her, my lip curling up in nostalgia as I note how much I've matured—mentally and physically. The woman that stares back at me reminds me of my growth and how much I've accomplished. Younger me was angry all the time, always infuriated with the way life was for her and her family. But now my anger has simmered into determination that reaches to the skies. I've reunited with my family, especially Nico. I've met my friends whom I can call family now. And I've met a man who cherishes every centimeter of me.

As much hell that's brewing outside, I am content with my life, with my growth, and with my maturity. I'm *content*.

Younger me grins, tilting her head to the side and studying

my features. As she's about to open her mouth to speak, though, a shadow appears behind her, approaching like a ghost. It corners and encircles around her, diverging from the darkness and molding into a figure. An unbelievably jaw-dropping figure that immediately conjures flames within my bones.

His gray eyes and hair glint back at me, a blood-boiling sneer growing on him. I physically have to hold myself back from clashing my knuckles against the slick mirror and do it over and over again until blood smears the transparent glass. Jax might have killed him in the physical form, but it seems as if his presence still lingers in my mind.

"Blaire Cohen." His voice is slithery, abominable, and approaches my heart like a disease. "Lovely to meet you again."

Go away! I want to scream at him. *Leave me alone!*

I instead stand here, lifeless and dull. Unwilling to move. Unwilling to breathe.

He hovers behind the younger me, his breath entering my ear. I gasp, turning around, but no one and nothing is behind me. Just darkness. But in the mirror, he's there. Behind me. A terrified younger me can't move either.

His disgusting hands trace my shoulders, and I feel them on me. She probably feels them too. I want to push him away from me, but I can't. I want her to push him away, but she can't either.

His lips are close to my skin, dipping his eyes to the side of my face. "Remember when I told you your life will get worse for you? Well, I meant every part of it. It does get worse for you. And I'll make sure it will."

And then, in one shaky breath of mine, he brings a knife—seemingly out of nowhere—and slashes it against the base of my throat.

I let out a quavering gasp, hastily bringing my trembling hand to where I feel blood trickling down my collarbone. But nothing seems to be on my hand. I just feel the blood seeping through my skin—but no physical indication of it is present.

Meanwhile, me in the mirror looks down at her throat smeared with blood and falls over with a silent thud.

And all I am left with is the presence of Tobias—his eyes on me and laughing wildly. Each laugh becomes increasingly sinister and rampages through my bones. I can't bear the sight of him anymore.

So I turn around and run.

Desperate breaths and gasps escape out of me as I sprint from the crucifying image of my worst nightmare. The cool water, which seems to be lightning striking my legs, doesn't bother me much. All I am determined to do is run, and run, and run.

And run.

But suddenly—I am met with a wall.

My torso collides with it first, and I fall back with a thud, my back hitting the liquid brewing from the transparent ground. I grit my teeth, clenching my spine and shriveling into a ball. I begin to let out a startling sob, but a commotion occurs in front of me on the other side of the invisible wall.

I hold my breath as Tobias, the same ghostly figure as before, originates from thin air and stares down at me, kneeling by my side. All we have between us is the wall, and I don't know whether I want to tear it down and pummel him with my bare hands or hope for an opaque wall where I don't have to see his demeaning and searing eyes.

"Go away," I try to say, but it merely comes out as a desperate choke transpiring from my tightened throat.

He shakes his head slightly. "Now why would I do that when I finally have you in my sight?"

My lip is trembling. *I* am trembling.

"Are you gonna hurt me?"

He sighs, cocking his head and standing up straight. Tobias reveals an object coated in a gleaming jet black color—the same color as my surroundings. I first found peace in the darkness, but now I feel nothing but unease that trembles like a shattering earthquake—growing at every terrifying millisecond.

His eyes narrow at me, coruscating with amusement. And then, he says five words—just five words—but those five words alone are enough to shatter my bones:

"It's not you I'll hurt."

And then, he turns around and walks away.

I inch to the clear wall, grazing my hands along it, desperate to know what he meant. But my yearnings are answered as four of the people I love the most in this world originate from thin air, kneeling to the ground in a straight line—their eyes leering into me.

The breath that squeezes out of my throat enters every crevice of my environment.

Tobias circles around them, his eyes indecisive as he paws the object clung to his side. "Hmm, who is up first? Shall I go with the little girl first? Or maybe I should start with the men first?"

"Get away from them!" I shriek, my eyes scorching with tears.

He ignores my desperate remarks and makes his way to my father. He stands behind him, bringing the metal object and pressing the gaping hole of it to the back of my dad's head. He grins, fingering the trigger, and pulls back.

My father falls to the ground with a *thud*, his skill cracking with the impact.

Before I can react, he travels down the line and shoots my mother. Then my sister. And lastly—my brother.

Tears blur my vision. I'm melting to the ground. I can't breathe.

They are all fallen forward, their heads bloodied and bodies splayed in such a terrifying manner that it engraves into my brain.

Tobias brings the slick black gun into his pocket again and

steps in front of the puddles of blood, making his way toward me.

I would move back in fear, but my legs are inactive. My thoughts are too.

When he reaches the wall, he kneels down again, his face eerily close to mine. I feel his hot breath traveling past the barrier and entering my veins. I'm shaking, tears dripping down my cheeks and hanging by my jaw, sporadically plopping onto my open palms.

His lips stretch out into a diabolical grin, tearing through his cheeks and tearing through my heart shattered into incalculable pieces.

"As much as you've dedicated your life to protecting them," he says, "you won't be able to. I know you won't."

Screams rip out of my chest as I tear my eyes open.

I sob with heaving breaths, each periodic scream raspy and rattling my throat. I bring my knees to my chest, digging my fingers into my thighs as I scream into them, ramming my teeth into the flesh. I bite down onto my skin, trembling with every movement, and I begin to taste liquid. I pull back, heaving and out of breath. Sweet blood trickles down my thighs and I abruptly wipe it away, my hands bloodied.

I scream again.

Eventually, my throat becomes so hoarse I have to stop screaming. So I level my breaths, my chest heaving in and out. But my heart is beating at a million miles per hour. *I don't know* how to calm myself.

So I turn and expect to see Jax. Expect to dive into his torso and bring his strong arms around me. Expect to feel his soft breath on the top of my head. Expect to trace my fingers along the curve of his carved jaw and bring it to his impeccable lips.

Expect to blend into him, into his presence, into his figure that brings me out of my internal hell.

But he isn't there.

The emptiness from his side of the bed is like a knife entering my chest. It tears through my insides and leaves me vulnerable and exposed.

A tear trickles down my cheek as I run my hand across his pillow, unbelievably gutted at his absence. Maybe he had to go to the bathroom. Maybe he just wanted a glass of water from the kitchen. Or maybe he went to the living room and wanted some fresh air.

I wait five minutes. He does not show up.

I grip the blanket in my hands and tear it off me, grunting to myself as I sob into my hands. Where did he go? I want him to tell me my nightmare was just a nightmare—that it wasn't real. I want his gray eyes to console me. I want to feel his soft lips on me—not just my lips, but everywhere I've desired them to touch. To feel. To caress. I want him to hug me so tight I'm embedded in his soul. I've become so unbelievably attached to him I can't stand a second without him. I *need* him.

But I also can't help but wonder . . . where did he go? Did he become tired of me and leave his room? Why didn't he wake me up or tell me? Or maybe . . . someone took him from me. Maybe kidnapped him. Tortured him, even. God, if anyone laid their hands on my man, then I would rip their eyes out with my bare hands.

The gaping emptiness in this room is too much for me to bear. So instead of dwelling on Jax's disappearance, I bring the blanket with me as I get up and wrap it around me. Every step I take out the door is marked with reluctance. I can't sit here and wait for him. What if he never shows up?

So I make my way to my family's room.

The door is unlocked, as I purposefully left it before. The entire building is secure anyway. I open the door slowly, revealing a dark room almost the same layout of Jax's. And I close it behind me, wiping my tears away and going down the hallway.

I peer inside my siblings' room first. From the cracked door, I see Em's hand is hanging down the edge of the bed, her mouth gaping open as snores erupt out of her. I would've been next to her. On the other hand, Nico is sprawled across the majority of the bed, one arm hung behind his head and the other clinging onto his chest. The snores that come out of him are the sounds of a threatened bear growling.

I can't help but smile and cry at the same time. Poor Em. How can she even sleep with our brother snoring like that?

Finally, I walk past their room and make my way to my parents' room. They are sleeping on separate sides of the bed, but they're facing each other—their breaths even. It brings me comfort to see them safe and sound, being here rather in our closeted home that was barely a home to begin with. My family deserves the most luxurious home of all. And I will make sure they get it one day.

Tightening my hold of the blanket around me, the excess of it trailing behind me like a shadow, I bring myself to the front of bed and crawl through the middle of it. I insert myself between my parents, landing on the soft mattress and feeling the pillow encasing the back of my head. Seconds later, they stir, and their half-awake eyes gape at me confusingly.

"*Mija?*" my mama whispers. "What are you doing here?"

"Is everything okay?" my papa adds.

I shake my head slightly, forcing my tears back because I don't want to worry my parents with them. "Everything is okay," I lie. "I just had a nightmare."

"Aw, Blaire." Mama drapes her hand across my chest, snuggling against my shoulder. "I'm sorry to hear that. You can sleep with us the entire night, if you want."

I nod immediately, my heart swooning. "Yeah. That's what I want."

The wound in my heart is healed as my mother kisses my cheek and caresses my jaw. My father rubs his hand on my shoulder and whispers to me that I am a strong woman, that I am beautiful, and that my family will always be here for me.

I sigh, closing my eyes and relishing in my parents' presence. It is my mission and my utmost determination to keep my family alive and safe, especially with the unwanted presence of the ERUSA.

Tobias is wrong; I'll be able to keep my family safe. Even if it means sacrificing my own life.

14

PROPOSITION

JAX

"LIEUTENANT REAVES IS WAITING for us at the headquarters. We must hurry."

Silver cuffs are clung around my wrists, and I grit my teeth, attempting to tear them apart.

The soldier in the front lets out a gruff laugh. "Nice try, Mr. Remington."

I look at the front, noticing the man turned to me, clad in a jet-black uniform and his face completely hidden in a gleaming black mask. A small label is engraved onto his breast pocket. It reads **ERUSA**, and it is a brazen font with a blazing blue color.

I am currently sprawled across the backseat of a moving car, the engine rumbling as it cruises down the Detroitian streets. It is eerily silent, except for the thousands of questions ramming into my mind.

"Why am I here?" I finally speak for the first time since I was brought here.

The soldier beside him, currently driving, adjusts his gloved hand on the steering wheel. "I am afraid we cannot answer that question."

I frown. "Why the hell not?"

"It is confidential."

"Confidential, my ass. You weirdos kidnapped me out of nowhere, and now you expect me to just sit tight like an obedient little child? Yeah, no, you're insane—"

I suddenly feel cool metal pressed in between my eyebrows. The soldier's gloved finger presses back on the trigger, a loud click resounding against my skin. The last time a gun was pressed against me was seven months ago, when I was kidnapped by the Subversives and Vi interrogated me the entire day. I remember just how frightened I felt, in a moment of vulnerability where I had no choice but to submit.

Such as now.

"To think the beloved President Remington's son would've at least had some manners. But considering your sinful actions on the fourth of December, I'd have to say I'm not surprised at your childish behavior either.

"Be quiet for the remainder of the ride." He brings the gun down, and I release a held-in breath. "Otherwise, I'll have the bits of your brain splattered across the windows."

I cross my arms, frowning as I sit ram-rod straight and lean against the window. I like my brain way too much to let it get blown into pieces, so I'd much rather obey and sit tight. Even though these guys scare the living shit out of me.

Five long minutes later, we arrive at the craning headquarters—in the heart of the city. Soldiers are lined around the parameters, studying our approaching vehicle and making way for us. I stare out the window, speechless, and wince every time distant gunshots, screams, and cries are heard. It's only been barely a day since the ERUSA took over Detroit, and it seems as if many people have died in just this small time period. I can't even imagine how much damage they can do in just this summer alone.

We drive past the gates slowly opening. The vehicle stops at the curb of the headquarters, and the soldier driving brings the window down. The distant screams and cries and gunshots are not so distant anymore.

He leans against the door and says to the soldier approaching, "I'm Comrade Hernandez and beside me is Comrade Bennett. The subject is in the back."

The ERUSA soldier by the curb nods once and allows us to go forward. After closing the window, the engine hums back to life as the tires tread against the smooth marbled-tilings. Mounds of trees hover over us, grazing against the roof of the vehicle. And, as the vehicle enters the round-a-bout, I am met with a tall and jagged building architecturally designed to look like a pin needle, except it's thicker at the bottom and becomes increasingly thin as one would venture to the top. The exterior is a shimmery silver that glints against the gleaming moon peering over us all. This is, of course, the Detroitian headquarters. The headquarters wasn't exactly built until after the formation of the newly reformed Detroit—after struggling to swim past the Dark Ages. The self-appointed members of the Detroitian government transformed this building into a government board meeting location, where everyone would convene to talk about any rising issues.

Of course, this was all informed by Layla. If it weren't for her, I would be a headless deer wandering amongst the night.

Comrade Hernandez and Bennett exit the vehicle and open the door on the right for me. As I make my way *peacefully* out of the car, they tug on my forearm and lug me forward. I wince, instinctively swatting the men away. "Damn, no need to be so harsh," I grumble.

They ignore my complaints the entire time we walk into the

headquarters. By then, my remarks have ceased and now I am left staring at the inside like a child inside of a candy store.

The Subversives and I already saw the headquarters when we first arrived here, but that was the last time ever. Now, this is my second time, and the breathtaking beauty of this place is still, well, *breathtaking*. A chandelier speckled with golden lights dangles above us, clinking as the wind unravels into the lobby. The flooring beneath my shoes I hurriedly put on before I was forced to come here feels hard and is the same color as Mallory's skin—beige. In front of us are numerous halls, amassing past elevators, decorations, and pictures depicting the endearing history and growth of Detroit.

We walk past the lobby and into the elevator. The two soldiers stand beside me, and every now and then, from the corner of my eye, I notice their heads moving slightly toward my handcuffed hands. These *bastards*. First they tear me away from my girlfriend and now they keep staring at me, as if I would have the actual guts to leave. Even if I wanted to, I would've done it a long ass time ago.

The elevator slowly ascends to the top. I clench my fists at my sides, thinking back to the precious time I spent with Blaire before I was lugged here against my will. I yearn to be by her side again. Just being in her presence is enough to console me for days. And—God—I can't even imagine how she would feel if she supposedly woke up in the middle of the night and saw that I wasn't there. I hate to see her upset.

Suddenly, the elevator jolts to a stop. The doors sift open, revealing a vast hallway drowning in glimmering marble. When we walk forward, I gape at the dozens of twinkling chandeliers that amass the ceilings. Everywhere around me are decorations seeming to be carved from gold itself. And the elegant music in the background rings into my ears. God, this entire floor must've taken a while to decorate and finalize—especially during the Dark Ages.

Hernandez and Bennett lead me to a door wedged in the far corner of the expansive floor. It is plated in a shimmering bronze color, towering over me and covering almost a fourth of the wall. As Bennett goes to open the door, I notice the thinly plated words **CHARLOTTE LEVINE** situated in the middle of the door have been scratched and ripped out and replaced with an unseemingly terrifying replacement.

The first thing I see when the door opens is a bookcase covering the entire wall. Thousands of intriguing covers are displayed to me, and I immediately think of Blaire. *Man, she would've squealed with delight seeing this shit.* My eyes trail over next to a small couch situated in front of a sleek black TV. Thousands of portraits of Charlotte Levine and her daughter are displayed to us, alongside many others of the city. Finally, I study the white-stained glass table in the middle of the room, adorned with a tiny house plant, a cup of pens and pencils, and various stacks of papers covering the entire table.

And the frightening woman standing by the desk chair behind it.

A lump grows in my throat as I acknowledge her eyes narrowed on me—and the way she twirls a thin blue pen in her paper-thin hands. Her whitish-blonde hair unravels at her sides, framing her harsh and sharp features. And she curtly clears her throat, pulling at the tips of her blazer.

"Take his handcuffs off, Comrade Hernandez," she says.

Without a word, he comes to me and releases the handcuffs digging into my wrists. I release an inaudible sigh and roll my neck, my gut tightening at the quite unfortunate situation I have landed myself in. Instead of wordlessly following that stupid ERUSA soldier, I should've just kicked him in the groin and slammed the door in his face. Or grabbed that rifle from his hand and pointed it at him, or something. I don't know—I feel like I should've just brought up a fight instead of being a coward and following the soldier around like a goddamn puppy. That way, I could've been spending my entire night with Blaire, wrapped up in her comforting arms. God, how much I miss her and her body and her smile and just *everything* about her.

When Hernandez steps back with the handcuffs in his gloved hands, Veronica nods once. "You and Comrade Bennett may leave."

The two men mutter out a "thank you, Lieutenant Reaves" and make their way out the door.

And close it.

"Sit down, please," she says.

I scoff. "Thanks, but no thanks."

"I don't want any trouble with you, Mr. Remington. I just want you to sit and have an adult conversation with me. You *are* an adult, if I'm right?"

I clench my jaw. "Yes. I'm twenty-one."

"Ah." She grins slightly. "You grew up so fast. I swear you were fourteen just yesterday." A moment of silence weighs into the room, and she gestures at the chair by my side again. "Take a seat, please. Let's chat. No harm in doing so, right?"

Eventually, I give in and sit down. Since I've already gone through so much trouble to get here, I might as well make the best of it.

When I sit down, I lean back in the chair and sigh. Veronica sits herself too and intertwines her fingers, leaning forward and tilting her head at me. God, this woman terrifies the living crap out of me—with those inhumane icy blue eyes and sharp jaw of hers. I am wholeheartedly convinced she isn't a human. She must be genetically engineered to look like a hybrid, or a screwed up version of a she-wolf. And sometimes, I can't help but imagine . . . how can a frightening woman like her give birth to such a sweet and warm girl like Mallory? It honestly doesn't make sense to me sometimes.

She speaks moments later. "Do you know the details of how the new D.C. society was formed?"

"Yes." I shrug. "I learned about it in my history class a couple of years ago."

"But do you know the details of it? Do you know truly just how life-changing it was?"

I frown. "No, not really."

At that, Veronica chuckles, but doesn't open her mouth at all in doing so. "Of course you don't. The education system doesn't really care about educating their students about the true aspects of our society anyway." She takes a deep breath and looks at me dead in the eye. "Let me explain to you the truth of our society, and how we formed such a wonderful system that should be established in every corner of our country.

"The Dark Ages, as you should be aware of, consisted of the Second Great Depression and the civil war our country endured. It went on for a couple of years and it all came to a mutual close when the rich and the poor in our country decided to go their own ways. But in D.C., the booming capital of the nation, us rich people were adamant to not let the poor people escape our wrath like that. You see, they were the reason for our nation's downfall. Our stock market and economy plummeted because of their inability to pay their debts and contribute to their end of their responsibilities. Of course we would make them pay and get our vengeance.

"So, the remaining rich people in D.C. came together in the ruins of our beloved city and came up with a plan to tighten our hold on these ungrateful individuals. We formed a revamped version of the government and immediately began the new society in 2038, after much planning. We did think to eradicate all of those who had incredible debt and a low salary during the Dark Ages, but we thought of it to be too vile and repulsive. Instead, we found it more convenient to weave them into our reimagined society as pawns in our new board game."

"And you guys—of course—decided to separate us into the

Rich and the Poor?" I scowl. "Only because your egos were threatened?"

"It was not a matter of egos, my dear," she says calmly. "It was solely to do with a matter to serve our country."

"In what way *did* you guys serve our country? Separating us all is not the solution because all it does is create even more wars and distress."

"Because a certain group of individuals refuse to be tied down."

"See, that's where you're wrong." I spring up from my seat and glare down at her. "You self-appointed people believe that these so-called 'poor people' are the reason for the economic depression when, in reality, it was probably because consumer spending and overall investments decreased. That is a team effort, rather than a group of people you're bunching together only because they weren't wealthy. Do you know how insulting that is to them and our country alone? Just admit that you believe your pride is being threatened and you refuse to live in a country that's falling apart at the seams."

"Sit down," she grits through her teeth. "I did not bring you here to argue on the economical aspects of our past."

"You're the one who started it," I grumble, reluctantly taking a seat.

Veronica plays with the blue pen in her rough and bony hands. Her sullen eyes drill into me as she says, "Look, Jax. I don't want to get off on the wrong footing with you."

"Bit too late for that," I murmur.

"And I don't want to make this night stressful and irritating for us too," she emphasizes. "I know you're very confused by how the past two days have been, just like my daughter. I am, of course, very upset with both of you for siding with these rebels, but that is a topic for later. Right now, I want to talk to you about the real reason you are here."

I raise my eyebrow. "Which is . . .?"

She takes a deep breath in, her cracked lips parting slightly as she drums her finger lightly against the edge of the stained-glass table. "The ERUSA are determined to reinforce our ideals we enforced in D.C., except it's not just the division of the Rich and the Poor. It is now those who are Impure and Pure. Impures are anyone who are Poor and any Detroitian who was directly and indirectly involved with the Subversives and the remaining Poor population's arrival here."

"What you're doing is useless and a waste of your time, Veronica," I say tiredly.

"It is Mrs. Reaves for you, as it always has been," she growls. "And neither is it useless nor a waste of my time. I am just carrying on with your father's duties except I will do it much better than he did."

"I'm sure he'd be happy to hear that."

She cocks her head, her pencil-thin eyebrows pinched together in irritation. "As I was stating before, the ERUSA is determined to carry out its goal during its entire stay here. Once we've fully inputted the ERUSA's system in Detroit, we will reconvene with remaining cities and build up our country brick by brick and stone by stone. I couldn't care less if it takes two years, maybe even twenty. I will do whatever it takes to rebuild our country.

"And that is why I need you," she concludes, setting the blue pen down.

My eyes widen as her words settle into my mind like heavy clay. "Me? What the hell do you want from me?"

"Just one thing. I can get you assigned to my request right now. It is quite urgent."

I shake my head. "I never told you I want to be a part of your stupid request. I just want to know . . . why me?"

Veronica presses her lips together and answers five long seconds later. "You know, I never liked you. I always questioned you and your personality. I always wondered how such a disheveled person like you could be related to such a prestigious man. All in all, you were utterly repugnant."

I roll my eyes. "Anything else you might want to add?"

"But you made my daughter happy, in whatever bizarre way you did," she concedes. "All Adam and I wanted was for her to be pleased with her life, and she always was when she was with you. I don't know why, but because of that, I allowed you to be friends with her. We would do anything for her happiness."

When she tells me that, I am met with a sudden recollection of Mallory revealing to me that she had feelings for me—when we were escaping the Guards as Subversives in our bunker and she and I were keeping watch that night. In all honesty, I was shocked. I had not even a tiny voice in my head that repeatedly shouted to me that Mallory liked me as more than a friend. I genuinely believed she thought very highly of me—but just as friends.

Mallory and I are way past that conversation, though, which relieves me because I can only think of her as my best friend and nothing more. Mallory reassures me she feels the same way too, which I can tell by her fervent desire for Blaire and me to be together. We have healthy boundaries established, and I am glad that we are now open with each other.

Veronica's voice startles me and ceases my thoughts. "As I said before, while you were distasteful as a person, you had some good qualities to you too, which is why I think of you as a Pure blood."

My hands immediately clench the chair's arms. *"What?"*

"You are the son of Tobias Remington."

"Were," I emphasize. "I do not identify myself as a Remington anymore."

"That is foolish to say. You can try to run away from your bloodline as much as you want, but you are still one whether you like it or not. And besides, your birth certificate and overall records name you as a Remington. Therefore, you are one."

"Can't you just leave this Pure and Impure bullshit behind and move on already?" I sigh. "I get that you're possibly upset about your husband's death. I really do get it. But that doesn't give you the right to unleash hell on such a beautiful city that took forever to rebuild itself after the Dark Ages. And, most of all, you can't be so determined to create this totalitarian society that you would shoot your own daughter if you don't get your own way. Are you not the slightest bit worried about her?"

"First of all," she says slowly, "she will live. Second of all, this is not only about my husband's death. And third of all . . . I don't care whether I have the right or not. I am the leader of the ERUSA and Detroit now too. What you say will not affect me at all.

"Thus, you must listen and believe me when I say you are a Pure blood because, as surprising as it may seem, you have leadership qualities in you. While your sinful actions against your father were quite harrowing, I was overall pleased with your passion. I believe that passion can come in handy if you join my side."

"You're crazy as hell," I grumble under my breath.

"Spy on the Detroitian military for me," she blurts out.

I almost jump out of my seat, blood jamming through my veins as my knuckles turn searingly white from how tight I clench the chair's arms. *What the actual hell?*

"How do I know about them, you must be wondering?" She pretends to ponder. "Do you really believe I would have zero idea of the estranged Detroitian military coming together—or rather, *reforming*—to fight against us? I have taken over the headquarters, where there are cameras in every nook and cranny of this place—even in Windsor. I know and see all, Mr. Remington."

"You're joking."

"I am not. I know every single thing going on in this city and outside of it too, but I am not going to attack. Not yet, at least. I want to gather all of my cards and use them wisely."

"Why are you telling me this?" My chest rises in and out. "What if I go back and tell everyone about your proposition?"

"You won't."

"And how are you so sure about that?"

"Because you are going to accept it right now, and you will pledge to obey me for the time being."

"Yeah, and I have a head growing out of my ass."

"You know, I really do not appreciate your immature commentaries," she seethes. "I just want you to acknowledge and accept my proposition. I know you all met with the military this morning, so you have no way out of this. All you have to do is act nice with them and report back to me on a weekly basis because I need to be several steps ahead of them at all times."

I don't even wait for her to finish speaking when I say, "I will never, and I am never going to accept your proposition. You're out of your goddamn mind."

I get up from my chair and start to storm out the door. I could care less about her proposition. There is no way in hell I would ever betray my family. No way.

"I see that you and Blaire Cohen are getting closer nowadays."

I stop in my tracks. And turn around.

"What the hell do you mean by that?"

"I'm assuming she is your girlfriend? And that she means a lot to you, correct?"

"Stop it."

"I guess she does, then." She chuckles underneath her breath. "So I am also assuming you would be very upset if something happened to her and that you would sacrifice your own pride for her?"

I clamp my mouth shut. I hate this woman with my absolute life.

Veronica narrows her eyes at me, her pupils swarming in a puddle of victory. "How do you feel knowing that walking out on me means her life will be threatened? That I would kill her?"

My feet are like tree roots embedding into the Earth's grounds. "You wouldn't."

"Oh, but I would. Anything for the ERUSA."

"If you even put a finger on her, then I swear on my life I will kill you myself."

"Well, if that's the case, then accept my proposition." She pauses. "If you want her to be spared."

I clench my jaw, feeling a wave of rage unravel through me, dying to be let out.

Veronica continues to study me, her eyes like slimy worms leaching into my soul. "All you have to do is accept my request and spy for me. That is all. And I can promise you I will not put a hand on Blaire. Just do this one thing for me, and I will spare her."

I run my hand across my bicep, letting out a low and strangled breath. There's no way I am going to accept her request. It is extremely delusional of her to ask that—thinking I am just going to up and leave everyone and join that wicked witch's side. Like hell I ever would.

But *Blaire.*

Just the thought of Veronica or anyone else inflicting pain on her brings such unbearable misery to me. She has already been through so much, and the last thing I want for her is to go through hell all over again.

I close my eyes, and gradually open them. Think to myself for a moment. And think one more time.

I hate what I'm about to do.

I hate that I'm about to sit down and accept her offer.

I hate that I'm about to vow secrecy and loyalty to her.

I hate that I'm going to spy on the Reformers to relay information to her.

And I hate that I'm betraying my friends who I had to prove so much to in order to even have them trust me just the slightest.

But I have to do this, whether I like it or not because Blaire's life is being threatened.

And after everything we've been through, I cannot risk that right now . . . especially because I *know* Veronica is not bluffing. She *would* kill Blaire if she got in her way even in the slightest— even if she was the smallest obstacle in her path.

I know she would.

15

ASSEMBLE

BLAIRE

EVERYONE IS GATHERED BY the foyer, indulged in conversations and light breakfast foods. Em and Tamia are sitting by the stairs, as Em guides her on how to eat a bagel. Layla, Nico, and Vi are standing by the front door, huddled in a tight circle as they're probably discussing our plan for today, which is to start our training at the Reformers' facility. And Mallory, Jeremiah, and I are in the middle of the room, talking about just how crazy life has been and it's barely been a week. Everyone seems to be using the company of others to alleviate their own worries that have basically been eating us up after the ERUSA's forced residing in Detroit.

All except Jax.

Ever since we all gathered by the foyer ten minutes ago, he's been leaning against the back wall, one foot propped against it and hands shoved into the pockets of his baggy camo pants. His chin is dipped into the base of his neck, and his chest rises in and out—slowly—as he closes his eyes to himself.

I quickly excuse myself to Mallory and Jeremiah and make my way to him.

I know it's probably not the best idea to pelt him with questions, but I am curious to know where he was last night. Or more so worried about him. He hasn't been himself this morning, which confuses me because he was acting rather normal last night. Something must've happened.

When he sees me walking toward him, he straightens up and smiles at me. However, I've memorized all his facial expressions quite thoroughly, so I am well aware he is faking that smile just to reassure me. I don't know whether that frustrates or saddens me. Maybe a little bit of both.

"Hey," I whisper, standing in front of him and craning my neck to look him in the eye. "Is everything okay?"

"Yeah," he says a bit too quickly. His gray eyes that are usually so radiant aren't radiating anymore. "Everything is okay, beautiful. Why?"

I sigh, inching toward him until we are almost torso-to-torso. "You left in the middle of the night," I say. "I'm sure something is bothering you if that's the case."

He shakes his head slightly, angling his head to mine. "I'm so sorry. I didn't mean to leave you like that. I was just . . . getting some fresh air. I had a horrible nightmare."

I did, too, I think to myself. *But I didn't leave you like you did.*

Another accusation lingers in my mind, in which I blurt out, "Is it me? Am I the problem?"

His eyes suddenly widen as he leans down to my height and cups my face with his soft hands, instantly bringing it inches to his beautiful features. It physically pains me sometimes just how beautiful he is. It's as if he was made in the stars and brought down to the world like an iridescent angel.

"Never in a million years would you ever be the problem." There's an urging and aching to his voice. "I can promise you that."

Electricity jolts into my veins and jumpstarts my heart as he presses a soft kiss to my lips. He pulls back, but only slightly so our lips are still touching. "Again, I'm sorry for acting weird. I'm still adjusting to this whole new situation. But I promise I'll become the man you deserve very soon. I will."

Before I can respond, he grabs my hand—interlacing our fingers together—and leads me to the others. Believe me, I am still shaken and hypnotized by his words—let alone his addictive lips—but I still feel a voice lurking in the back of my mind imploring me I shouldn't believe him so easily . . . that there is something he knows that he refuses to tell me.

We leave for the Detroitian military base as soon as an eerily familiar female voice rings into the implanted speakers around us.

"Please rise for the ERUSA pledge."

We look around at each other, frozen in our place.

"Dear Great Members of Society, it is hereby declared that I will adhere to the ERUSA, by the ERUSA, and for the ERUSA. All Pure Bloods are United, while all of Impure will be Separated. Beautiful America will be Cleansed of all Impure, of all non-ERUSA. Failure to Adhere to the ERUSA will result in the Shedding of Blood and Skin. Therefore, I will Adhere, I will Pledge, and I will Obey. Amen."

A thick and heavy silence like clotting blood fills into my throat.

"That's going to be hard to get used to," Mal whispers as we climb into the jeep.

Vi, who is driving this time, revs the engine as she looks at her with great intensity. "Who said we had to get used to it?"

Her words resonate in my mind as she drives past the driveway originating from our relocated home and the fissured roads. I turn around and notice the close-shuttered windows, where my parents, Em, and Tamia must be. They will be safely residing here while we spend our time at the military base, and if anything were to occur to them, then the safety bracelets on their wrist will release a signal to one of us. We do think it is unnecessary to keep them away from us, but we decided there is no reason for them to see our training because, well, I don't think it'll really interest them. Especially Em, who practically screeches when she even senses an oncoming fight.

The entire drive consists of Vi veering past ERUSA vehicles and wholly avoiding driving into the city. The chaos has increased significantly today, as I see flames and smoke billowing out of buildings and amalgamating into the gleaming white clouds. One of those buildings is probably the refuge, and my gut physically twists as I realize that we unfortunately were not able to save everyone. We already struggled with saving everyone when we first arrived here, and now the same situation is catching up to us. And I feel incredibly helpless and selfish driving away from the chaos when I know damn well I should be there, fighting against the ERUSA and reclaiming our territory.

But I am a part of the Subversives—*again.* Which means I am a part of a team, and I must cooperate with everyone.

We reach the base in less than ten minutes, only because Vi drove like a madman, and we quickly trample inside the gaping entrance. After we check in with security, we traverse through the narrowing hallways and reach the commonplace, where the entire area is still bustling in and out with people. We veer past the commonplace and enter a wooden door in the far left, making way to a large training room that interconnects with private sparring stations, shooting facilities, and massive gyms.

I feel my stomach tightening just looking at this place. The entire training room itself must be three times bigger than the Subversives' bunker.

As Layla, Nico, Jeremiah, Vi, Mal, Jax, and I stand here, we hear a familiar shuffling of heavy combat boots and a deep voice rattling into the air. "You made it on time."

We all turn to Commander Thatcher, who has her thin lips set into a straight line. Wrinkles amass her forehead as strands of her short brown hair fall onto her eyebrows. "Training will begin very shortly. Please take a seat by the benches to my left and wait for the soldiers to arrive. Let me know if you have any questions."

She stalks to the sparring stations to the left, keenly watching a man and an even larger man circling around each other, arms held up to their chests in defense. As they spend the next ten seconds wandering around each other and refusing to engage in combat, Commander Thatcher flares her nostrils and yells at the men, "Quit prancing around like goddamn chickens and fight each other, for Christ's sake!"

Jax lets out a low whistle beside me. "That woman scares the shit out of me." He smirks and turns to Vi. "Kinda reminds me of you."

She scowls and smacks his forehead with the back of her hand. He winces, muttering profanities underneath his breath.

Once we've seated ourselves on the benches and wait for a couple of minutes, we hear light footsteps originating from where we came in. We turn to the door and see a familiar stream of red traveling down someone's back, and flaring green eyes tracing the proximity of the room. The tight jetblack romper on this person outlines all their curves and edges, and a dose of jealousy and insecurity courses through me. *How does one even* get *a body like that?* All I have going for me are my long tan legs and my rather generous posterior.

But this woman has *everything* going for her. She has me glancing at Jax every now and then too, hoping he's not enamored by her presence. But when I see he's not even looking at her and is instead rubbing his forehead with a grimace on his mouth, I feel a bit more relieved.

She sits besides Vi, crossing her long legs and studying her nails, which are smeared in the same color as her romper. When she notices us staring at her, she raises her well-threaded eyebrows and purses her medium-sized lips together. "I'm sorry, have we met before?" she says in a small yet judgmental tone with a semi-Russian accent.

"Yeah," Mal says, who sits behind her with Layla and Jeremiah on the same bench as her. "We were there when you came to the base and told Commander Thatcher that you wanted to join the military." She pauses and then murmurs, "And the other fifteen times we met you too."

"Oh." Renata chuckles to herself. "That's quite interesting. I swear we haven't met before. Maybe it's because I meet so many people everyday."

"Prissy bitch," Vi mutters to herself.

"I'm sorry, I couldn't quite catch that?" She looks at her with genuine confusion.

"Oh." Vi looks at her for a split second and brings her eyes back to the ground. "Don't worry about it."

Renata nods and looks over at Layla. She straightens up and leans forward to her. "You're Layla Morgan, aren't you?"

She grins, dark and thick curly locks falling onto her glistening brown eyes. "That's me. We've met a couple of times before."

"Yes, you seem pretty familiar to me," she says. "You used to come over to the headquarters frequently to discuss matters about the refuge with us. My mother admired you a lot." Her voice suddenly cracks, and she shakes her head, sadly smiling to herself. "My mother was a very appreciative person."

"I'm sorry for your loss," I breathe out.

Everyone echoes my words, except for Vi, who just whispers it to herself. Renata holds a shaky hand up to her heart and grins, flashing her flawless teeth. *Damn, what about her* isn't *flawless?* "Thank you," she whispers. "You guys are so sweet." She sniffles and quickly consoles herself. "I'm assuming you are all here for the first training session too, correct?"

"Yes, we are," Jax says. "We are the Subversives."

"Oh, the *Subversives.*" Renata snaps her fingers with realization. "I've been trying to place my finger on who you guys are. You were just too familiar to me."

As Renata goes on about her familiarity with us, even though she said before she swore before she'd never seen us in the first place, Commander Thatcher appears in front of us and clears her throat. Renata's chatter ceases and she straightens herself up.

"I see that you've arrived," Commander Thatcher says. "Did you find your way around here easily?"

"Yes, I did." Renata nods eagerly. "The place is becoming easier to navigate."

"That's nice to hear." She pauses and looks around the training room. "All right, let me get started with the orientation. Since this is your first training session, you will just be training amongst yourselves. Once I *know* you have passed that level, only then will you be ready to train with the other soldiers and especially the best ones here.

"In regards to my best soldiers, AJ and Annie will be here shortly to commence your training. They, alongside the other top soldiers in the vicinity, will be guiding you with the equipment as you slowly get used to it and eventually participate in combat. Until then, we will wait for AJ and Annie to arrive so we can get started as soon as possible." Commander Thatcher walks back into the entryway and stuffs her strong hands into the pocket of her uniform. "Time is an essential and delicate substance, and it will not be wasted in this compound."

"Yet another batch of trainees I have to hear you say that to." We turn to the side where the deep voice comes from. AJ and Annie emerge from a set of doors, gleaming at Commander Thatcher's sight.

"AJ and Annie." She nods once. "Pleasure to see you here."

"No, the pleasure is mine," Annie says, grinning.

They turn to us, standing side by side with their arms clung against their chests. AJ, dressed in a tight black shirt that reveals his taut and gleaming tan muscles, nods once in Annie's direction. She salutes her brother and jogs over to the gym on our left.

AJ speaks moments later. "While my sister prepares the gym for you guys, I'm gonna briefly explain what to expect from our training sessions." He pulls his arms back and paces back and forth slowly as he starts to speak again. "We, as the Detroitian military, plan to reclaim our territory and fight against the ERUSA in a month when we are *all* ready to step on the battlegrounds. That is why we expect you all to be fully prepared to join us on the battlegrounds too.

"So, in this time period, you will engage in heavy combat amongst yourselves before you eventually join the rest of the comrades. I am well aware you are the Subversives and have helped a good majority of the people escape the ruins of D.C., but you all lack military and professional skills. Therefore, I will be guiding you until then.

"Are there any questions?" AJ stops in his tracks and looks at us, his golden eyes lingering over me for a bit too long. I hold my breath as he sets his jaw and cocks his head, his gaze never leaving mine.

I immediately look away and inch closer to Jax, clinging onto his bicep. *Sorry, AJ. I already have a man.*

His eyes leave mine as he looks at Renata, who has her hand up. "Yes, Ms. Levine?" He clears his throat.

She pushes her flowing red hair to the side and tilts her heart-shaped head. "What if you don't have any combat training at all? What would you do then?"

AJ suddenly looks like somebody punched him in the gut. "What? You don't have combat training?"

"Yeah." Renata presses her lips together. "Is that okay?"

He looks over at Commander Thatcher with desperation, and his eyes seem to say, *What the hell is going on?*

Commander Thatcher leers her hard, cold eyes on him. *I'll explain later.*

AJ looks back at Renata and sighs, his broad shoulders sulking. "That's fine. I guess we'll just pay extra attention to you."

She grins, winking at him. "Not a problem for me."

Besides her, Vi turns to us and dryly mouths, *Get me out of here.*

AJ, who has still been stomaching what Renata was insinuating, nods slowly and leers his eyes to us. "Any other questions?"

We all shake our heads.

"Awesome." He claps his hands together. "Let's all go over to the gym now."

We all stand up from the benches and make our way to the tall set of see-through doors that AJ glides his strong forearm against, pushing it open. A rush of cool air smacks my cheeks as I take in the strong smell of rubber and metal. Weights clank and people grunt in the background as we tread over to the main entrance of the gym. This is, of course, just one of the many gyms here because it is rumored thousands of soldiers reside in this massive compound alone.

AJ stops us in our tracks and studies us, clenching his jaw and furrowing his dark, thick brows. "I'm gonna split you guys up into teams, based on what Commander Thatcher decided for herself." He points to the tall woman behind us, who seemed to have crept up on us like a ghost. "This is all random and doesn't designate any physical differences between you all. Everyone understand?"

We nod.

"Great." AJ clears his throat and clicks his tongue against the roof of his mouth. "The first group is Mallory and Vienna, and you guys will be with Brady by the cardio station for the time being."

As they disperse to their designated stations, AJ glances at the red-haired woman playing with the material of her skin-tight romper. "Renata, you will be alone with Reynolds by the yoga mats because you have to first stretch out your muscles and prepare for combat before participating in any physically demanding activities.

"Jeremiah and Nicolas, you will be with Annie by the weight station." He glances over at me and the man beside me. "And Jax and Blaire, you will be with me by the other weight station."

My stomach squeezes as I realize just how awkward this situation is going to be. First of all, Jax told me he is not fond of AJ. AJ seems to stare at me a bit too much these days, and it has me hating yet worrying for him at the same time. Is he not aware Jax will literally kill him if he keeps this up? But then again, I don't think he's much aware of our relationship. Maybe I should make that known to him, so he can finally get the hint and leave me alone.

"And Layla will be with me," Commander Thatcher interjects, "Since she is not training and she's only here to watch."

Jax and I follow AJ down the dimly lit corridor as the others disperse to their designated stations. As he and I walk torso-to-torso behind AJ, I feel his hand slightly graze and linger around mine. My heart stutters as I look up to his gleaming gray eyes, twinkling with a hint of amusement. *Watch this,* he mouths.

He brings his other hand to the back of AJ's head and forms it in a way so that only his middle finger is shown. I stifle a laugh as Jax holds both middle fingers to his head now, as AJ is, of course, completely oblivious to his actions.

However, AJ weirdly catches onto our shenanigans in the back and turns around in a swift motion. Jax immediately clamps his mouth shut and brings both of his hands to his sides as quickly as he can.

AJ stops in his tracks and glares at Jax, slightly angling his head to his. It kind of humors me that AJ has to physically look up at him, even though AJ is definitely tall himself.

"Is there a problem, Mr. Remington?" he asks in a dry and accusing tone.

"Nope," Jax drawls out, using all his might to not burst out in laughter. "Everything's fine back here."

AJ narrows his eyes at him and looks over at me again, his expression marked with disappointment and a hint of jealousy.

He turns around and starts walking again. We follow behind him, hand-in-hand now, still stifling our laughter.

16

APPREHEND

JAX

I REALLY MEANT IT when I told Blaire I hate that AJ guy.

Does he not get the hint whenever he stares at Blaire and she looks away from him? Does he not understand she wants nothing to do with him? But then again, this may be my fault too because I never let him know that we're a couple. I should probably let this asshat know that this woman is *mine.*

After our intensive training session ended for the first hour, we were set to go on break. Blaire excused herself to the bathroom, and I sat myself by the bench, running a white towel across my damp shirt. I hate to say it, but AJ's session definitely got me sweating and panting all over the place. My muscles are still clenched up from the deadlifts I did, and I guess these are more effective than the workouts I've been doing incessantly on my own. Even though settling into Detroit and taking care of refugees took a huge chunk of my time, I still managed to hit the gym and work on my physique. I've had no choice but to, only because my father taunted me relentlessly in my mind.

I guess this is now my time to retain my desired physique

and possibly exceed my expectations. This was something I've always wanted since I was a pre-teen, and because of that, I used to workout with my father. He used to teach me all his routines and how he maintained his physique. I hate to say it, but that son of a bitch really knew how to keep himself in shape. He was, overall, a good father whenever he wanted to be. Whenever he didn't want to, though . . . that's when things got traumatizing.

Sighing, I place the white towel beside me and stand up, my calves tense and my abs tightened. AJ emerges from the storage closet with a disinfectant spray and a white cloth in his hand. When he starts to clean the equipment, his eyes narrowed at the tiny spots of sweat speckled everywhere, I stand up from the bench and make my way to him. It's time to let this asshole know what he needs to know. If he keeps this up, then he might just lose all his teeth. Who knows?

I gruffly clear my throat, shoving my hands into the pockets of my pants and glaring at him. He looks at me with raised eyebrows and sets his spray and cloth to the side. "Yes, Jax? Is everything all right?"

"Um, no, actually." I chuckle humorlessly. "Nothing's all right."

He frowns. "Excuse me?"

"You heard me."

"Then what's the problem?"

I intake a sharp breath. "You. You're the problem."

His facial expression drops as he steps toward me, his golden eyes narrowed angrily. "What did you just say?"

"I said"—I look down at him—"you. Are. The. Problem."

AJ stares at me in disbelief and shakes his head, chuckling to himself. "Please enlighten me. Why am *I* the problem when all I've been doing is helping you with your training?"

I snort. "Damn, are you really that stupid? Does being an asshole eat away at your brain cells? Or were you dropped a lot as a kid?"

"Look, I don't appreciate your attitude," he growls. "Just tell me what the hell's going on."

"You keep staring at her!" I snarl. "Even though it is quite obvious she wants nothing to do with you!"

He sets his lips into a straight line. "You're talking about Blaire, aren't you?"

"Yeah," I spit out. "My *girlfriend*."

I expect him to look regretful all of a sudden—or at least seem a little bit shocked—but instead, he just grins in delight. "Oh, I'm already aware of that."

I clench my jaw and lower my tone. "What the hell are you talking about?"

AJ looks a bit too pleased with himself. "I am well aware you guys are a couple. That doesn't mean I can't flirt with her every now and then. She's not your property."

I curl my fists tightly by my sides, preparing to smash his face into smithereens. "I never said she was my property because she isn't. I know she can think for herself. But I just don't appreciate you doing all this knowing *damn well* she's with me. I think you're making a fool out of yourself."

"My image is none of your concern. I can do whatever I want whenever I'd like. If I want to admire your girlfriend, then I am free to do that."

I snort out a laugh. "Why? Do you expect she's going to up and leave me just because *you're* interested in her?"

AJ crosses his arms over his chest and shrugs. "Maybe."

A flash of rage runs through my veins like a lightning bolt. "You take that back, shithead."

"Nope." He smiles irritatingly. "There is a major chance she'll have interest in me and leave you one day. You never know—"

"Take that back!" I yell, shoving him back with my shaking hands.

He stumbles back a little, chuckling to himself, and shakes

his head in disbelief. "Seriously, Remington? You want to do this right now?" AJ cocks his head. "Let's do it."

And, in the blink of an eye, he marches to me and brings his arm back, prepared to hit me.

Until I hear a familiar voice approaching from the other side of the gym. "Stop right now!"

AJ stops in his tracks, looking like a child who got caught stealing the last cookie from the cookie jar. I freeze in place, my chest rising in and out in amalgamated fear and anger.

Vi runs to us while Mal and Jeremiah jog behind her. Her nostrils are flared as she steps in between us and shoves us apart, her eyes narrowed in disappointment. "Can't you two just set aside your testosterone for once and at least *try* to get along?"

We stare at her, speechless.

She scoffs and rolls her eyes, smacking the back of our heads one by one. "You guys are *idiots*. And besides, we have bigger things to worry about than fighting for a girl who clearly"—she gives AJ an unidentified look—"is in a happy relationship right now. So I would suggest you leave them alone because you have no idea how long it took for them to get together.

"And *you*." She shoves a finger onto my chest and glares at me. "I don't know what's been going on with you lately, but you need to get your shit together. The last thing Blaire needs to see is her boyfriend fighting with the best soldier in this compound. Get it together, Jax, before I snitch on you to Thatcher. And God knows how she'll handle your childish ass."

I sulk my shoulders in defeat, letting out a solemn sigh. She's right. What the hell *am* I doing, cornering some dude for just *looking* at Blaire? This isn't me. And the disappointing looks from Mal and Jeremiah and *especially* Vi tell me that I do need to get my shit together.

If only they knew just how much I've been through in the past twelve hours.

Veronica's words are still echoing into my mind and taunting me every corner I pass. I still don't know whether it was the right decision to accept her request, but what other choice did I have? If I refused, then she would've ordered one of her comrades to shoot Blaire, if not her family and the Subversives. I couldn't risk doing that to them, especially her. I wouldn't dare do or accept anything that would risk their lives.

So I had to do this. And it's been eating away at my mind lately.

Once our situation washes away, Vi, Mal, and Jeremiah go back to their designated stations as AJ continues to clean. Blaire suddenly emerges from the bathroom, looking beautiful—as usual—and makes her way to me. And I can't help but think that AJ is wrong in so many ways. Blaire would never leave me. She would forever stay by my side. And AJ would never know how to treat her right because I've been through hell and back with her. We're Bonnie and Clyde—partners in crime. It would be against the laws of the universe if Blaire ended up with anybody else except me—especially with that son of a bitch who thinks he's *so cool* only because he has a couple of tattoos and can fight. I really couldn't care less about him.

I'm taller than him anyway.

I set aside my fifty-pound dumbbell after I finish my reps. Sweat clings to every inch and crevice of my body as I lean forward, jarring breaths escaping my throat. I prop my elbows on my thighs and silently crave water, even just a mere droplet of it.

However, it seems as if my pleas are telepathically heard from Mallory, who walks over to me from the yoga mats with a plastic water bottle in her hand. She arches her eyebrow and thrusts it to me. "You looked like you needed this," she says, a hint of amusement glinting in her tone.

"Thanks," I gasp out, taking the bottle from her and water-falling it to my mouth. I end up drinking and swallowing every drop of water in this bottle and douse the very little left on my face, relishing in the coolness. It's been a while since I've worked out, and after today, I'm going to need everything it takes to keep myself healthy and my muscles growing.

I stand up and hand the bottle back to her. "You're a life-saver, Mallory," I say.

"Ah, stop it." She takes it from me and throws it into a nearby trash can. "When I see a friend in need, I'll do anything it takes to help them."

I playfully nudge her shoulder as we walk over to the benches. "And *that* is why you're my best friend."

"Because I'm so nice?" She smirks.

"That, and you'd be there for me no matter what."

"Like I have been for the past several years I've known you." She grins as we sit on the bench. I stretch my legs out as she crosses hers, and she sends me a friendly look. "How was your day today?"

"Well, besides AJ getting on my nerves"—I sigh—"it was, overall, pretty great, but also very tiring. I'm just not-so patiently waiting for lunch."

"Same." Mallory groans. "Today's training beat the actual life out of me. If this goes on any further, I might just drop dead."

I snort. "Me and you both."

She chuckles lightly and turns her head to me. "Can you believe how much our life has changed and it's barely been a week?"

"No, I can't. It all feels like a giant nightmare to me."

"Tell me about it," she murmurs.

I press my lips together and glance at her, leaning the back of my head against the wall. "Hey, Mallory?"

Her ocean-like eyes land on me. "Yeah, Jax?"

I take a deep breath in. "How are *you* holding up? Especially because, well, your mother is leading an entire organization that has basically taken over Detroit. And also because . . ." I wince. "She shot you."

Mallory leers her eyes away from me and looks up at the ceiling, slowly shaking her head in disgust. "I feel terrible. I want to throw up every time I think about my mom and how she's the reason we're in this situation in the first place." She runs her hand across her exposed thigh, still covered in a slightly bloodied roll of gauze. "Why would she do this to me? And even worst of all, why would she do this to me *and* feel absolutely zero remorse for it? Does she not love me anymore? Only because I disagree with her on how our society should be? Am I really that disgraceful to her?"

"Hey," I whisper, inching to her and rubbing her shoulder. "Your mom is an absolute asshole for doing that to you, you know that, right? Don't blame this on yourself, Mallory. You are nothing like her."

She sighs. "I know I'm not like her, but it still upsets me, Jax. Why couldn't I just have a normal mom? Why couldn't she just love and accept me for who I am? Is she really that upset with me to the point where she *shoots* me in the thigh?" She lets out a sad laugh. "I wish she could just move on and accept our society for what it is. Why did she have to disrupt the calm?"

"You know," I say, "I've wondered the same thing you're wondering right now. My father, as you and I both know, treated me horribly. He was the reason behind this scar." I point to the repugnant *thing* that has been clinging to my cheek since the incident. "He made my life so miserable, Mallory. But what can *I* do? The harm has been made. The damage has been done. Now I am left to carry his sins and his unwanted memories in my mind."

She smiles sadly at me. "Wow, we have really terrible parents."

I chuckle, poking her arm. "Tell me about it."

Mallory starts to play with her blonde hair and sulks in her spot. "I just wish you would've told me."

"Told you what?"

"That your father used to hurt you," she says. "When I asked you about it that day we were on watch in D.C., you refused to bring it up with me." Her eyes flash with pain, and a wave of sadness hits my chest like a punch to my gut. "But you told *Blaire* about it. And I get it. You probably felt more comfortable telling her about it, which is totally fine. But . . . I'm your best friend, Jax. Believe it or not, I *know you.* I'm not saying your girl-friend doesn't know you, but you need to realize that you can trust me too."

I frown and place a hand on top of hers. *Damn, what an asshole I am. What the hell was I even thinking?* "I'm so sorry, Mallory. I didn't even mean to make you feel like that. I promise to open up to you more now. I really do."

"Good." She scoffs. "I was starting to think you secretly hated me."

I immediately shake my head. *"Never* would I ever hate you. Not in this lifetime, and not even in the next."

And at this moment, something in her eyes changes. Before they were so calm, like waves lapping against the shore, but now they are rampaging with blue flames. The size of her pupils have changed slightly, but before I can examine them more, she looks away from me and seemingly murmurs to herself.

"I just realized that Vi was calling me over before," she breathes out. "I'm gonna go now. Thanks for everything, Jax."

As she quickly springs up from the bench and prepares to walk away, I grab her forearm and pull her back to me. Alarmed and taken aback, she turns to me, her face flushed red.

I furrow my brows at her. "Before you go, Mallory . . . I just wanted to let you know that I will always be here for you no matter what. I want to be that person you can always rely on in the darkest moments of your life. I really do."

She bites her lip, slowly edging away from me. "That means a lot to me, Jax. And thanks for listening to me rant about my mom."

"Of course," I say. "That's what friends are for, right?"

Mallory purses her lips together, her eyes full of something I can't seem to put my finger on. "Right," she murmurs, and slowly walks away.

17

COMRADES

BLAIRE

"Make sure to twist your hips and chest toward your target."

I draw my lips into a thin line and rest my head against the rubbery material of the punching bag as Vi makes her way to me. She stands behind the punching bag in front of me and jerks her hand with an incomprehensible gesture. "Do it again."

"I'm tired, Vi."

"You've only been doing this for ten minutes. There's no way you can be tired already."

"Well, I am."

She narrows her eyes into tiny slits. "Just do a few more punches. Now I don't wanna hear any more whining from you."

I sigh, stepping back from the punching bag and slowly rolling my neck. My knuckles are pounding and aching, even with the protection of boxing gloves. But the back of my neck and the ridges of my shoulders ache the most. I haven't done intensive training like this in almost a year—*none of us* have. My muscles are just not used to this.

Almost like a second instinct, I glance down at the green

stone still hanging against my collarbone. Ever since Jax gave me this present of mine, I haven't dared to take it off. Even in the shower I keep it on. Even in a goddamn tsunami I'll have it with me. It just feels morally wrong to take off this beauty. I've tried once, just because I wanted to preserve it and not let it wither away due to the harsh heat, but I've always failed. My fingers have always hesitantly lingered by the clasp and defeatedly brought themselves down. Even *they* are unwilling to let this beauty loose from my skin.

So, just for this green stone, I push through.

I plant my feet firmly—spread apart to a certain distance—and the soles of my tennis shoes dig into the hard concrete ground. I curl my hands into tight fists, engulfed by the triple-layered boxing gloves. I take two deep breaths in and out, pushing my shoulders back and sucking my stomach in.

Breathing slowly, I glue my eyes onto the target in front of me with Vi holding onto it from behind. She looks at me the entire time and nods once. I nod back at her.

And I punch.

Harsh grunts escape out of me as my right fist collides with the rigid material, making sure to keep my wrists straight and my elbows tight. Satisfied with the earth-shattering sound of a *smack,* I punch with my right fist again. Move around, work my feet. Channel my breathing. Narrow my eyes and puff my chest.

And punch. Over and over again.

Five minutes later of non-stop punching, Vi brings out her hand with a startled expression embedded in her feline features. "All right, that's enough. You can go on break now."

"Thanks," I gasp out, bringing my hands to my knees and digging my face into the crook of my neck.

Vi walks over to me and crosses her arms. "Man, you really gotta get in shape."

I look up at her with an annoyed expression, still breathing heavily. "And how shall I do that?"

"Just work out more," she suggests.

"Easy for you to say. You've worked out plenty in the gym at our refuge while the rest of us haven't."

"Actually, Jeremiah and I did. I was surprised Jax didn't join us. He was probably fighting his own demons at the time."

I sigh. "Yeah, probably. He told me he's still upset about his father and what he did to him."

Vi sighs. "Not surprised about that one. That must've been traumatizing as hell for him."

"It *was*," I confirm. "I hate seeing him upset like that. He doesn't deserve any pain."

Vi makes a fake gagging noise. "Enough with this sappy couple shit. I'm sick and tired of it."

I laugh, standing up straight and nudging her shoulder. "C'mon, Vi. You can't keep on having a pessimistic attitude toward relationships. Say, when *will* you find your special someone?"

"Never," she says angrily. "Relationships are overrated and a complete waste of time."

"Only a person who secretly wants to be in a relationship would say that."

"Shut the hell up." She rolls her eyes and walks away, her cheeks flustered.

I follow after her, still laughing. "Okay, fine. I'm sorry. If you're perfectly fine being single, then I respect that."

"Thank you," she says, shaking her head. "God, I thought you were annoying already as a single woman, but now that you're taken, it's even worse."

"Oh, stop it. You *love* me."

"I do not."

"Do too!"

She groans and shouts out to Jeremiah, who's been intensively running on the treadmill for the past thirty minutes, "Can you please tell Blaire to leave me alone or else I'm gonna smash her face into pieces?"

He barks out a breathless laugh and yells, "I'd pay to see that!"

"Jeremiah!" I hiss, playfully rolling my eyes.

Vi crosses her arms over her chest and tilts her chin at me. "Are you done bothering me now? I'm tryna grab a quick snack."

"We had lunch barely two hours ago."

She raises her eyebrows suggestively at me. "So?" As I start to speak, Vi clenches her jaw and impatiently taps her foot against the floor. "Incoming people behind you," she murmurs underneath her breath.

I turn around and see AJ, Renata, and Annie walking toward us. They wave at us, and I wave back enthusiastically. Vi waves too, but without any trace of enthusiasm.

"How's your training going?" Annie asks, propping her hands on her hips.

"Pretty great," I say. "Vi and I were about to grab a snack."

"Actually, *I* was the only one grabbing a snack. You're just tagging along to annoy the life outta me."

"Hah!" Renata snorts out a laugh. "You're funny."

Vi scowls at her. "That wasn't meant to be—you know what, never mind."

The three of them crowd around us. I see from the corner of my eye that Vi is about to make a run for it, but I grab her forearm and lug her to everyone else. She shoots me a threatening look that runs along the lines of, *Touch me again, and I will murder you with my bare hands.*

I grin at them, ignoring the daggers from Vi's eyes drilling into the side of my head. "I just wanted to thank you guys for helping us with training on the first day. It's only because of you that we will be able to take down the ERUSA."

"Thanks, but I think you're giving us too much credit," AJ says, his gleaming golden eyes landing on me. "You also put in a lot of work. I honestly find your progress really admirable." His lips curl up into a lopsided smile, and my stomach churns at his gaze.

Thankfully, Renata's voice distracts me from AJ's eyes on me. "I think we all have put in lots of work. If we keep this up, then we can most definitely take down those imbeciles."

"Yeah, those *sons of bitches* who think it's just so hilarious that they've taken over our city," Vi grumbles. And suddenly, Renata gives her a condescending look. Vi cocks her head at her. "What's the problem?"

"Oh, nothing." Renata's tone is terse. "I just don't like people cursing."

A short chuckle escapes Vi's mouth. "You don't like people *cursing?* What are you, a mormon?"

Renata raises one perfect eyebrow. "What's that?"

" . . . You don't know what a mormon is? You know what—I really can't do this with you anymore. Why the hell do you not allow cursing? You do know that we are all adults here, right?"

"Oh, I know," she says. "I just think cursing is unnecessary. You can express your feelings in a much healthier way, rather than saying inappropriate words."

Vi closes her eyes to herself and takes a deep breath in. *I just know she's restraining herself from physically hurting Renata.* "Look, Renata—"

"Ren."

She blinks once. "What?"

"I don't go by Renata anymore. I established a nickname for myself . . . which is Ren." She sends her a bright smile.

I share a confused look with AJ and Annie. Looks like they're just as confused—and slightly terrified—as me.

Vi grits her teeth. "Okay, *Ren* . . . I don't know what enclosed bubble you lived in, but in the real world, people curse. *A lot.* It is inevitable you will run across people who will drop 'f' bombs like it's nothing. So you can't control what comes out of people's mouths." Vi takes a step toward Renata—or rather, *Ren*—and looks down at her with a challenging look engraved in her brown eyes. "Especially mine."

She nods once, bringing her hands up in surrender. "Okay. I will respect that. But from now on, I want you to refrain yourself from cursing. Trust me, it will transform your life."

"I'm not gonna—"

"Vi," I hiss, nudging her shoulder. "Just let it go."

She takes another deep breath in and speaks in a rushed tone. "Okay. *Fine.* I will watch my language. Happy?"

Ren sends her a victorious look. "Yes, *very* happy."

Once that supposedly interesting conversation ends, we talk about the plans for the rest of the month.

"Since training went exceptionally well for everyone," Annie says, "we will start with sparring at the end of this week. If the results show up to be great, then we can initiate our ranks against the ERUSA maybe as early as the second week of July."

"That early?" I ask.

"Yeah," AJ says. "The earlier the better, since God knows what the ERUSA are up to down in Detroit. Sometimes I feel so helpless just staying here in our compound while there are dozens of people dying everyday because they didn't follow Veronica's rules."

"How do you know about that?" Vi asks.

"Commander Thatcher has hidden cameras in every corner in Detroit," Annie responds. "We've been cooped up in here for years, so of course we are more than prepared for taking down the ERUSA. We just have to gather as many trained soldiers as possible, and we will have very little to worry about."

"Unless Veronica turns out to be ten steps ahead of us," Vi says.

"There's no way she can be." AJ shakes his head. "She doesn't even know where we, as a military, are located."

"She took over our headquarters as soon as my mother died,"

Ren says with a crack to her voice. "That's what I was told by my bodyguards as they took me to the safety bunker away from the city. And in those headquarters, there are cameras everywhere."

AJ's body tenses. "Do any of those cameras look into our military base?"

"I don't know. I'm just aware that there are cameras in general."

"Well, that's just wonderful," Vi says sarcastically.

Ren swivels her head to her and looks at her with an upturned chin. "That is not wonderful."

Vi raises her eyebrows, chuckling to herself. "That was sarcasm. Jesus."

"Oh." She picks at her outfit's fabric by her torso. "What does that mean?"

AJ's mouth gapes open. "You don't know what sarcasm is?"

"Nope." Ren sighs.

"Sarcasm is when you say something in a mocking tone. It's not meant to be taken literally," I say.

"Oh, that makes sense," she says. "Thanks, uh . . ."

"Blaire."

"Yes, *Blaire*. Um, thanks for explaining that to me." Ren pushes her red hair to the side. "I didn't attend school in Russia, so I'm not really aware of these terms."

An abruptness hangs from her mouth, and she presses her lips together and looks up at the ceiling. Renata's life is still ambiguous to us all, since she was an escapee from Russia's strict regime. Charlotte took her in because she felt sympathetic toward her struggles, and she was like the mother she never had. No one is aware of who her biological parents are and what they were like, and I'm pretty sure Ren intends to keep it that way.

"So," Annie says awkwardly, "shall we go on break? Everybody else is waiting there."

"Everybody, as in Jax too, right?" I ask.

"Yes, Blaire, your hunk-of-a boyfriend is there." Vi smirks. "There's no need to get so worked up."

"I'm not worked up," I say defensively.

Annie snickers, tucking a short dark strand behind her ear. "How did you guys even handle each other in D.C.?"

"We didn't," Vi clarifies. "I had to restrain myself from punching one of these idiots in the goddamn face every five minutes."

"What did I say?" Ren glares at her threateningly.

Vi groans. "*Goddamn* is probably the least horrible cuss word out there."

"All cuss words are horrible," she says.

"No, there's some that are worse, such as bitch, shit, fu—"

"Enough!" Ren shrieks, flailing her arms and running to the door.

Vi chortles, her eyes crinkling with amusement. "Can you believe that a twenty-three-year-old grown woman would ever cringe at cuss words? Jesus Christ." She walks over to the exit, still laughing to herself.

Just leaving me and the twins.

I look at them suggestively. "Well, looks like Vi and Ren will get along just fine."

Annie chuckles. "I love Vi's personality, though. It's super . . ."

"Interesting?" AJ suggests.

"Yeah, I guess you can say that."

I grin. "I can't believe I've known that woman for almost a year. It still amazes me to this day."

"Would you say that you're close with her?" Annie asks.

I wince. "Eh, it honestly depends on her mood. Today is actually one of the days when she's in a good mood."

"That's her in a *good mood?*" AJ shrieks.

"Yeah. When she's in a bad mood, it's just . . ." I shiver in fear. "It's sort of terrifying."

"I can only imagine," Annie says breathlessly.

I chuckle, remembering all the times I wrongfully crossed Vi. "Anyway, enough about her. What about you guys? Would you say you're pretty close with each other?"

They share glances with each other. "I guess so," AJ says. "It honestly depends on our mood too."

"Even though he's most definitely the grumpy one." Annie grins.

"You take that back." He frowns.

I laugh. "Who's the oldest?"

"It's me," Annie says in a victorious tone.

"By only two minutes," AJ murmurs underneath his breath.

"Doesn't make much of a difference, though."

I smile to myself as they bicker back and forth. It sort of reminds me of my relationship with Em and Nico, except ours have gotten so bad our parents had to step in and rip us apart.

Something crackles beneath AJ's pants. He brings out a walkie-talkie from his pocket, which relays back a message from Commander Thatcher. "Come to the commonplace with the others right now. Over."

He says into the device, "Gotcha. Over and out."

As AJ slips the walkie-talkie into his pocket, I say, "I thought we're done for the day."

"We're done with training," Annie confirms. "But Commander Thatcher has some things to talk about." She walks to the exit door, leaving me and AJ in the middle of the gym.

He raises one dark eyebrow, a lazy smile growing on his lips. "I suggest you come too, if you don't wanna get your head ripped off by the Commander."

I grimace as I follow AJ out the door. He's right. I wouldn't want to be on the wrong side of that woman. God knows what would happen to me then.

18

BURDEN

JAX

THE NIGHT ARRIVES, AND I am appointed back to the head-quarters to meet Veronica. Obviously against my will.

When Hernandez showed up at my room door again, I didn't do much to fight back. Blaire was sleeping in her own room tonight because apparently Em got mad at her for leaving her that one night she was with me, and I don't know whether I should be upset or relieved about that. Upset that I won't be able to hold her in my arms in the dark anymore? Or relieved so I can leave the property in peace?

The car ride to the headquarters goes by in the blink of an eye, and before I know it, the building like a jagged needle appears in front of me like a figment of my imagination. The shining exterior gleams against the moon, now partly hidden beneath the wispy clouds, and it beckons to me, calling my name.

With Hernandez and Bennett at my side again, we walk past the entrance and into the building, cool air from the vents clashing against my skin. I contemplate heavily about grabbing the back of Hernandez's head and smashing his face against the wall while I kick Bennett in the crotch with all my might and make a run for it, but I realize I probably shouldn't commit those actions because they're armed to the bone. Meanwhile, I'm only here in a loose white shirt and gray shorts.

After the awkward elevator ride to the sixth floor, as the two soldiers beside me said we'd be going, we tread past the marbled hallways and into the large double doors. I step inside the office, heart beating by my throat, and Hernandez and Bennett stand behind me.

"Lieutenant Reaves," Bennett says, "I have the subject with me."

Subject? I scoff to myself. *What am I, a volunteer for a science experiment?*

The shuffling from the other side of the office piques my attention. A flash of flowing white hair, almost like a lightning bolt, rushes past me and appears in front of me, affixed with a pale face showcasing cold blue eyes that are *so blue* I question whether they are just colored contacts.

The pair of cold blue eyes open and close. "Take a seat, Jax. Make yourself comfortable too, if need be." The eyes waver over to the men behind me. "You may leave, Comrades."

After an abrupt "thank you, Lieutenant Reaves," there is a shuffling of boots and eventually a slamming of a door.

All oxygen leaves my system as I take a seat in front of the stained glass table, so speechless my lips feel to be physically sealed.

The lanky woman in front of me takes a seat too.

And speaks moments later.

"Would you like anything to drink? I have a coffee brewer and a couple of breakfast snacks."

I clench my jaw. "No, thanks. I'm good."

"Are you sure? I know it's nearly midnight, but that shouldn't stop you from having a delicious bagel."

I leer my eyes at Veronica. "Why are you being so nice to me? I thought you hated me?"

Now chuckling, she says, "I never hated you, Jax. I only doubted you, and that was only in regards to the friendship you formed with my daughter. But hate? That's a very strong word, my dear. I wouldn't say I hate you. If anything, I admire you."

"You . . . admire me?" I drawl out.

"Only because you are Tobias's son."

"Were."

"Are," she counters, shaking her head. "I thought we went over this, Jax. You are still your father's son, whether or not you mentally emancipated yourself from him. In your records, you're still his son, so I will refer to you as such."

I curl my hands into fists, veins growing on my forearms as I restrain myself with all my might from setting this room on fire with the lit candle on her desk and charging out of the door— right after I slam the door close behind me. And from the outside, I will satisfyingly listen to her screams as the flames engulf her, consuming her ghostly presence.

But I can't do that. Because if my attempt were to fail, then she would hurt Blaire. I'd rather take a hike to hell than see her in pain.

"Now, enough of that." Her words bring me out of my thoughts. "Do you have any updates for me?"

I freeze in place, my hands slowly uncurling and my fears slowly unraveling.

She cocks her head at me, the pits of her glacier-like eyes searing into my soul. "You agreed to my request, my dear. All I expect from you is just a run-down of what's happening in that military bunker. The cameras I have implemented here can only show the outside of the base, not the inside. And worse yet, the cameras that show the home you were appointed to with the rebels does not reveal the audio. I am in the dark here," she says. "So fill me in, please."

I work my jaw, lightly rapping my knuckles against the arm of the chair I'm sulking in. My mind is a whirlwind of thoughts and my heart is rampaging with emotions that flood through my veins. Maybe I shouldn't say anything to her. What if she's just bluffing and, even if I do reveal what the Reformers are up to, she's still going to do something to Blaire? I shouldn't trust Veronica so easily. I shouldn't trust her at *all*.

Moments later, I shake my head.

Veronica lowers her eyes from me, leans forward, and finally looks at me again. The only thing I can hear right now is the quiet shuffling of her feet beneath the desk and the beating of my heart rattling my bones.

Her cracked lips open, and she says in a slow and calm tone, "Don't do this right now, Jax. Provide me information. Need I remind you of what consequences lie ahead of your failure to serve me?"

"I already know," I grumble. "Either way you will not get your hands on Blaire. Do you know how long it took to push past my fears and ask her to be mine? I hopelessly thought about her for months after we settled here, and it was just inevitable I was gonna hit my breaking point and finally do what I needed to do a long ass time ago. But I did it, and she feels the same way as me." I try to ignore the shakiness in my voice. "I endured the strongest of storms, traveled the most dangerous of roads, and fought the most terrifying of battles to finally call her mine. And now you're telling me that I'm just gonna leave and *betray her* after one little request from you?" I shake my head, biting the inside of my cheek. "Yeah, not gonna happen."

Veronica's response is swift and brusque like a gust of wind slapping my face. "I couldn't care less about your sappy romance with that rebel whose brother is the reason why we're in this turmoil to begin with. I just want to hear about any information you have from the Reformers. I need to know." She grasps onto the table tightly. *"Now."*

Heat inches up my throat and spreads across my face, my throat swelling up and tightening. Whether that is from anger or frustration—I'm not really sure. But what I do know is that I have a lot to say to this irritable woman. I have so many insults and threats lodged up in my mind that my head physically starts to hurt from how much I hide away. I want to say so much to her, but somehow I can't. Because the stabbing reminder of what Veronica might do to Blaire is gnashing into my mind. And for the sake of our relationship, I am going to succumb to Veronica's desires.

Just for now.

Bile rises at the back of my throat as I strain out, "We're training right now."

The glory in her eyes fuels my hatred for her more. "Really?"

"Yes." I gulp. "We're preparing for battle against . . . against the ERUSA."

"Interesting." One eyebrow of her's arches up. "Do tell more."

Tell her more? I don't want to relay everything to her. The Detroitian army spent years rebuilding its foundation, and I am not going to be the asshole that destroys it for them in a heartbeat.

I reluctantly shake my head. "No can do."

"You—!" She fists her hands and starts to say something else to me, but she draws her lips into a straight line and inaudibly murmurs something to herself. "You know what? It's fine." Her voice enters the crevices of my bones and chills me to the core. "You're just being reluctant with me right now because you don't want to betray your peers. I get it.

"I'll be nice this one time and release you. But the next time I call you over, you must relay *everything* to me. If not, then your special one will be killed, and not even by my Comrades." She leans forward, her cracked lips parted slightly. "I will murder her with my own bare hands. Whether I will strangle her to death, kidnap her and starve her in the middle of the forest, or simply send three consecutive bullets to her head—that is still yet to be determined. But *I* will do it, Mr. Remington. You know damn well that I will."

———

As soon as I am dropped off by Hernandez and Bennett by the front of our relocated home, I march up to my room, swing the door open, slam it shut, and take three heaving breaths before utter chaos overcomes me.

I grit my teeth, suppressing a strained scream. I need to throw something. I need to punch something, *someone*—I don't know. I just want to unleash my anger.

A vase is perched on the kitchen counter.

I trudge over there, feeling serrated breaths dig through my insides like a knife, and grab the bottom of the vase. Weigh it in my hand. Cock my head and square my jaw.

And I throw it across the room.

It immediately shatters against the living room wall, inches from the sliding glass doors leading to the patio. Shards splatter everywhere, and I step back into the dining table, fearful of myself. Fearful of my behavior. What the hell am I doing? This isn't who I am. I don't go into random outbursts like this.

I push off the dining table and walk into the bathroom, adamant to get my shit together. The door shuts behind me, and I flick the lights on.

I almost hiss as I notice myself in the mirror.

My dark hair is unkempt, unruly, and flat-out hideous. My eyes are like storm clouds looming amongst the naked atmosphere—dreary and unnerving. My tan skin is red and spotted from sweat, and I claw at it, terrified at this image of me. This is not me. This isn't who I am.

And that's when I notice it.

That goddamn scar.

A tentative finger of mine grazes it, feeling the roughness and jaggedness of the drawn-on line. The bright crimson color has faded into a color almost the same as my skin's, except it's slightly darker and more prominent. It's still there. It's *always* been there.

I want it off me . . . *now*.

I dig my fingers into the scar and scratch at it, gritting my teeth and grunting. I add another finger and scratch more. More and more fingers until my entire hand attempts to rub away the one horrible thing engraved into not just my skin, but my life too. Nails dig into my scar, and instead of seeing my face crystal clear and empty of that wretched line, all I see instead is it even more bloodied and more prominent than ever.

My fists tighten against the curve of the sink and I start the water from the faucet with an abrupt flick of my hand. I pool the streaming water into my shaking hands and splash it against my face, cooling my skin and stopping the blood streaming from my scar.

At this point, water has drenched my shirt too, so I tear it off me and throw it at the mirror. As it falls to the bathroom floor with a silent thud, I begin to clash my fists against the glass. I pound against it, thrusting my entire body forward as I scream my heart out. I don't care if the others hear me. Hell, I don't care if Veronica hears me.

I could honestly give zero shits.

The clashing and pounding of my fists against the mirror creates a crack in it, but I still don't stop. Blood—just like the blood still pouring from my scar—peers from my hands and streams down my forearms. The broken shards of glass are falling to the floor around me, bloodied and lifeless.

I pound against the mirror one last time.

And I finally stop—breathless and aching.

My entire body is trembling, barely able to hold itself up.

Veins run up and down my hands and grow on my abdomen, and I grit my teeth, holding onto the front of the sink and dipping my chin down. Breathing in and out.

Breathe.

Once my heart-rate steadies, I look up at the mirror, seeing broken images of myself from the shattered mirror. Blood is smeared across like streaks of paint against a canvas, but it's not beautiful. It's not awe striking.

It's rather horrendous. And it frightens the hell out of me.

Still holding onto the sink and attempting to look at a shattered version of myself, I feel a rush of cool air enter my veins. I freeze in place, my bones tightening and my muscles hardening. My entire heart heaves so tightly it's about to shatter—just like the mirror in front of me.

A hushed voice enters my ear.

No matter how hard you try, you'll never get away from me. Never.

19

CALAMITOUS

BLAIRE

"GET YOUR ASS OUT of bed—right *now!*"

I gasp awake, clinging to my blanket as I blearily look up at an exasperated Vi. Her unruly black and red short hair looks disheveled about her face, and she frustratingly blows out a low breath. I look around, seeing that the rest of my family has started to wake up too. Well, all except Em, who can sleep in a hurricane itself without batting a damn eye.

"Vienna, why in the world are you here?" My mama asks, arching one thin eyebrow. It's already unfortunate enough making Vi upset, but my mother is a completely different story. She may seem all nice at first, but the moment someone wrongs her, consider them *done.*

Vi hurriedly turns to her. "It's an emergency, and I'm gonna need your daughter." She glances over at a half-awake Nico. "And her brother too."

"I'm not letting them go anywhere until you tell me what's going on," my papa grumbles.

She groans to herself, shooting her widened eyes at my

parents. "Barely two minutes ago, Layla came barging into mine and Mallory's room and told us that Commander Thatcher wants us, or the Subversives, in Detroit. Apparently there's a major execution going on there, and we have to stop it."

"*What?*" a suddenly awakened Nico shrieks. "I thought we weren't showing ourselves to the Detroitian public until the Reformers were ready as well?"

"That's what I thought too," Vi says. "But I guess we follow whatever Thatcher says."

"*Commander* Thatcher," I correct her.

She annoyingly cocks her head at me. "She's not here right now, so I couldn't care less. But anyway, we need to go."

"We never allowed them to go," my dad says.

I send my parents a reassuring glance. "We will be fine. We've been in worse situations."

"I don't care, *mija*," my mama hisses. "You and your brother are not risking your life again for some so-called emergency."

"This is our *job*, Mom!" Nico shoots out of bed. "I know you're scared to lose us, but we will be fine. We know how to handle these situations. I've killed countless Guards before. I've survived D.C. prison. I know how to do this, I promise."

My mama tilts her head, her lips twitching as she contemplates. "Fine. You can go."

"Thank you," Nico says breathlessly.

"But if you ever raise your voice at me like that another time, I will make you go through D.C. prison all over again."

His face flushes to a deep red color. "Sorry, Mama. That won't happen again."

As I stifle a snort, my mama's enraging brown eyes land on me. "You especially, Blaire. People like Vienna and Nicolas have been in extreme fighting situations. You have not. I need you to stay safe, too—if not the most. Just because you're turning twenty soon and you have a boyfriend, doesn't mean you can go around like a headless chicken."

My throat constricts at the sourness surrounding the word "boyfriend." *Damn, I still have to have* that *conversation with her.* "I got it, Mama," I whisper.

"Great," she says, turning to Vi. "You may take them."

At that, Vi immediately jumps to her feet and lugs us out the door. Once it shuts behind us, she lets out a breath and turns to us. "Now that that shenanigan is over . . . we have to get a move on."

"Why do we have to go to this execution when there have been plenty in the past few days?" I ask as we trample out the front door.

"I guess Thatcher finally allowed us to go out in Detroit," Vi says, "since we are a part of her military."

"So why just us Subversives and not the Reformers too?" Nico asks.

Vi closes the front door behind us as we stand in the lobby. "Thatcher just wants us there because, according to her, we have been in more conflicting situations than them in the past few years. So if any issues arise now, she wants us there. But when they are ready to step out and announce themselves to Detroit, we will join them." When she sees the confused expression on our faces, she raises her hands up in defense. "Her words, not mine."

Suddenly, Jeremiah, Mallory, and Jax barge from Jax's room. They jog to us, and Jeremiah immediately says, "There are back up armors and weapons in the jeep we will go in as I drive us to the center of Detroit, so put them on before we reach there."

"Okay," I say. "Wait, why isn't Layla coming?"

"She's with Tamia, since we don't want her to be alone," he says. "God, I hate leaving them behind."

"We'll be fine, Jeremiah," Mallory reassures him. "All we have to do is resolve the conflict and make our way to the base safely."

"What if they follow us there?" Nico asks.

"We'll just kill them," Vi says ambiguously, making her way to the stairs. She gives us an impatient look as we stand there, watching her speechlessly. "Well, don't just stand there. *Come!*"

As we run down the stairs, my heart throbbing in my chest, I inch over to Jax, who hasn't spoken a word since. His faded scar is not so faded anymore; instead, it's semi bloodied. My stomach churns at his unreadable eyes as they land on me. He smiles at me, but his eyes are as dull as ever. "Hey. What a day it's been so far, huh?"

I ignore his words and grab his forearm, but I stop us in our tracks as my eyes trail down to the rolls of gauze wrapped around his fists. Speckled spots of blood line the soft white material, and my veins pound with fury as I breathlessly say to him, "Who did this to you?"

His eyebrows furrow as he slowly shakes his head. "Nobody did this to me, Blaire."

"Then why the hell are your fists wrapped in gauze?"

He opens his mouth to say something, but is stopped by a furious Vi who speed-walks to us like a charging bull. "Are you kidding me right now?" She scoffs, painfully lugging us both out the door with her strong hands tightened around our wrists and refusing to hear our remarks. "Now is *not* the time for sappy couple shit. People are *dying*. Jesus Christ."

The bulky navy blue armor weighs down on my chest as the jeep rolls to a stop in a discreet alleyway. My gloved fingers nervously dance on my thighs, my heart jamming into my lungs and pounding its way out of my throat. *I'm gonna throw up, I'm gonna throw up, I'm gonna—*

"Hey." Jax's soft voice interrupts me out of thoughts as he brings his gloved hand on top of mine and squeezes it—his hand easily engulfing mine. "You will be okay," he murmurs, giving me both a heart-warming and heart-melting smile.

I try to speak, but all I do instead is nod and give him a tiny smile, forcing my bile down my throat. *It's not me I'm worried about,* I want to tell him. *I'm worried about you. I want to know why your scar and hands are bloodied.*

We all climb out of the vehicle, the gravel beneath us crunching against our heavy combat boots. Commotion is near, and the distant crying has me squeezing my eyes shut as I aimlessly walk down the alleyway with the others. I hold onto the rifle set against my chest with my dear life. I haven't shot anything or anyone ever since D.C. God knows if I'll make it out alive.

Jax, who is behind me, grasps my lower back and whispers into my ear, "I know you're nervous right now, so I just wanna let you know that I'm here for you."

I glance over at Jax with an apologetic expression. "I'm sorry, but that's not helping my anxiety go away."

He curses to himself and tightens his hold on my back. "All right. Then I'll say this . . . you are strong. You are brave. And you are unstoppable. If you can survive D.C., then we can survive this. Just stay courageous for me, please. I promise you'll come out of this alive."

I take a deep breath in, weighing in his words. "Thanks, Jax. That helped a lot."

"Seriously?"

"Yes, seriously. You're the best."

He smiles, shrugging afterwards. "Hmm, yeah. You're right. I *am* the best."

As I go to roll my eyes playfully, Vi, who is behind Nico, looks at me and Jax with widened eyes and hisses, "Keep it down back there!"

We immediately clamp our mouths shut and follow after the others.

As Nico continues to lead us, he cocks his gun and gestures his head forward. We circle around him as he whispers to us, "Remember what we talked about. This is incredibly crucial, so don't mess this up. I wanna be alive and intact after this. Got it?"

"Got it," we whisper.

Nico immediately goes to the front with Jeremiah trailing behind. Mallory and I are behind them, and Vi and Jax are behind us.

Seconds pass until Nico gives us the green-light.

And we charge forward.

The alleyway transforms into a ten-lane road blocked off by ERUSA vehicles. The vehicles in the back honk their horns and their tires squeal as they angrily leave the scene. As I sprint forward, my breathing delayed and my heart thrusting against my chest, I feel my jaw slowly dropping from the scene that unravels in front of me.

An ERUSA soldier. Holding a gun up to the back of a little girl's head.

With Veronica in front of her.

Around the soldier, the little girl, and Veronica is a large crowd, huddling around the commotion. There are tears shed. Screams heard. People held back by other soldiers. Heavy heat breathing on my neck. Crawling down my spine and setting my insides on fire.

As soon as we point our guns at them, the ERUSA soldiers do the same. A couple of them come charging at us, but Nico shouts, "Lower your weapons, *now!* We just want to talk."

"Not until you lower yours, *Subversive*," one of the soldiers hisses.

From where I stand, I see Nico slowly nod moments later. He turns to us and says, "Lower your weapons. We can handle this in a much less violent way."

We reluctantly lower our weapons. He *is* the boss.

Nico sets his rifle to the side and gestures to their weapons still raised at us. "Your turn," he says dryly.

Seconds later, they lower theirs.

Jeremiah steps forward, his dark brown eyes darting back and forth toward the ERUSA soldier still pointing their gun to the back of the little girl's head. "What the hell is he doing?"

"This girl broke one of my rules," Veronica says. "She was wearing a skimpy tank top and shorts that barely covered her thighs. Inappropriate clothes are not permitted here, especially for an innocent ten-year-old such as you."

"It was really hot," she whimpers, her hands grasping her bloodied thighs. *Veronica is sick. So sick.*

"Shut up," the soldier behind her growls, nudging the tip of the gun to the back of her skull. She silently starts to cry, her lips trembling as tears rapidly stream down her cheeks.

"Stop this right now," Vi hisses, raising her hand up in defense. "All we want for you is to leave this innocent girl alone. If anything, we want you to leave *us* alone and leave this city as soon as you can. We don't need a female version of Tobias running around."

"Don't you dare insult our late president *ever again.*" Veronica's eyes are widened and such a translucent bright blue that they're almost a glacier white. Suddenly, she looks over at Jax, who inches closer to me. "Do you hear this, Mr. Remington? They're insulting your father."

I don't even have to look at Jax to know he's rolling his eyes right now. And he doesn't even hesitate when he says, "Get out of here, Veronica. Enough is enough."

Her seething eyes sear into him for a bit too long, a meaning hidden beneath the depths of her pupils that I can't seem to decipher. He stills behind me, his breathing low and quiet.

So quiet.

"I'm not going anywhere," she responds, looking back over to the trembling little girl. "I want to spread a message to those who dare to defy the ERUSA, who dare to defy *me*. It was only inevitable that we would rise from the ruins of D.C. and show you imbeciles that we are not to be messed with—that we are the *true* American citizens. This is not just a matter of the Rich and the Poor anymore . . ." Veronica's long and pale hair sways against the stiff wind as she ambles forward, her eyes darting to the little girl who's curling and shriveling to the ground, drowning her sobs into the paved road.

"This is a matter of justice and revenge," she finishes off.

Our guns still by our sides, we stand there, speechless, wavering as we take in Veronica's words. Tobias's extreme hatred for us had no embedded reason to it; it was based on pure allegiance to society and his reputation, which is all he ever stood for.

But Veronica? Her hatred is deep and running into her veins. She has a reason. An unfortunately terrifying reason.

She gestures her hand to the soldier who still has the shimmering black gun raised to the back of the girl's forehead. "Carry on, Comrade Hernandez."

For some reason, Jax stiffens behind me.

The soldier grabs the back of the girl's shirt and pulls her up, digging the trigger of the gun into her skull. Her face is red and streaming in tears, and my heart squeezes tightly, my limbs melting to the ground. *We need to do something about this . . . now.*

Suddenly, the blonde-headed and petite girl beside me pushes her gun to the side and steps toward her mother. "Leave her alone," Mal says, her voice slightly trembling as she steps past Nico and curls her hands into fists by her side. "You shouldn't do this, Mom. *Please.*"

"Mallory, go away," Veronica hisses immediately, turning to her daughter. "Or else I will shoot your other thigh."

She clamps her mouth shut, tears brimming her eyes as she stays put. Hesitation curls at her insides, and I know she wants to scream and shout at her mom. I know she wants to prove to her that she is not to be messed with. I know she wants her mother to step down and let her dad rest in peace.

She really does.

Veronica points at her accusingly, her pale skin shimmering against the intense sunrays. "I'll never forgive you for what you did. It's a sin to leave your parents at such a young age. All we did was shower you with love and care. That's all we did, Mallory. And yet, you being the ungrateful brat you are, you were still unsatisfied with our love and left us. You left our society. You left your best friend, Jax."

"Mom, *stop*," Mal croaks out, her bottom lip trembling.

"And because of that," Veronica continues, "you are the most selfish human being I have met. I am ashamed to be your mother."

Mal rapidly blinks, tears sprinting past her eyes and dribbling down her chin. I know one day she will be able to release this anger inside of her—this anger that's been settled within the nook and cranny of her veins for too long. They are flames burgeoning in her chest, unfurling into the mightiest of collisions. A raging and uncontrollable collision.

But they are deep and buried inside of her. I know Mal at this point. Something is stopping her from releasing her rage, and she's infuriated with herself. For letting this obstacle impede her.

Her pink cotton candy lips curl into a frown, her chest rising in and out. "Leave. Her. Alone." Hesitatingly, she tightens her hold on the rifle tugged against her padded torso. "Or else I will shoot you, too."

A harsh grunt leaves Veronica's mouth, followed by a slight curl to her lip—similar to the shape and curve of her daughter's. I've always found comfort in Mal's soothing ocean eyes, but Veronica's gives me nothing but a sharp twinge to my gut. They are lifeless glaciers lodged in the furthest corner of this earth, submerged in freezing snow and falling sleet.

Her ghostly voice haunts my ear and sends venom to my soul. "Like you'd ever have the guts for that."

And in the blink of an eye—too fast even for the stealthy Vi and the strong Jeremiah—she gives the soldier holding up the gun to the little girl a swift glance.

"Shoot the betrayer."

The bullet plunges into the poor little girl's skull too fast. Too, *too* fast.

Even lightning wouldn't be fast enough.

There is a moment of heavy, stuffy, and seething silence crawling down my throat and lodging my insides. It suffocates me, irritates me, frustrates me. Even Jax's hand on my lower back doesn't soothe me. And he *always* soothes me.

I thought it was over then. I really thought that egregious noise followed after the silent thud of the little girl would be it.

But it isn't. Of *course* it isn't.

Because multiple gun shots initiate around us, almost like the clash of a stick to a drum—beating and booming into my ears. I'm alarmed at first, thinking the ERUSA is shooting at us.

But some of them have fallen to the ground, bullets piercing into their flesh and Veronica kneeling by their sides.

I twist my head to the side, noting a mass of soldiers—dressed in navy blue uniforms with the letter "D" engraved into their breastbone—hurtling toward us, rifles pointed at the woman piercingly white all around. White hair, white eyes, white skin.

White, screeching noises.

Hurtling white pain pierces into my gut—of realization that this is it. This is the beginning.

The beginning of an end.

20

PREDICAMENT

JAX

MY EARS BLEED AT the multiple claps of gunshots, transcending and cascading amongst the hot stuffy air. They swarm around me like clouds of dust spiked with deadly intentions, and once they've lodged themselves into as many ERUSA soldiers as they can, they fall to the ground, blood seeping past their flesh and silently trailing against the cracked roads.

The line of Reformers come rushing in, rifles cocked in their gloved hands and resting against their padded chests. I look down at our skimpy uniform in comparison to theirs—a gleaming blue against the beating sun and strapped with artillery to the goddamn *bone.* For someone who was supposed to reveal themselves to Detroitian society in a significant time from now, I am quite surprised their uniforms are much more advanced than ours.

My jaw falls. *Wait . . . why* are *they here?*

Before I can question their actions much longer, I feel a harsh pull on my elbow. "Stop staring and take shelter!" Vi hisses at me, lugging a speechless Blaire with her too. "Come on!"

The Subversives and I go over to the alleyway—where our jeep is—and gawk at the overwhelming line of soldiers. They're shoulder-to-shoulder, mouths drawn into a straight line and eyes lifeless, and parade past the swarming vehicles with rapid gunshots searing past the rifles propped in their hands. I recognize a few familiar faces already. Annie commandeering the line forward, her short jet-black hair flinging past her broad and strong shoulders. Her rather irritating yet weirdly coordinated twin brother trails behind her, grappling the pistols lodged in each hand and looking around frantically.

And Commander Thatcher, once driving a large jeep into the middle of the commotion, jumps out of the vehicle and twists her neck around, analyzing her troops. "March forward and annihilate as many ERUSA's as you can!" Her eyes narrow into tiny slits. "I got the scrawny blonde woman."

Veronica, or rather the *scrawny blonde woman*, grabs hold of the rifles slung against the limp ERUSA soldiers around her, her fists and jaw and every facial muscle tightened. She grits her teeth at the strong woman ahead of her, adorned in a navy blue uniform decorated with medals and lapels so intricate my puny eyes are unable to see them all.

"Just surrender already, Reaves," Commander Thatcher says in a tone so harsh, so demanding. "It's not worth wasting all this blood and energy on an army incomparable to yours."

"The Detroitian military, right?" Veronica scoffs. "I thought you guys were hiding for years, only because your army was falling apart. So, in actuality, you should be scared of *mine*."

As Commander Thatcher begins to reply, I feel another harsh pull on my shoulder, a hand too familiar to my liking. I turn around, inches away from a pale-faced woman affixed with narrowed, cold eyes. "Stop standing so close to the commotion," she hisses, "unless you want your head blown off."

I nod wordlessly, following after her. The others are gathered by the jeep, frantically running their hands through their hair and discussing amongst themselves. When Vi and I come around, she whisper-yells to the others, "We need to help the Reformers."

"You mean the people who didn't even bother to tell us they were gonna show up in the first place?" Jeremiah cocks his head.

"Look, I'm not really happy with this situation either," Nico says, "but Vienna is right. It is our duty as the Subversives to help when it is needed. Whether we like it or not."

"But *how?*" Blaire emphasizes, inching to my side. "We still have training going on. We don't even know whether we're fully prepared to go on grounds in the first place."

"There's no other choice," Mal says, leaning against the front of the jeep. "We have to at least try our best."

"And how will we do that?" I voice out.

"With our help."

I turn around to an incoming AJ, sweat basking on his caramel skin and his eyes, almost a hazy yellow, land on us with a trace of determination hidden beneath his pupils. He sets his pistols to the side and impatiently glances at us. "We need to split up."

"Yeah, that's not a good idea," I murmur.

"You're not the boss, *I* am." AJ narrows his eyes at me. "So I suggest you keep your mouth shut, asshole."

"Don't talk to him like that," Blaire hisses underneath her breath. For some reason, a rush of feelings filter through my veins. *God, she really is the one for me.*

Immediately, AJ's face reddens and he shakes his head, chuckling. "Sorry for my attitude, Blaire. I'm just really stressed right now and want you all to understand that it is imperative that we split up. That way, we can cover more ground and reduce the chances of us being seen in a giant group."

"To an extent, he's right," Jeremiah says. "How should we split up?"

AJ starts pointing rapidly. "Nicolas and Mallory, you will be by the frontline of the Reformers. Position yourselves there according to your intuitions. Vienna, you will be with Annie by the other frontline. Jax and Jeremiah, you will be by the outermost of the Reformers and you will watch for any incoming ERUSA soldiers. Judging by what Veronica is saying to Commander Thatcher, she ordered more of her troops to come here—so we must hurry up. And Blaire—his eyes flicker to hers for a concise moment—"you're with me behind Commander Thatcher."

All air leaves my lungs—like someone sent a punch to my gut. *Oh*, hell no.

I shake my head, linking my arm with hers. "Yeah, not on my watch are you getting near her, shithead."

AJ works his jaw, a smirk growing on his mouth. God, how *badly* I want to wipe that annoying smirk off his face with a quick punch to his face. That would shut him right up.

"Listen here, Jax." He takes a silent step toward me. "There is a possibility of a battle right now—after many years of peacetime. Is my partnership with Blaire really a major concern of yours?"

"Yes," I say with no hesitation.

"Dude," Vi hisses, jabbing at my side, "now is *not* the time to be the overprotective and jealous boyfriend."

"I'm not—"

"Yes, you are," she grits through her teeth. "You can act however you wanna act toward AJ later, but right now you're gonna have to push your overprotective tendencies to the side and allow Blaire to be with AJ. I'm sure she'll be safe with him."

I sigh, my heart deflating with every breath. God, I hate to admit that Vi's right. Now is not the time to let my feelings of AJ conflict with my relationship with Blaire. Besides, I trust her to not do anything with him. So there's no reason for me to feel this shit right now.

I look down at Blaire, whose eyes plead for not just my trust in her, but for our lives too. "Okay." I nod. "But if he ever puts his hands on you—"

"Then I'll slit his throat." Blaire's lips twitch into a smile.

I grin. If there was nobody else here, then hell, would I kiss the absolute life out of her.

After a quick peck on my cheek, her grip loosens on my arm, a stab of pain slashing through my gut as we stand besides our partner for the time being. Jeremiah is next to me, his dark brown eyes drilled forward at the heated conversation unloading between Veronica and Commander Thatcher. I know Jeremiah wants to step in and resolve the conflict. While he is a very intimidating man and could probably rip me into shreds, he has a heart within him and all that heart wants is peace and prosperity.

It's what all of our hearts desired—until the devil in disguise came and tore it away from us. Like a mother from her child. A sun from its rays. A painter from their canvas. And a body without a heart.

It's useless. It's all just . . . *nothing.* A deep pit of nothingness that expands into a grave galaxy of loneliness and despair. Of hopeless desires and pitiful needs—cascading amongst the naked and clear strokes of a certain jab to a gut, realizing all this was for *nothing.*

But even for nothing, we can still fight for something. Whether it be the end of a rainbow or simply crossing the road, our battle can still be fought for something.

After Blaire and I exchange long glances, AJ grips the pistols again and acknowledges the rifles and other weapons strapped on us. "I know you all barely trained, but try to remember how you fought as a Subversive back in D.C. Got it?"

"Got it," we all echo.

"Great." He clears his throat and veers his head back to the opening crack of the alley, revealing us to the entrance of hell. "Let's move forward when I count down from three. Three, two, one . . . *go!*"

My legs move before my brain processes what's going on. A rush of adrenaline pumps through my veins, my breathing full of vitality as we disperse in different directions. Vi, Mallory, and Nicolas sprint past me and Jeremiah and position themselves by the line of Reformers. Blaire and AJ—whose teeth I still want to knock out—stop by Commander Thatcher and kneel beside her, eyes narrowed and guns cocked in their gloved hands.

And Jeremiah and I tread past the glowering Veronica and lower ourselves by the outside ranks. My heart thrashes and thrusts against my chest, thudding against my ribcage at this point. I press my lips together, sending Jeremiah an acknowledging glance as we brace ourselves for impact.

A victorious Veronica gleams at the sight of her oncoming soldiers parading past the clearing and into the line of vehicles stopped at the commotion. With the sun beating on my neck, I squint at the furious soldiers, bullets from their guns springing at us.

We duck and cover behind the ranks, my finger resting against the tip of the trigger—just in case. The screams and shouts from the soldiers—from both sides—are like deathly tunes cast to my soul. I don't want to hear it, but nonetheless, it is engraved into my ears. It is engraved into the pits of the soul and has me gritting my teeth in utter revulsion—bile threatening to spew from my throat. It is like cannons exploding through the air, each trail of dust left behind deadly and vile.

Jeremiah stands up beside me, gun upholstered in his strong arms and his eyes narrowed as he aims at the ERUSA soldiers coming at us. *Shit!* As I fumble to steady myself and aim the soldiers, Jeremiah has already begun to shoot at them. The noise of the gunshots tremble into my veins and leave me shaken, my knees almost buckling. I want to get away from these earth-trembling noises as much as I can, but I physically cannot move. My feet are planted on the ground, becoming one with the roots and the dirt sifting into the grounds.

How *can* he do this so effortlessly, though? Then again, he was a Guard. Hell, I don't even know why he needs to go through training when he's trained beyond belief. That man can shoot like never before. And sure, I can shoot too, but only at peaceful deers nipping at the grass below their hooves. Never was I ever trained to shoot at moving bodies of flesh armed beyond what my eyes can interpret.

Reality shifts into my mind as I notice a soldier nearing me, his steel-gray eyes narrowed and his gun pointed at my temple. I press my lips together, and in a swift motion, I bring the tip of my rifle to his exposed jaw—and with great pressure amongst myself and a determined Jeremiah, I bring myself to shoot him.

With bated breath, I watch him fall back, blood seeping from his gaping wound. It is only seconds later he gets back up to his feet, his breathing ragged and his nostrils flared as he narrows his eyes at me. As a string of curses leave my mouth and I begin to shoot at him again, Jeremiah's large hand grasps my forearm and lugs me back—where a narrow alleyway leads to the train station.

"We need to fall back," Jeremiah grits out, his eyes darting at the numerous ERUSA soldiers cornering us. My heart leaps up to my throat, my mind running in thousands of directions. I start to stammer about Blaire, who I cannot see from this crowded position and cannot hear either from the never-ending gunshots and shouts of cries, but Jeremiah interrupts me by saying, "She will be fine. *Trust me.* She's with the finest soldier in the Detroitian compound. But good lord—Jax, we *need* to fall back and make a goddamn run for it."

A desert resides in the center of my throat. I nod moments later, squeezing my eyes shut for a split second. "Okay."

Jeremiah nods once, and in one swift motion, he runs in the opposite direction.

And I follow behind him, my heart beating at my throat and my legs running so fast I start to lose control of them. The wind howls at my ear, entering my system and chilling my veins. I clench my fists tight, pumping them as I feel the ERUSA soldiers nearing at my heels. In order to avoid their oncoming bullets, I turn around halfway and shoot rapidly at them, praying to God at least one of my bullets pierces through them. Some of them are shot, but only in minor places where they can easily pull themselves together for a quick moment and carry on. *Oh, goddammit.*

Amongst all the chaos, my eyes linger over to Blaire in the far distance, shielding herself behind AJ, who rapidly shoots at the ERUSA soldiers cornering them. It seems as if the others are assisting them too, while Veronica and Commander Thatcher continue with their constant rebuttals. I know I hate AJ with all my guts, but it is only this one time that I hope he protects her because I am not there with her for this one moment.

She *needs* to be safe.

As the scene closes in the far distance, I take a deep breath in and continue to shoot at the soldiers whilst running and running and running as the hot, stuffy wind drives me forward. Thankful to the winding roads, I can catch up to Jeremiah's fast pace, which is surprising considering his amputated leg. Then again, he must have had years of practice with his robotic leg, so it must not even concern him at this point.

I huff out another breath, struggling to run synchronously with this he-robot of a man. I'm dead serious when I say I'm going to ask Jeremiah what his workout routine is—after this whole shenanigan is over.

Due to the adrenaline pumping through our veins and mine and Jeremiah's repeated attempts to shoot the ERUSA soldiers charging behind us, we manage to outrun them and catch the oncoming train heading toward Dearborn. Lungs heavy with pumping blood, we heave ourselves onto the platform and into one of the cars. I immediately fall back on one of the leather seats, holding my head in my hands and breathing in and out. Slowly, but with great meaning.

What the hell just happened?

I spread my legs, closing my eyes and setting my gun to the side. Thanks to the fast speed of the train, we should be able to escape the chaos for now. Once we are near the outskirts of Detroit, we will leave the train—even when it's running—and make our way back to the scene. There, we can probably have a better outlook on this entire situation.

By then, I set my weapons to the side and unbutton the upper half of my uniform. All the padding and shields fall off my torso and plunge to the ground of the train which rattles against the steel railings. Jeremiah in the seat ahead of me seems to be doing the same. Thankfully no one else is on this train, or else it would be rather frightening for them to see two men dressed head-to-toe in military uniform and sweating their asses off.

All Jeremiah and I have on now are the black undershirt with our baggy camo pants, the cuffs wedged underneath jet-black combat boots. Jeremiah makes his way to the seat next to mine—just the aisle separating us. He runs his hand across his face, sweat gleaming against his brow. "Let's catch our breath for a bit," he says. "At least until we lose track of the soldiers."

"That sounds like a plan," I say breathlessly.

He cocks his head at me, a grin growing on him suddenly. "Man, if it weren't for your mini argument with AJ then maybe we could be in a better place right now."

"Look, I'm sorry," I grumble. "He just gets on my goddamn nerves."

Jeremiah chuckles. "I'm just joking, Jax. And besides, I understand where you're coming from. If someone was getting all close with my Layla too, then God knows whether they'd be intact afterwards."

I snort. "Finally, *someone* gets it."

His grin deepens, and as he starts to say something else, the train car shakes slightly as I stumble against my seat. I peer at where the commotion came from—right at the entrance.

Lines of ERUSA soldiers entering from the cars behind us are now entering our car.

"Shit," I hiss. "What the hell do we do?"

"Hide," Jeremiah says immediately, lodging all seventy-eight inches of him semi-underneath his seat. I do the same, grunting to myself and cursing every time the metal rod inserted at the bottom of the leather seat clashes against the back of my skull.

Once we situate ourselves, I hold my breath as I feel the soldiers coming to us—like silent ghosts. I know hiding from them isn't the most effective solution, but it's efficient for now. At least it gives us enough time to prepare to fight against the neverending trail of ERUSA soldiers. It'll give us enough time to gather our weapons and our wits and fight against all odds as we clash with the enemy. And for a hot minute, I think it is possible—that we might *just* be able to win this sole battle.

But the split second of eye contact I share with Jeremiah tells a story more convincing than mine . . .

There's no way in hell we're getting out of this alive.

21

BOURGEON

BLAIRE

THE SCREECHES OF FLYING bullets and frantic citizens ring into my ears. I grit my teeth, tears threatening to escape my eyes, but I swallow them down, just like I swallow my unavoidable fears. My hands fumble for the trigger of the rifle I cling onto—the only thing that can possibly protect me from this impending doom hole. Then again, even *that* may not be enough, judging by the innumerable ERUSA soldiers spewing past Veronica and sprinting to us like water shooting out of a faucet.

How the hell are we going to win this battle?

In situations like these, I would usually go to my boyfriend for emotional support—for something no one else can offer to me. His hugs and his words are unlike any others, even in comparison to my mother, who has been calming my nerves since the day I was able to read. But Jax is not here. He is with Jeremiah, and God knows where they are. And I am unfortunately stuck with AJ—who isn't that bad to begin with. I just want Jax with me, and no one else.

AJ kneels beside me, pushing a solid shield ahead of him and covering the both of us. As I sit here, cowering to the ground, he sighs and raises one dark eyebrow at me. "Scared?"

"Very," I mutter.

One side of his lip twitches up. Whether it is with amusement or pity—that I have no idea. "I don't blame you. It's been months since you've held a gun, right?"

Bullets continue to whizz past my ears, and some even lodge into the seemingly bullet-proof shield ahead of us. "Yeah, it has been months." I sigh, my shoulders sulking. "I do know how to fight, I just can't bring myself to."

"Hey, that's okay," he says, looking around. "We can take a break, if you want."

I shake my head, vehement and unwilling. "No, I don't want to take a break. I'll never be able to face my fears that way."

"Okay, that's fine too." AJ raises his hands in defense, a grin inflicting on his lips. "Whatever suits you."

"Thanks." I pause. "Do *you* need a break?"

As AJ starts to speak, someone's hand on my shoulder startles me. A yelp leaves my mouth as I jump in my sitting position and turn around, and I am met with a panting Vi who brings Mal and Ren with her.

Wait . . . *Ren?*

"I'm confused too," Vi says dryly as she acknowledges the bewildered look embedded on my face. She kneels beside me, putting half of her body weight on mine and dragging sharp breaths in and out of her. "God, I need a breather."

"You can stay here behind the shield as long as you need," AJ says. "Is my sister up there?"

"Yes, she is," Mal responds. "She's doing a really great job holding up the ranks, alongside the other soldiers, Nicolas, and Commander Thatcher too."

He sends Mal a grateful look. "Thanks for the update. Sometimes it scares me to see Annie up there. I know she's more than capable of defending and fighting for herself, but it still terrifies me. I don't want anything to happen to her."

"Nothing will happen to her," I reassure him. "Annie is a great soldier. I'm sure she will be fine."

"I sure hope you're right," he drawls, leaning back against the wall of the abandoned shop we've been propped against. As Mal brings up her shield and combines it with ours, Vi holds a gun on standby if a soldier were to come here. But as of now, we're in the clear. Thanks to Annie, Nico, and Commander Thatcher, that is.

A flash of red meets my eye and falls on my lap as the pale-skinned and freckled woman takes a slow breath in and adjusts herself on the ground. She scrunches her nose as she timidly sits on the dirt, scoffing with indeterminable disgust. "Can we move to a different location?" Ren murmurs, her full lips pressed together in disdain.

"No," Vi spits out. "If your prissy ass can't handle a little bit of dirt, then I suggest you go on the battlefield. Maybe the smell of blood and soot will be more to your liking."

"*Vi,*" Mal hisses out, anchoring her injured thigh ahead of her. "Don't do this right now."

"What?" She scowls at her. "You mean humbling her? Because that should've been done a long ass time ago."

"Look, I don't know what you have against me," Ren starts, "but I am a pretty nice woman. I love long walks by the beach, I love playing board games, I love doing makeup—"

"Oh, *please*—"

"And I love making friends." Ren's eyebrows raise in question. "Let's be friends, Vienna. It shouldn't be too bad, right?"

Vi rolls her eyes, pressing her knees to her chest. "See, the thing about me is that I don't *make friends*, let alone have them. I only have acquaintances. I've learned quite the hard way that building close bonds with others often leads to disappointment and eventually—heartbreak." She clears her throat stoically. "So I suggest you leave me alone, m'kay?"

Ren looks at us desperately. *What should I do?* Her eyes seem to plead.

Mal and I just shrug. *Trust us . . . you should just let it be.*

Moments of silence pass by in the suffocating air, cascading amongst the trails of smoke and the intense heat of the sun. Ren has accepted her defeat and quietly hums to herself. Vi inches away from her and holds on tight to her rifle still. AJ does the same, his eyes drilled on the hoard of soldiers fighting and clashing against each other. Mal has her injured thigh propped on me now, pushing her matty blonde hair to the side. And I lean against the battered shop walls, lightly banging my head against it as I silently wish for this constant ringing to go away.

Please go away.

But it doesn't go away. Instead, the ringing intensifies—bombards into my eardrums and rattles my soul. The ringing multiples, nothing but jarring staticity and searing into my veins. That's when I realize the ringing is nearing, followed by several soldiers who have somehow found their way past their hoarding battlefield and onto the sidelines—where we are.

Oh, no.

They immediately start shooting at us, bullets springing against the shields with a high-pitched vibrant noise. AJ pulls himself up to his feet, narrowing his eyes at the soldiers and shooting at them. In the blink of an eye, some of them are punctured and stumble back. Vi, by this time, has gotten up and shoots at them too.

As Vi and AJ attempt to take care of the ever-growing soldiers, I finger the trigger, the pad of my thumb cupping the butt of the rifle. It glides itself among the smooth exterior of the weapon—familiarizing itself.

Ren cowers to the ground, grasping her flowing red hair as she gasps out, "I can't do this. I can't handle this anymore."

"Then why are you here?" Vi scowls as she continues to shoot rapidly at the incoming ERUSA soldiers.

"Because I wanted to support you all. And I wanted to stand up against the people who killed my mother." Ren's tone is surprisingly sharp and jagged. "That's all I wanted to do."

"Look, I get that you wanted to support us and stand up for your mother," AJ says from the other end, "but you shouldn't risk your life like this. This is not just something you can do in your sleep. This is something that requires years of training. At least the Subversives had first-hand experience in D.C., but you have not, Renata. That's why we suggested for you to stay back in the first place, but you kept on insisting and we allowed you to come."

She huffs out a low breath. "Well, now I wish you didn't allow me to come because I hate it here."

From my peripheral vision, I notice Vi rolling her eyes and pushing her shoulders back as she continues to shoot at the soldiers. "Prissy bitch," she mutters underneath her breath.

I jut my jaw forward, still trembling as I push myself off the ground. Ren holds onto the shop's wall behind us, whimpering to herself. Mal is still kneeling, merely because of her injury, but still shoots at the impending soldiers from where she is.

So what the hell am I doing? I should be fighting back too. I should be shooting at the soldiers too. I shouldn't be standing here, wordless, dumbfounded, and acting like the universe has stolen every single limb and movement in my legs. There is no excuse for me. I am not injured like Mal. I am not inexperienced like Ren. I have shot at people before—and without any hesitation too. The version of me back then was so brave, so determined to fight even though she never stepped foot out of her house before. So why am I acting like this right now, when I sure as hell have zero excuses?

I have zero excuses.

I finger the trigger again, finding myself slowly getting

acquainted with the curve of the material and the edge of the lining. I've pressed against many triggers before. I've unleashed plenty of bullets before. I've heard several gunshots before. This shouldn't be new to me. This should be child's play to me— something I can do even in my sleep.

I just have to unleash this hidden fire inside of me. Right now, this fire is nothing but a flickering flame, struggling to stay lit. But I want it to be the way it was before—burning, raging, uncontrollable, and bourgeoning. Younger Blaire's soul was enraging with flames, seething and scathing past her insides and controlling her mind. Now my fire has lessened and has become a devoid being. I want it to be flourishing again, though. I want it to soar past my veins and fly into the wind, hurling out of my mouth in trails of smoke—like the smoke amalgamating into the air and whisking into the fat, puffy white clouds.

I'll flourish again. I'll relight this flickering flame again. I *will*.

But it all starts from here. It is either now or never.

I decide to go with the former . . . and pull back on the trigger.

The sound that leaves my rifle encroaches into my veins, buries itself into my soul, and disperses its remnants into the beating valleys of my heart. It's louder than any sound I've heard before—louder than the scream that left my throat when Nico was being pulled away by the Guards. Louder than the sole bomb blast that occured after we were supposed to get executed. And louder than the scream that erupted from Ren's throat when Charlotte Levine's bloodied and lifeless figure fell to a thud on the stage.

Loud, loud, *loud*.

So loud I start to relish in it—start to relish in the soldier who falls to the ground as a result of my action—and I desire to pull the trigger again.

And again, and *again*.

22

FIGMENT

JAX

"WHAT THE HELL DO we do?" I whisper to Jeremiah as I hear the growing heavy footsteps of the ERUSA soldiers.

"We have to fight," he whispers back, so slowly and so lowly I have to crane my head forward—but not too forward as well. Otherwise, one of these soldiers walking down the lanky aisle will notice my face poking out and will most likely shoot at me. And I like my face way too much for that shit to happen.

Two beats of silence pass by, and I watch Jeremiah reach for the rifle with his large hands. They aren't trembling like mine are. They're determined to fight. Determined to prevail. He clenches his hard jaw, adjusting himself with the stealthiest of movements and sends me another look.

Let's do this, his eyes tell me.

And just like a bolt of lightning, he stands up, leans against the back of the seat, and shoots rapidly at the soldiers. From where I am, I hear the heavy falling of bodies and the strangled cries of the ERUSA. I blearily look up at Jeremiah—while I defensively hold up the rifle in my hand. No way in hell am I just going to let him fight all several dozens of the soldiers. No matter how strong he may be, I'm still going to help. Whether he needs it or not.

But for some reason, my feet disagree with my mind. They stay put, glued to the ground, and unwilling to move. As much as I am determined to fight, simultaneously, I *can't*. The last time I was involved in heavy fighting was when I killed my father, and I sure as hell don't want to be in the sight of blood and tears again. But that is not a choice for me anymore; this is my life now, and this is what I'm obliged to do—fight even if demons and nightmares constantly pounce at my mind.

Jeremiah's words that come out of his mouth next are a confirmation for my pending actions. "C'mon, Jax! Only a little boy would sit and cower like that. Are you a boy or a man, huh?" he says breathlessly between firing gunshots. "What are you?"

At this moment, my surroundings blur and I furrow my brows, lowering my head in thought. My father used to ask me that. He used to ask me—constantly—if I was a boy or a man. If I was a cowardly little boy who would much rather hide in the shadows than be an outstanding man fighting anyone who gets in his way. He used to taunt me with that question, chant it to me and grin in delight whenever I struggled to stutter out a response.

He died thinking of me as nothing but a little boy. And that is my biggest regret in life—not letting him know that I am instead a *man*. I don't want to be in the shadows. I don't want to cower, hide, and stutter. I want to stand, seek, and yell.

I am a man.

A drive of adrenaline rushes through my veins as I stand up, my legs grounding the shaky floors of the train. I grasp the butt of my rifle with the cusp of my hand and narrow my eyes at the flailing soldiers trapped on the train—counting at least twenty of them. Five are seemingly dead, and the rest alive.

And I press on the trigger.

It's satisfying, to say the least—watching the soldiers fall to the ground with the same balance as a fly completely out of control. The train shakes with every enemy of mine that thuds against the hard floor in a fast movement. Trees whizz past the trembling windows, and I immediately note that we will be in Dearborn at least in the next several minutes. That is why Jeremiah and I *have* to escape this train well and alive before then.

Nonetheless, there are still plenty of soldiers that remain, and I must gather my will and energy if I want to make it out of this hellhole in one goddamn piece. So, I grasp onto the head of the leather seat, leering myself over the edge until my legs are basically grounding the seat. The butt of the rifle is wedged underneath my arms, and I narrow my eyes, squeezing my fingers around the trigger and pulling back whenever a soldier comes in my line of sight. I think back to when my dad used to take me hunting—which was rare, considering he was just *too busy* to be a normal father to me. Even though that man irritated the hell out of me, I must admit, his skills were pretty useful.

The most memorable tip he told me was to never tremble because the animal—or rather in this situation, the *soldier*—can easily sense the perpetrator's fear and use it against them. Fear, other than love, is the strongest emotion any human can harness, and if anyone were to detect it even in a one-mile radius, then—in the simplest terms possible—they're basically screwed.

I keep that tip in mind as I grit my teeth, my chest vibrating with the intense noise the gun rumbles with every pull of the trigger. The never-ending trail of bullets flying out of the hole of the rifle pierces into almost every soldier I can see—my eyes perfectly fixated on my target whenever it is needed. I am a man. I don't ever cower, and nor do I ever fear.

Unfortunately, the gun gives off a distinctive clicking noise, and no bullets spew out as I rapidly pull and pull and pull on the trigger. The soldiers are nearing, and I have no idea what to do.

Neither does Jeremiah, who also seems to have run out of ammunition.

"Shit," I grumble to myself, throwing my rifle against the window and frustratingly running my hands through my matted hair. I turn to Jeremiah, who has sprung out of his seat and curls his fists, veins bulging from his biceps. "Are you seriously about to fight them with your bare hands?"

Right before Jeremiah rams his fist into the cusp of the soldier's neck that is in front of him, he turns to me with a raging emotion glinting in his cocoa eyes. "Well, it's either that, or giving up."

His words remain hung up in the air, and before I can even react, he swings his arm back and lunges the core of his knuckles into the soldier's neck. A satisfying crunch reverberates into the stifling and humid air, and he stumbles back, a warbled groan leaving his mouth.

Well, that is until Jeremiah snatches the Barrett M82 out of the ERUSA soldier's hand, points it at him, and shoots at him innumerably. It's disgusting to watch his face turn into battered and broken pieces of flesh and skull—blood spewing onto the seats around him.

Damn. That is both revolting yet pleasing at the same time.

However, it is unfortunate that I have lost my attention and completely overlooked the strong soldier stomping over to me and grabbing the hem of my shirt with both of his gloved hands —and sending a swift punch to my jaw. My vision turns white, and I let out a husky groan, falling against the back of the seat in front of me. I'm suddenly on all fours, pulling at the ground, and gritting my teeth as I try to push the overwhelming pain away. *Ignore it, Jax. Just ignore it already.*

I slowly get up to my feet, marching over to the soldier head-on, my eyes flashing with fury. My chest rises in and out as he pulls at the rifle wedged underneath his armpit and aims it at me. I am met with the gaping hole—right where the bullet would plunge from—pointed at me, and it is fortunate that I duck in time. The shell flies over my head and clashes against the window behind, sending millions of glass shards sifting to the ground.

I take this moment in time to grab the waist of the man and push him to the ground, and that's when I send dozens of blows to his puny little face. It doesn't take much time for him to limpen beneath my figure. For his pulse to cease, too.

One down, many more to go.

I don't know what demon or rather foreign entity has invaded my system, but it's pretty damn exhilarating because I haven't felt this high before in my entire life—smashing people's skulls into smithereens. Grabbing their gun and shooting at them. Or kicking them in the gut until they eventually start puking blood. Maybe it's because I'm so determined to prove to my dead father that I am a man. Prove to him that I am not a damn coward. *Not* one at all.

It is several dead soldiers later that we are left with two. Jeremiah is currently handling one just fine on his own—pretty much strangling the man to death—and the other stands in front of me, his darkened eyes never leaving my face. He's run out of ammunition too, so this battle will be pretty fair and square. Either way, it doesn't really matter to me. I've killed plenty of soldiers here who were armed to the bone.

I eye the metal rod poking out beneath the leather seat that's near me. I yank it out of its spot, weighing it in my hand with a curiosity that both pleases and scares me. This should do the trick.

Pulling myself up to my feet, a wave of adrenaline rushes through my body—trembling like an earthquake and crashing over like a tsunami. My heavy combat boots pound against the aisle of the train as I roll and circle the rod in my hand, whirling it around me and never trailing my sight away from the wretched soldier. Dangerous intentions wander in my mind. So dangerous it enthralls me.

When I am near the man, he brings his arm back to swing at me, and the moment his fist nears mine, I grab it with my free hand and twist it—simultaneously sending a kick to his gut. He groans, stumbling back slightly, but regains himself fast enough to push the square of my chest and drive quite a strong uppercut to my chin. My head almost snaps back from the force, but I immediately regain myself by grounding my feet to the floor and taking deep breaths in and out. I feel thick and hot blood coating the entrance of my mouth, and I spit out whatever's in my mouth to the edge of the man's leather combat boots.

I wipe the blood coating my lips with the back of my hand and send the soldier a challenging grin. "Come at me, you jackass. I dare you."

As his raging eyes never leave my face, I notice the man conforms into an amorphous entity. I start to think I'm going insane, and maybe my lack of sleep contributes heavily to what I see in front of me now, but I swear he's so real. So tangible. And it scares the absolute shit out of me.

His narrowed gray eyes, thick, dark eyebrows, and sunken features are the first thing I see. That, and the gaping wound presented in the center of his broad chest.

My heart leaps to my throat.

He walks toward me, his graying hair gleaming against the flickering dim lights of the moving train. An annoying grin has stretched upon his lips, and the same scar I drew on him—right before I plunged the knife into him—stares at me as if it had eyes of its own.

"Hello, son." Blood from his gaping wound on his chest drips to the bottom of his feet as he cocks his head at me. "You've grown a lot since the last time we met."

I don't say a single word.

He chuckles, shaking his head slightly. "It's okay. You don't have to answer. I understand that you're a bit shaken meeting me like this. Especially since our last interaction was a bit . . . unpredictable."

"Leave me alone," I grunt out, my grip on the rod tightening.

The flame in his stormy eyes flickers, his ghostly presence consuming my veins. "Now, why would I do that, when we've finally reconvened? I miss you, son. No matter the sin you committed."

"I didn't commit a single sin. I did what was needed. I did what was best for everyone."

"And yet, you're in a moving train splattered with blood and shards of glass, right in front of the person you've been avoiding all along." The muscle in his jaw twitches. "But you can't avoid me, Jax. No matter how many times you kill me and throw me to the side like some piece of trash, I will always come back. I will always remind you of the *sin* you committed."

"Again," I hiss, "I didn't commit a single sin."

"You murdered me!" His voice comes out like a demonic growl, rushing through me like a gust of wind. "You murdered your goddamn father! I raised you. I fed you. I nurtured you. I taught you. I motivated you. I worshiped you. And better yet, I *loved* you when no one else did. Love is not something you can get from the streets. It's a rare principle. A diamond people have been searching for years. You should've been damn happy you had that love when no one else did. But you weren't." He laughs a sad laugh. "You were an ungrateful brat who wrongfully thought you weren't meant to be like me. I don't know who told you those lies, but they were wrong.

"Don't you get it? You're like *me.* You're the carbon copy of me. Admit it, Jax. As much as you killed me both mentally and physically, you are me. As much as you pushed away becoming president and joined the wrong side, you are me. And as much as you chase this so-called dream of yours and think you're so smart for being this so-called independent man, *you are me."* He takes a brave step toward me, his eyebrows pushed up. "Admit it."

I shake my head once, twice, and so many more times my head starts to hurt. "No," I whisper, a wave of tears threatening to escape my eyes but I push them down my throat—gulp them down and throw them away, just like I've thrown all my emotions away lately. "I am not like you, Tobias. I am my own person. I am not like you. *I am not.*"

The curl to his lip upsets me, bringing a sense of foreboding into my veins. His eyes are full of disappointment, just like they've always been when they look at me. As much as he tells me he loves me and misses me, he actually doesn't. He's only saying that to taunt me—feeding me false nothings and expecting me to succumb to his desires. But I'm not stupid. I'm not dependent on him. I have a mind of my own, whether he likes it or not.

He steps toward me again, so close to me that we are almost torso-to-torso. And I hate it. I want to kill him again. I want to tear his body into pieces and dispose of him into a shredder. He deserves the worst out of the *worst.*

His lip twitches angrily as he whispers to me, "I should've dragged that knife into your heart instead."

And, without any warning, he brings his hand to my face and claws his fingers against my bloodied scar.

A pained howl leaves my mouth, and I feel fresh blood dripping down my face again. *Shit!* I bring my hand to my cheek, feeling dark, thick red liquid coating my flesh. It disgusts me. *Really* disgusts and saddens me.

I look at the entity in front of me. I don't see the soldier anymore. I see my worst enemy and nightmare instead.

I don't even hesitate when I bring the rod back and drive it to his temple with such speed and force that when it hits him, he flies three rows back. I don't even hesitate when I throw the rod behind me, march to him, grasp the hem of his collar, and smash his body against the window next to me, even more shards of glass falling to the ground and coating his thick, graying hair. I don't even hesitate when I clasp both of my shaking hands to his neck and squeeze as if my life depended on it. I don't even hesitate to push his bobbing head out, trees still whizzing by and lights flooding in. I don't even hesitate when I say "I hate you" over and over again, one tear slowly trailing down my bloody cheek.

I don't even hesitate at all.

His eyes are red with pain, anger, frustration, and disappointment. "How could you, Jax? How could you ever betray me like this?"

My hold on him tightens. "I never betrayed you. *You* betrayed me. You say that you love me, and you miss me, but you really don't."

"I do."

"You *don't*."

"*I do*," he emphasizes, his nostrils flaring. "You are dim-witted and stubborn, so of course you don't see that. You're too busy frolicking behind your girlfriend, who's just as dim-witted and stubborn as you—if not more."

My vision turns hazy and my blood runs cold with ire. "Don't say that about her, you bitch."

"She will leave you, just like everyone else has," he says with a dangerous edge. "And it's what you deserve. You deserve nothing but a cold, isolated life because of the numerous sins you committed. *That* is what you deserve."

My hands are shaking against his cold neck, and purple veins sprout on the cusp of his neck as his eyes almost bulge out of its sockets. I want to kill him again. I really do.

"Go ahead and do it," he says, seeming to read my mind. "Kill me however many times you want. But you'll never get rid of me. You won't."

My wounded soul suddenly burns alive, crackling flames

and red, red, *red*. My hold tightens and tightens on the wretched man, the outside light peering in and the whisking wind brushing against my face and hissing against my wounds.

Outside, I notice an incoming pole displaying the Detroitian flag, rumpling against the air.

And I bring his body out the window even more, allowing the back of his skull to collide against the pole, immediately jerking forward and detaching from its neck.

Blood splatters and sprays against my face.

My vision slowly unhazes as I wipe the blood away—mine and his—and I see a blurred Jeremiah standing above a dead soldier, looking at me, concern and pride amassing his features.

All that remains in the air and in my sight is my heavy breathing, a decapitated and marred male soldier slumped in the seat in front of me, and the aching words the figment of my imagination taunted to me endlessly.

2 3

TOGETHER

BLAIRE

THE LIGHTS OF THE infirmary glare down on me, almost blinding me in the process.

As I groan to myself, shielding my eyes away, I place my hand over the wound that amasses my lower stomach. During the battle, my torso was exposed from the shield and an ERUSA soldier noticed it, so he took it to his advantage and shot me there. I had to stay there for the longest ten minutes ever, in *such* pain, and it was fortunate that we drove the ERUSA soldiers back—alongside an infuriated Veronica—and shot at them even as we made our way to the Detroitian army underground bunker. Since the land is in Windsor territory and in a completely different expanse, the ERUSA are not allowed to enter the premises—unless they were to colonize it by force. Luckily, our ranks were too powerful compared to theirs, and it would've been downright idiotic of them to challenge us.

Everyone immediately rushed me to the infirmary—or so that is what Mal told me, since I was entirely knocked out. It was only ten minutes ago that I woke up from the heavily inducing drugs the doctors gave me, and now my fingers are grazing the sutured wound, wincing every time I hit a sensitive spot.

The entire time I was awake, though, I kept thinking about Jax. Hell, I *still* am. No one has heard a word from either him or Jeremiah, since they had to separate from us due to most of the ERUSA soldiers chasing after them. I've been gnawing on my fingernails since, hoping and hoping and *hoping* nothing happened to Jax. I might just lose my shit if something did.

Five minutes later—or seemingly five *eternities* later—Vi opens the opalescent infirmary door and steps inside, her black and red hair slicked back into a tiny ponytail. Her sunken and tired brown eyes glance over at me, unreadable and bringing a heavy weight to my heart. "They're here," she says.

"Really?" I sit up in my hospital bed, wincing with every movement. "Are they okay?"

"Yes. Luckily, they're not impaled, decapitated, or lacking any important body parts." She sighs, leaning against the door-frame. "How are you holding up?"

"Pretty decent, I think. But I couldn't care less about myself. I just want to see him."

"You mean your boyfriend?" Vi rolls her eyes. "God, I wish I could go back in time when you two hated each other."

"Oh, stop it. You know you secretly wanted us together."

She doesn't say a single word. *That's what I thought.*

"Anyway"—she clears her throat—"besides them finally reaching the compound, I also wanted to let you know Jax is coming to you . . . right now, actually."

"Seriously?" My heart rate suddenly fastens.

"Wait, he's not coming to you. He's actually *rushing* to you. Seriously. He's pushing past people as if they were trash on the side of the road. Acting like he has a wife in labor." She lets out a sharp breath—and I assume it to be an attempted chuckle.

I raise my eyebrows, heat rushing to my face. "He's running to *me?* Is he really that worried about me?"

"Blaire." She cocks her head at me. "Are you forgetting the fact that he's completely obsessed with you? He almost lost his shit when AJ suggested you pair up with him."

I jut my chin forward in thought. *Well, when you put it that way . . .*

Vi impatiently waves a hand at me. "Whatever. I just wanted to let you know about that."

As she starts to leave, I blurt out, "Are *you* okay, though?"

Normally, Vi would make a dry joke and move on with her day, but this time, she instead ever so slightly shakes her head, dread and a remembrance of her past trauma overcoming her feline features. "Am I ever okay?" she says in a small voice. And before I can even say anything, she closes the door on me.

I take a heavy breath in, my fingers still dancing on my wound. I have so much respect for Vi—so much I can't even measure it at this point. Whenever I find myself complaining about my past and how much turmoil I underwent in D.C., I immediately remind myself that there are plenty of other people who have gone through even more trauma—such as Vi. She lost her entire family in front of her own eyes, for God's sake. And I applaud her for still carrying on with her life and pushing that horrible memory to the back of her mind because if it were me in that situation, I wouldn't be as strong as her. Hell, I would basically go numb and isolate myself from the world.

As I start to lean back on my pillow, there is a soft knock at the door. "Blaire?" A familiar deep voice echoes through the cracks of the closed door. "It's me. Jax."

My heart races at a million miles per hour. "It's open," I say in a small voice, hoping he heard me.

Moments later, the door quivers open, revealing Jax and his flawless self. Flawless gray eyes, flawless tan skin, flawless hair, flawless *everything*. So flawless it's almost unbelievable. Even amongst the dozens of bruises, scars, and blemishes on his flesh, I still think he's flawless.

He sends me a small smile as he closes the door behind him and ambles to me. He sits on the edge of the hospital bed, bringing his bruised hand to my knee. He moves it against my knee in a slow and soothing manner, and suddenly, my stomach is a raging zoo.

"Hi," he says, still smiling slightly.

"Hey," I say back, smirking at him afterwards. "Vi told me you pushed through people just to see me."

Jax chuckles to himself. "I did."

"How did you even find out about my condition?"

"Mallory told me as soon as Jeremiah and I stepped into the compound. Before she even finished speaking to me, I *sprinted* over to the infirmary. I was freaking the hell out."

I raise my eyebrows at him amusingly. "So I've heard."

His grin deepens. "How are you holding up, though? And how were you even shot?" I explain to him the story, and he immediately frowns. The way his eyebrows are pushed together in frustration both frightens yet intrigues me. "Were you exposed when you were shot?"

"I was in the heat of the moment," I start off.

"That doesn't give you an excuse to get yourself shot and potentially killed." He lets out an uneasy sigh and tugs at the bottom of my shirt. "Let me see."

My heart pounds through the flimsy fabric of my cotton top. "Right now?"

"Yes, right now." Jax raises his eyebrows at me, his fingers unwilling to let go. "I don't want to hear any excuses, Blaire. Let me see."

I start to refute his words, but seeing the unwavering eye contact from him makes me sigh out in defeat and give in to his desires. It's okay, I'll just show it to him. The only reason I don't want to show him in the first place is because I *know* he will freak out.

Which is exactly what he does.

When he slowly pulls up at my shirt, revealing only my torso, his eyes widen at the dried blood splotched across my lower stomach and ceasing around the curve of my hip. My pants are low, barely hanging on my hips—only to let my wound "breathe," as stated by the doctor. Normally, I would be completely fine if someone was assessing me like this. But this is Jax, whose otherworldly gray eyes can possibly mesmerize anyone in a five-feet radius. And his light touch isn't exactly helping my intense rush of adrenaline either.

The muscle in his jaw twitches as he drinks in my exposed stomach. "Lay down," he murmurs.

"What?" I furrow my brows at him.

"Lay down," he says again, gesturing to the bed beneath me. "You shouldn't be sitting up right now. Especially with a wound like that."

"I'm sorry, Dr. Remington," I say jokingly. "I'll lay down."

As my head hits the pillow, he hovers around me, no trace of amusement wandering around in his pupils. Normally it would be Jax joking and definitely not me, but in this case the tables have been turned quite extraordinarily because I attempted to crack a joke to hopefully lift the disdainful environment—but Jax is frowning at me, his eyebrows pushed together like steel plates.

"Don't joke with me," he mutters. "This is a serious matter, Blaire. If you weren't brought here on time then . . ." He curses underneath his breath. "Shit. I don't even want to think about it."

I press my lips together and place my hand on top of his, planted on the sheets. "Look, Jax. I'm fine, I promise. The doctor himself said that I'll be released in a couple of hours. I just have to rest and regain my vitals until then."

"You were almost *killed*," he says in a low voice, leaning into me. "How do you not understand the extremity of that situation? I can't afford to lose you."

"I can't afford to lose you either, Jax," I whisper. "But we're in this together, and you need to understand this is the life we have to live now. It might just be an everyday thing that one of us will get shot. I don't like the thought of it either, but that's just our life now and there's nothing we can do about it." I inch toward him, cupping his face with both of my hands. "As long as we trust and believe in each other, then that's all that matters. Do you trust and believe in me?"

I barely even finish the sentence when he says, "More than anything out there, yes."

"Same goes for me. So let's move on from this injury of mine and keep on kicking ass." I cock my head at him. "Yeah?"

His lips stretch into a small smile, dimples creasing. "Yeah."

Suddenly, he brings me back on the bed and sits next to me, his arm and thigh grazing mine. My heart stutters at our close proximity and the warmth radiating from his skin. It takes every part of me to not turn to him and kiss him as if my life depended on it, but I decide that in an environment such as this, that is most likely inappropriate. And if my mother were to barge in on us in a compromising position such as that, then consider me dead meat.

I bring my hand slowly down his forearm and place mine on top of his, running my fingers over the veins amassing his strong hands. "Hey, Jax?" I whisper.

"Yes, Blaire?" he whispers back.

I dare to look at him, my heart about to crawl up my throat. "Is everything okay?"

He looks at me with an unreadable expression, but he masks it with an abrupt grin. "Well, besides you almost getting yourself killed, I'd say I'm doing pretty decent."

I sigh, cocking my head. "Are you sure? Because you haven't been acting like . . . well, *yourself* lately."

He frowns at me. "What do you mean?"

I speak several moments later, attempting to gather my thoughts. "Ever since the night you left me while we were sleeping together, you've been MIA more frequently—both mentally and physically. And I'm honestly just worried about you, Jax. I know it's been hard for the both of us lately, so I want to be here for you. You know you can talk to me about anything, right?"

"Of course I can," he says almost immediately. "I just . . ." He sighs, rubbing his forehead with his free hand, feeling oddly conflicted. "Life has just been kinda hard, y'know? What with the world kinda falling apart at its seams. It's just hard to go on with my day, knowing others are struggling and dying every single day. Maybe . . . things would be different if I didn't kill my father and we lived our same life in D.C. Maybe even *better.*"

"That's not true," I say vehemently. "You can't say that when you have no idea what it's like to be a Poor person. Granted I can't really compare my lifestyle as a Poor to how my life is now, but they're both bad. And I think that's all that matters. Also . . . why are you still beating yourself up for what happened last year?"

"I don't know," he stammers. "It's still on my mind, Blaire. And I don't know what to do about it."

I sigh, looking into his eyes. "Y'know, Jax? You're not the only one struggling like this. I am too."

"Really?" He straightens up in alarm. "What do you mean?"

"Well . . . I had a nightmare about him the other day."

When I finish explaining the nightmare to him, he curses to himself, grabbing my hand and squeezing it tightly. "God, I'm so sorry, Blaire. I'm so sorry you had that nightmare."

"Don't be sorry." I frown at him afterwards. "That's the only nightmare I've had so far, but something tells me that's not the end. That there's more."

He lets out a low breath, his grip never loosening. "I'm always here if you need me. You know that right?"

I give him a sad smile. "Of course. Same goes for you too."

His eyebrows weirdly scrunch together, almost as if he is having an internal battle. "Yeah. I know."

We don't say anything for what seems like forever, and I like it that way. I like how we're comfortable being silent with each other—how we can prosper in the quietude together. Others need chaos or loudness to keep them going, but Jax and I are not like that. Every now and then, we yearn for peace and quiet because our lives have become so chaotic—so raucous. And now that we have an opportunity for peace and quiet, Jax and I are taking advantage of that. *Together.*

I lean on his shoulder, bringing my hand to his bicep and squeezing it, letting him know that I am here and I will never leave him. He responds to me silently by bringing his head on top of mine, still holding onto my hand and breathing in and out. So calmly and so slowly.

I match my breathing to his and revel in his warmth. Letting him know, again and again, that we will be okay.

It is now midnight, and Jeremiah, Vi, and I have gathered in the foyer downstairs. We were going to bring Mal and Jax, but Mal is still recovering from her injury and I want Jax to rest, especially after our conversation this afternoon. So I didn't even bother to check in on him because I know he'll want space.

We are seated in a mini triangle, my back against the wall so I don't put too much pressure on my wounded torso and Vi and Jeremiah facing me, sitting side-by-side. A dim light hums in the background, and it is dead silent, nothing but our breathing heard. I don't exactly know why we gathered here. Well, first it was Vi and Jeremiah who were sitting together, but I came outside to get some fresh air because Nico was snoring really loudly and they invited me to sit with them. I don't know whether it was from pity or they genuinely want me here, but I couldn't care less right now because too much is pounding at my mind.

Too. Much.

It is Jeremiah who breaks the silence.

"Do you think Veronica will hijack the compound now?" he asks.

I shake my head. "Layla told me she can't, since Windsor is technically its own territory."

Vi raises her eyebrows at me, bringing her knees to her chest. "Do you really think that would stop her, though?" At our lack of response, she lets out a humorless chuckle. "That's what I thought."

"How do we stop that then?" I ponder.

"That's Thatcher's issue, not ours," she affirms. "All we have to worry about is fighting against them when the time arises."

"I don't want to spend the rest of my life fighting against them, Vi." Jeremiah frowns at her. "I have a wife and a daughter to look after. I don't want to be gone the entire day, fighting. I want to spend time with them too."

"At least they're alive," she snarls, sending him a look that could possibly kill millions. "I have absolutely no one, Jeremiah. Be grateful that they're intact and weren't murdered right in front of your own goddamn eyes."

"Okay, I'm sorry." He defensively raises his hands. "You had a terrible childhood that no person should ever go through. I really am sorry, Vi. But your life is different from mine. I have a family to protect, and I'm sure as hell gonna be by their sides after being torn from them for years. You can't possibly make me feel bad for that."

Vi grits her teeth, impatiently waving her hand at him. "I'm not tryna make you feel bad for it. I'm just saying that you should be grateful that they're alive. That's all."

"I am more than grateful. Okay? Now can we move past this topic and onto something that is better use of our time?"

She purses her lips together, contemplating. "Sure."

"Good." Jeremiah sighs. "As I was saying before . . . I don't want to be in battles everyday and fend for my goddamn life. And I know you guys don't either. So instead of pushing all of these issues on Commander Thatcher, we need to step up too. We are not just Subversives anymore. We're part of the Reformers now."

"They didn't even tell us they were going to show up on the battlefield," she says coldly. "How can we even be a part of them if they don't even treat us properly?"

"Commander Thatcher specifically told us that they decided at the last minute it was the best decision to interfere," Jeremiah explains. "I know they were planning to be incognito and gain their power in peace so they can fight against the ERUSA properly, but I guess desperate times call for desperate measures. And besides, we should be happy they showed up. Otherwise, we would've been killed on that damn battlefield."

"I still don't trust them." She shakes her head. "I don't care whether or not they're on our side—I don't trust them at *all*. Especially after they lied to us like that."

To some extent, I agree with both Jeremiah and Vi. I agree with Jeremiah because the Reformers are all we have, and without them, we would've been obliterated within mere seconds. It doesn't matter whether or not they showed up unannounced; we need them, and it is a fact. But, also . . . Vi is right too. We don't know much about the Reformers, let alone Commander Thatcher. It has only been a week since chaos ensued upon Detroit, and only a week since Layla introduced us to them. We can't trust them yet. Hell, it took days for me to even follow along with what Vi and the other Subversives were ordering to me during our time in D.C.

But we have no other choice but to follow the Reformers. Because if not for them, then we wouldn't be alive right now.

"I know they're not trustworthy," I start off, "but who else *can* we trust? There's only six of us, and there are thousands of ERUSA soldiers. There's only so much we can do alone. And I know that the Reformers showed up unannounced and expected us to follow their orders, but they are an established military. We are just a self-made organization."

"The one your *brother* made." Vi narrows her eyes at me.

"Yes, I know." I sigh. "I know he spent a lot of time and energy behind making the Subversives. But you have to admit that the Detroitian military has been established for dozens of years. The only reason they ceased their operations was because there was a large peacetime before the ERUSA took over. But now they are expected to step in again after this foreign group of people has invaded our city, so of course they will lead us. They are trained—both professionally and physically. I do agree with you, Vi, but I agree with Jeremiah more."

Followed by a glorious look from Jeremiah, Vi's lip curls in disdain as she scowls at me. "God, I hate how right you can be sometimes."

I grin at her. "Hey, blame it on Nico. He's the one who taught me these things."

She rolls her eyes at me, fighting a smile.

Afterwards, we talk about our battle today and what both the Reformers and the ERUSA might have in store for us. "How's your injury doing?" Jeremiah asks me.

"Decent, I'd say." I graze my fingers around the gauze wrapped around my torso, feeling a distinct gash of pain every time I feel the injury. "Since the bullet was extracted, I am bound to feel some pain for a bit, but the doctor advised me to stack up on some pain meds for the time being, so I should heal pretty quickly."

"Good," Vi says, "because you need to do the most training."

"Because I'm out of shape, right?" I frown at her.

She shrugs. "Maybe, maybe not."

Jeremiah nudges her shoulder. "Vi!"

"What? It's the truth. If you want to join the Reformers so badly, then you have to be built to the bone. Like your boyfriend, for example."

"He worked out three times a day when we first settled in Detroit," Jeremiah says.

"Seriously?" I ask. *I had absolutely no idea. Maybe because we could barely bring ourselves to talk to each other back then.*

"Yeah," Vi says. "Woke up at five in the morning for early morning cardio. Did upper body in the afternoon. And ended with lower body at night. Sunday was the only day he didn't work out."

I raise my eyebrows at her. "Wow. I cannot believe I didn't know that."

"Well, now you know." She sends me an unreadable expression.

As a wave of silence overcomes us, Jeremiah clears his throat. "Jax fought pretty well on the train today," he says, bringing his amputated leg out. I study the plaid pajama pants strung up to reveal his glimmering silver prosthetic, intricacies of metal wrapped and interwoven together. "I've never seen him fight like that before."

"Wait, seriously?" I ask, suddenly intrigued. "Maybe he just felt a rush of adrenaline out of nowhere."

"Adrenaline seems like child's play in this situation." His dark and thick eyebrows raise at me. "*No one* would have fought like him. He killed dozens of ERUSA soldiers in just a matter of minutes. I myself could never do that. Something must've been on his mind."

"You know, now that we're on the topic"—Vi straightens herself—"don't you think he's been acting a little weird lately? Mal is acting the same, too."

"Well, Mal has a reason to act weird," Jeremiah points out.

"True," she whispers. "Jax doesn't, though. If he was like this when we stepped foot in Detroit, then I wouldn't question it much because he *killed* his father, for Christ's sake. But this is right after Veronica and the ERUSA took over Detroit. Something must've happened."

As her words weigh in my mind, settling like battering rain to my skull, I can't help but think to myself the same thing, too. What if Jax has been lying to me all this time and something is actually on his mind? And, as much it physically disgusts me to think this, but what if his feelings toward me have dissipated and he's distancing from me, so he wouldn't have to break my heart?

I immediately force myself out of my thoughts. What the hell am I thinking? Jax is the most forward man I know. He wouldn't lie to me, and he would tell me if something's going on. Tobias is just on his mind. That is all.

That is all.

24

EXACTION

JAX

"NICE TO SEE YOU again, Mr. Remington," Veronica says, her skin just as pallid as the lights above me.

I enclose my fists and rap them against the armchair I'm sitting in—the same one I was in last time. It's unfortunately time for my weekly session with Veronica, and at this point, I am just sick and tired of her presence. I'm already upset that I wasn't able to open up to Blaire about my nightmares, especially the *living* nightmare I had of my father and when I "killed" him again. I don't know why I wasn't able to, but maybe it was because both him and Veronica were eating away at my mind. And I hate that. At this point, I would do *anything* to get rid of my father and especially Veronica after seeing her more often than I would've liked to these past two weeks.

However, the thin knife displayed against her marbled desk dissipates all of my angering thoughts.

"I see that you have noticed the knife," she says again in a cold and inhuman tone. "Aren't you wondering why it's there?"

Even at my lack of response, Veronica continues to speak. "It's for something I need to show you. To *prove* to you."

"Prove *what* to me?" I scowl.

Her translucent and startling blue eyes sear into me. "That I am not to be messed with. You haven't been treating me right, Jax. You have been more loyal to the Reformers than to me—than to the ERUSA. That's not fair."

"I don't care, Veronica," I spit out. "I will tell you as many details as I want. Besides, there's no point in me relaying everything to you if you can barely look into the compound—which isn't right to begin with because that is in Windsor territory. You don't have control there."

"Do you think I care about that? Let alone these so-called rules?" She chuckles, but it is without any trace of humor. "Like I've said before, I am not going to invade certain territories abruptly. I am gathering my kings and queens before I make my move. I am bringing forth a sense of submissiveness only until my forces are gathered. Only then can I call checkmate. Only then can I obtain my victory."

"None of that will happen," I snarl, my knuckles turning white from how tight I hold onto the armchair. "You are instead going to draw back and release your forces. Surrender and allow us to live in peace. *Please.* There is no need to fight for something you're not gonna have control over in the first place."

She brings forth no response, no acknowledgment, and no emotions to my words. Her face is unreadable, her pupils constricting and her lips drawn into a thin line. It terrifies me, just how calm she can be from the outside. But on the inside I know damn well there's a storm raging inside her—a storm more dangerous than an asteroid that can obliterate every nook and cranny of our world. She is nothing but a cracked vase, each fragment an opening to the demons inside—lurking like unwanted pesticides.

I feel Veronica's cold eyes searing into me as she says, "When the Center blew up into smithereens and I lost consciousness for several minutes, I thought that it was the end. That after we tried so hard to put the Poor folks in their righteous places, they somehow prevailed. While most of the other Rich people believed it so, I, on the other hand, refused. So I forced myself awake and dragged myself through the rubbles, just to find my dead husband across from me." She pauses. "Thousands of emotions unraveled through me, but only one was prominent . . . utter *rage*. I didn't bother to shed a single tear. Why should I when I could just channel all my feelings into *rage, rage, rage?*

"So, I pushed myself through the remains and rubbles and conjured as many living people as I could and took them to the government's emergency underground bunker. It also turned out you all and the remaining Poor population left for Detroit, leaving us all in the ruins of our beloved city. That I have to admit was a clever decision. But your mistake lies in the fact that you all were so confident in thinking we wouldn't chase after you. We *had* to chase after you. Like hell we would let you all run off like that. While we were all recovering in the bunker, at the same time, I couldn't help but feel this intense desire to avenge and avenge and avenge. So I sought a way to search after the Poor and the rebels that left us in the dust. But there were barely any of us alive. There weren't enough Guards to even form a plan involving the usage of guns or violence anyway. So I had to resort to greater methods instead."

This woman needs extreme help, I can't help but think to myself.

"Adam and I were, of course, very close to Tobias, so one chilly February night, I went through the White House ruins, desperate to find at least one remaining city. There were so many that remained, but ever since the Dark Ages, we all separated and minded our own business. After such a destructive war, we didn't dare to cross paths again. But I didn't care much about that. Why would I?

"Many hours later, I found the documents that provided the locations to the remaining cities. Since you all were in Detroit, I searched for cities on the east coast so I can easily gather everyone and form tactics for ways we can serve our revenge to the best of our ability. I contacted the leaders of several cities. After I explained our situation to them, they told me they were more than willing to help—only if their names wouldn't be involved in the act itself. I promised them as such.

"So, we all met up in the ruins of D.C. Their militaries were stronger than we could've ever sought them to be. We got along just fine—better than I had presumed—and soon enough, we were known as the Elite Regiment of the United States of America. It felt much more satisfying knowing we were part of this new syndicate, combined merely to enforce our ideals on those who have done us wrong. I knew at that moment . . . we were going to prevail. *I* was going to prevail and serve justice for Adam—the man who saved thousands of lives, just to end up on the wrong side of these ungrateful humans."

As I struggle to stomach all the information Veronica threw at me, she says again, "The reason I told you this is to remind you that nothing you say or do will stop me from having revenge. I've watched from the sidelines way too long now. That's why I am not executing the Poor and the Impure—as much as I want to. Because I've waited too long just to get rid of the issue in a matter of seconds. What's the fun in that? I'd much rather make the torture so slow and agonizing that it *burns* for them."

"Just stop," I whisper harshly. "Stop all of this *right now.*"

Veronica clenches her jaw at my words, takes a sharp breath in, and her mouth twitches as she says, "Dear, please come out."

My face falls, and I lean forward in both interest and fear. *Dear? Don't tell me . . .*

The door adjacent to Veronica's desk creaks open, revealing familiar blue eyes—but not as cold and calculating as her mother's. Her's are instead warm, welcoming, and resembles the lapping waves of an ocean shore. Her cheeks are a bright pink tint, and she looks down at the ground, taking two small steps forward and closing the storage door behind her.

"I'm sure you are well acquainted with my daughter, Mallory," Veronica says dryly, her pupils now swarming in a pool of victory.

My blood is boiling deep inside my veins as I snarl at her, "Leave her out of this. She is upset with this situation to begin with."

"I can do whatever I want with her, Jax. She is my daughter. I couldn't care less if she's uncomfortable or upset with a certain situation. That is her issue. All I have brought her here for is to make and prove a statement to you."

"*Screw* your statement! Let her go. You can leave me here, but let Mallory go. She already has enough on her plate."

"Why are you so quick to sacrifice yourself and let her free?" Veronica asks.

I look over at Mallory, and she does the same, bringing both of her hands clad against her torso and biting her lip nervously. This is the woman that's been by my side when no one else was —when my father treated me like shit day and night. When I lived in a home that was nowhere close to how a home should actually feel. When I lived in a body I felt as if it didn't belong to me.

In all honesty, Mallory treated me like a rare diamond when no one else did. And for that, I will forever be indebted to her.

"She's my close friend," I say to Veronica. "She's always been there for me, so of course I will be there for her."

"And you're saying this knowing she left you that one night?" she adds, challenging me with a raised, thin eyebrow. "She didn't even hesitate to leave you, Jax. If you think about it, she was *never* there for you. She used you and threw you away like a rag and left you *and her family* just for her own benefit."

When her words sift into my mind, I dare to look at Mallory again, but I am unexpectedly met with her drowning in tears, shivering and trembling as she silently sobs to herself. "I only left because I didn't belong in that house . . . with you guys." Mallory sniffles, and the pain emanating from her pupils cracks my heart into innumerable pieces. "It wasn't because of Jax. If anything, he would be the only reason why I would even think to stay."

Veronica shakes her head once, and then twice. "We showered you with nothing but love and care. What more could you possibly want? Are you seriously that bratty and self-centered?"

"Don't say that to her," I mutter under my breath. "She's neither of those things."

"You're *still* defending her?" She scoffs to herself. "To think you would have at least an ounce of dignity left in you. I guess it all left the moment you brought that knife down on your father."

I clench my jaw, biting the inside of my cheek so hard I swear I start to taste blood. The only thing stopping me from grabbing that thin-bladed knife on the edge of her desk is Mallory. The last thing I want to do is murder someone's mother right in front of them. No matter how much Mallory hates her, I would *never* do that to her. Not with her here, at least.

The knife I've been eyeing for a while lands in Veronica's palm, and she squeezes the handle of it with her fist, the blade pointed toward me. "Remember when I said I wanted to prove just how extreme my wrath is to you? Well, this is it, Jax. This is a test of your loyalty to me, and if you do not comply, then I won't be very happy. And you have yet to see the worst of me. This will barely scrape the surface of how much damage I can *truly* do."

In just two heartbeats, she looks over at her daughter, trembling in the slightest of movements. "Mallory, dear, please stand in front of the table and face Jax."

When the word *dear* comes out of Veronica's mouth, Mallory cringes and reluctantly brings herself in front of the table, facing me and doing whatever it takes to not look me in the eye. We are only two arm lengths away, and the trepidation emanating from her is so strong it reaches me, too. I understand her fear. I understand it all.

Veronica leans forward against the table and props her bony hands around Mallory's hips, her face eerily close to her neck. Every time she lets out a breath, Mallory's lip trembles like the Earth's core, sniffling and mumbling to herself.

I slowly stand up, hoping my knees don't give out. "What the hell are you doing?" I angrily ask Veronica.

"I don't think you truly understand just how much I value honesty and loyalty." The words leaving her mouth are chilled—making my blood run cold. "When you first came here, Jax, you pledged to me that you would serve me. I've expected that much from you since. However, I was met with disappointment when I realized you were giving me curt feedback and constantly sided with the Reformers over the ERUSA. What I expected you to do was spy on them and relay sacred information to me, not betray me after surrendering yourself to this beloved organization. And because of your behavior, I must challenge you and solidify whether or not I should offer you a second chance."

My eyes narrow at her frail fingers still grasping the handle of the knife—

And bringing the tip of the blade to the center of her neck.

No, no, no, no!

"If you promise, again, to serve me, to relay information to me, and to never betray me, only then will I not slit Mallory's throat." Her conniving and lifeless eyes trail over my stunned figure in one swift motion. "The choice is up to you, Jax."

The shimmery edge of the blade idly rests against the sensitive part of Mallory's neck, and if Veronica were to dig it in even in the slightest, then that would be the end of it. As much as I want to refuse, I can't afford to because I am *not* letting Mallory die. There's not even a way for her to escape this situation any other way because Veronica has her locked in one position. And, unfortunately, if she were to move in the slightest in any sort of direction, then her *own damn mother* won't even hesitate to plunge that blade into her flesh.

As I stand here, weighing the consequences while my mind runs around in a neverending manner, Mallory opens her mouth to speak. "Don't do it, Jax," she whispers. "It's okay."

"No, it's not okay," I hiss, digging my fingers through my hair.

"You shouldn't give any information to her," she grits out, streams of tears running down her cheek and hanging by her chin. "That's not right to you or to us."

"Shut up," Veronica snarls, now digging the blade into her flesh. Mallory lets out a choked gasp, clawing at her mother's arm. "Don't you dare say a damn word."

"Stop it!" I gasp, watching a sliver of blood peering from her skin and dripping onto the thick blade. "Shit, I'll follow your goddamn rules! I promise!"

"Jax, no!" Mal yells in between shaky sobs.

"Do you promise to be loyal?" Veronica says in a low voice.

"Yes, for God's sake, *yes.*" My breathing is now uneven, sharp, and ragged. "Just please take that goddamn knife away from her . . . *now.*"

Immediately, she releases the knife from Mallory's neck and her hand, and I breathlessly watch it clang to the ground, tiny splotches of blood staining the ground beneath me. Mallory lets out one last gasp, desperately reaching for her throat and falling to the ground, sobbing uncontrollably. I don't even hesitate to kneel down with her, rubbing her back and attempting to console her. "It's going to be okay," I tell her hurriedly. "Breathe, Mallory. *Breathe.*"

While Mallory lets go of herself on the floor, crying so much my heart cracks even more in the process, I look up at a gleaming Veronica, no sense of regret or remorse smeared across her features. All I see is pale skin, clear eyes, and cracked lips turned upward in a way that brings fire to my soul— unleashes a beast in my veins.

"Now that I have granted you this second chance, Jax, I expect you to be loyal to me and *fully* explain whatever the hell is going on in that compound. There's only so much I can see from this place. I am relying on you, and now that I see your allegiance with my daughter, I will appoint her to your position as well. You both were born into Pure families with no trace of Poor or Impure blood; therefore, I grant you both as spies for the ERUSA. It is your duty and responsibility to serve and feed me information. Do whatever you need to do to get as much information as possible, but make sure in the end, when I bring you to the headquarters next week, you have information for me.

"And remember the certain consequences if you fail to adhere." Her eyes slither over to me. "You especially have a lot on the line, Jax, such as your beloved girlfriend. Remember her when you think to betray me, and hopefully that will set you straight to obey regardless of your unnatural tendencies. But"— she pauses, her tone conquering my insides—"no more chances will be given from here. Because from here on out, all you have waiting for you on the other side are your consequences and a deep pit of hell. Keep that in mind if you merely even think to betray me."

25

DECLARE

BLAIRE

"THATCHER IS CALLING ALL of us over to make a statement," Vi says as she walks toward me.

"What kind of statement?" I ask as I let go of the dumbbells in my hands, sweat basking on the back of my neck.

"I don't know. I think it's about how we're going to line our forces against the ERUSA. It's happening in about five minutes, so I suggest we leave now and gather in the commonplace."

I nod and as soon as I pack up my workout equipment, Vi and I exit the gym and make our way to the commonplace. Trails of chatter erupt around us as we emerge amongst hundreds of other soldiers. They gather by the bottom floor of the commonplace while Commander Thatcher remains at the open top floor, looking down past the railing and acknowledging the numerous people gathered to see her. AJ, Annie, and the other top soldiers stand behind her in a straight line, their features neutral and their hands clad beside them. Commander Thatcher has never conjured us up like this before, so I do wonder what this could possibly be about.

While we wait, Jax, Mal, Jeremiah, Nico, and Layla come over to us. Jax immediately stands beside me and grabs my hand, interlacing our fingers together. He gives me a half-smile, his gray eyes glinting at me. On the other hand, Nico scowls at us and stands next to Vi, a sour look etched across his features.

Great, another member in my family who still has not gotten used to my relationship.

Once the five minutes breeze by, Commander Thatcher raises her hand in one swift motion, her eyes drilling into us. It's quite difficult in any other situation to shut up hundreds and *hundreds* of people, especially riled up and confused soldiers, but in this situation, everyone silences as soon as she lifts her hand. Her face is as neutral as ever, and yet she is more than capable of quieting the entire commonplace. *Damn.*

"Good afternoon, soldiers," Thatcher says, her deep voice rattling into the atmosphere. "I know most of you were engaged in either combat or working out in the gym, so as soon as this speech concludes, you may go on with your normal duties. But as of now, I request for your undivided attention because this speech is imperative to not only us Reformers, but to the entirety of Detroit as well." She pauses, continuing to look down at us like we are nothing but her obedient servants.

"It has been almost two weeks since we fought the ERUSA," Thatcher continues. "I know it was a last-minute decision, particularly because we felt indebted to help the Subversives and not leave them in the dust, for it is our job to help when it is needed. It is quite evident that we, alongside the Subversives, have won that battle, but it is also quite evident another battle will likely be on the way. Veronica Reaves is unfortunately someone who doesn't give up very easily, so it is imperative that we emphasize our daily training so we, as a military, can defend our land and drive back the enemy.

"However, ever since that battle, I have come to a realization and an ultimate decision." The audience murmurs quietly, clearly on edge for what Thatcher could possibly say. "Due to the intensity of that conflict, I do not want to risk losing our troops that we spent *years* building upon. Therefore, it is hereby declared by me that we will remain on the defensive side, rather than being the offender. We will not initiate any attacks against the ERUSA, and we will instead defend our homeland and hope to resolve future conflicts in a peaceful way."

At her words, an uproar and protest unleashes in the crowd, people hurtling out rebuttals and ultimate repugnancy to Thatcher's speech. Jax's grip on my hand tightens as the intensity of the audience increases, soldiers pushing past us like water sprouting from a faucet. Simultaneously, I can't help but disagree with her statement, too. There is no point to be on the defensive side because it is overall just asking for further attacks from the ERUSA. That just makes us seem more submissive and vulnerable to Veronica. I don't know why the hell Thatcher would even propose that. Because then, what is the purpose of the military? It's not just to defend, but it's also to *protect*. And protecting requires attacking, especially against a woman like Veronica.

"Silence!" Annie yells, attempting to quieten the audience like Thatcher had at first, but that is to no avail. The audience continues to cry, protest, and scream, and from what I also see, some soldiers have begun to climb up the stairs to where Commander Thatcher is standing.

Immediately, a clap of thunder resounds into the room, and us, including the rest of the audience, cry out in shock. I clasp my hands to my ears, wincing to myself as the earth-shattering *bang* rings into my veins, resounding into my mind. *What the hell was that noise?*

I look up and see AJ pointing the rifle at the wall ahead of him, a gaping hole incised into the wood. Smoke unfurls out of the opening of the rifle, and wordlessly, he throws the weapon to the ground, falling with a reverberating thud. His hard jaw is clenched, and he rolls his neck, his dull eyes landing on the speechless individuals. A thick silence stuffs itself into the atmosphere, taking away everyone's ability to cry, protest, scream. *Breathe,* even.

"I am highly disappointed by this reaction," Thatcher says calmly, but her eyes are raging with flames instead. "I am your Commander, and it was disrespectful of you all to react like that. Whatever I say you must follow, whether you like it or not. I knew people would be upset by this, but I was not aware the reaction would be this childish." She tuts, her hazel eyes perusing across the room. "Number one rule of being a part of the Detroitian military is serving your Commander. If the rule were to be broken—or even *threatened* to be broken—again, then I won't be so willing to offer another chance.

"The reason for my proposal is because I do not want to stoop down to the ERUSA's level. We must take a higher road and not succumb to our animalistic tendencies. We must be level-headed and defend our land like the professional individuals we are. Like I have seen in that battle two weeks ago, it was disheartening to see the lives of our well-rounded soldiers threatened. Thankfully, no one died from their injuries, but there were plenty of injuries involved. It could've been worse, and in order to avoid that end, we must be defensive, not offensive.

"That is all for my speech today." Thatcher clears her throat and stuffs her strong hands into her camo pants. "You may go on with your day now as you wish. But remember to keep any foul words of me and my proposition out of your mouth. If I or any of my fine soldiers beside me were to hear any insults in any way today, then dire consequences will be lined up for you. The choice is yours to make."

I shove the pant leg up my thigh, cursing to myself as I shimmy the pair of jeans up my hips and button at my waist. *First thing on my workout list is to lose my posterior fat.* Once I wear my jeans, I throw on a loose gray shirt and make my way out of the changing room. After yet another painstaking day of training with the Reformers, I already have muscle aches in *various* parts of my body. It's already difficult enough for me to walk down the corridor itself, especially with a healing wound, and I immediately scoff at my poor decision to wear jeans today.

First thing I see as I set foot in the corridor is Mallory, who has her leg propped up on the bench she's sitting on and leans against the wall, closing her eyes. I sit on the bench in front of her so I don't invade her personal space and take a deep breath in.

"How's your injury?" I ask.

Mallory opens one eye and eventually the other as she sighs. "Could be better. What about you?"

"Same. It's only been two weeks since I've gotten this *thing* and I'm already sick of it."

She chuckles. "I feel the same way too. I hate the pitiful looks I get from people whenever I train in the compound. Someone even came up to me the other day and requested for me to just stretch. How long can I stretch when I clearly want to be a part of training as well?" Mal frowns. "I just want to be taken seriously for once. I bet if Vi got this injury then no one would bat an eyelash at her."

"Uh, Mal, have you *met* Vi?" I raise my eyebrow at her. "She's basically a robot. She has no emotions, let alone any reaction to human nature in general. Of course people wouldn't bat an eyelash at her."

She snorts. "Yeah, you're definitely right about that."

"Of course I am," I say, but I wince afterwards. "Also, don't tell Vi I said that about her."

Mal lets out a giggle. "Don't worry, Blaire. I won't."

I grin at her. "God, we really haven't had much time to talk in private, huh?"

"We really haven't. I miss the quality time you and I used to have together."

"Me too. I would do anything to go back in time to the good old days."

"Yeah, before my mother hijacked Detroit."

I frown at her. "How are you holding up with that? Has she interacted with you in any way so far?"

Mal's face falls for a second, but she clears her throat and says, "No. Not really."

"Seriously?" I ask, appalled.

"Yeah." She shrugs. "You'd think she would at least say *something* to me, or even apologize for putting a bullet into my thigh. But nope." Her voice trails off. "Not a single word from her."

"Gosh, that's terrible."

"I know. And I can't help but think that maybe, just maybe, if I hadn't left that night, then . . . I don't know. Life would probably be different right now."

"Are you blaming this on yourself?" My mouth gapes open in shock. "Mal, this is in no way *your fault.* You can't possibly blame yourself for prioritizing your needs over society's."

"Of course I'm gonna blame myself, Blaire. It's because of my selfish tendencies that we are in this major issue. If I had just accepted my parents' conditional love, then we would not be in this situation." She hesitates to say the next sentence. "Jax's father treated him horribly but he still stayed. I *am* selfish."

"Mallory," I sound out her name. "Listen to me. Jax's situation was different from yours. It was completely your choice to leave, and I'm personally glad you took up that choice. You made a bold statement by running away, and I admire you for it. Do you know how much of an inspiration you are? We all think you're so strong and brave, Mal. But I don't know why you're throwing yourself under the bus for your mother's actions.

Don't treat yourself like that. Treat yourself like you are a rare beauty because you are. Again, Mal, this is *not your fault.* Okay?"

Her voice wavers, her eyes watering. "I don't know, Blaire. It's gonna take me a while to understand that. But right now, I don't feel so good about myself. I don't think I ever will."

God, just hearing her say that breaks my heart into a million pieces. *Mallory deserves so much better. She doesn't deserve a shitty mother like Veronica.* "I understand that it'll take a while," I say. "And I'm not gonna force my viewpoint and other's viewpoints on you. But I do want to say this, and I mean it from the bottom of my heart . . . *none of this is your fault.* I swear on my entire family, Mal."

"Oh, no, don't say that." She squeezes her eyes shut.

"But it's the damn truth. You are not like your mother. You and your mother are not connected in any way. Trust me, I've had this talk with Jax too because he struggled with the exact same thing, so you know damn well that *I mean this.* You are your own person, Mal. Don't ever let anyone diminish your individual qualities."

I rush over to her and give her a hug, resting my chin atop her shoulder and feeling her body tremble with tears. "Thank you," she sobs. "Thank you for helping me get through this. I love you, Blaire. You're the most amazing friend I can ever ask for."

"I love you too, Mal." I rub her back. "We're in this together, okay? And before you know it, life will be back to normal. I promise."

Once she wipes her tears away and gives me a reassuring smile, we talk about other topics. Obviously not as concerning as the one major topic that's been swirling around our minds for weeks on end, but it's still something to get our minds off the hell impending upon us. Like for one, she asks me about Jax and how we're doing. I tell her that we're doing great, but it has been pretty hard to prioritize our relationship while preparing for battle. Mal reassures me that he and I will be okay, that life in general will be okay. I know she's always wanted Jax and I to get together because, as Jax told me, she was the one who urged him to ask me out.

But this time, as she gives me advice about our relationship, I can't help but notice a different tone to her voice.

Suddenly, the others emerge from the changing room and we make our way to the jeep, ready to go home and rest. It's rather a calm day in Detroit—not many people are getting slaughtered by the ERUSA for breaking one of their rules—so I guess we can take advantage of this calm before it eventually goes away in a snap of a finger.

For some reason, I get a gut feeling that I should enjoy the calm while it lasts.

26

DISPATCH

JAX

Utensils clatter around me as I seat myself next to Jeremiah, who is sitting in front of Vi. They look up at me simultaneously and each give me a single nod as I let my plate collide with the top of the table, a sigh releasing from me.

"What's with the bruises on your knuckles?" Jeremiah asks me as he stuffs a spoonful of soup into his mouth.

"Got a bit too carried away with the punching bag." I snort.

"I'm sure Blaire will be thrilled to hear that," Vi mutters right before she gulps down a handful of water from her glass.

"She already knows," I wince. "And you're right. She *wasn't* thrilled to hear or see that."

"Well, that's Blaire." Jeremiah chuckles. "But anyway, how's everyone's time here at the compound going?"

"Decent," Vi says curtly. "Training's a bit too easy for me, though."

"Of course it is." I smirk at her. "Since you're a goddess made out of steel anyway."

"Hah, very funny." She rolls her eyes at me. "The only reason training is easy for me is because I've been through the worst situations. Hell, at this point, Thatcher can give me a paper and a pen and expect me to draw a rainbow, or something."

"*Commander* Thatcher, Vi," Jeremiah interrupts. "You've been saying it wrong for weeks on end."

"Do I look like I care? And besides, she's not here to hear me now, right?"

"Yeah, but that woman may have cameras around us. You never know." I shrug.

"Still," she says, "I don't care. It's not that big of a deal. Anyone can become Commander these days."

Jeremiah slowly turns to me, his brown eyes glinting with amusement. "Is that . . . *jealousy* I'm hearing from her?"

I let out a loud laugh. "God, who knew Vi would be jealous of anyone. I thought you were the almighty goddess of steel."

"Oh, shut the hell up," she grumbles at us. "I'm *not* jealous. Why would I even be in the first place?"

"I don't know, you tell me," I singsong. "Commander Thatcher's just the leader of the well-renowned Detroitian military for five years straight *and* is one of the most decorated soldiers here. I'd say that's definitely worth getting jealous over."

"Last time I'm saying this." She narrows her eyes at me. "I'm *not* jealous. I got better things to worry about, okay? And if we're talking about jealousy then I don't think you guys should be pointing fingers at me. I think we should be focusing more on you instead, *Jax.*"

I raise my eyebrows at her. "And what could you possibly mean by that?"

"Uh, hello? Don't you always shoot daggers with your eyes at the back of AJ's head every time he walks past you?" Vi chortles as she props her foot up at the edge of the table, picking up the sandwich and eating it after she says, "Man, if looks could kill then that dude would turn into ashes within seconds."

"Look, I'm not jealous of AJ at *all,*" I say, frowning in the process. "What's there to be jealous about anyway? He's just some regular guy."

"Yeah," Jeremiah interjects, "just some regular guy that's coincidentally the best soldier in the Detroitian military."

"I'm only *upset* with him," I emphasize, "because he's getting on my nerves."

"Because he keeps trying to talk to Blaire, right?" Vi fights off a smile.

"Yes! And it annoys the hell out of me. Why can't he just get the hint that she's clearly uncomfortable with him and move onto some other woman? I'm pretty sure Ren's interested in him anyway."

"Ren and AJ *together*?" Jeremiah snorts. "Wouldn't that be chaotic as hell?"

"I don't know, nor do I care," I stammer. "I would do anything to get that shithead away from Blaire. He's just too damn weird and creepy."

"Him? Or you?" Vi chuckles.

"Oh, screw you." I frown, stuffing a mouthful of mashed potatoes into my mouth.

As Jeremiah chuckles to himself, I lean back in my seat, scanning the entire cafeteria. Since it's rush hour, there are plenty of people gathered here, either grabbing their food from the daily buffet or seating themselves at the booths. The high-beam ceiling encloses over us, coated in a mixture of an off-white and murky brown color, casting a yellow-ish beam of light toward us. The background chatters are easy to cast myself away in. The attempt to get away from the thoughts and questions and demons pelting at my mind even to this day.

The meetings I've had with Veronica so far have consisted of nothing but her squeezing information out of me as if I am an innocent fruit and she were a ruthless blender, throwing my vulnerable self into her blades and slashing through my insides with relentless brutality. I hate to admit it, but I gave in to her.

Not in a deep and concerning amount, though, only enough to keep her interest piqued. Like I haven't mentioned us going on the defensive side now. I've only mentioned that we've been training everyday, and I plan to keep it that way until I conjure up the proper plan to get me out of this horrible nightmare.

To make matters worse, Mallory is a part of this unfortunate situation now, which means I *have* to formulate a plan as soon as possible—just to make sure she doesn't end up in her mother's permanent wrath. Veronica is traumatizing as hell, and I really don't want Mallory to endure that shit. She doesn't deserve that.

"Did you hear Thatcher's gonna start sparring soon?" Vi blurts out.

"No," Jeremiah and I both say.

"Well, now you do," she says. "I don't know why she's starting it off so late, though. We should've started sparring a long ass time ago. God knows when a surprise attack will occur, so we better be safe than sorry."

"We're already sorry regarding the proposal she made with her speech three days ago," I lower my voice. "Going defensive? Seriously? Now that's just a free ride to heaven."

"There's no way we can object to that, though," Jeremiah winces. "She's the *Commander,* for God's sake."

"But she's not a dictator, right?" Vi cocks her head at him. "That means we can definitely voice our opinions to her."

"And get executed by her and her minions?" I suck in a sharp breath. "Yeah, I'm good."

"I don't care what you say. I'm gonna voice my opinion to her at least by the end of today."

Jeremiah and I both stare at her in surprise. "Vi, are you sure?" he asks her. "Commander Thatcher is capable of so much."

"Well, so am I." She glares at him, finishing up her lunch and jumping out of her seat to throw her food away.

However, the moment her food's thrown into the large trash bin by the exit of the cafeteria, a loud wailing sound ensues across the parameters. It travels in and out of my ears with elongated reverberations, cornering into my soul and sending shivers up my spine. The entire crowd cries out in pain, hissing at the screeches and shrieks sifting across multiple rooms.

"This is a level five emergency. I repeat this is a level five emergency." A robotic female voice enters the cafeteria through the speakers anchored into the high beam walls. "There is a breach on the premises and all soldiers must gear up and report to the send-off posts. Please report there immediately. Thank you."

27

STEADFAST

BLAIRE

SOMEONE SHOVES A PLETHORA of gear my way, and I overwhelmingly stare at the pile—wondering how the hell I'm going to wear all this in less than a minute. The women around me in the locker room seem to know what they're doing as they quickly shove the clothes on them and rush out of the room. The sirens that ensued while Mal and I were training are still going on, blaring into my eardrums and thrumming into my veins.

"Camo pants, bulletproof vest, body pads, combat boots, helmet, gloves, goggles, and your mask." Vi's voice grows closer as she urges the gear to me. "It's now or never, Cohen. C'mon."

Hurriedly, I put on the gear as she states it one more time, impatience prominent on her features. As I dress, wearing the gear on top of my workout clothes, I notice she's clad in the same uniform as me. Navy blue gear engulfs her, and all I can see are her cold and harsh brown eyes. But even those will be covered once we make our way out into the commotion because of the eye goggles perched on her helmet. The only way to set her apart from the others is her last name engraved on the proximity of her upper right breast: **POWERS.**

The heat in the room rises the more I shove the gear onto myself, and once I am finished, I give her an unsteady look. "All right. I'm done," I gasp out.

Before I even finish speaking, she grabs my upper arm with such intensity I almost wince and lugs me out the locker room. "Because of your slow ass, we'll be in the back. It'll take forever to get ourselves in the upper ranks."

"Why would we even want to be in the upper ranks in the first place?" I murmur. "That's an ultimate death wish."

As we rush over to the docking area, she gives me a narrowed glance. "Not if we play this game right."

Confused by the ambiguity of her words, we jog over to the docking area, where thousands of soldiers are currently employed. At the very front are other soldiers marching forward, pointing their rifles to the opening of the field. I narrow my eyes at the scene, noticing our enemy moving like lightning bolts, clanging their bullets onto our territory. Infuriating jet-black armor with **ERUSA** emblazoned across it.

Suddenly, Vi shoves a rifle almost half my weight into my arms, and I almost fall backwards, clinging onto the butt of it. "Careful there," she says dryly, weighing her rifle in her gloved hands. "If you stumble around even more, then Thatcher won't even send you into battle in the first place."

"Everyone's going," I wheeze out, the bulk of the armor weighing down on me. "It'd be kinda embarrassing if I was the only one not thrown into battle."

She clicks her tongue at me. "Exactly."

As we settle into our ranks, I frantically look around for a familiar bed of dark hair and searing gray eyes, and I gasp as I see him rows away from me, two soldiers away from Nico. I get a horrible feeling that we're going to be separated during battle, since Commander Thatcher wants us to spread out when we drizzle over to the battlefield above us. It's going to be like *hell* not being with Jax.

When I start to call for him, Vi violently nudges my rib with her pointy elbow. "We're going up," she whispers to me. "So I suggest you stop staring at your boyfriend and get your shit together. *Now.*"

The ranks move forward, and my heart beats at my neck, my lips drying like a parched desert. Sirens hum into the atmosphere, and distant gunshots grow louder and louder, each startling noise leading to me clutching the rifle a bit tighter. With every solid and taut movement from the other soldiers, I feel my limbs weaken, melting into a puddle and slowly drifting away into an abundance of incalculable emotions. God knows how this battle is going to end. We barely won the other one a week ago.

As we near the clearing, I shove the butt of the rifle up my right underarm and dig my pointer finger at the cusp of the trigger, edging the harsh material of it. The sun blinds my vision, and immediate heat travels up my spine, heavy breaths dragging out of me. This is all on us now. We must defend our base against the enemy.

All stated by Commander Thatcher, though. But I don't want to defend. I want to *fight back.*

When our rank urges forward, I see the Commander rapidly moving her arm in different directions, navigating the soldiers to different parameters. As she eyes our line of soldiers, she juts her arm forward and shouts, "Grab the shields and fall back quarter of a mile! If they shoot at you, *don't* shoot back! Defend the ranks and yourself! No shooting back at them unless I order you to!"

I grab the shield lying at my feet and cradle it in my arms, hiding behind the transparent glass which seems to weigh more than the crust of the Earth. Heavy silence falls into my being, and I take two quick breaths in, praying to myself we all make it back alive.

And we charge forward.

Immediately bullets rampage into us from all directions, and I frantically shield myself from them, pulling the goggles down to my aching eyes. The raging sunrays simmer down as the shades cover me, and my breath escapes into the thin cloth covering my mouth, ragged and barely there.

"Keep up, Blaire!" Vi shouts as she sprints past me. "You're falling back!"

With panic bubbling up in my chest, I abruptly turn around and see my entire back is exposed, our entire rank ahead of me, and the ERUSA soldiers slowly catching up to us with bullets springing into my shields. Thankfully my shield is able to reflect the bullets, but this is all I have. This is all I can truly rely on.

I turn back around and feel the speed of my legs shift beneath me, adrenaline and fear both riding in my veins, the noises around me engulfed in gleaming waters. The sunrays beat above us, and I already feel sweat carving on my face, my lips dry and grazing the shimmery mask. My feet move like snakes beneath the grass, slithering past the roots and sneaking up to the ranks, running behind Vi. As long as I'm near her, I'll be fine.

When we reach our stopping mark, we gather by the gleaming grass—trees hovering over us like dark storm clouds in the night—and shove our shields forward. The bullets pounce onto our shields, and the soldiers come at us, unwilling to fall back.

"There's at least hundreds of them," Vi whispers as she settles in beside me. "We need to fight back."

"Commander Thatcher won't allow us to." I shake my head.

"*Screw* what she thinks!" she hisses. "If we listen to her for the time being then we're gonna get our asses killed. We need to go with our guts. I'm not tryna get killed out here."

"I don't want to be killed either. But as much as we want to think for ourselves, we *can't* because we are part of a damn military and if we disagree with anything the Commander says, then she will throw us to the wolves."

Vi repeatedly shakes her head. "This is bullshit," she murmurs. "Layla should not have brought us here. If anything, we would've been fine on our own."

As her words settle in my mind and the bullets continue to rampage into the thick glass covering all dozen of us, my eyes land on another rank settled diagonally, in the same position as ours. But what intrigues me the most is seeing Jax hiding behind his shield, his arm hesitantly going up to the body of his rifle. Even though everything but his eyes are concealed, I can still spot him a mile away, only because of his distinct mannerisms. The way he moves after thinking to himself, forming an entire plan in that mind of his. Taking in the entire environment with his curious eyes, narrowed ahead of him and darting back and forth. He's tactical. Watching. *Speculative.* That's how I can notice him.

I weigh the rifle in my head, debating whether Vi is right. I feel as if, to some extent, maybe she is. Maybe we are making a huge mistake sitting here, defensive, while the ranks up front are getting annihilated by the ERUSA. We're damn lucky for being back here, but I feel useless—a bit too privileged. People are dying out there. *Our* people are dying out there.

Suddenly, a strong gloved hand lands on my shoulder.

A small shriek leaves my mouth as I raise the rifle to where the hand came from, but all I see are frightened golden eyes staring back at me. "Whoa, Blaire!" AJ gasps out. "Relax! I'm on your side."

"Oh," I whisper, pushing my rifle back down and heat creeping up my neck. "Sorry."

"It's okay." He sits beside me, blood splotched on his vest, his breaths just as clipped as his oncoming words. "I don't blame you for raising that gun at me. Never know who exactly can come up at you, you know?"

For a moment no one really speaks; all there remains in the air are the continuous gunshots and cries of death hurtling into the atmosphere.

"Why is your vest so bloodied?" Vi breaks the silence between us.

A frown grows on him as he sulks forward, slinging his forearms onto his lifted knees. "Many soldiers of ours died up there. One of them even died in my arms. It was terrible."

"Oh gosh," I murmur. "And we're still not allowed to fight back?"

He shakes his head. "Commander Thatcher won't allow us to. I would say something about it, but she's not exactly the most open-minded person in the world."

"Wait, you agree with us?" Vi raises her eyebrows at him.

"Uh, yeah. Why?"

"Because I thought you were her devoted servant or something." She scoffs.

"I'm not her devoted servant."

Vi and I stare at him expectantly.

"*Anyway* . . . to an extent, I don't agree with her. Hell, I disagreed with her the moment she brought up the idea to us— mentally, of course."

"You should still say something about it," I say.

"I thought I told you that she's not an open-minded person."

"At least give it a shot," Vi says. "You are her most favorite person in the world."

He snorts. "Yeah, like that's gonna do anything."

"Well, maybe you can voice your opinion here," I say.

AJ looks over at me, eyebrows raised. "What do you mean by that?"

I straighten myself up, feeling the wounded muscles by my torso constrict. "Well, the situation is kinda bad right now. A lot of soldiers from our side have been shot and killed. It's clearly evident that we need to raise our weapons too, whether Commander Thatcher allows it or not."

"God knows what she would do to me then, Blaire."

"Well, that's certainly better than getting murdered in plain sight," Vi hisses. "C'mon, AJ! You're our last hope. The moment you raise your weapon and lead us through this battle, then everyone else will. And if things were to go well, then maybe Commander Thatcher won't be upset with you." One side of her lip curls up beguilingly. "Maybe one day she'll consider promoting you as Commander. Who the hell knows?"

His golden eyes fall to the ground, narrowing in thought. In the past three weeks I've known AJ, to be honest, I've never seen him so vulnerable and exposed, especially amongst us. He's always been hidden in Commander Thatcher's shadows, voicing whatever she voices and reflecting whatever she reflects. But it was never about him. And now that this perfect opportunity is being handed over to him on a silver platter, of *course* he's going to consider it. This is a moment he's been waiting for since forever.

He grumbles underneath his breath, "Fine. We'll attack."

"Seriously?" Vi and I say simultaneously.

"Yeah." He chuckles. "You guys won. Happy?"

"Yes, very happy," Vi says hurriedly. "Now can we just shoot some of these goddamn ERUSA soldiers already? My finger is itching to pull on the trigger."

"Yes, yes, give me a second." AJ anchors himself up against the shield, leering past the people in our ranks ahead of us and giving us a determined look—his eyes the same color of the sun beating above me. "I know we haven't done much training, so I want you guys to stay behind me for now."

"Oh, bullshit—"

"Just listen to me, Vienna," he urges. "I've heard you Subversives were downright spectacular in D.C., and that's amazing and all, but this is a full-blown battle. It's been a while since you all fought people—let alone experienced soldiers. Preferably I don't want you guys to jump into battle just yet, but I'm only allowing it because I know you're determined to. Just stay behind me." His glowing and radiating eyes land on me. "Please."

Moments later, I sigh defeatedly and nod. "Okay. We'll stay behind you."

"Great." I don't even have to see him without his mask on to know that he's grinning. AJ then looks over at a reluctant Vi, who refuses to look at him. "What do you say, Powers? Do you accept my proposition?"

She pushes the helmet down on her skull, encasing her short black and red hair framing her perfectly carved features. Her eyes narrow and then they roll as she says, "I guess I accept."

"Awesome." He claps his hand and then grasps his rifle under his arm. "Again, stay behind me. Once I know and see that you guys are ready to go on your own, then you're more than welcome to. Got it?"

"Got it," we echo. Vi is still reluctant, of course. But it's progress.

As we huddle behind AJ, positioning ourselves simultaneously, I can't help but hear AJ mutter to himself, "God, she's gonna rip my insides apart."

The beating of my heart thuds into my veins and transpires to my eardrums, rattling my organs and my mind. A large cramp settles in my stomach, and it must be from my wound, clearly agitated by the heat and the numerous layers of clothing. Also, I barely ate anything because I wanted to train instead. But as I sit here, gritting my teeth and wincing, I realize just how much of a stupid mistake I made.

But I'm not here to chastise myself. I'm here to motivate myself to strive forward. To persevere. To *fight*.

Fight for what we've been desiring.

It all happens in a matter of seconds.

Before, I never really understood why AJ was named the best soldier in the compound. I thought he was just some mysterious guy with tattoos who always showed a bit too much interest in me. But never did I think that *he* would be capable of being the top soldier in a whole ass military. Even though he was named as such, I just never believed it.

Hell, I believe it now. Too, *too* much now.

I watch in awe as AJ jumps past the rank faster than the speed of lightning, digs his knees into the grass murky with dirt and blood, and lets out a guttural war cry as loads and loads and loads of bullets fly out of the gaping hole of his rifle—all the while holding the glass shield. He darts back and forth in sporadic measures, methodically raising his head to the soldiers in front of him and releasing yet another round of bullets. It's an infinite process that both intrigues and terrifies me.

Yeah, he's *definitely* the best soldier in the compound.

It is seconds later that Vi springs behind him, following his traces and shooting at the soldiers too. I've known since the very beginning that Vi is exceptionally skilled at combat—and at this point, I would love to know where and how she trained. There's no way she learned those tactical movements and measures and motives from training as a Subversive. I know there's more to her life than what she told me that night—when I had basically pried it out of her. But I know, beneath that hard exterior of her, is a woman with a bright and gleaming heart specifically reserved for Matthew, Isaiah, and Jessica. The people she got so very little time with.

I prepare myself to line behind them, but it's exceptionally mesmerizing to watch Vi and AJ fight. Honestly, AJ might have to watch himself these days because Vi has overpowered him at this point and kills three soldiers in just a mere heartbeat.

I tap my foot against the ground, edge the trigger again—after turning the safety off—and push my knees up the ground and sprint sprint *sprint* over to AJ and Vi.

I've always let my mind control my heart. I thought my mind was logical and practical, which would lead me to far better outcomes in life. I believed following my heart would just be a means to an eventually unfortunate end. That's why I never even bothered to.

But this time, I don't follow that rule of mine.

Instead, I break it. Break it like a flimsy piece of wood with a resounding *snap* and send the splinters to the ground.

Because I want to follow my heart this time. Maybe it has an outcome for me that I've never expected before. Never *seen* before.

And as I repeatedly pull back on the trigger, screeching into my mask and allowing my cries to drift into the hot, humid air, I wholly follow my heart. I follow it like a lone bird, intrigued by that one puffy, white cloud floating against a pale blue sky, and never look back.

28

ADMONISH

JAX

"WHERE ARE THOSE NOISES coming from?" Nicolas asks as he frantically looks past the shield, squinting whenever a cloud of dust formulates around us.

"I don't know," Annie says, attempting to look too. "It's too hazy to tell."

I hold onto the shield, my knuckles turning into a pale white as I grind on my molars. It's only been a minute since we've heard the gunshots coming from our end—obviously from the transpiring end. Bullets still collide with our protectors, but I get the unabating fear that one of these bullets is just going to come crashing past the glass and lodge into my heart. And I won't even have a second to regain myself—to hold onto the light before it eventually dissipates. Life, as rare as it may seem, is fleeting and execrable. Once that bomb is triggered, then prepare to go up in flames.

As Annie peers past the pervasive dust emanating from the maelstrom around us, I steal a glance at Nicolas, who grounds his knees to the murky and wet grass and pushes his mask down to catch his breath—but he immediately regrets it once he starts hacking his lungs out, leaning forward and wheezing out ragged breaths, and pushing the mask up again.

I look over at him, debating whether or not I should step in and help him, or comfort him with my words from here. Eventually I decide neither of those options are ideal because Nicolas has a great hatred for me now . . . all because I'm dating his younger sister. How do I know that? Well, whenever I pass by him and attempt to say a simple "hi," he scoffs and pushes past me. And he never did that to me before. I get that he's unbelievably overprotective over Blaire after being separated from her for so many years, but it legitimately appalls me that he's acting as if I insulted his hair, or something. Which I would never even dare to do or merely even think of because—let's be honest— Nicolas's hair is unbelievably amazing.

Right when he catches my glance, I feel someone nagging at my shoulder. I turn to where it occurred, face-to-face with a panting Annie. "It's AJ, Vienna, and Blaire."

Suddenly, my world comes crashing down.

"What?" Nicolas and I both screech.

"Yes. They're at the front lines and they're just . . . shooting at the soldiers rapidly. Completely exposed, too." At her words, I push past Annie and attempt to make a beeline past the shields, but she pushes me down square in the chest, and I fall back to a thud, my ass hitting the ground a little bit too harshly. "What do you think you're doing? You will get yourself killed out there."

"I couldn't care less about myself right now. For God's sake, my goddamn *girlfriend's* out there."

"We will come up with a plan to get them out of there in a bit, Jax. But you can't make impulsive decisions like this. This is a life or death situation."

"Aren't you the slightest bit worried for them?" My chest rises in and out, about to explode in rage. "It's okay if you don't care for Blaire, or even Vi. But AJ? He's your brother. I'm surprised you're not volunteering to step in for him either."

"Of *course* I'm worried about him." Her voice is laced with iciness as she leans down to me, her sizzling golden eyes searing into my soul and strands of unruly dark hair curling around the nape of her neck. "But I trust AJ enough to know that he can defend himself. Just like you can trust Blaire and Vienna enough to do the same. I think you're underestimating just how skilled they are. Trust me, I've seen them train for the past few weeks. So, Jax, I suggest you compose yourself for the time being and let me handle this situation. Just give me two minutes. All right?"

I work my jaw and stare down at my feet, overwhelming emotions surging into me like a tsunami crashing and thundering onto shore. To an extent, Annie is right. Blaire and Vi *are* more than capable of defending themselves. If anything, both of them combined can override and dominate me in a damn heartbeat. They really can.

But what I'm most worried about is losing them—especially Blaire. God, if I lost her, especially against that enraging she-devil, then it'll be like a part of me was lost as well. Because she gets me more than anybody has ever gotten me before. It is as if the universe made her just for *me*—tailored to goddamn perfection. But little did this universe know that, while intending to give her a flawless life, they granted her a life filled with hell— each moment in her life utterly painful and repugnant.

That's why I'm here, though. To rid all tensions and anxieties from her. To reassure her that *I'm here* and I'm not going anywhere. Where else would I go anyway? Even if I tried to leave, my footsteps would always come tracing back to hers.

I rap my fingers against the ground as I look over at Nicolas again, but this time his eyes are glued onto me. Slowly, he nods, and my heart restarts and sputters to life in one single moment. I know Nicolas well enough to assume he's more than worried for her too. He's survived the extremities of D.C., knowing his family, especially Blaire, was missing him everyday. He just doesn't want her to go through pain again. That's all.

But he also trusts Blaire enough to let her fend for herself. As if she was a bird in a cage her entire life, enduring the moments that led up to *this* single moment was her fighting past the bars and stretching her wings out into the gaping unknown —letting her gleaming target be whatever she desires.

My throat is dry as I rasp out, "Fine. We'll let them be there."

Annie gives me a single nod, her eyes gleaming with appreciation. "Thank you. And don't worry, I'll make sure they're safe."

However, before she even finishes speaking, a pounding stream of thunder rolls through the atmosphere, and I grimace, expecting it to be another round of gunshots coming our way, but it's instead a vehicle of our own. And eventually *multiple* vehicles of the Reformers, encased in a thick exterior and spewing out bullets of their own. They fly at the surrounding ERUSA, and what occurs is a gruesome sight of its own. Blood splattering everywhere, splashing onto the ground already wet with sweat to begin with and condescending against the beating sun. Guts come flying out next—from the bodies of our enemies —and I leer my eyes away, bile washing and forming at the back of my throat. *Jesus Christ.*

The rumbling of the thick tires treading against the crunching grass draws my attention, and I blearily look at the scene unraveling in front of my own eyes. A furious Commander Thatcher decked in the same gear as us—if not more—raises her rifle at the ERUSA soldiers and bellows out, "I order you to leave my premise *now!* This is a trespassing of military territory and that is in a different country itself. If you are not to leave in the next thirty seconds, then I will release the trigger bombs in my jeep right now. The moment these bombs land on the ground, they will explode, and we all know what happens from there."

"Crap," Annie whispers, but definitely loud enough for me to hear. "We gotta go."

"If we go into the compound then the ERUSA will come following us," Nico says.

"Did you not hear what Commander Thatcher just said?" I gape at him. "She has goddamn *bombs* with her. We will be blown into pieces when those things even make the littlest of contact with the ground. We *need* to make a run for it."

"What about the others?" Nico asks. "Not just Blaire, Vi, and AJ, but Jeremiah and Mallory too. Where are they to begin with?"

"They're at the front, so they'll be the safest," Annie says. "But we'll make sure to bring the other three with us. I promise."

She doesn't even wait for a response from us as she pulls herself up to her feet and sprints toward where Blaire, AJ, and Vi are. We follow behind her, my veins pounding and my limbs throbbing as bullets cascade into my upheld shield.

Their bodies are hazy figures in the distance, clouds of dust impending upon my sight. I push the goggles down from my helmet, which immediately covers my eyes, and rapidly blink out the slowly dissipating haziness. My heart rides in my throat as we quickly trek over to them, their figures more visible and fervent in our sight.

Blaire glances over at me and flies up to her feet, leaving her post and running to my side. She slams into my chest and holds me up with her arms that curl around my torso. I hold her tight, grasping her helmet, and she says breathlessly, "I'm so glad to see you're okay."

"Me too," I say, holding her because she is my life. She *is* life. "Let's go back now, all right? Let's get away from this place."

She rapidly nods against my chest and releases from me, her bright green eyes gleaming against the sizzling sunrays scorching against my skin. Blaire grabs my gloved hand, lurches toward the compound and shouts to the others, "Let's go!"

Everyone runs over to the base, the remote control to open the entrance in Annie's hand as AJ calls over any alive and present soldiers to us. It physically pains me to see the soldiers splayed on the ground, their eyes open yet no trace of life evident. It's horrifying to think that some of these soldiers had a life outside of the military. Had motives. Desires. Fears. Strengths. Weaknesses. Goals. Maybe a loved one. A couple of children, too. And a life they would always look forward to coming back to once this mayhem was over. But their dreams and aspirations were stripped of them in a heartbeat, and now they're just figments of the universe—floating and nonexistent. It's terrifying how such a significant figure on this earth can be reduced to nothing but a mere unmoving and lifeless molecule the minute that heart of theirs stops beating.

Three bullets slamming into my shield startle me out of my thoughts as my hold on Blaire tightens. More and more soldiers join us, but it's a horrifyingly smaller number compared to when we first came here. Jeremiah and Mallory join our side too, which eases some of my nerves to begin with. At least *we're* all alive. God knows about the injuries, but we're alive. That's all that matters.

Once we escape the mound of ERUSA soldiers that slowly retreat from the premise—but there are of course those that still stubbornly remain—we climb into the gaping entrance Annie just activated, and we all pour inside, determined to fend off any of the ERUSA's who dare to get near our premise. So far, though, the coast is clear.

In the thirty seconds it takes to escape the battlefield, we peer from the docking grounds a hazy glimpse of Commander Thatcher's vehicle rolling inside the parameters with her vehicles trailing in last. She fends them off with the best of her ability, mounding three shields on her own, and not even coming close to spewing any bullets at them. *How does one even have that kind of self-control?*

"Hurry in, Commander Thatcher!" AJ yells. "Before they close in on us!"

When her vehicle rolls inside, she jumps out of the back, toils three jet-black items the same size as her palm and hurdles it forward into the smoky abyss with all her might. The moment the bomb contacts the grounds the remaining ERUSA soldiers obdurately stand on, a ground-shaking rumble encounters the air—and she simultaneously reaches into her decorated belt to press a button, allowing the double-doored entrance the size of a family home's forefront to immediately simmer shut.

The grounds beneath our feet shake, and we hold onto each other, grimacing every time a roaring gust of explosive wind pounds against the steel-barring entrance that can possibly endure the thickest of storms.

We immediately strip off our helmets, mask, goggles, and rifles, picking at our bloodied uniforms—whether that be ours or another's. But I don't think that really matters to any of us because we're all just grateful to be alive. Unlike the others whose lives were unfortunately taken in a snap of a finger.

Blaire gives me an uneasy glance and sidles up to me, leaning the side of her head onto my shoulder. I lean into her too, communicating with my unspoken words that she is okay and safe now. We are *all* safe now.

Commander Thatcher's heavy boots thump and thump against the concrete floor still shaking from the impending explosions. "The explosions are enough to kill someone in a matter of seconds, but not enough to eradicate an underground base made of steel. We should be safe here."

"What about our soldiers that died out there?" someone voices out in a bitter manner. "What about them, Commander?"

"In the military," she starts, "people are bound to lose their lives. It is a sad truth that cannot be avoided."

"That's bullshit," Vi mutters to herself.

Thankfully Commander Thatcher does not hear her remark

from her distance. *Oh, thank God. Otherwise, another battle would break out, but this time it would be between the two scariest women in the world.*

She cocks her head at us, setting her rifle to the side and planting her feet shoulder-to-shoulder. "As a good-willed Commander, I will make sure to dedicate our fallen soldiers this evening. Until then, I suggest you all resume your normal activities. You may go to the infirmary and check yourself in there for someone to heal your wounds, if that is necessary. Do what you think is best, as long as you're not lounging around." Her hazel eyes wander over us one last time, each movement measured and careful. "Sorry to break it to you all, but this is your life now. Being a part of the military does not mean rainbows and sunshine. It means back-breaking labor for our country that has never failed us and against the so-called American citizens that *have* failed us.

"I know it's also been a while since we've stepped out into battle, so, believe it or not, I understand that most of you are traumatized by what you just encountered. But, again, this is your life now, and I hate to put it bluntly, but you're gonna have to deal with it."

Slowly, everyone disperses from the compound entrance, silently absorbing her words—but before anyone has exited the area, she yells out, "Wait!" Everyone stops in their tracks, wondering what the hell Commander Thatcher has to say now. "Don't be so eager to leave. I have yet another thing to announce.

"I specifically instructed everyone to remain on the defensive side from here on out. As a Commander, I expect everyone to abide by my proposition. However"—her eyes sidle onto us— "some people decided to pull a so-called heroic stunt and completely disregard my statement in the first place. Even my utmost trusted soldier in this compound."

Beside me, AJ tenses in both fear and disappointment.

Commander Thatcher clenches her jaw, shaking her head ever-so slightly. "Some people just don't learn, do they? Lessons must unfortunately be taught to those ungrateful individuals who are too immature and impulsive to begin with." Her eyes harden on Blaire, Vi, and AJ in a matter of seconds. "And that's why I order Powers, Cohen, and Iyer to report to my office for a private conversation in ten minutes. Just to remind you of why you're here; not to break rules and go about your business the way *you* prefer. No, not at all. You are instead here to serve and obey. That is all. The rest of you may leave."

29

HOPE

BLAIRE

VI AND AJ SHUFFLE in beside me, and we sit on the creaky wooden chairs coated in a glimmery gray. Affixed directly in front of us is an oak table glinting against the searing LED lights burning above us. It creates a constant humming sound that I soon find myself getting sick of.

Commander Thatcher settles in on the looming black office chair perched against the curve of her desk, facing us and a not-so amused look etched onto her grave features. Wrinkles amass her forehead, and she rubs at the back of her neck, strands of short brown hair falling onto her eyes.

"Everyone is aware of the Detroitian military history, if I am not mistaken?" Her voice filters into the room, and I claw at my thighs, clenching my jaw. *We're wholeheartedly doomed.* When we nod, she leans back in her chair, the legs creaking against the hardwood floor. "Well, I call bullshit because what I saw up there were three idiots going against my word. Do you know how long it took me to get here and receive the prestige and respect I have now?" She leans forward, her lip curled, seething.

"It took me *innumerable* years. Even though I was the most dedicated and skilled soldier in the compound, as a mere eighteen-year-old too, I was not considered for the Commander position until almost two decades later. Think about that for a second.

"This military was not easy to form and maintain either. Among all the isolated cities in our broken country, our military is the most predominant of them all. Now think of the pressure I have—I have to form this flawless group of ranks and carve out the strongest of soldiers to even think of preparing for another possible war if, God forbid, that happens again. Think of that for just a second, will you?

"I have expectations for my soldiers. That is *all* I request of you." Her muscles constrict against her tight uniform, exemplifying her broad chest, and her tired eyes rake over each of us. "But I am highly disappointed in all of you. Utterly ashamed right now. Especially you, Iyer." Like lightning bolts, her eyes move in a split second over to AJ. "You're my most trusted companion here. Now I don't know whether that title remains the same anymore."

"I'm sorry, Commander Thatcher," AJ says, dropping his chin limply to his chest. "I did not mean to upset you."

"Even if that's not what you meant, it still happened. I gave clear-cut instructions, Iyer. *Don't fire at the ERUSA.* It's not Pig Latin, for Christ's sake."

"Why are you so determined to not fire at them?" Vi speaks up suddenly. My muscles tense as I cringe to myself. *Oh, I knew this was going to happen . . .*

"Excuse me?" Commander Thatcher slightly leans forward. "Were you just questioning my motives?"

"Never meant it in that way," she says in a clipped tone. "Just a genuine question."

"Ah." The coldness in her eyes never leaves. "Well, in that case, I would answer your question, but I'm afraid to let you know that I already answered it during the speech. Were you not paying attention?"

"Oh, I was. I just found it incredibly stupid and boring."

"Vi," I hiss, slightly nudging her elbow. "Quit it."

"Please, what is she gonna do? Torture me?" She snorts. "I've dealt with worse."

"Is that the case?" Commander Thatcher challenges her by jutting her chin forward and crossing her arms over her chest. "Then enlighten me. What exactly have you dealt with?"

Vi takes one sharp breath in until a stream of words rush through her mouth. "In prison, I was drowned and forced to breathe for minutes on end, weights were dropped on my stomach, I was starved for almost a week, they gave me almost zero water to drink, I was forced to live in my puddle of vomit and sweat and tears, and I was incredibly isolated that I went into a deep hole of insanity."

"My husband committed suicide only two years into our marriage," Commander Thatcher blurts out. "I was pregnant with my daughter, and I drank myself into misery by his sudden death to the point where I miscarried. Through many failed pregnancies, I finally gave birth to two who were healthy, but I lost parental rights over them because of my history with alcohol. Now I don't know where they are"—she takes a heavy breath in—"or whether they're alive."

Vi takes a deep breath in, but she immediately composes herself by saying, "My entire family was murdered in front of my own eyes."

"My husband wrote me a suicide letter where he detailed that he killed himself because of me."

Vi immediately clamps her mouth shut, angling her jaw to the ground and rapping her fingers against the armchair.

My mouth remains agape, my throat dry, parched, and itching with despair. *Whoa . . . what the hell did I just hear?* How can someone even go through so much baggage of pain and misery combined in such a short time period? Is that why the most stoic and cold-hearted of people endure the most emotional baggage? Because they have so much to lug on their shoulders, it's much easier to not carry their hearts on their sleeves?

"I'm not saying I've dealt with more trauma than you," Commander Thatcher says, not a speck of tears found swarming in her emotionless eyes. "I'm just letting you know that you are not the only ones with trauma, Powers. In a world like this, *everyone* has trauma. The world only cares for itself, not for those who take up its space. It's inevitable to endure the sort of pain where you become cold to this world because that's the only way to escape your past trauma. Trust me, I know. But that does not give you the excuse to act like a dim-witted narcissist who only cares about themselves and not for others. That's not how it works here."

"I'm not a dim-witted narcissist," Vi grits out. "I was just asking a simple question."

"A simple question for which I answered already."

"Your answer still doesn't make sense, though."

"I am not going to argue with you, Powers," Commander Thatcher sounds out. "I know you're a smart and skilled soldier. I've been watching you train and combat with the others and your training is phenomenal. I know you can think for yourself. But what you did with Cohen and Iyer was unnecessary. The reason why I was against firing at them is because that fuels them even more to attack our area again. We were lucky they were only by the field and not inside our compound. Now that you all fired at them without *my permission,* they will come back angrier and more determined to destroy us."

"Our numbers were decreasing, though," I say for the first time during this conversation. "We had no choice but to fire."

"That's not your decision to make, Cohen." Her eyes linger over me, her mouth hung open in thought. "I know our numbers were decreasing, and while I do value my soldiers plenty, it is also their duty to sacrifice. I would sacrifice too, if the opportunity arose. Being a soldier does not mean to rapidly fire at whatever comes your way; it means to defend and not stoop down to the enemy's level. Because firing back doesn't make us any better than them.

"I'll release you for now," she says, and we share confused looks with each other. *She's letting us go?* "The only reason I am is because you all had good intentions behind firing at the ERUSA, even though that was against everything I said. Take this lecture as a warning for what's to come. You are dismissed." Slowly, we get up from our seats, speechless with only the sound of the chair legs scraping against the hardwood floor. As we make our way out to the door, though, we are interrupted by Commander Thatcher's voice again. "Cohen?"

My heart leaps up to my throat as I turn to her. "Yes, Commander Thatcher?"

"Stay back for a second," she says, gesturing to the chair that I was sitting in. "There's something I need to discuss with you."

Not a squeak leaves my throat as I look over at Vi and AJ. All they do is raise their eyebrows, slowly making their way out of the room and whispering to me, *Good luck.*

I take a deep breath in and turn back to the Commander. *Great.*

"Is everything all right?" I ask as I take a seat. "Did I do something wrong . . . again?"

"No," she says bluntly. "You did nothing of the sort. I only brought you here because, well . . . this conversation was long overdue anyway." When she sees the confusion drawn on my features, she sighs and leans back, propping her feet atop her desk. "I'm sure you're aware now that I didn't have the most glorious past, right?"

I nod, remembering the horrifying details she spewed out to

us not too long ago. "Yes, and I'm sorry to hear you went through that. I can't even imagine how that'd be."

Commander Thatcher doesn't say anything in regards to my attempt to console her. "I was twenty-one and my husband was twenty-three when we eloped. We were both in the military and we had our wedding here"—she looks around her—"because my parents disapproved of him. He was an amazing man, Cohen. He was the love of my life. I couldn't imagine a life without him.

"Now imagine . . ." She clears her throat. "Imagine being only two years into your marriage with the *love of your life* and suddenly hearing from another soldier—on a bright July afternoon, mind you—that your husband drowned himself in the bathtub that morning and he wrote in his suicide note to you that *you were the reason* he was depressed—with no explanation provided. I refused to eat, sleep, or speak for days. Alcohol became my best friend then. And at that point I didn't even feel like living anymore, but the only reason I carried on was because I wanted to be Commander. And even worse of all, I became pregnant. I tried to stop drinking, but my addiction was too much that I miscarried. From there, I went into rehab here in Detroit for about a couple of months, and I came back better and pregnant again. I gave birth to two beautiful children—one boy and one girl. Once I came back from maternity leave, I reentered the military and visited my children to the best of my ability. Life was starting to become good . . . up until that point.

"I was shocked and upset when I saw authorities crashing into my home and taking my babies away from me. They were only toddlers—just two years apart. That day was the day I last shed a tear," she says under her breath. "Since then, there have been no updates on where they are, how they're doing, who's taking care of them—nothing of the sort." She levels her eyes at me. "I want nothing more than to get them back. I'll do *anything* to get them back."

A still silence roams in the air, and my throat is itchy with tears, which I force down my throat. "That sounds . . . terrible," I rasp out. "Words can't even explain how much sorrow I feel for you."

She nods once, her lips drawn into a thin line. I leer my eyes to the ground, unable to center on the intensity emanating from her eyes.

Almost a minute passes until she speaks again.

"Only one person stood by my side while my life was falling apart."

I look back at her, feeling the hard weight of the peridot stone pressing onto my skin. "Who?"

A gust of air rushes through the vents above, and I can feel my limbs weakening the moment she says, "Marianna Gonzalez."

My face slackens, my tongue lapping back and forth in my mouth with thought. *What?*

I shake my head, stammering out, "How . . . how was my mama—"

"Let me explain," she interrupts, her chin bobbing up as she swallows. "I met your mother in D.C. when I was employed to help with the disputes there. At that time my children were taken away from me, so I had no desire to make friends or even associate with anyone. I just wanted to do my part in the military, and that is all. However, I met your mother while walking around the city there. During that time, we were undergoing the Dark Ages, so the tensions between the upper and lower classes were too much to bear. The situation was easier to handle in Detroit because it didn't have much emphasis on the political aspect, but in D.C., of course, *everything* was about politics.

"I met Marianna at the markets there, and she was nothing but a sweetheart, even when I was cold and ruthless to her. I ran into her at the markets everyday, and I always hated seeing her because she just . . . made me feel emotions after a very long time. I hated to admit it, but her persistence to always see me and tell me stories about her life or anything, really . . . it made me feel a whole lot better. But I didn't want to.

"Eventually, I gave in to her and thawed the ice I lodged between us. And before you know it, we became the best of friends." One corner of her lip tugs up. "Since we were both Hispanic, it was easy to bond with her. We were in our twenties —full-grown adults, at that—and there were still moments when her parents yelled at us to keep it down in her room." She shakes her head, almost chuckling to herself. "God, she made me forget all my past trauma. Mari was the reason I felt alive after so long.

"Our two-year friendship came to an end when I was employed back in Detroit. It was like hell leaving her," she grits through her teeth. "And that was the end of it. I haven't seen her since then." Suddenly, Commander Thatcher looks up at me, passion and pride gleaming over her pupils. "Now, imagine my surprise when I see the carbon copy of Mari come into the Detroitian compound. You are such a splitting image of her that it terrifies me. I didn't know how to confront you about this. About the friendship I had with your mother. And what terrified me the most was not just your looks being like her's, but your personality too. Mari was the most passionate, intelligent, and driven woman I knew . . . just like you, Blaire. You are *just* like your mother. The woman I dream of being reunited with every single waking moment of my life.

"I know this was a lot to dump on you. I know you're still trying to reel in from not just my life story, but from this whole ERUSA situation in its entirety too." She lets out a sad laugh. "That's okay. I get it. But I just . . . I just want one request from you. Can you . . ." She presses her lips together. "Can you find some way to bring us together? I wish you could bring her here but you can't because outsiders are not allowed. But I really want to see her, Blaire. I want to see your mother and let her know that her best friend is here. Just talk to her about it. Tell her what I told you. And then ask her to tell you all the stories. About her, about me, and about us. I promise you there's another side of your mother that you don't know."

My mind is nothing but a fuzzy entity, buzzing with thousands of emotions and thoughts. *My mama and Commander Thatcher were best friends?* I can't seem to make much sense of what I just heard. I don't even know what to think right now.

"I . . ." I gulp. "Okay. I'll talk to my mama about our conversation tonight and I'll let you know what she says."

I've never seen Commander Thatcher smile in the past two weeks until this very moment. Her eyes light up like lights twinkling against the side of the streets, enlightening the earth's core. Her lips spread out, revealing her bright white teeth and lines creasing into the side of her lips. She grins the entire time, her lips twitching every now and then. "Thank you. I appreciate it." Once she sniffles, she clears her throat and shakes her head to herself. "Don't tell anyone but your family about this conversation. Especially what I told you about my past. Got it?"

"Got it," I say, my voice wavering from what I've just heard.

As I leave her office, her voice interrupts me. "Wait, Blaire. One more thing."

"Yes, Commander Thatcher?" I turn, my eyebrows pinched together.

Like a line of ink trailing across paper, her lips curl into a small smile. "Call me Heidi instead."

30

BREAKTHROUGH

JAX

I WIPE THE SWEAT rusting from my blade and toss it in the bin, deep and ragged breaths dragging out of my system. Clatters of equipment and grunts of soldiers resonate in the background, which clearly indicates toward the end of the day. Many people just want to finish strong so they can feel somewhat accomplished by the end of the day; and many other people, like me, become increasingly tired throughout the day and just want to go home and sleep.

Which is exactly what I'm dealing with right now.

There remains only a few people in the gym, and unfortunately, one of the few is AJ. He just finished one of his workouts and is now walking away from there, rubbing a white towel at his neck. Ever since his secretive conversation with Commander Thatcher, he's been frowning the entire time and barely saying a word to anyone. Maybe he's just upset at himself for betraying the one person he's supposed to be loyal to at his employment here. Or maybe he just feels like a terrible role model to the other soldiers.

That sounds like his problem, not mine, I think to myself.

As he nears me, I can't help but study his features and the bruises on his jaw. His eyes look beyond tired, and his usually lively golden eyes are nothing but dull blobs of nothingness. It's like someone reached into his soul, snatched it right out of him, and shredded it into pieces. Leaving him with nothing but a pile of his own bones and flesh.

AJ's eyes snap up at me, and I immediately drag my sight to the clock on the ceiling behind him, whistling a wavering tune. *Shit!*

"What time is it?" I nervously blurt out, still staring at the clock and ignoring a silently boiling AJ walking toward me. "It's been a very long day, y'know? Training, combating, working out, and obviously we can't forget the whole fiasco that occurred this morning." I let out a nervous chuckle. "Talk about a complete turn of events, eh?"

"Why are you talking to me?" he grumbles, stopping in his tracks and leveling his vision up to mine.

"Why not?" I shrug. "You've been alone for several hours. You won't even talk to your sister. I'd say you need a friend."

He snorts. "Please, like I want *you* to be my friend. Besides, don't you hate my guts?"

"Whoa." I cock my head at him, grinning. "*Hate* is a pretty intense word you're using there, buddy. I'd say a word more appropriate would probably be, well . . . *dislike.* Yes. Dislike is definitely more appropriate in this situation."

"Oh, don't flatter me, Jax," he mutters, sizing up to me. "I know what you're trying to do."

"What?" I'm still grinning.

"You're trying to get on my nerves, and because I'm not in a good mood, you're using it to your advantage."

"Now, c'mon, AJ. Don't think so low of me. I'd *never* do that to you. I mean, yeah, I do dislike you because you're trying to steal my girlfriend from me, but I think we can put that to the side and be mature adults. You *are* an adult . . . right?"

"Yeah." He glares at me. "I'm older than you."

"Seriously?"

"Yes."

"How much older?"

"I'm twenty-two."

"Really? I swear you were, like, seventeen."

"Seventeen? For Christ's sake, are you insulting me?"

"Nope, not at all. I swear you look seventeen."

"Okay, *enough!*" He snarls, pushing a finger deep into my chest that I feel nudging at my bones. "Please, for the love of God, shut the *hell* up so I can just get through my day peacefully. I've already had a lot going on lately. Jesus Christ, you're so annoying."

"Shit, man." I scowl at him, pushing his finger away. "Relax, okay? I was just playin' with you. You don't have to act like you have a stick up your ass because you had a bad day. We all have bad days, and it's okay to be upset. That doesn't mean you act like a douchebag to others. Damn."

Red flares across his tanned cheeks, and he shakes his head once, twice—almost in disbelief. He presses his lips together and stuffs his hands into his pockets. "God, I think you're right. I *have* been a douchebag."

I raise my eyebrows at him. "Wait, say that again?"

"Say what?"

"What you just said. That you think I'm r . . ."

"Oh, you've gotta be kidding me."

"C'mon, please!" I grin at him. "This is a once-in-a-lifetime moment."

"Who's the douchebag now?" He rolls his eyes at me.

"Okay, I'm sorry." I start to walk forward by the exit, which he does too. "You may carry on with your little spiel."

"All right." He takes a deep breath in. "Yes, I have been upset.

I mean, can you blame me? Commander Thatcher lectured me —when she called Blaire, Vienna, and I in—that she trusted me the most when all I did was betray her in the end. What kind of soldier *does* that? I have a reputation to maintain in this compound, which I destroyed with my own hands. When I came out of her office, I could barely look Annie in the eye. I just *know* she's disappointed in me. I just know *everyone's* disappointed in me."

"Enough of this sappy shit," I grumble. "Do you even know what bullshit you're spitting out right now? No one is disappointed in you, for God's sake. If anything, people think more highly of you."

"You're very funny."

"Actually, for once, I'm being serious." I look over at him. "You did something that took *balls.* People will have loads of respect for you."

"Yeah, well, I don't think that," he says. "I've never gone against a single word Commander Thatcher has said. Even when I had the burning desire to disagree with her, I still didn't. So I don't know why I rebelled in this situation."

"Because you saw our people dying. Because you realized just how bad the situation was."

"Maybe, maybe not. But either way, it would've been a lose-lose situation. And now I don't know how to get past my mistake. I can barely talk to anyone. Hell, I can barely stand within a five-feet radius of Commander Thatcher. I just know she's mad as hell at me right now."

"Okay, now you're just being dramatic," I say, pushing against the exit door and entering a narrow and dimly lit hallway. "There's no need to assume shit. Just go on with your normal routine and *talk* to people. You're not really creating the best image of yourself while acting like a shithead."

"I don't want to act like a shithead."

"So get your crap together and *man up.* Own up to what you

committed and move on. Don't just whine and pout like you are now. It disgusts the hell out of me."

"You know, you're very good at lifting other people's self-esteem," he says, clearly sarcastic.

"What do you want me to do?" I drawl out. "Drown you in sappy shit? Sing you bedtime stories and lure you into a magical sleep with sheep jumping past fences? That's not gonna teach you shit, AJ. I'm telling it to you as it is. Man to man."

"Since when did you ever want to help me?" He shoots me an unimpressed look. "I thought you disliked me because you're afraid I might steal Blaire away from you?"

"I'm not *afraid* about that." I scoff.

AJ suggestively raises his eyebrows at me.

"I'm *not*."

"Mm-hmm."

I huff, flipping him off in the process.

He grins, shoving my finger away with the back of his hand. I roll my eyes, tucking my hands into my pocket and walking alongside the very same man I wanted to punch the hell out of just a week ago.

We walk past soldiers healing in the infirmary, and a frown grows on my lips as I recount how terrible the entire battle was. In D.C. we were all able to escape with barely a scratch, but the battles here are getting more dire. More *intense*. It makes us a bit more protective of ourselves because we went through so much to come here . . . just for it to bite us in the ass. Is this what we get for standing up for ourselves?

Moments later, I see Annie coming out of the infirmary and running into us, her eyes widened at AJ walking with me. *Yeah, I'm sorta surprised too.*

"Hey, guys," she says in a slow and contemplative tone. "Where are you headed off to?"

"Well, I'm about to leave in a little," I say. "This guy, on the other hand, is just creepily following me along."

"Shut up," AJ grumbles, jamming his elbow into my ribs. It hurts like hell, but I'd rather die than suggest to him in any way that he caused me pain.

Annie's golden eyes glaze over me, and then her twin brother. Now that I see them standing in front of each other, I can acknowledge their similarities and what sets them apart. They're almost the same height, but AJ must be an inch or two taller. They have the same skin tone, but Annie has a mole on her neck. They have the same smile, but Annie's eyes crinkle when she smiles. But that's the only difference between them, besides their completely polar opposite personalities.

It's sort of entertaining to watch them interact, even though they came out of the same womb at almost the same time—with Annie being the oldest. All I know is, from my limited knowledge as an only child, they get along pretty damn well in comparison to other siblings. I know Blaire, Nico, and Em get into an argument everyday, but it always ends up in them hugging each other and calling it a truce. But I've never seen AJ and Annie argue, or even act distant toward each other. That's why it semi-bothers me that AJ is refusing to talk to Annie because he's too in his head.

Suddenly, I get an amazing idea.

"Hey, Annie?" I say, cocking my head.

"Yes?"

"Your brother has something he wants to tell you."

From my peripheral vision, I notice AJ's face slackening.

"Tell me what?"

"I don't know." I smirk at him. "I guess you'll find out from him."

"Oh." Annie looks over at AJ. "Is everything okay?"

"Uh, yeah." When I start glaring at him, he sighs exaggeratingly and says, "All right, fine. I'm not okay. Um . . . I just want to let you know that I've been kinda avoiding you because, well,

I think that both you and Commander Thatcher think that I'm a disappointment." He clears his throat. "That's all."

"What?" She frowns at him. "Why would we be disappointed in you?"

"Because I fired at the ERUSA without Commander Thatcher's permission."

Annie starts to chuckle. "AJ, I honestly forgot that happened. Why are you still thinking about that?"

"I don't know. I just hate letting people down."

"You haven't let *anyone* down. Not me, and not the Commander. You're just too hard on yourself."

"I'm not hard on myself."

Annie and I glare at AJ suggestively.

"Okay, fine. Maybe you're right. Maybe I just need to take a breather and move on."

"That's exactly what I told him," I say to Annie. "But does he listen? Nope, of course he doesn't."

"Because he's super hot-headed and stubborn." She scoffs. "He's way too in his head."

"That's why you're the better sibling."

"Hey!" AJ snarls. "You guys teaming up against me is not making me feel any better."

"Sorry." She chuckles. "But anyway, no one is disappointed by you. What's done is done. All you can do is move on now." A frown suddenly grows on her lips, which concerns me because I've almost never seen Annie upset. "Do you remember what *amma* and *baba* used to tell us?"

Wordlessly, AJ nods, his features hardened and his jaw clenched.

"They used to tell us that your self-worth is like the sun," she tells him anyway. "When your self-worth is high, you shine your rays on everyone, and you immediately make people happy because *you're* happy. But the moment you think lowly of yourself, storm clouds will appear and you will rain and thunder on everyone. You're still shining beneath the clouds, but you have to push those clouds away to be shining your rays on everyone again. So, *push* those clouds away, AJ. Don't let anything or anyone stop you, not even yourself.

"Don't do this only for me, for Commander Thatcher, or for the military as a whole. Do this for *amma* and *baba.* Because they were the only ones who looked after us when we ourselves were unable to."

AJ's features, which were first hardened like a block of ice, thaws at Annie's words and a certain mentioning of an *amma* and a *baba.* He slowly nods and murmurs, "You're right. Thank you, Annie."

Her frown transforms into a playful smile. "C'mon, drop the nice guy act. Since when have *you* ever said thank you to me?"

He chuckles, pulling her in for a side-hug.

Annie eventually goes her own way, leaving AJ and I to walk through the hallway again. We're only just a couple of steps away from the docking area, where the others are probably waiting to go back home, which I am concerningly excited about because this day was *too much* for various reasons.

I clear my throat, hoping to make conversation amongst our awkward silence. "So, who was Annie talking about when she gave you that advice? Those people that she mentioned?"

"Oh," he says curtly, avoiding any sort of eye contact with me. "Just our parents."

When he doesn't elaborate any further, I take it as a hint and instead decide to ease the tension-filled air. "Well, I feel bad for them because they had to raise *you.* That must've been hell for them."

All he does is chuckle, but his eyes are as dull as ever.

Two long minutes later, we reach the docking area where the others are perched by the jeep: Mallory, Jeremiah, Vi, and Blaire. When I make eye contact with Blaire, she doesn't even smile at me; instead all she does is raise one confused brow and gesture between me and AJ.

Yeah, I don't know what the hell's going on either.

I turn to him and cross my arms over my chest. "Before I go, I just want to let you know that just because I gave you advice, doesn't mean we're friends. Hell, we're not even acquaintances."

AJ props his hands on his hips and sighs. "Fine by me."

"Yep," I say. "Also, try not to do anything stupid while I'm gone. I know that would be very hard for you."

He smirks. "Same goes for you."

I frown at him, and he laughs.

When I step away from him, walk over to the jeep and eventually climb onto it, Vi nudges my shoulder and asks me, "Since when did you guys get along?"

31

TENDERNESS

BLAIRE

JAX INTERTWINES HIS FINGERS with mine, leaning his cheek against my shoulder and releasing a low breath that echoes throughout the empty foyer. It's nearing midnight, so we took this as an opportunity to relish in each other's presence, without an entire battle interrupting us.

"Hey," he whispers.

"Hi," I whisper back.

"I've missed you." He looks up at me, deep storm clouds brewing in the pits of his mesmerizing eyes. His lips drag up into a beam, framing his cheeks and bringing light to his tired features. He removed the bandage from his scar just before arriving at our secret abode, which reveals the vicious scrapings and blood framing his cheek. I still wonder why his scar deepened, but I'm too exhausted to bombard him with any questions. Hell, I barely have the energy to *breathe.* "How are you?" he asks me.

"Pretty good," I say. "Well, except for the fact that Commander Thatcher lectured me, Vi, and AJ this evening."

Jax winces. "How did that go?"

As I'm about to tell him how our conversation went, I stop in my tracks and remember that Commander Thatcher—or better yet, *Heidi*—was best friends with my mom. I do plan to tell my family about our encounter, but I don't know how exactly to state it. My parents are already reluctant with me and Nico joining the military, and me having a whole ass boyfriend too, so I don't want to add to their list of stresses. Though I'm not sure about that because my mama might be enthralled to find out her long-lost best friend is here all along. Maybe she's not too upset about moving to Detroit because Heidi is here. *God, I'm still not used to the fact that her name is Heidi, and she told me to call her that, too. Has the world gone nuts?*

I look down at Jax, feeling his body leaning against mine and his face so close to mine I have to physically restrain myself from kissing him. How am I supposed to keep this secret from him? He's a trustworthy guy—otherwise I wouldn't be with him. I'll just tell him and then emphasize that he shouldn't tell anyone.

And so, I tell him.

When I finish, I notice his eyes are widened and his mouth is agape, his eyebrows pushed together in thought. "Her . . . her name is Heidi? And her husband . . . her children . . . best friends with your mom . . . what the hell?" he murmurs.

"Yeah," I say. "That's exactly how I feel right now."

He sighs, pausing a few seconds before he speaks. "Do you plan to tell your mom about it?"

"I do. I just don't know when."

Jax's hold on my hand tightens. "You'll know when the time is right." Suddenly, he grins again. "Just like I did when I was thinking of asking you to be my girlfriend."

I smile. "I can't believe it's been almost a month since we got together."

"Tell me about it." He grins lazily. "Can't believe you've stuck with my annoying ass for one whole month."

"I can't believe it either."

"Hey!" He frowns. "You weren't supposed to agree with me. You were supposed to reassure me, like all loving girlfriends are supposed to do."

"Oh, you want me to reassure you?" I climb on top of him, straddling him and trailing one finger lazily down where his sternum is. "I'll reassure you all you want, Jax."

He sucks in a deep breath, his lower body tensing and his gray eyes teasing. "Oh, God. You might just kill me if you keep this up, beautiful."

I laugh into his mouth, and he immediately smashes our lips together. We instantly mold into each other, my hand resting on his chest as I grasp at his shirt hungrily. His movements are eager, frantic, and desperate, bringing his hand to the back of my head and grasping my hair, grasping my heart in his unforgettable presence for him to cherish and hold. *I'll gladly give my heart to him.*

I don't know how long it's been since we've been intertwined in each other's arms and mouths in the corner of the foyer, not caring if anyone walks in on us as our hands travel up and each other's bodies like curious sailors seeking the unknown sea. A rush of buried emotions thuds and pounds at my heart and streams through my veins—adrenaline, passion, desperation, desire, happiness . . . and another one I can't seem to put my finger on.

"Where have you been?"

I wince at my mama's confrontational tone as I slowly close the door. *I should've known this conversation was to come.*

My mama stands in front of me, worry drawn on her

features as she walks over to me in the entrance of our room. Sleepiness is prominent in her eyes, so I'm assuming she must have woken up by my entrance—which I'm confused by because she's quite a heavy sleeper.

"I was . . . just getting some fresh air," I say quietly, stepping past her and hoping to end this conversation as soon as possible. Unfortunately, she grabs onto my forearm, making me stop in my tracks.

She raises her eyebrows at me. "Don't lie to me, *mija*. I am not someone you can fool very easily."

I sigh, already accepting my defeat. *What was I thinking? Did I seriously believe I could ever deceive my mother?*

"Okay," I whisper. "I was with Jax."

Even though I am unable to meet her eyes, I can still notice from my peripheral vision that she's grinning ear-to-ear—and it's not with happiness. It's rather from victory.

"You mean your new boyfriend, right? The boy you never bothered to tell me about? You're supposed to tell your mama everything."

"Look, I'm sorry, Mama. The only reason I didn't tell you was because I didn't want you to get . . . well, *mad* at me."

She cocks her head at me. "Why would I get mad at you?"

"Because every time I hang out with him, both you and Papa give me a dirty look."

My mama lets out a short laugh. "That's how every parent is. We're all overprotective. But that doesn't mean we don't want you to be happy."

"What's going on here?" My papa peers into the living room and widens his eyes at us. "Is everything okay?"

"Yes, actually," she says. "We were just talking about Jax, Blaire's boyfriend."

"Oh my God."

"Don't be embarrassed, Blaire. I'm glad you're opening up to us. Come, let's sit on the couch and we can talk about it." She ushers me over to the living room and pushes me down on the couch. "Come here, David. Let's talk to her."

"Marianna, I'm sure we can do this another day," he murmurs, yawning afterwards.

"It's either now or never," she says in a stern voice. Reluctantly, he comes over, sleepily muttering to himself and sitting on the armchair in front of us.

Thankfully the room is dark so my parents can't see me blushing.

"Mama?" I blurt out. As much as I appreciate my parents for not lecturing me for having a boyfriend, I need to tell her about Heidi. I wanted to tell them another day, but since they're both awake and ready to hear me say *something,* I might as well do it now so I can get it off my chest.

"Yes, *mija?*"

"We can't talk about Jax right now because I have something else to tell you."

My dad frowns from the armchair. "What is it?"

"Well . . ." I fidget to myself. "I had a conversation with the military Commander this evening, and she told me that she wanted to be reunited with her best friend again." I look at my mom beside me, anxiety clawing at my insides. "Her name's Commander Heidi Thatcher. Does that name seem familiar to you?"

Immediately, my mama's bottom lip wobbles—one, two, three tears escaping from her saddened and hopeful eyes. "Heidi?" she whimpers. "Is that my Heidi?"

"Yes." I place my hand over hers as my papa walks over and rubs my mama's shoulder.

"What . . . what else did she say?"

"She said I remind her of you. Everything about me. My personality, my looks . . . everything."

"Oh my gosh," she sobs, bringing her hands to her face and shaking. As we comfort her, she says again, "When . . . when can I see her?"

"I don't know, Mama. You can't go to the Detroitian compound because it's restricted to all outsiders, though I'll see if there's anything I can do from my end. Commander Thatcher's also very busy with training the soldiers and fending off the ERUSA. It might be a while 'til you'll see her again," I say honestly.

"That's okay." She clears her throat. "I'll wait as long as I have to. I thought that . . . she wouldn't want anything to do with me. That's probably why she left for Detroit all of a sudden."

"No, Mama. She left because she was deployed in Detroit."

"Really?" She sighs. "I thought she hated me. That's what I thought even as we relocated here. Even then I still hoped that she would remember *you* are *my* daughter and find some way to bring us together again. And she did." She grins. "She did."

I smile at her, leaning my head on her shoulder as my papa says, "They were the dynamic duo back then."

"Really?" I look over at him.

"Yes. I met your mother just a year before she met Heidi, and I swear she started spending more time with her than me." He chuckles. "I started to get jealous because I liked your mother so much back then, but she was always with Heidi. Gosh, what a time it was, right, Marianna?"

"Yeah." She sighs ruefully.

When silence settles in on us, I clear my throat and say, "Heidi also said that there was a lot about you I don't know, and that I should ask you about any stories you have."

"Oh, really?" she mutters. "Wow, she really talked to you about this, huh?"

"She did. So tell me, Mama," I say to her eagerly. "Tell me about your stories."

"Well . . . all right. I'll tell you." She cozies in beside me, as my father leans on her shoulder too. Just three people, together, relishing in each other's warmth. "I'm sure she told you that she was very cold to me when we first met, while I was more welcoming. I always wondered why she acted that way to me, but as I later found out, it was because she had a terrible past. I have to admit, I in no way had as such the traumatic life that she did because, while it is very traumatizing to lose your parents during the Dark Ages, it's not as traumatizing as losing your entire family. So, in some way, I understood her coldness.

"I was only an English teacher back then at a nearby high school, and I didn't have many friends. The only friend I had was Heidi, and we could somewhat relate because we were both Hispanic, but in no way connected to our culture." She giggles. "My parents always yelled at me for never connecting to my Argentinian culture, and I always brushed them off because, as a first-generation child, you're just more focused on American culture. It's a sad truth, and it was my situation. Yet I wish I was more connected so I could teach you more about it." Mama gives me a sad smile.

"Days flew by, and Heidi and I became very close. We both shared our hatred of the world around us, and one day, I decided to lead a protest in D.C." My eyebrows raise at her statement. *She led a protest in D.C.?* "It was obviously a very last minute decision, but every moment I spent with Heidi fueled my hatred for the government. So, me, Heidi, and your papa led a pretty monstrous protest in D.C."

"It was massive," he adds. "We were on the frontlines, and as I turned around to look at who was joining us, I saw mounds and mounds of people joining, both the wealthy and poor alike. We were infuriated with the government's way of dealing with our economic crisis, and that was to divide us.

"For a while, the protest went great . . . until the police showed up out of nowhere and tased us. Pepper-sprayed us. Beat us with their bare fists." His Adam's apple bobs as he gulps. "It was very terrifying, but at the same time, it was exhilarating to just go out there and express our opinions."

"Wow," I whisper. "Is that why Heidi told me I'm just like

you, Mama? Because you were part of a protest against the government?"

"Yes." She nods. "Because *you* are part of your own generation's protest, and it makes me so proud to see that you and your brother are on the same page. Maybe Em one day can join too, but I think she's more intrigued by the healthcare side." Mama winks.

I chuckle, imagining a curious and intelligent Em tending to her patients. "I can't believe there was this whole other side to you and Papa. Why would you keep this from me?"

"It wasn't intentional," she says. "I did it just to protect you and keep you safe. I didn't want to inspire you to form protests of your own because, well, getting tased and pepper-sprayed isn't the most pleasant thing out there. But when I heard of you joining the Subversives that Nico *himself* formed . . . it made me have faith in society again—and that your generation will create a better world that my generation was unable to. That's why I've been overprotective with you, Blaire. Because I don't want you to suffer like I did."

"I'm not gonna suffer, Mama. I'm under great care by the Reformers, and I'm learning very helpful life skills from them. I can even fight against Nico now." I grin. "And Jax makes sure I'm safe too. Believe it or not, he's very overprotective of me, just like I am of him and you guys too."

My papa furrows his thick bushy graying brows at me. "There's no need to worry about us, sweetheart."

"I mean, to an extent, I have to," I whisper. "I'm gone most of the day, and all you have to keep you company is Em, and even she must be getting sick and tired of being stuck here all day. How long can you guys stay here with Layla and Tamia anyway? And there's no guarantee this place is one-hundred percent safe either. *Anything can happen.* That's why I'm gonna ask Heidi if she can bring you guys over to the bunker for extra safety one of these days."

"No, *mija,* you don't have to do that." My mama cups my cheek. "See, this is another thing we have in common: we worry about others too much. I've begun to tell myself this, and you should too . . . stop worrying about others more than yourself. You are a rare and precious diamond, and the moment you begin to wither even in the slightest, you will shatter into pieces. Treat yourself kindly. You shouldn't wrack your mind by worrying about others."

I gleam at her, tears brimming my eyes. "I love you, Mama." I look over at my papa, holding onto his hand. "I love you too, Papa."

And we sit there in the darkness, half-sleep and hugging each other so tightly I begin to lose feeling in my limbs. It must be minutes later that I fall asleep, my exhaustion overcoming me like a pervasive fog perusing the sky. I feel my papa lifting me and carrying me over to Em and Nico's room, planting me in the middle of them. They both kiss my forehead, shortly before gleaming at a sleeping Em and Nico, and my mama whispers to me, "We will be safe. Don't worry."

32

MUSE

JAX

I MIGHT BE ONE of the very few people in the world who hate to sleep.

For many, sleep is an exit from reality and a way to recharge themselves after such a draining day. It is hours upon hours of white noise, black sight, and calming blue waves lapping into their ears as they enter a nonresponsive state.

For me, though? It is *hell*.

As soon as my eyes close, my father appears. Not one night has passed that I've had a peaceful sleep. And every time, when he shows up, it is seven hours of relentless torture—whether it be physical, verbal, or mental. Sometimes, he tortures me so much I can't even wake up. It's as if I'm stuck in that vulnerable state forever, taunted by a figment of my imagination and an unearthly presence that leaves me frozen in my bones. Like a sleep paralysis demon . . . but in the shape of my father.

The air is still with very little wind rushing around. The trees barely move, nothing more than immobile giants. My feet dangle over the edge of the building, and I look down at the ground floors under me. If I wanted to, I could jump. I could end my nightmares right here, and right now, just by jumping and calling an end to my painful journey.

But I eventually decide that I don't think Blaire and the others will be very pleased to hear in the morning that I jumped off a damn building.

I've been coming here for the past several weeks, ever since I smashed my fist through the mirror that one night. Sleep is something I've been avoiding for the longest time. As soon as we reach the bunker, I gulp three cups of coffee and run on that the entire day. And I *hate* coffee.

I'm only drinking it to avoid my father.

In the far distance, I still hear sirens that have been occurring ever since the invasion. The Detroitian police and emergency services have been trying to fend off the ERUSA to the best of their ability, but even their numbers are decreasing, so all the people can rely on is the Reformers. However, we are currently falling apart at the seams because the ERUSA attacked us just this very afternoon, and now Commander Thatcher's defensive plan is on the fence.

I remember when Blaire told me—barely an hour ago—about Commander Thatcher's backstory and her desire to reconvene with her best friend, or Blaire's mom, again. Oh, and not to mention the fact that her real name is *Heidi.* No offense to her, but Heidi is more of a name a kind-hearted person would have, and she is nowhere close to being identified as kind-hearted.

Before I can dive into my thoughts any further, I hear a shuffling of combat boots behind me. I turn around, just to see Vi by the ladder, pulling herself up and arching her eyebrow at me. "What are you doing here?"

"What are *you* doing here?" I arch my eyebrow back.

"I asked you first." She gives me a death glare. *Damn, I can't ever argue with that death glare of hers.*

"I always come here," I say, gesturing to the city and the sights. "I have been for almost a month now."

"Oh." Vi sits beside me, just two arm's length away. Her unruly black and red hair frames her tired features, her pale skin the same shade as the moon. "This is my first time here. I just wanted to check it out and smoke a 'lil." She pulls out a lighter and a pack of cigarettes from her pocket. She takes one out of the box, props it between her pointer and middle finger, and brings the tip to the lighter exhibiting a lone flame. Immediately, a scorching smell encircles me as she brings the cigarette to her mouth, inhales, and releases it from her mouth, smoke leaving both her lips and her nostrils. Her tightened figure loosens—seemingly from relief. When she sees me staring at her, she leans back and offers it to me. "You want one?"

I shake my head.

"C'mon, just one puff."

"Seriously, Vi. I'm good." She shrugs and goes to smoke again. I cock my head at her. "You know those things can kill you, right?"

Mid-smoke, she looks over at me with hooded eyes. "Like I have much to live for."

I frown at her. "Damn. That was dark as hell."

"It's the truth. I don't have anyone."

"What the hell do you mean? You have us."

"And who is *us*?"

"Me, Blaire, Mallory, Jeremiah, I guess AJ, Annie, and Ren."

"You and Blaire have each other, Mallory has you, Jeremiah has Layla, AJ and Annie have each other, and I hate Ren's guts."

"C'mon, Vi. You don't even know her well enough to say that."

"I don't need to know her well enough to establish my own opinion of her, and frankly, I don't have a very high one." She smokes again.

"Well, if you don't like Ren, then that's okay—but you can't just say you don't have us when, in reality, *you do.* We've always been there for you."

"It's not about whether or not you guys are here for me." Vi lets out a long string of smoke from her slightly parted mouth. "It's about who truly gets me, understands me like no other, and no offense to any of you, but none of you get me. Only one person did and . . ." She shakes her head to herself, gnawing on the butt of her cigarette.

"Finish that sentence," I urge her.

"No. I'm good."

"Vi, c'mon. You can talk to me about your thoughts. Open up to me, please. I know I may not get you, but I can *listen* to you."

She clenches her jaw and drills her eyes into me. "Like anyone would ever want to listen to me open up about my damn feelings."

"*I do,*" I emphasize. "C'mon, Vi. I am your friend, you have to admit it. You and I, we've both come so far. It was just seven months ago that you kicked me in the balls for acting like a douchebag which I don't blame you for. You had to do what you had to do. But we're on the same page now. We're all going through the same thing, and we've grown closer during these dark times. You can't just be closed off to me. That's not fair to me."

Her brown eyes glaze over me, wavering and, for once, not stern. She presses her lips together, shakes her head, and smokes again, this time elongating the time when she exhales. The smoke prancing out of her mouth flies off into the distance like a flock of birds carried away by the dim atmosphere. "Fine," Vi says. "I'll tell you. Just don't . . . don't bring this conversation up again with me, or anyone else. I don't need to be reminded of what drags me down every second of my life."

I keep quiet, only nodding. I don't want to challenge her, especially when she's finally opening up to me after all these months. I know she's told everyone about her past except me, which I think may have to do with the fact that I'm Tobias's son, but we're way past that point because Vi should know I'm *not like him.*

Vi loosely dangles the joint from her lips, her eyes reddening from either oncoming tears or the effect of smoking whatever the hell she's smoking. Eventually I decide that the latter sounds more realistic than the former because Vi is made out of steel, and people made out of steel don't cry.

She removes the cigarette from her mouth and says, "I had a little brother. His name was Matthew."

And she tells me everything. How she and Matthew were four years apart yet could relate to each other more than anything. How they were both so loving and warm-hearted toward each other and their parents, even though their living situation wasn't the most enlightening. She says Matthew was the light in her soul that lit up the path in front of her; it made her feel more hopeful, more determined to travel through our ambiguous society. But, as she tells me with not a single crack in her voice or a tear sprinting down her cheek, her time spent with Matthew came to a sharp close the moment the authorities came banging on her door and shot her entire family because they were Chinese, and at that time, they were America's worst enemy.

Vi was in the bathroom, but she was frozen . . . her feet were glued to the ground. Not only did she mourn her brother, but she mourned her parents, for they were killed too. Jessica, who taught her how to love. Isaiah, who was not even Chinese but was killed for *knowing* them, taught her how to persevere. And her brother, who taught her how to have *hope.* But the moment they left the world, all those emotions in her quickly faded away.

She tells me that she left through the gaping window in the bathroom and didn't look back once. As a frightened fourteen-year-old with no sense of fighting skills, she didn't know how to stand up to the Guards. So she did what is every human's instinct when something threatening is in their vicinity: *run.* Vi ran past the villages and was starting to go somewhere before the Guards captured her and threw her in jail. She escaped each time with various concocted plans—each going successfully. But every time she was caught by those Guards again and treated even worse, yet she escaped. Came back with more tattoos. More piercings. More determination. But fewer emotions.

When she finishes, Vi studies the burning and destroyed city ahead of us, not much to cherish about Detroit. All that remains is a gleaming headquarters with a few buildings still, somehow, standing. She drags her bony fingers across the texture of the cigarette in her hand and stuffs it into her mouth again. She lazily glances over at me, strands of her short hair flying onto her dull eyes. "Now you know why I like to smoke. It's the only way I can stop thinking about them. They're the only ones who've given me love."

"Oh, c'mon, don't say that, Vi. Plenty of other people will give you love, if you just let them."

"It's not that damn easy, Jax."

"Yes, it is." I straighten myself. "Have you considered getting in a relationship?"

She scowls at me. "Relationships are a complete waste of my time."

"Enough with the pessimism, Vi. Just think about it for a second. There has to be someone in the entire Detroitian compound that interests you. Is there some guy you have your eye on? Just don't let it be AJ, he's too damn annoying."

She slowly raises her eyebrows, nodding once and saying slowly, "What if I told you I don't like any guy there?"

"Oh, well, that's okay. Is there a guy in Detroit you like?"

"God, what don't you get?" she grumbles. "I don't like any guys."

Her eyes piercing into my soul terrifies the shit out of me. "What do you mean?"

She stares at me suggestively.

I stare at her back.

She stares at me for a couple more seconds before she curses to herself and hisses, "I bat for the other team, you dumbass."

When the meaning of her words settles in my mind, my mouth gapes open as I whisper, "Oh."

"Yeah."

"I didn't know you, uh . . ."

"Yeah."

"Damn," I whisper. "Does anyone else know?"

"Everyone except you."

"What?" I yelp. "How did you tell them before me?"

"I didn't tell them, exactly. They just figured it out on their own because, well, they're not a dumbass like you."

I scowl at her. "Gee, thanks."

She rolls her eyes at me. "Anyway, now you know why it's hard for me to find love. I don't care for it much in the first place, and my options are narrow as hell."

"Well, that's okay, Vi. You'll find someone. I promise."

"I don't know about that, Jax. I don't know if love is gonna be something I'll get one of these days."

At her words, I sigh and scoot closer to her. When I do, she raises her eyebrows at me.

I grin. "If you're worried I'm gonna push you off the building, then you don't need to worry about that. I'm only going to hug you."

Her face immediately falls. "*Hug* me? Why the hell would you wanna do that?"

I frown at her. "To *comfort* you? Isn't that what friends do when they're sad?"

She scoffs. "First of all, I'm not sad. And second of all, you're not my friend."

"Oh, cut the bullshit. We're friends, Vi. You can think whatever the hell you wanna think, but you know I'm right." As she starts to protest, I wrap my arms around her, about to plant my chin on her shoulders, but she suddenly pushes me back by the center of my chest. I fall back on my ass, inches away from the edge. I peer over the ground beneath me, gulp, and give Vi a terrified look. "What the hell was that for? You almost killed me!"

"Because you tried to hug me," she says. "I don't like hugs. Or physical touch in general."

"It was a kind gesture, Vi. I don't care if you like it or not. That doesn't give you the right to almost push me off a *goddamn building.*"

"Whatever." She rolls her eyes at me, not even caring a bit about my almost-death. "Are you happy now that I told you about my life? Will you leave me alone now?"

"Yes, I will." I grin at her.

While we bask in the not-so silent atmosphere, reverberating with distant crackles of fires by the beating heart of Detroit, I clench my jaw and think of my encounters with Veronica lately. It's been almost two weeks since she's been pulling me to the side—at this point, our meetings have grown to two days a week now—and not only me, but she brings in Mallory too. We sit side by side, cornered by her mother who, clearly, is eager for information out of us. Mallory and I have a nonverbal agreement to not reveal anything that can damage the Reformers' overall growth and development, so we continue to stall with static information, and we sometimes even take the risk by making things up. Anything to keep Veronica entertained—however long that may be.

I just don't know how we're going to get ourselves out of this situation. If I brought up the possibility of assassinating Veronica then that would just lead to a shitstorm. I don't know how Mallory would feel about killing her mother, and just because she hates her guts, that doesn't exactly correlate to wanting death for her. There are soldiers standing outside our door, and if they were to hear their beloved Lieutenant shriek in pain in any way, then they would kill us in a heartbeat. That would just cause more of an uproar, and, in conclusion, the situation will get even worse.

So . . . how the hell *do* I get myself out of this mess?

To make matters worse, I feel so incredibly terrible for lying to Blaire. I can tell by her facial expressions sometimes that she's genuinely getting suspicious of my behavior, which, of course she would. I've been making excuses to not sleep with her so she doesn't find out about my altercation with Veronica. I would one-hundred percent tell Blaire *everything* if Veronica hadn't threatened her life. And I'm not daring to risk it because she almost killed her own damn daughter. My heart is ripping apart just at the thought of what sinister things Veronica could possibly do to Blaire.

"Hey, Vi?" I blurt out. I know I can't talk to her about Veronica because *no one* knows or will know about that whole situation, but I can talk to her about Blaire. Hopefully get some insight on our relationship because Vi knows Blaire and I pretty well. I just need *something* to ease my mind.

"What?" she grumbles to me.

"Can I talk to you about something?"

"No."

"What? Why?"

"Because I came up here to smoke. Not hear jibber jabber."

"This'll only last for five minutes. I promise."

"Like your talkative ass would ever shut up in five minutes."

"I mean it, Vi. Seriously."

She clenches her jaw, narrows her eyes at me, and sighs what seems like one long minute later. "God, fine. *Five minutes only.* Got it?"

"Yes." I take a deep breath in and face her, my limbs aching with every movement. "So . . . I need relationship advice."

An amused smile takes up over her face, startling me because she only smiles five times a year, as it seems. "From me?"

"Yes."

"You need relationship advice . . . from me?" She chuckles. "You have Mallory, Jeremiah, or—hell—even *Ren* to give you relationship advice, and from all those people . . . you're choosing me? Are you all right in the head?"

"Yes, I'm just fine," I hiss. "I'm asking you because you're the only person awake and closest to me. Jesus."

"Okay, that's what I thought."

"Anyway . . ." I sigh. "I just need your input on something." She silently gestures for me to carry on, impatience drawn on her features. "So, obviously Blaire and I have been dating for a while now. Things are getting pretty serious, and we're attached by the hip. But, uh . . . at the same time, battles are going on. We're constantly training, there are surprise attacks from the ERUSA every now and then, and our lives are basically getting busier and more stressful. And with all this going on, I just can't help but wonder . . . are Blaire and I gonna be able to survive this while being together? It's just so difficult to prioritize our relationship while the world is falling apart at the seams, and I don't want *us* to be thrown to the wolves the moment life gets worse. I want to be with her forever, I really do. But I don't want the things beyond my control to affect our relationship. That's all.

"So, I was just wondering . . . do *you* think we'll make it through? Me and her? I just want an outsider's perspective because, well, you see more than I do. Just give me whatever you got. Anything to ease my mind."

I expect Vi to make fun of me, or, even worse, chastise me for thinking so much over a damn relationship. However, she doesn't do any of those things; instead, she nods once, clicks her tongue, and looks over at me, her eyes gleaming against the gleaming moonlight. "When I heard about you guys kissing in D.C. and barely interacting with each other in Detroit . . . a small part of me was pissed. I knew you guys couldn't keep your hands off each other let alone not go a single day without talking to the other person, so it infuriated me that you and her were being distant. Why make things more complicated than they need to be? If you both had just confronted your feelings on the spot, then your relationship would've been easier. It would've been seven months of a stress-free relationship without full-blown battles going on. But what's done is done, and we cannot erase the past.

"Now, I'm not a relationship expert, but I will say this . . . no matter how rough it gets, don't let go of her." Her words are almost slurred now, dragging out in long syllables as she plays with the joint in her hands. "I know Veronica's acting like a bitch and there's a whole ass shitstorm goin' on, but that shouldn't stop you guys from being together. Love truly is rare these days, and you shouldn't avoid it. You should embrace it because, well, you're privileged, Jax. You're privileged to have someone by your side that loves you. *Embrace* it."

My vision goes hazy and my cheeks redden.

Love.

I have been prancing around that word for so long because last time a person claimed to love me, it was coated in fakeness. It was designed to stab through my heart, just like he had stabbed through my cheek and literally scarred me forever. I've been avoiding love since because it is deceivingly beautiful. Mesmerizing on the outside, nothing but world-shattering pain on the inside.

But the way Vi describes it . . . it beguiles me, especially in regards to Blaire. I definitely like her, but when I think about loving her, it's a vast universe with just me, and just her, and no one else. And I want that feeling—so damn bad.

"Are you saying we love each other?" I stammer out.

"Yes," she says immediately. "Don't even argue with me on this one. She loves you. You love her. I don't give a damn if you're barely a month into the relationship. Labels don't define shit when it comes to feelings. Labels are just meant to restrict you, just meant to make you believe in a false notion that love has to do with how well you know someone. Well, that's wrong because love isn't that.

"What I know from the love I was given by my family is that love is the connection you feel with the other person. It's as if their soul fits with yours, like puzzle pieces. The moment you click, you know it's love. An alarm goes off in your mind, telling you that this person is your other half, and there's no time to waste. Love is a fleeting moment, and it should never be pushed to the side. And I'm tellin' you, I see that with you and Blaire. The connection you guys share . . . well, it almost startles me. Honestly, it makes me jealous too. You're so unbelievably privileged because you have someone you can share a connection with. That's why I don't want you to let go of her. Make the most that you can in times like these because I learned that the hard way. Oh, I really did. So, admit that you love her, right now, and admit that this is what you want, regardless of the circumstances."

I don't know what to be more surprised by: Vi's surprisingly great relationship advice, or the groundbreaking emotions surging past my soul and unleashing into my heart. She is right. I'm way too in my head about this situation, and I need to accept it as it is. I need to stay with her and enjoy our moments together, however long they may last. As much as we want to be together forever with our loved ones, it is unfortunately not possible. We are mortal. We should enjoy as much as we can, before death comes knocking at our door. That's why I want to admire Blaire like she's the rarest diamond and study all her intricacies, all her passions, all her sorrows, and all her motives.

It's quite obvious I want her more than anything, so I'm not letting her go. Even if the entire world is falling apart.

The word *love* also tickles my lips, seducing me to my surrender. As much as I don't want to admit it, just for my sake, I do want to love. I want to offer my heart to a woman who is my other half and gets me more than myself—and that woman is Blaire. She understands me, and I understand her, and because of that, our connection is a burning and bright oasis oozing with passion. I feel more connected to her than to the roots of this earth because, well, she does complete me, and like Vi said, she's the other puzzle piece.

I don't know why I didn't realize this sooner.

It doesn't matter if we were together for only three weeks, three days, or three seconds. Love does *not* correlate with time. It correlates with that connection, and because of that, I do have love to share. I have plenty to give to Blaire.

My lips part open slowly, and a small breath of seemingly relief escapes out of me. "I love Blaire, and this is what I want. Regardless of the circumstances."

33

AUROUS

BLAIRE

IT IS THE TWENTY-SECOND of July, and training has never been as intense as it is now. We, as in the Subversives, have been getting to the compound at 6 a.m. lately, and we get back home sometimes at 10 p.m. That is with the strict curfew Veronica has placed for a month now, alongside the other strict rules in place, which are difficult to maneuver past, but somehow, we do. Life just has been hard lately, each moment increasing with difficulties. I'm praying for the day we are liberated from Veronica's wrath, and we can live in peace again.

The treadmill slows to a stop as my arms cling onto the handlebars, sweat clinging to my skin. I grab the water bottle stuffed into the holder, unscrew the cap, and dump the water into my mouth, shaking it until everything is emptied. In the several weeks I've been training, I've noticed a change to my body and my stamina in its entirety too, even with this damn injury, which, surprisingly, is healing pretty well. Before I could barely run two miles without wheezing and becoming out of breath, and now I can go ten miles without doing that—which I just now accomplished.

The others, too, have improved with their training. Jeremiah and Vi have had the least improvement because, well, they've always been good at the physical aspects of training, but I've seen significant changes in Mal and Jax. Mal's thigh injury has improved to the point where she doesn't even need the bandaging anymore; thus, she can now partake in the heavy training with us. And Jax honed down on his skills with legitimate combatting, which he was at an advantage with because he's incredibly strong to begin with.

I exit the treadmill, getting a hold of my breathing as I see AJ emerging from the entrance doors. His golden eyes scan the gym, and they just so happen to land on me. I have no choice but to awkwardly wave him over, as he grins and makes his way to me.

"Intense workout session, I'm assuming?" he says with a smile on his face.

"Very," I gasp out. "Where are the others?"

"They're all in the break room, taking a breather. You wanna join them?"

"No, I'm good."

He chuckles. "Did you get into a fight with them?"

"No." I smile. "Just want some time to myself, that's all."

AJ raises his hands in defense. "No worries. I get that." We walk past the treadmill and by the weights, where AJ sets himself up. His jet-black hair frames his strong features as he grabs a dumbbell and grunts as he starts his reps. "How have you been doing lately?" he asks me. "Is your injury healing now?"

"It is, actually. I might get the bandaging removed sometime this week."

"That's great to hear." Five seconds of silence pass by before he speaks again. "You know what, Blaire? I'm very proud of you."

I cock my head at him. "Why is that?"

He drops his dumbbell on the rack after his reps finish, and he grabs another set. "Because, since the time I first met you, you've improved a lot. You had no idea what you were doing before, and several weeks have passed by, and you're an absolute *beast.* I think Commander Thatcher might put you on the frontlines now."

"You're just saying that," I mutter, oddly red now.

"It's true," he emphasizes. "You're one of the most determined people I know. Seriously."

"Thanks. That means a lot to me, AJ. And I've gotta say, you're pretty determined too. How did you even learn to fight like that?"

He grins, his eyes softening. "Years and years of training here. Not to mention that I had no choice but to train."

"What do you mean by that?"

"My life was difficult back then," he says with a low tone. "Annie and I were orphans, going in and out of foster homes repeatedly. During that time, our love for the military grew because there was no one to protect us, so we wanted to protect others so they wouldn't feel as vulnerable as we felt."

"Oh, gosh," I murmur. "I'm so sorry."

He kindly waves me off. "Don't be. There are just some aspects of my life I can't control. You know what I mean?"

"Yeah, I unfortunately do." I cock my head at him, taking a deep breath in. "Were you guys at least treated well in your foster homes?"

"Sometimes, yeah. Some were good, some were not. I don't think Annie and I really cared about that, though, because all we wanted was a roof above our heads. Love, warmth, and a caring family was the least of our worries because we just wanted to survive a life without our parents." He clenches his jaw, his sorrowful eyes never leaving mine. "They were killed in a car crash when Annie and I were five-year-olds . . . so we really didn't get to spend much time with them."

"Oh, my gosh," I whisper, going up to him and placing a consoling hand on his shoulder. "AJ, I'm so sorry."

"Again, there's no need to be sorry." He gives me a sad smile. "I only spent five years with them, which honestly isn't enough time to get to know your parents. The only way I can only remember them is through the motivational and inspirational things they used to tell us before they passed away. So, whenever Annie or I feel down, we remind each other of what our parents used to say to keep us going." Suddenly, he frowns. "I just wish I got to spend more time with them. That's all."

Hearing this makes me really grateful for my parents being alive and well. "I bet they would be really proud of you and Annie," I say.

He smiles at me again. "Thanks, Blaire."

We remain there in silence, our breathing synchronized. I look into his sad golden eyes, almost a gleaming yellow. They feel and look like bright rays of sun, so endearing and so calm. I truly feel nothing but sorrow for AJ. He and Annie deserve parents who look after them, who inspire and motivate them to this day.

AJ clears his throat, giving me a crooked smile. "I'm sure Jax will be really happy to see this."

I can't help but laugh. "He just gets really overprotective sometimes. That's all."

"I don't blame him. He has a really beautiful girlfriend."

There is no hint of humor or even lightheartedness in his words; instead, his expression is as serious as ever, and his lips are slightly parted as he looks down at me, his thick eyelashes framing his strong features. He takes one step toward me, brings his hand out and places it on my cheek.

Immediately, I blurt out, "AJ, don't—"

"I know," he whispers. "I know you have a boyfriend, and I know you guys both like each other a lot. I know I'm gonna have to see you guys together and deal with it because, well, I know I have zero chances. But that's okay. I'll try to get over you, but I just . . . I just want to enjoy the alone time I have with you." He sighs. "Please?"

My throat is parched, my breathing stuck in my throat, and I stammer, "Okay. That's fine."

"Thank you." He pauses. "I'm sorry for putting you in this position. I'm sure no one would be happy to hear that some random guy is fawning over them while they're in a whole ass relationship."

"AJ, please don't say sorry. If anything, I should be."

"Why are *you* sorry? I'm the one who likes you."

"But I'm hurting you. And I hate hurting people."

"This is not your fault, though," he says. "This is all on me. I should've just controlled my feelings, but instead they . . . they went haywire."

I open my mouth up to speak but am immediately interrupted by a distant screeching noise taking over the speakers.

"Good afternoon, Detroitian soldiers." I recognize that voice to be Commander Thatcher's. "I hope everyone's training is going well and that you have visited the memorial for our fallen soldiers during the past two battles we've had against the ERUSA. The main reason for this announcement, though, is to inform you that we will be lining up our troops in Detroit where our enemy has been for the past month. Enough citizens have been killed there, and we must set our foot down now.

"As expected, you must remain on the defensive side and refrain from shooting at the soldiers. We do not want to give reasons for Veronica Reaves to attack us any further; we want to end our rift with them on as much of an amicable note as we can. Thank you."

34

ENDEARMENT

JAX

THE MOON GLEAMS ABOVE us, puffy white clouds cascading against the night. Crickets chirp in the background amongst the still, stuffy air, and I walk hand-in-hand with Blaire, trekking against the fissured roads that lead to our safety home. I know Veronica can see every movement we're making, but she can't hear what comes out of my mouth next.

"I hate Veronica," I murmur to Blaire.

She looks over at me, a frown drawn on her lips. "Me too. We could've been enjoying our summer right now, but instead just enjoying in *general* can possibly get us killed."

"I just want to kill her in plain sight," I whisper immediately after she finishes her sentence. "She deserves to get stabbed five million times in a row."

"Hey, uh, Jax?" she whispers to me.

"Yeah?"

"I know you're upset with her, but you may want to ease the grip a little."

"Oh," I murmur, easing my grip on her. "I'm sorry, beautiful."

"It's okay." She leans on my bicep as we walk over to the home. "I find it attractive when you get all mad like that anyway."

I turn my head to her with a lopsided grin plastered on my face. "Yeah?"

She nods, smirking.

"Well, looks like I'll just get mad more often now."

She chuckles. I join too.

Blaire and I just came back from a brisk walk, and now we're on our way to our rooms, meaning to sleep, but our energy is still vibrant. No matter how drained we are, our energy somehow remains unusually high when we're with each other.

We enter the foyer and stop by my door. She releases a tiny breath, inches away from me. "You seem really tired lately. Are you okay?"

"Am I ever okay?" I give her a sad smile.

She playfully punches my shoulder. "Don't say that. You're getting better with your nightmares, right?"

"Kinda, but they still show up randomly, and when they show up . . . they're really traumatizing."

Blaire sighs ruefully, gently placing her hand on my naked bicep and squeezing it. I love it when she does that. "Do you want me to sleep with you? Em and Nico are probably passed out right now, so I can assure you they won't even notice my absence. I just want to be with you, Jax. I want to comfort you in your darkest moments."

I press my lips together, feeling my limbs physically melting at her endearing green eyes. Because of her, green has become my favorite color.

How can I ever say no to her? Veronica most likely won't recruit me at the headquarters tonight because she called me yesterday for yet another awkward session. What could she possibly want from me now? I might as well spend this time alone with Blaire, especially since she wants it too.

"I would love that," I whisper.

She grins, intertwining our hands together and gesturing for me to open the door. Once I do, we walk inside, greeted by darkness. I close the door shut slightly, my heart beating so hard in my chest as I face her. She looks so beautiful even in darkness, even when light can't display her mesmerizing beauty. Her short dark hair I desire to run my fingers through. Those lips of her I can't get enough of. That soft olive-colored skin I feel at every hesitant gesture. And that smile that weakens my knees, weakens my bones. If I was an artist, I would paint that smile of hers and keep it all to myself.

Ever since I realized I love her, she's been in my mind even when I'm not aware of it. Just seeing her in front of me is enough to squeeze out all the air from my lungs. How can someone ever have this much power over me? But then again, this is *Blaire Cohen*. The most gorgeous woman to ever walk this earth.

Goddammit. I need to tell her that I love her. I've held this in for a couple of days already, and I'm afraid if I hold it in any longer then I *will* explode.

She slowly blinks up at me. "What happened?"

I release a shaky breath, taking one step toward her. "Nothing. I just . . . I want to tell you something."

"Okay," she murmurs, looking up at me with curious and hypnotizing forest-like eyes.

Gradually, I take one, two, three steps toward her, and then one more until we are chest-to-chest. I feel our hearts ramming into each other like vehicle collisions, each impact thrusting through my bones. My fingers have a mind of their own as they grasp the peridot stone still resting idly against the top of her chest. She *still* has not taken it off to this day.

"Most couples have had happy encounters with each other," I start off, "but me and you? Oh, we hated each other's guts at first. We wanted to rip each other's heads off because, well, we simply came from different backgrounds. You despised anyone who was Rich, and I was blinded by my father and listened to whatever he told me to do. Nobody would've guessed that it would be *us,* out of all the other people in the world, that would end up together. Funny how life works, right?

"What's also funny is that . . . no matter how much I hated you in the beginning, I still thought you were the most beautiful girl I've ever seen. And I'm being completely honest when I say that, even when I knew you as Marie Davis, I thought you were beautiful. You've had me mesmerized by your looks since then, Blaire. That's how much power you have over me. Even when I didn't even know who you were and even when I despised you because you despised *me,* I *still* thought you were beautiful."

I take a shaky breath in. "I slowly fell for you in D.C., and I was purely amazed when we kissed the day we left from there. It was all I could think about during that train ride. But the moment we reached there . . . it was as if everything changed and we were strangers again. I don't know what it was, but we just acknowledged each other normally, as if we didn't have our first kiss not too long ago. I get that we were busy adjusting to the Detroitian lifestyle and helping the refugees, but we just didn't have time for each other. It was also just my luck that I fell for you even harder in those seven months we barely acknowledged each other.

"But then, the Summer Solstice Festival came, and everything changed. I finally had the courage to confess my feelings and ask you to be mine, but then the ERUSA took over. Thank God we are so attracted to each other that even a full-blown mini-war wouldn't tear us apart," I whisper, chuckling as I study her lips pushed into a deep smile. "Yet in those moments that the world constantly pushed and pulled at us, we *still* persevered. And it was just inevitable that my feelings would strengthen so much for you that I . . . I found love for you."

Her lips part open as a shaky gasp leaves her mouth, but I

keep on speaking. I need to keep on speaking. "You know I struggled to love my father so much because, well, he didn't treat me right. He gave me a goddamn scar when I was a teenager because I refused to go to a rally of his. Obviously I'm really hesitant now to love someone, or even be that vulnerable with anyone. I felt the same in the beginning of this relationship too, if I'm being honest. I forced myself to not fall in love with you because I didn't want to get hurt again. Of course you're not my father and you wouldn't hurt me, but I still was protective of myself. I didn't want to wound my heart any further.

"I was so incredibly wrong, though, because I've fallen so hard for you it physically *hurts*. I never loved a person this much, Blaire. I think of nothing but you when the word *love* comes through my mind. When I imagine my future, I imagine it with you and nobody else. I know this is a lot to dump on you, so I understand if you're slightly overwhelmed. I would be too. I just . . . I had to tell you this. I had to tell you that I love you. I love you so much that I want to design a world where it is just you and me and no one else. Everyone can think I'm crazy, but I couldn't care less. My love for you is just too great to explain in words, Blaire. I love you. I love you more than the size of this earth, this universe, and anything else bigger than that. And that's a lot of love right there."

When I finish speaking, I am breathless, my chest erratically rising in and out. My eyes scan her features, silently begging for her to say *something*. Please say something.

She gnaws at her bottom lip, her expression truly unreadable. I feel like three years go by until Blaire opens her mouth to speak, her eyes never leaving mine. Suddenly, to my surprise, her mouth curls into a lopsided grin. "Your ego."

I frown at her. "What?"

"You said you love me more than anything else bigger than the universe. I think that could be your ego."

I scoff, playfully rolling my eyes at her. "Ha ha. Very funny."

She laughs, grabbing ahold of my shirt and bringing every-thing but our lips together. Her expression is serious now, wedged beneath intricate layers of emotions. Her eyes are animated too, almost gleaming with tears. As I'm about to beg her not to cry, she whispers almost inaudibly, "I love you too, Jax. I've loved you for a while actually, but I never came to terms with it until you just now confessed. I don't know how to explain it, but as you revealed your love, a light flickered inside of me, and I've never felt so eager to tell you."

I suddenly feel the urge to cry tears of joy. "Seriously?"

She nods furiously. "Seriously."

I grin ear-to-ear, my cheeks almost starting to hurt. "You don't understand, Blaire. I'm so happy to hear that. I'm so happy to hear you love me too."

"Of course I do," she urges. "You make me feel like no one else, Jax."

Something unleashes in my chest. An unexplainable feeling. "What do I make you feel?"

She brings her lips even closer to mine, but they're *still* not touching. I don't think I can handle this anymore. "You make me feel everything," she whispers with a dangerous edge to her tone. "Everything that no normal girl would feel."

I bring my hand to her cheek, pressing our lips slightly together, but still not kissing. "Show me what you feel, Blaire. Right here and right now."

Immediately, she clashes her lips to mine, and I kiss her back just as hard, an unattainable urgency clawing at my heart. I hold onto the underside of her jaw, my fingers grasping at the nape of her neck as she brings her hands to my back, clawing at my thin cotton shirt. I want her to rip it off me. *All of it.* I don't want these cotton boundaries between us.

We slowly make our way to my bedroom, our lips never leaving one another's. We crash into sofas, walls, doors, some-times injuring ourselves too, but we don't care. I gnaw at her bottom lip, tugging at it softly as she moans into my mouth. Something awakens in my lower body—a feeling I've been desiring for the longest of time. My feet lead her to the edge of the bed, and we both fall on the mattress, her straddling me. I kiss her neck, marking my territory as my fingers crawl underneath her shirt, feeling her soft skin. Her fingers grasp my neck as she moans into my ear, a sound I want to hear over and over again. I know she wants her shirt off her too. I know she wants zero boundaries between us too. I want her; she wants me. Nothing can beat the desire a boy and a girl have for each other —especially pent-up desire.

As I tease my fingers at the hem of her shirt, she desperately and breathlessly whispers into my ear, "Just take it off me already."

I drag my lips up and across her neck until they meet her ear. "Are you sure?" I rasp out.

"Yes," she begs. *"Yes."*

Immediately, I rip the shirt off her, and she tugs at mine, which flies over my head too. Our lips meet each other again in such desperation that it almost astounds me. My ears burn at her breaths escaping into my mouth, lips molding and melting like a cataclystic alchemy, a scientific wonder. She claws at my back, her nails digging into my skin—which I love. I want her to scratch at my back even *more.* We release from each other soon enough, just to catch a breather. Both of our upper bodies are completely exposed, and I study her body with such interest. She is a book I want to read front to back and devour every word inscribed onto her pages.

From my peripheral vision, I notice her cheeks are flushed red. I immediately look up at her, and I mean every word that comes out of my mouth when I say, "I don't think the word *beautiful* can describe you anymore because you're too other-worldly for that."

She grins at me, whispering into my mouth that she loves me

and lazily kisses me again, and again, and again—all over my lips and sporadically over my scar.

I grab ahold of her naked and warm back and bring her onto the bed, the back of her head hitting the pillow. Slowly, we tug the remaining clothes off us until there is nothing left. We are vulnerable, nothing can be hidden, everything is exposed to us.

Everything.

I lean over her, pressing my body over hers and kissing every inch of her face. Then I kiss her lips, her neck, her collarbone, and the more I go down, the more her body rises and falls.

Her body beneath mine feels so ethereal. Flawless.

I hover over her, our faces and bodies so close that I feel her soul emerging into mine. This is the woman I love, the woman I've always loved but never dared to come to terms with. I've learned, though, that I'm not going to run away from my feelings. I'm going to embrace them, cherish them, and embrace and cherish the woman I have in front of me—the woman I'm so unbelievably lucky to call mine. To hold her in my arms and let her know that, no matter what's going on in this world and no matter how much limited time we have, we will still make it. I'll make sure of it.

I press a soft kiss on her forehead, on her nose, on her top lip, and then her bottom.

And I show her just how much I love her.

35

RECOLLECTION

BLAIRE

A SOFT KISS LANDS on my shoulder. "Good morning, beautiful," a raspy voice says behind me, wrapping his arm around my waist. My skin warms as I look down at his strong hand grasping my stomach, remembering that same strong hand shamelessly exploring my body last night.

Jax turns me around so we are face-to-face, for which I shyly inch the comforter up over my mouth. He raises his eyebrows at me, asking me with his soothing gray eyes what the matter is.

"Morning breath," I mutter.

"Ah." He chuckles, kissing my forehead. "You're worried about morning breath after everything we did last night?"

"Uh . . . yes."

He grins bashfully, dimples creasing his cheek. "You don't have to be shy with me, but if you're really worried about morning breath, then we can go brush right now."

"Yeah, I'm more than willing to do that."

Jax laughs as he collides his hand with mine, intertwining our fingers together. He pulls me up and lugs me behind him, the comforter clinging onto me until I get up off the bed. Now we are completely exposed, and it takes all of my might to not stare at Jax's finely built physique and strong legs. His *extremely* strong legs. I already did enough of that last night.

When we reach the bathroom, we throw on our clothes from last night and begin to brush, hip-to-hip, and I lean on his arm, completely enamored by him. His dark hair is lazily draped over him, random disheveled strands inching down his forehead. His sizzling gray eyes are centered on me in the mirror, and my skin burns from his sight on me. I wouldn't mind throwing myself on him—right here and right now—but it is almost 6 a.m., and we're going to have to leave soon. Until then, I'm going to enjoy the alone time I have with Jax before we are thrown into the real world again. Amongst the chaos occurring in the real world, it's nice to escape it all with someone you trust. With someone you've shared a good amount of your emotional and physical self.

Once we finish brushing, he escorts me to the living room as I prepare to go to my room. Before I can go though, he kisses me deeply, freezing my limbs. He releases after another kiss on my bottom lip. "I hate to see you go," he whispers.

"Me too." I sigh. "But I have to leave. My parents are gonna wake up soon, and it's gonna be really awkward to explain to them why I was in your room the entire night."

"You're right." He winces, but then he smiles down at me. "I'm just glad we got to spend some time together at least. This makes me believe in us—that we will be able to make it even with everything going on."

We stand there in silence as a beam of light slowly trickles into the room. His warm-toned skin glows, his pupils swarming with emotions I want to delve myself in. I don't think I've ever felt this attached to a person before.

He wraps his arms around me without a warning, and my head lands on his hard chest, feeling his heart beating wildly against his flesh. From the first day he made me feel his heart-beat, it's still beating fast. At this point, I start to think it's beating even faster too.

Although I don't know whether it's beating because of happiness . . . or fear.

Jeremiah, Mal, Vi, Jax, and I gather in the breakroom. It wasn't a profound decision to all gather here simultaneously, but rather an unspoken agreement. Spending a good portion of my day with strangers is exhausting, and sometimes it is imperative to reconvene with familiar faces again. Especially after undergoing numerous surprise attacks from the ERUSA.

We sit around the long oval table that's in the center of the room. Jax is, of course, beside me and rubbing the inside of my thigh beneath the table. We have been inseparable ever since this morning, and I can't even imagine spending the entirety of my day with anyone else. He brings me peace and comfort, and vice versa. And that is all someone needs when the world is quite literally falling apart.

"I feel like she's gonna attack again," Vi says. "I don't know, I just *feel* it."

"Oh, let's not manifest it for ourselves now," Jeremiah hisses at her.

"I'm serious, though. The last time she and her troops attacked us was during the battle on the field. It's been weirdly quiet lately. I know something is on the way."

"Well, if she *does* attack," Jax says, "then we're blaming this on you."

Vi rolls her eyes, flipping him off in the process.

"To some extent," Mal blurts out, "Vi is right. My mom will attack soon. She is the type of woman to gather all her kings, queens, and aces and use them all at once instead of attacking us here and there. The only reason she did attack us before is because her power was threatened. But we have been living sort of peacefully for a while, so it's inevitable she's going to unleash everything before we know it. She's my mom"—she pauses—"I know her more than I need or want to."

"Veronica does seem like the kind of woman to respond like that," I say, "so we need to be prepared no matter what."

"Well, that's what we've been doing for the past month," Vi hisses. "We've been training every single day from the crack of dawn to dusk. Hell, if Jeremiah himself says every single day that he's tired, then that's when you know we've been tiring ourselves out. I say we don't even give her the possibility or time to attack and we attack first."

"Why don't you try saying that to Commander Thatcher instead?" Jax asks sarcastically. "I'm sure she'd be thrilled to hear you want to attack them first because, clearly, she's still clinging onto the defensive approach."

"God, I don't know why she's being so dead set about that still," Vi grumbles.

"It's because she doesn't want us to seem like the bad people," Jeremiah says. "So we don't have blood on our hands."

"Well, that's damn idiotic because that's just an easy way to get wiped out by the ERUSA. I swear, if I was Commander instead, then we would be in a much better place right now."

"Vi, keep it down," Mal urges her. "I'm pretty sure she can hear everything you're saying from the speakers and cameras implanted around here."

"Do I look like I care, Mallory?" Vi sounds her name out dryly. "I'll go up to her right now and say that right to her face. I really don't give a shit."

Jax snorts. "She would kill you in a heartbeat."

"No, she wouldn't." Vi raises her eyebrows at him. "Since she apparently doesn't want 'blood on her hands'."

"Look, Vi," Jeremiah starts off, "how about this? We'll wait for a week and see what defensive strategies she has set up. If they don't go well, we will voice our opinions *with you* and tell her that we need to be on the offensive too so our numbers don't deteriorate."

"I'm not waiting a whole ass week. Do you have any idea how much our forces will weaken by then? Okay, let's say Veronica attacks us again, right?" She stands up from her seat and looks at us with widened eyes. "Let's say that, this time, she drives her forces into the compound and starts shooting at us like madmen. Do you really think only defending ourselves is really going to do much? There's no point in having the most technologically advanced weapons in the nation if we're just not gonna use them in the end. We are gonna get *slaughtered* if we only defend, guys. What don't you get?"

"I get what you're saying," Jeremiah says, running his fingers through his scruffy beard. "I really do. But do you not understand that Commander Thatcher will not listen to a single word you or anyone else will say until she is physically proven wrong? That's why I'm telling you to wait and be patient."

"Yeah." Vi rolls her eyes. "Let's just wait and be patient and get annihilated in the process. That sounds pretty great, right?"

"Oh, don't use that attitude with me—"

"I'll use whatever attitude I wanna use—"

"Guys!" Mal yelps, frustration drawn on her features. "Now is not the time to argue! This is a *break* room, not a *stress* room. Let's just relax, pull ourselves together, and carry on with this conversation like adults. Okay?"

Vi sits back down, grumbling to herself and murmuring, "He started it."

Jeremiah shoots her an annoyed look.

Moments later, Mal turns to me and says, "Has Commander Thatcher talked to you about her strategies and line up for the time being? She hasn't announced anything publicly to us yet, but maybe she's told you something because you guys have been meeting up in private lately."

Jax turns to me with his eyebrows pushed together as I let out a defeated sigh. "No, she hasn't talked to me about that at all."

"Then what the hell does she even talk to you about every single damn day?" Vi huffs out.

I shrug. "Just how my day's going. That's all."

"Well, if that's the case then why doesn't she meet with everyone in private then?"

"Vi, lay off her," Jax hisses.

"And why are you jumping to her rescue? Is there something you know that we don't?"

"She just tells me private things I cannot tell anyone else," I grit out.

"Are you teaming up with her? Are you secretly agreeing with her defensive tactics?"

"I'm not. We just have completely different conversations—that's all. Now can we please talk about something else?"

She grumbles, takes a deep breath in, and narrows her eyes at me, which they seem to say to me, *I'm on to you.*

We sit in silence, aside from the distant chatter outside of the break room door. Jax continues to rub the inside of my thigh and a bit more vehemently now that Vi came onto me about Heidi and I meeting more these days. We were afraid people would be suspicious about our daily meetings, which are more like hangouts really, and we're not secretly teaming up against the others. Instead, Heidi tells me stories about her and my mama—how they did practically everything together. I don't ever get tired of her stories because it gives me a better understanding and insight of my mother, and I see a side of her I've never seen before. Like I never knew before she led that one protest with Heidi and my papa. I also never knew they used to sneak out past government curfew and go down to the garden nearby and stare at the beautiful plants and other shrubberies. Honestly, I *yearn* for the moment Heidi calls me down to her office where we engage in daily conversations about the dynamic duo: Heidi Thatcher and Marianna Gonzalez.

The only person who knows about our "meetings" to this day is Jax, who's kept his word to keep quiet about it since then. I'd say the trust between us is pretty astronomical, and I know that if something came up I would tell him in a heartbeat. I hope he feels the same way for me, too.

"Now that I think about it," Mal blurts out, "this is probably the first time in a while us Subversives gathered alone."

"But Nicolas is not here, and he's a Subversive," Jeremiah says.

"I know, but I meant the Subversives that handled D.C. *without* Nicolas. That alone was the most terrifying thing I've ever been through."

"I agree with Mal," Vi says. "Honestly, I still get nightmares about that whole day when Dylan revealed himself to be Zachary. I never felt so betrayed in my entire life."

"Same," I breathe out. "It terrifies me to think that we had a traitor living among us the entire time and we had no idea."

"I hate to say it, but that asshole really played his role well." Jeremiah frowns.

We nod in agreement, and it is only a few seconds later that Vi says, "I don't know if it's just me, but I feel like both Zachary and Tobias have never really left. I feel like they're roaming around us still, even though we killed them."

Besides me, Jax whispers something to himself that I can't quite understand.

"God, I just feel so bad for you guys sometimes," Jeremiah says to Jax and Mal.

"Why?" she asks.

"Because, well, Jax's father was the sole reason D.C. was in shambles and completely divided, and Mallory's mother is now vowing revenge on those who she believes are the 'reason' for the Rich's downfall. That must be an extremely terrible thing to live with every single day."

"It is," Jax and Mal say at the same time, and they both share embarrassed looks. Her cheeks especially flush deeply, and she shies her eyes away from him.

"Anyway," Vi says, "is our conversation finished here? I want to hit my max today."

As she gets up to leave, Jeremiah stops her in her tracks by saying, "Whoa, wait! Where do you think you're going?"

She frowns at him. "Didn't I just say I want to hit my max?"

"You can do that after I announce a certain something to the others . . ."

Vi slowly takes a deep breath in and hisses to him, "Oh, *hell* no. Don't you dare say a single word about that."

"About what?" Jax asks.

"Nothing. There's absolutely *nothing* going on."

"It's her birthday today." Jeremiah grins at her.

"What?" Both Jax, Mal, and I say at the same time. How could I ever forget Vi's birthday? I was the one who pried it out of her that one night we were on watch in the forest.

"Jesus Christ, it's really not that big of a deal," she murmurs.

"Uh, yeah, it is!" Mal yelps. "You're turning twenty-three on the twenty-third. I'd say that calls for a celebration."

"Um, *no* celebration will be going on. I would much rather spend today hitting my max. So, if you would let me go and do that, then I would really appreciate it—"

"Where do you think you're going?" Jax's voice makes Vi stop in her tracks again. "We're not gonna let you spend your birthday alone. And why did you never remind us of your birthday?"

"Because I hate birthdays."

"Why?"

"They are just a constant reminder that I'm aging at this very moment and I am slowly getting closer and closer to my inevitable death."

"God, you're so pessimistic," Jax grumbles.

"I'm not pessimistic, I'm *realistic*," she emphasizes as she makes her way to the door. "Now, if you would excuse me, I'm gonna hit my *damn max* already while you guys *don't* prepare any celebrations or surprises for me. Got it?"

"Got it," we say simultaneously.

"Good." She nods once and closes the door behind her.

Ten seconds pass by until Jax blurts out, "Let's ask Annie if they have a cake lying around."

Suddenly, we all burst into laughter, and for just this small moment, there are no worries on my mind.

36

SOLICITUDE

JAX

"WE WILL DRIVE OUR forces into Detroit next week," Commander Thatcher says once she has gathered us all into the commonplace. "Enough training has been done, and I feel as if we are more than ready to defend ourselves against the ERUSA. In the time being, though, I would like to work on lining our forces based on your ability to defend when necessary."

From the balcony she stands upon, she gestures to AJ, or her rather annoying right-hand man. He ambles to her as she says, "Iyer over here will be calling the defense line ups that we have conjured. Please stand accordingly as he announces your name."

My grip on Blaire's hand tightens as AJ starts to read off the paper in his hands. She's hip-to-hip with me, as we have been since yesterday when we . . . got a little *intimate*, I'd say. The sweet memories of that night roll into my mind and diminish the numerous worries unraveling through me—such as Veronica still not initiating a meeting with me and me still getting nightmares about my father. Granted I did not have a nightmare about him yesterday, so I'm not too worried about that lately, but Veronica? Normally she would communicate with me, but our lack of meetings worries me because I'm afraid she has something worse up her sleeve. And now that Mallory is aware of her devious plans too, I'm even *more* afraid.

" . . . We have the Subversives listed for our first line-up. Please make your way to the front if your name is Nicolas Cohen, Blaire Cohen, Vienna Powers, Jeremiah Morgan, Jax Remington, and Mallory Reaves."

It's already convenient enough that we're together anyway, as we share confused looks with each other. We are ushered over to the front as Annie rearranges us. Vi is in the center with Jeremiah next to her, Nicolas on the other side, me next to Jeremiah, Blaire next to Nicolas, and Mallory next to me. It's pretty evident Commander Thatcher pre-arranged us by our ability to fight and defend, and it's also pretty evident she's putting the Subversives in the front because, well, we're their biggest advocate.

Once the rest of the soldiers line-up behind us—all 1,089 soldiers filling up the commonplace to the brim—Commander Thatcher stands in front of Vi, who looks at her dead in the eye. We celebrated her birthday yesterday, which she wasn't so thrilled by because she did explicitly state that she didn't want a celebration, but I couldn't help but feel incredibly indebted to her because she's been through a lot in twenty-three years. I couldn't imagine having such a wonderful and caring family and being stripped of them in a heartbeat because they were a certain race. It both disgusts and saddens me, and I really hope Vi realizes one day that she has people, no matter if we're not blood-related. Family is not defined by blood; it's instead defined by trust and companionship.

I learned that the hard way.

"Since your day here has almost ended, you may quickly wrap up your training and prepare to leave. But I must remind you that you have a duty here, which is to serve and protect this city. We only encompass Detroit, but ERUSA is of D.C. and several other cities that have survived the Dark Ages. If their forces were to combine further, then we *will* be annihilated. If we want to avoid that, we must defend our land to our last breath. Remember, we only have guns if we need to use them, not *want* to use them. When time calls, we will fire back. As of now, though, we must take the higher road and avoid violence because the more blood involved, the higher the chance we'll have more wars. In order to break this chain, we must think maturely about this."

I notice Jeremiah's hand jerking out to Vi's forearm in an attempt to stop her remarks. *The moment Vi refutes Commander Thatcher's words is the moment hell will rain upon us.*

"That is all I have for now," she says. "You may leave to complete your desired tasks. We will meet tomorrow morning at the same time per usual and practice forming into our line-ups and initiating post sign-ups 'til then. You are dismissed."

As she starts to dismiss us, I hear a female voice beside me spark to life. "Wait. I have something to say."

Oh, God . . . it's Vi.

Murmurs erupt in the air as Commander Thatcher turns to her slowly, cocking her head at her. "Yes, Powers?"

Vi clenches her jaw, stepping forward to the Commander. Jeremiah knows it is hopeless to stop her. Judging by her hard and cold eyes, *nothing* will be able to stop her. Not even a goddamn earthquake, at this point.

Mallory leans in to me as she whispers, "Is it just me, or are you scared to see what's gonna happen next?"

I wait a few moments until I whisper back, "Trust me, it's not just you."

As I look back at the commotion, I see Vi and the Commander are only a foot or two apart, their eyes drilled into each other. "Well, go ahead, Powers. Say what it is you need to say."

"Well . . . it's about your defensive strategy."

Shit. Shit, shit, shit.

"What about it? C'mon, I don't have all day here."

"I think it's stupid," Vi blurts out.

Yep. We're definitely screwed now. Best to evacuate before the room explodes.

Once Commander Thatcher interprets her words, she lets out a sharp and humorless laugh. "Yes, you already told me that before. C'mon, enough with the jokes now."

"I'm not joking. I really do mean that it's stupid. Plain and simple as that."

"Hey, watch your mouth," she hisses. "I don't care how good of a soldier you are. I am in charge here, and you have no right to speak to me like that."

"Just like you have no right to put our lives in danger, just because you don't want us to attack," Vi growls. "Remember when the ERUSA first attacked us and you got mad at us for shooting at them? Yeah, you *shouldn't* have yelled at us because we did the right thing. If we just stayed put like idiots then we would've been shot dead. Thank God we didn't listen to you."

"Powers," the Commander enunciates. "That is enough."

"Yes, please, Vi," Nico whispers to her from the side. "We can discuss this later and not in front of everyone. Just please. Cool off and forget about it, okay?"

"No, I can't and *won't* forget about it. I am not gonna sit here and remain silent as if she's some sort of dictator. I am allowed to express my opinions, okay? And my opinion is that we need to fight back for once. We are walking into death every moment we don't press on a trigger. Just imagine how many lives we wouldn't have lost if we just *fired back*. What do you say about that, everybody?" she voices to the others.

Surprisingly, large shouts from the crowd erupt. *Damn, Vi really knows how to get a crowd riled up.*

"Do you hear that?" Vi narrows her eyes at Commander

Thatcher. "Look how many people you've silenced. Is this the military you want? Because if that's what you want, then I don't want to be a part of this shit."

Vi huffs, not even bothering to wait for a response as she storms off into one of the many hallways.

No one speaks for five minutes straight. Not until Commander Thatcher says that we are dismissed, and we leave —of course, *silently*—our minds still reeling in what Vi told Commander Thatcher. I agree with what she said, but I would much rather keep it to myself than pull the shit Vi did. Then again, she *is* Vi, and she never holds anything back. Which, in all honesty, takes a lot of guts.

As we are dismissed, we make our way to the locker room to pick up our equipment. Once we grab everything, we go over to the loading docks where our jeep is. The sun peers into the battlefield, which is still drenched in singed grass and gives off a burning smell from the battle we had weeks ago, even to this day. Once we climb into the jeep, with Nicolas driving, we make our way out of the dock and into the street where the murky hot air nips at my skin. Blaire curls up beside me, her tan skin gleaming against the sunrays and closes her eyes, tightening her grip on my bicep. I lean my cheek on the top of her head and find sleep too, even though I struggle to at night.

Eventually, we reach the home which still stands to this day. Layla, Tamia, Blaire's parents and Emilia greet us as we park by the front. Emilia goes up to Blaire and hugs her tightly, murmuring that she misses her. She pulls in a reluctant Nicolas, who gives in and hugs them too. Their parents laugh at their encounter, joining in as well.

I can't help but look at them with both happiness and a hint of jealousy.

We make our way inside the home and into the foyer where it separates into our different rooms. Blaire tells me she's going to spend some time with her family, which I completely understand because we've just been too busy lately. After I give her a quick kiss on the cheek, with Emilia wiggling her eyebrows at her, we disperse into different directions.

Throughout the day, we all meet up in the foyer and discuss our life so far. Jeremiah, Layla, and Tamia have been doing great, besides Layla and Tamia being upset about not seeing Jeremiah often these days. Luckily he reassures them that, when life calms down, he will spend more time with them. Vi states that her life has been going how it usually goes . . . *boring.* Mallory says her thigh is doing better and her hatred for her mother grows everyday. Blaire jokingly says she wants to sleep somewhere else tonight because her family is apparently "too annoying," and I say that my father is not on my mind as much anymore—which is a complete lie. I only said that to avoid the worries from others because, as much as I appreciate everyone caring for me, I just want to deal with this on my own. That's why I only told Blaire and Mallory.

Once my most dreaded time of day arrives, I sit on the couch in the living room, prying my eyes open even though sleep is most definitely knocking at my door. For tonight, and just like every other tonight, I want that door to remain shut because behind it is the devil disguised as my father. Even though he's nothing but a disintegrated pile of flesh and bones, he's still on my mind. And I don't know why.

I sure as hell know it's not because of my guilt.

Suddenly, I hear a knock on the door, and not the sleep one. It's my *actual* door. I sigh as I make my way there, hoping it's Blaire to console me.

Instead, it's Mallory, her big blue eyes looking up at me. "Hi," she says. "I'm sorry to bother you. I just, uh . . . I just wanted to see what you were up to. And I also couldn't sleep."

"Oh, that's fine," I say, allowing her to come inside. "And honestly, me too."

"Is it because of your nightmares?"

"Yeah."

"That's okay," she says. "I'll be here if that makes you feel any better."

I can't help but notice her lifeless eyes, glassy and one-dimensional. She slowly sits on the couch, and I sit across from her on the armchair. I clear my throat. "Is everything okay, Mallory?"

"What?" She blinks at me. "Oh, yeah. I'm fine."

I cock my head at her, unconvinced.

"Okay, fine, I lied." Mallory sulks in her seat. "I'm not doing okay at all."

"Is it because of your mom?"

"Of course. It's *always* been about my mother ever since she arrived here and hijacked the entire place. I just . . . I just wish she accepted her defeat and went along with her life. And I know she's upset about my father, but that doesn't give her the right to ruin the lives of thousands of people. I'm upset too, but I didn't let my anger and frustration control me. She's just such a hard-willed, stubborn, and self-centered person. Even if God Himself was telling her not to do these things, she *still* would not listen. That's how stubborn she is."

"Yeah, that definitely sounds like your mom." I sigh.

"Right? But anyway, just hearing her torturing and killing all these people brings so much pain to me. You and I both know that she's a very dangerous woman, especially when her priorities are harmed, but I never knew her determination ran to such a deep extent that she'd terrorize and harm innocent people. I feel so incredibly helpless when I hear that, Jax. And I can't help but blame myself too. Maybe if I didn't leave my parents that one night then maybe life would be so different right now. This is all my fault, Jax—"

"Okay, Mallory, now you're just saying bullshit," I say hurriedly. "*None* of those things are true. You made the right decision by leaving your parents because they never treated you right. And just because they spoiled you with riches and materialistic things doesn't mean that you should still stick by their side no matter what. They gave you zero *emotional* love, Mallory. So of course you had every right to leave. You followed your heart when I struggled to. That, I think, is the most badass thing I ever heard."

Her eyes slowly meet mine. "Really?"

"Yes!" I chuckle. "Do you know how irritated I would get toward your mom when you used to complain to me that she yelled at you for not doing something she wanted? I never understood as a kid why you always defended her. She's not the mother you deserve, Mallory. If anything, she doesn't even deserve the right to be called your mom."

"I think you're right," she says slowly. "From now on, I'll stop calling her my mom. I'll call her . . . Veronica. That's it."

"That's exactly what I want to hear." I smile at her.

She slowly smiles back at me. "What about you? Are your nightmares at least getting any better?"

"Kinda," I mutter. "They're of course still there, but they're on and off. Sometimes they're mildly terrifying, sometimes they're extremely traumatizing. Sometimes they show up every day of a week, sometimes they don't show up for days on end. It's entirely random and there's no warning when they come."

"What are the nightmares about, if you don't mind saying?"

"They're about *everything*, Mallory. I'm either getting suffocated, drowned, kicked, punched, taunted, tortured, terrorized, you name it. And it's all done by my father with a scar on his cheek and his torso bloodied. Sometimes it's so bad I feel it even when I wake up—his shadow, his presence, *everything*."

"Oh, gosh," she murmurs. "I'm so sorry, Jax."

"No need to say sorry. I just . . . I just really want the nightmares to go away already. I can't handle them anymore."

"They'll go away soon. I promise." Her lip twitches into a smile, and I can't help but smile back. Of course Blaire gives me more than enough love and comfort than I need, but the love and comfort she gives me is with passion and need. The love and comfort Mallory gives me is familial because she's known me even when I didn't know myself.

"Hey, Jax?" she blurts out.

"Yes, Mallory?"

"Are, uh . . . are things going well with you and Blaire?"

I nod immediately. "Things are absolutely amazing with her. Why?"

"I was just wondering." Weirdly, her cheeks redden. "I'm truly glad to hear things are going amazing with her. You deserve happiness more than anything. I just hope she's treating you well, too." I don't know if it's my tired eyes, but I swear I just saw her lip tremble just the slightest bit. "I know how much you struggled with finding yourself and being happy, especially when you used to live with your parents, so I hope you found all of those things now. I really do."

When her words radiate into my mind, I lean forward as I grin with her. "Thank you, Mallory. I really appreciate it. And I hope you find someone, too. You deserve just as much happiness as you want for me, if not more."

She immediately brings her eyes to the ground, shaking her head slightly. "I don't know whether I'll find someone."

I frown at her. "What do you mean? Of course you will."

Mallory now shakes her head vehemently. "No, I won't, Jax. How can I when I—"

Suddenly, three small knocks pound against the door.

Mallory and I share confused looks as I slowly get up toward the door. When I open it just a crack, I notice a sliver of an arm clad in jet-black armor. My heart sinks as I crack it open even more, meeting Comrade Bennett, the man who's been bringing me to my terrorizing hell since I set foot in this place.

He peers inside and almost cocks his head at us. "Quite convenient to see you both here."

"What the hell do you want?" I murmur tiredly.

He chuckles shortly afterwards. "Funny you should ask. Lieutenant Reaves wants to meet with you and her daughter."

37

SKEPTICISM

BLAIRE

TOBIAS SHOWS UP IN my nightmares for the second time.

As I jerk awake, tossing and turning in bed, Em wakes up from her deep slumber and nudges my shoulder with a poking finger. "Can you not do that, B?" she murmurs. "I'm trying to sleep."

"Sorry," I breathe out, drenched in sweat. "It's really hot in here."

"Then go to the foyer so you can get some fresh air." She turns around to the other side and curls into her blanket even more. "Maybe that will help."

"I don't know if going to the foyer will make my negative thoughts go away," I whisper. I expect Em to console me, or at least rub my arm, but as I look over at her, I notice she's fallen asleep early, her lips curled down slightly with slumber. I sometimes feel terrible that I haven't been able to spend much time with her these days, but I know that is beyond my control because of what's happening around us. We just spent every single moment together when we lived in D.C., so it feels abnormal that Em and I haven't been together as much lately. I hope that, when life eventually and hopefully calms down, that will change.

Same with Nico, as I see almost passed out beside me. His hair—longer than mine now—is sprawled around him on his pillow, his mouth hung open as snores escape out of him. I find it almost unfair that I spent three years without him and, barely a year after I'm reunited with him, we are suddenly physically torn apart by a stubborn and hard-headed woman who's unhappy with the way things ended in D.C. Sometimes, I just wish we had more time together so I could ask him how and when he came up with the idea to start the Subversion Act. I want to get to know him more because, well, he would be a stranger to me if we hadn't had those several months in between to catch up. But there's still a lot in general I want and need to know about him because he's almost a part of me. If I don't know him very well, then I'll lose knowledge of myself too.

I get up out of bed by crawling through the middle, wincing every time the bed creaks with my hesitant movements. The last thing I want to do is wake up an irritated Em again, and I don't want to deal with that. It seems as if she's entering her cranky teenage phase now, which I know will be a headache to get through these days.

Once I climb out of bed, I make my way out the door with intentions to meet up with Jax. He's the only one who can calm me down and bring me out of my negative thoughts, which have been revolving around nothing but my worries for my family. Veronica is a very volatile and sneaky woman, and if anything triggers that mind of hers, then she won't hesitate to kill anyone in her way. I just hope it doesn't get to the point where my family succumbs to her wrath. I'd rather throw myself under the bus just for my family's safety.

As I go to knock on his door, I hear Vi's voice behind me. "Jax isn't here, and neither is Mallory."

I turn around to her slowly, my eyebrows pushed together in confusion. "Why?"

"God knows." She shrugs. "I just wanted to bring everyone together to discuss things because I can't sleep."

"I can't sleep either," I murmur.

"Well, welcome to the insomniac party," she says sarcastically, gesturing to a sluggish Jeremiah behind her.

He rolls his eyes at her. "You and Blaire are the only insomniacs because I was sleeping just peacefully before you dragged me out of bed. You would have woken up my girls if you made any more commotion."

"Well, I didn't, did I?" She smirks at him. "Besides, I did everyone a favor by getting you up out of bed. Nobody wants to hear the nasty things you and Layla are up to these days."

He scoffs shyly, almost seeming to blush beneath his ebony skin. "We haven't been doing anything *nasty* these days. Are you forgetting we have a child sleeping beside us?"

"True. But anyway, enough of that. I just wanted to talk to someone because I legitimately cannot sleep."

"*You* want to talk to someone?" Sarcasm drags out of my tone. "That's a new one."

"Screw you," she says as she flips me off and lugs Jeremiah and I over to a door that leads to no one's room.

"Where are you taking us?" Jeremiah asks.

"To the roof."

"The *roof*?" I mutter.

Vi doesn't say a single word as she pops the door open, hot and murky air flooding my veins. There's not much room to walk out here, except for a balcony that has a ladder attached to its side. She starts to climb up, for which Jeremiah and I confusingly follow behind her. When we reach the roof, my breath almost escapes out of my throat from the pictorial beauty of the outside.

My eyes narrow at the ins and outs of valleys and winding secluded roads that lead to the entrance of the booming city. Some buildings have collapsed from Veronica's wrath, but the beauty of Detroit is still captured, no matter how much she harms our home. Detroit is our home regardless of how it looks because it brought us happiness in much less time than D.C. ever did.

We sit ourselves by the edge of the roof, Vi in the middle and Jeremiah and I on either side of her. My feet dangle by the edge, and my heart jumps to my throat as I notice the height from where we're sitting. There is just a dark and shapeless pit of ground beneath us, and I can't even think of the consequences if one of us were to fall.

"I came up here a while ago," Vi blurts out.

"Really?" I ask.

"Yeah. I came up here with Jax." She turns to me slowly. "Didn't he tell you?"

I raise my eyebrows at her. "No, actually. He didn't tell me."

"Seriously?" Vi chuckles. "This is the first time I know something about Jax that you don't. Why didn't he tell you?"

"God knows," I murmur to myself. "I thought he told me everything."

"Maybe he forgot to tell you and just saw Vi when he came up here," Jeremiah says. "I'm pretty sure it wasn't done intentionally."

"Well, I hope you're right. I just . . . I'm a bit taken aback by that. That's all."

"Yeah, I would be too." Vi snorts.

"You're not really helping her right now." Jeremiah glares at her.

"No, it's okay. I'm fine." I brush them off. "Maybe you're right, Jeremiah. Maybe he just forgot to tell me."

"Well, if that's the case," Vi says, "then why didn't he tell you about him going somewhere with Mallory? As a matter of fact, why didn't he tell *anyone?*"

"Vi!" Jeremiah hisses.

"What? We need to get to the bottom of this, Jeremiah. I get that Jax and Mallory are good friends, but that doesn't mean they just roam around without telling us where they are."

"What if they're in trouble?" I say. "That could be the case too."

"The chances of them being in trouble are very low because neither Veronica nor the ERUSA soldiers are aware of our hideaway here. I doubt that is the case."

"Then where could they be?" I murmur to myself.

"I don't know, maybe they went for a walk," Jeremiah says. "I'm sure they'll be back soon."

"But what if they're not? And what if they didn't go for a walk?" More and more questions pelt into my mind. "I've noticed Jax and Mallory have been getting closer these days, but I didn't make much mind of it. I trust them more than I trust myself, so I never worried about them once. But now . . . I'm not so sure about that anymore."

"C'mon, Blaire, don't think that," Jeremiah attempts to soothe me. "Jax and Mallory would never betray you in any sort of way. If they went for a walk somewhere, then I can most assuredly tell you that they will be back. If not, then we will talk to Commander Thatcher and she will search for them. Okay?"

I let out a shaky breath. "Okay."

We talk about other topics, but I don't pay attention much because all I can think about is Jax and Mallory together, doing something I have no idea about. Now that I think about it, he has been vague with me on plenty of occasions, such as when his scar got bloodier, his hand was bruised, and he indirectly refused to sleep with me sometimes. But maybe that's because he's been struggling with his nightmares so he's too involved with his own issues and telling me about them is the least of his worries. I get that because I've felt like that sometimes too. Yet the moment I heard about Jax and Mallory being together and not telling anyone about it . . . I don't know whether I should brush this off anymore.

When I come back from our hangout and enter my room, I freeze by the doorway as I see Nico perched upright at the edge of the bed, long locks drawn over his face. He looks up at me instantly, his deep brown eyes pulsating even amongst the dim environment.

"Where were you?" he asks me simultaneously as I ask him, "Why are you awake?"

I chuckle as Nico says, "You first."

"I was on the roof with Vi and Jeremiah. You?"

He waits a couple of seconds before he says, "Couldn't sleep."

"Should've joined us then." I shrug. "You wanna sit outside in the living room with me? Since I can't really sleep as well." I point toward a sleeping Em, soft snores erupting from her mouth. "I don't wanna wake her up either."

"Sure. Let's go."

We make our way to the living room and sit on opposite sides of the couch. Nico plants his feet on the ground, leaning forward with his elbows digging into his knees. I, on the other hand, lean back against the armrest and lay across the couch, my feet inches away from him. The environment is still, peaceful, and just enough to make my thoughts a little less distracting. I've been thinking so much lately that it's just become . . . uncontrollable. Overwhelming, even. All I need is some alone time with the person I've been aching to spend time with the most.

"Y'know what's so sad?" I blurt out.

Nico looks over at me slowly. "What?"

I release a deep breath. "How I've spent several years searching for you, and right when I find you, we're thrown into this mess and life becomes hectic again. I just haven't been able to spend time with you lately, which I hate. I don't even . . . I don't even know you that well. Like, what's your favorite color? Your fears? Your goals? Your pet peeves? I don't know, Nico. The only thing I know about you is that you are the leader of the Subversives. Which really sucks."

He gives me a sad smile. "I know. It really does suck a lot, Bumble Bee. But hey, that's beyond our control, you know. Definitely not something you should worry too much about. But now that we're here . . . we can talk all night long. Catch up, if you wanna call it that."

I nod to myself slowly. "I would love that."

His grin deepens. "Great. Well, uh . . . what do you want to know? Do you really want to know my favorite color and things like that?"

"Of course. Anything will be fine with me."

"Okay, um . . . my favorite color is red because it reminds me of fire, and I love fire. My fear is losing you guys. My goal is to destroy the ERUSA. And my pet peeve is when people chew too loudly. What about you?"

"My favorite color is green—surprise, surprise." I chuckle. "My fear and goal is pretty much the same as yours. My pet peeve is different . . . I absolutely *hate it* when people lie. The truth is gonna come out anyway, so what's the point in lying? You're just making a fool out of yourself in the end."

"True," Nico says, laughing. "God, I almost forgot how hard-headed you are. Nothing ever goes past you, Bumble Bee. If you weren't a soldier then you'd pretty much be a detective instead."

"Oh, shut up." I chuckle. "I guess I just don't like any loose ends."

"Well, unfortunately"—Nico winces—"that's not how life works."

"Yeah. Unfortunately."

Silence.

"Hey, Nico?"

"Yeah?"

"I know you talked about this in the last *actual* conversation we had, which was probably months ago. But, uh . . . how are you doing? Like, actually? And I mean ever since you were in jail and escaped and stuff like that. I . . . I want you to know I'm here for you, Nico, and you can always open up to me whenever you want. I know we get into our stupid fights and disagreements here and there, but that's normal, y'know? Just know, deep down, I'm here for you . . . whether you like it or not—"

"Bumble Bee?"

". . . Yes?"

Nico chuckles softly. "Of course I know you're here for me, just like I know the same. And it's not that I don't want to open up to you. It's just, before, you had no idea how bad the world was and I wanted to keep it that way. I was afraid if I told you about my life then your viewpoint of the world would be ruined —way more than it was before. I didn't want to do that to you."

"But I've seen bad things now," I say desperately. "I've seen enough to understand your life in the past."

"I'm sorry, Bumble Bee, but you haven't." He sighs. "What I've seen and been through . . . it's traumatizing as hell. And I can only tell you about it in detail when I feel as if you're ready. But right now, I want you to be as innocent as you can be. Only because it's hard to be innocent in a world like this. So, enjoy it."

"But, Nico—"

"I'm serious. *Enjoy it.* I promise you . . . it's not gonna last long. Your innocence, I mean."

As I think about protesting again, I hear a soft female voice purr from the corner. "Guys?" *Em.* I look over to see her timid frame, tightly hugging the end of the hallway and peering over to where we sit. "Am I interrupting something?"

"Oh, no, not at all," Nico says, patting the space between us.

After Em sits cross-legged in the middle, she sighs, looking down at her knees. "I woke up and saw both of you guys were gone. So I came here because I heard noises. I hope it's okay . . . that I'm here."

"Em, of *course* it's okay," I say. "Why wouldn't it be?"

"Because . . ." She frowns to herself. "Because you guys are much older than me. And I'm only thirteen and stupid and my only friend is Tamia, but she can barely speak in full sentences. I don't know. I just . . . I get it if you guys don't like talking to me. I understand that I'm not as smart as you are. I really do."

My mind flashes in alarm. *What the hell? Does she really think this? God, I feel so bad now.* I quickly scoot over to her and grab her shoulder as I look into her eyes. "Em, what are you talking about? Nico and I love talking to you, and you're certainly not stupid. Where did you even get that from?"

"I don't know." She shrugs. "But you don't have to lie to me, B. Seriously. I won't be mad at all if you want to talk to Nico over me. I'm pretty sure you can have a better conversation with him than me."

"Okay, Em, please stop saying that stuff," Nico says hurriedly as he scoots over to her too. "Let me just say one thing, okay? You are smart. More than you ever know. I've noticed at the refuge lately that you've been helping the doctors and the nurses really well. You have such a knack for taking care of people that I genuinely see you becoming a doctor when you grow up. You are *so* talented, Em. Don't let yourself think otherwise."

She releases a low breath. "Really?"

"Yes, really," I say. "Nico and I love you very much. We never meant to exclude you. You were just asleep, and I didn't want to wake you up. That's all."

"Oh," she murmurs. "Well, yeah. That makes sense." Em pauses. "Thanks. I guess I'm just scared to lose you guys."

"You're not gonna lose us," Nico whispers. "Okay?" When she nods, he grins and pokes her ribs playfully. We all start to laugh, but not too loud because we don't want to wake our parents up.

Suddenly, we all hug each other, and nothing is said for a very long time. All I can hear, really, is our breathing, mixed together with unspoken fears. One thing I've learned tonight is that I have at least something in common with Nico and Em, which is we're all scared to lose each other.

As we relish in each other's presence, I pray to myself that that fear doesn't come true.

38

REPERCUSSION

JAX

MY HEART BEATS AT my throat as Mallory and I sit side-by-side across from her mother, her icy blue eyes glazing across us like paint streaking across a canvas, each stroke making it increasingly difficult for me to breathe. I don't know how Veronica is so capable of sucking out all the air and life out of a room. Maybe it's because she hasn't said a single word since we've been seated, just merely staring at us as if we were nothing but inconveniences to her.

From my peripheral vision, I see Mallory's legs twitching, her eyes raised at the ceiling as she refuses to look at her mother, which I'm not blaming her for because if that was my father sitting in front of us instead then I would do anything to avoid his eyes. Hell, I wouldn't even be here in the first place. I suck a deep breath in as I get a searing flashback of a nightmare I had the other day—something that's been engraved into my brain ever since it occurred. It was of my father squeezing my throat and drowning me underwater, holding on so tight my vision became spotty and my ears began to pop. His face was gleaming with sweat, and he had the bloody scar and the bloody chest which was all, of course, due to my actions. That was all the dream was, but when I woke up, my throat was raging red and I was gasping for air.

I haven't had a nightmare since that day. And I don't know what's to come next.

Veronica clears her throat, her skin like broken fragments of pale glass glistening against the humming lights. My attention diverts to her as I push my nightmares to the back of my mind. I don't know how today's going to go, but judging by her twitchy features, I'm assuming it won't be a walk in the park. If anything, it'll be a walk in the park that's engulfed in *flames.*

"Betrayal is something I always felt ever since I was a child," she starts off. "I felt betrayed when my father left me, my mother, and my older sister Clarissa when I was barely in grade school. I felt betrayed when my mother turned to narcotics and alcoholic substances and barely took care of me and Clarissa. I felt betrayed when my mother passed away from cancer due to her idiotic decisions and Clarissa and I were left to the streets. I felt betrayed when Clarissa left me because she found a rich lover and expected me to fend for myself."

She pauses, her cracked lips pressed together. "Even when I forced myself to get an education, be at the top of the class, and fall in love with Adam, betrayal still followed me like a shadow that clung to my side whether I liked it or not. I felt betrayed when my one and only daughter left us in the middle of the night because our love was apparently not enough for her. I felt betrayed when I found Adam dead beneath the ruins of D.C. because he vowed to always be with me, no matter the circumstances. And now I *especially* feel betrayed because my daughter and her close friend vowed to stay by my side and provide valuable information to me, when in reality you both have betrayed me by not doing either one of those things.

"I expected better of you," Veronica hisses. "I only wanted

the bare minimum and yet you failed to deliver that. What kind of accomplices are you? Betraying me even when I have gone through enough? That is truly a huge offense to me, the ERUSA, and the entirety of America's foundation."

"What does America's foundation have to do with this?" I blurt out. "This only has to do with us. If I don't want to report anything, then that only affects you."

"You *promised!*" Her pale hands bang against the wooden table she's seated at, a deep echo of the wood crackling throughout the room. "Promises and betrayals go hand-in-hand, Mr. Remington. When you break a promise, you form a betrayal. The line deepens and creates a fissure that will eventually spread throughout your flesh. The more and more people who promise to stay by your side, the more and more your wound deepens. And as of now, my wound has deepened so much that I feel it affecting my heart, my lungs, my *mind*. This betrayal will run deep with me. I won't ever forget about it."

"How about when you betrayed *me*, Mom?" Mallory grits out. "You don't have the right to insult me, make fun of me, or *shoot me* when all I did was follow my heart. Do you know how many sleepless nights I've had, knowing you are killing innocent people every day simply because Dad died? That isn't fair—"

"It's not only because of him. It's because of the sins both the Poor and you Subversives have committed. But mainly, it's because of *you*. You are the reason for everything that's been happening. If you hadn't left that night, we would've been a happy family and D.C. would remain the same. This all originates back to you, Mallory. I hope you know how much of an inconvenience you are. I am *ashamed* to be your mother. I brought you into this world so you can follow in your parents' footsteps, not run from them. That is an insult to the Reaves bloodline, and for that, I don't claim you as my own. You are not a part of me anymore. I wish you nothing but grievances and troubles in your future."

Mallory's breath audibly hitches as she clenches her fists. "You don't mean that."

"I mean it more than you think," she snarls. "You will struggle, Mallory, and you will realize too late that I was right, and you were wrong. You will be begging to come back in my arms again, and I gave you multiple chances before, but this time I'm not. This time I will ignore you and leave you to the wolves, just so you know how big of a mistake you made."

"Stop!" I grit out, my throat clawing with rage. "None of what you're saying is true. Instead of blaming your decisions on your daughter, how about you step up and admit *you're* the reason why we're here?"

"Careful there, Mr. Remington. Be aware of the very thin line you're walking across."

"I could give zero shits, Veronica. In all honesty, I'm *tired*. I'm tired of the way you've been treating me and now Mallory like damn puppets. We are not gonna be controlled by you, simply because you want to get revenge on those who have killed your husband and destroyed a society that was meant to be destroyed in the first place."

"Watch. Your. Mouth." She points her bony finger at me. "I think you're forgetting what your consequences will be if you speak like that to me any further."

"You're not gonna kill her." I let out a humorless laugh, standing up from my seat with such force that the chair almost flies back. "You say you're not like my father because he was all talk and never followed through, but in all honesty, you're just like him. You're just saying all these things to persuade people into following you when in reality, you're the biggest coward out of all of us. There's no way you have the guts to kill the little sister of the man who's leading the Subversives. The moment you do, even more chaos will form and people will be hellbent to assassinate you. You're attempting to make a bold move, Veronica, and it's not gonna go very well for you."

"Are you forgetting that I am the Lieutenant of the ERUSA?" Her not-so calm voice booms around us. "The ERUSA comprises multiple cities across the nation. There's no way your puny little army can ever take us down."

"You're speaking a bit too highly of your regime," I say calmly, holding onto the very little patience I have left. "I think you're underestimating us, Veronica. Wait until you see what we have planned for you."

Mallory is quiet the entire time, trembling and looking down at the ground. I want to stand up for not just her, but for everyone too—the Subversives, the Reformers, the Detroitian citizens, and for *all* of America. Veronica will not have authority over me anymore. I am not to be controlled, especially after how my father treated me.

"You're making a very terrible mistake, Mr. Remington. You had plenty of potential to be with the ERUSA because you are a very skilled and talented man. You could go so far when you're with us, rather than with that sorry bunch of people who are fighting for something they're never going to obtain in the first place. Think clearly for once. If you carry on with this idiotic behavior of yours then my respect for you will continue to decline. How can I ever respect a man who turns away from his bloodline and commits patricide?"

That's it.

I don't know what crawls into my throat and lodges into my insides, but it sure is enough to bring uncontrollable adrenaline coursing and pulsing through my veins. I charge up to Veronica, inches away from her face, and slam my hands against her desk, the wood rattling against my limbs. Her lips are zipped shut, but her eyes are a raging blue fire, each flame flickering like raining icicles. I want to kill her. I *need* to kill her.

Yet I control my urge because her daughter is behind me,

and I don't want to be branded as the man who kills without a second thought. I want to be smart about this. I want to say something that Veronica will remember even when she's killed and shipped off to Hell.

And so I do.

"Why would I ever give my bloodline respect when they hadn't given me an ounce of it? I have dignity, and I'm not gonna run myself over for some people who claimed to love me, when in reality they just wanted to exploit me for their own benefit. I value myself highly, Veronica, so that's why I killed my father. I am simply getting rid of people who are nothing but obstacles in not just my road, but other people's roads too. You've been nothing but a major stressor for Mallory, and the pain she goes through everyday pains me even more. Not to mention how you're stringing along *my girlfriend* who has done nothing wrong to begin with. You may want to kill her just to torture me, but you're not gonna kill her. You don't have the guts for that, and even if you did, your decision is not gonna land you in a good place.

"You're telling me to think clearly for once, but maybe you should tell yourself that. Maybe you should move on from your past and from all these people that have apparently betrayed you, and maybe you should stop harassing innocent people who are not the reason for your sadness. I suggest you go to therapy, Veronica. That's a much better decision than vowing revenge and making a whole shitshow out of this.

"Go ahead and do whatever the hell you wanna do. For all I care, go ahead and try to kill Blaire because you're gonna have to get through me, through Nicolas, through Vi, through Mallory, and through Jeremiah—and I'm telling you, we're much more powerful combined. But most importantly, I myself won't even let you in her presence. You can yell at me, punch me, torture me, whatever the hell you want to do—I really don't care anymore. Just please do us all a big favor by packing your bags and getting the fuck out of here. I don't want to see your fucking face ever again."

When I finish, I'm out of breath and my face is fuming red. I wipe my trembling mouth with the back of my hand and pace to the back of the room, my heart ramming against my chest. An eerie silence shifts into the room, dripping into my veins.

I turn back around and see Mallory looking at me with a small smile on her face. *I'm so proud of you,* she mouths.

I start to smile back at her, but I am interrupted by a pointy blade suddenly tipped to my chin, grazing my outstretched neck. A cold hand lands on my forearm, and even more cold eyes sear into me, so close to me. Making the slightest of movement puts me at so much risk for death.

"What I don't understand," she says, "is why you would say that to me. But you said what you had to say, which I will forever remember. I understand your intentions now, Mr. Remington, and I will let you have your intentions. I won't force you to be on my side anymore. I'll let you and Mallory free, and you can do whatever you like now.

"And you know what? You're right. I shouldn't kill Blaire. The decision is too uncanny and a bit controversial as well. Your girlfriend will be safe." Normally, I would breathe out in relief, but knowing this is Veronica, I *hold* my breath in, nervous for what's to come. "But that doesn't mean I don't have something else up my sleeve . . . so I suggest you watch yourself for the next few days, Mr. Remington. Life can change so much in the blink of an eye."

39

CONVERGE

BLAIRE

I DESPISE LISTENING TO the forced Pledge every single damn day.

Not one of us usually bothers to tune in to it, so we don't make much mind of it. But today? Every single word that screeches out of the outdoor speakers is like a constant punch to my gut. I hate being reminded of the world we are living in now which is wholly governed by a woman who just doesn't know how to control her emotions. I can't believe I'm thinking this, but Tobias seems like a saint now because he never made us do a pledge every morning.

As we start to climb into the jeep, I notice Jax and Mallory lugging behind me. Ever since Vi, Jeremiah, and I became worried and slightly suspicious of why they were both gone, I've been thinking about them the entire time. Why *were* they gone? And why are they suddenly here again, acting like nothing ever happened?

I'm not one to accuse Jax of anything, but I do want to ask him where he was at least. I have every right to ask him that, as his worried girlfriend. So, when he comes into the back row of the vehicle with me, I nudge his shoulder and ask him, "Hey, where were you last night?"

He glances at me for a second, giving me a smile that I *know* is completely fabricated. "Just went to get some fresh air," he says in a clipped tone.

"With *Mallory?*" I whisper to him.

"Yeah, I guess." Jax shrugs. "She couldn't sleep so she came up to me and we went on a walk by the lake. I was going to call you over too but you were asleep, so I didn't want to bother you."

"When was this?"

"Uh . . . around twelve-ish, I'd say."

"I was awake during that time." I raise my eyebrow at him. "Are you lying to me?"

"No, I'm not," he says to me hurriedly, wrapping his arm around my shoulder. "Why would I lie to you, Blaire? I swear I just went on a harmless walk with Mallory. And if you think we *did* anything, then I just want to assure you that we didn't." Jax lowers his voice, fully aware she is in front of us. "Mallory is just a friend of mine and nothing else. I only have feelings for you."

A whirlwind of thoughts and emotions enter my mind, and I debate to myself whether or not I should believe Jax. Sincerity is clearly emanating from his words, but his eyes are nervous, wavering. I've been intimate with this man before, so I can tell whether or not he's lying—which he's obviously doing in plain sight. What I just don't get, though, is *why* he would do that. What could possibly be so horrendous that he has to hide it from me?

"I don't know what to think anymore," I murmur, looking at the house that now flies behind us. "But I swear to God if you're lying"—I turn to look at him—"then I *will* kill you."

His jaw twitches and he sighs, nodding once. I expect some sort of sarcastic retort out of him, but his gray eyes are swarming in a puddle of defeat as he plants a peck on my lips and brings me closer to him. I reluctantly curl into him, breathing out a sigh of relief as I feel his warm and hard muscles constrict against me. For once I just want to forget about the inconsistencies in Jax's life here in Detroit so far and relish in his presence. Might as well hold onto him for as long as I can.

As the jeep continues to roll forward, the speaker screeches to life again.

"Good morning, Detroit." A very cold and familiar voice rings into the air. "It is ERUSA Leader Veronica Reaves, and I am here to make an announcement that everyone must gather by the headquarters for a public statement. This is a mandatory event, so when the ERUSA soldiers do a roll call of every person as they enter the premises and you're not there, then immediate plans for execution will be made. I expect everyone to be gathered at ten past eight. Thank you."

The jeep suddenly rolls to a stop with a sharp brake. "What the hell?" Vi hisses. "What could she possibly want to tell us now?"

"I don't know," Jeremiah says. "Should we contact Commander Thatcher and ask what we should do?"

"Obviously we have to attend it," I say. "If we don't then she won't hesitate to kill us."

"Not if we prepare to bring our forces there and kill her before she gets a chance to get her grimy hands on us," Vi grits out.

"First, let's talk to Commander Thatcher, all right?" Jeremiah says as he reaches into his pocket for his device. A droning ringtone hisses into the air, and suddenly, the line clicks. "Hello?" he says.

"I heard what Veronica said," Commander Thatcher's voice enters the jeep. "You guys go there, and we will follow behind you just in case we need to defend the city. Make sure to not instigate any attacks, even if she does. Don't be armed because that will come off as a threat to her, and threats are the last thing anyone needs right now. Act like a considerate citizen, and avoid any rough encounters."

As Jeremiah starts to respond to her, she hangs up. "Damn," he curses. "Looks like we really have to do this, huh?"

"Guess so," Nico murmurs.

"Do we leave everyone here?" Mal asks. "I mean, Blaire's family and Jeremiah's family too?"

"As expected, yes," Jax says. "Just so they can stay safe."

"I'll shoot a call to Layla real quick to inform her of what's going on," Jeremiah says as he frantically types on his device given by the Reformers. "By then, quickly drive to the city, Vi. Make sure you get there on time, too. Last thing we want to do is anger Veronica."

Vi salutes him silently and drives the jeep forward, the tires treading against the cracked roads. Slowly, the speed increases until the trees now whizz past us, parched of water. It's been a while since it has rained, hence why Layla was worried about the potential water drought. Hopefully it rains soon, so we have at least one less thing to worry about.

As I rest my head on Jax's chest, his hand rubbing my shoulder, I feel a myriad of emotions rush through me at all once. It's been a month since we've been together, and yet so much chaos is happening. Not only is Veronica Reaves marching around the city and assassinating anyone who does not adhere to her rules, but Jax has been quasi-closed off to me lately, and I don't know why. I don't want to be the type of girlfriend to pry at him and beg him to tell me his every thought, but I don't want him to lie to me either—for whatever reason that may be. I want him to trust me just like I trust him.

The silhouette of the Detroitian city increases in size the nearer we get. The entire shape and contrast of the metropolis is still intact, yet some buildings have been worn down due to the numerous attacks Veronica initiated for the past month. Hundreds of voices clatter around us as we enter the beating heart, curiosity taking the best of us as we frantically look around at the commotion. It's been a while since we've been in the city, so seeing the gut-wrenching conditions and the bleary atmosphere drives a knife into my chest. How can one ever cause so much distress at what was once a thriving place? There is not much originality and uniqueness anymore; it's all just a gray and frothing ball of despair.

There are trails and trails of citizens traveling lifelessly against the cracked sidewalks, ERUSA soldiers gathered at every nook and cranny to, I'm assuming, chaperone the streets. When they see our jeep cruising in the middle of the road, three ERUSA soldiers rush over to us and stand in front of the engine. Vi slams on the brakes and we lurch forward, my hold of Jax immediately releasing as my chest hits the seat in front of me. Thankfully Jax holds me back and pulls me almost onto his lap, and he reassuringly rubs my back. "Are you okay?" he says with worry.

"Yes, I'm fine," I murmur, my flesh burning at the impact.

The others in the front seem to be in distress as well, and Vi curses at the soldiers, "What the hell was that for?"

"Vehicle entry is not permitted by the headquarters," one of the soldiers say. "You must park on the side and walk from this originating point."

From the front, I see Vi about to refute their demand, but Nico holds up a hand and says, "Whatever you wish, soldier."

With that said, Vi reluctantly parks over to the side, the tire grazing the edge of the sidewalk. One by one, we climb out of the car, the thick murky air clinging onto our skin. Thank goodness the sky is smothered in gray, lofty clouds covering the bright and beating sun; otherwise, we'd all be puddles right now.

Once Vi locks the jeep, all six of us tread forward, the ERUSA soldiers behind following us at our heels. Jax urges me in front of him and he protectively stands behind me, grasping my shoulders. Mallory is beside me and she sends me a half-smile, yet when she sees Jax behind me, she meekly nods once and strays her eyes to the front of the road. Still, I can't seem to brush off the worries and wonders as to why Jax and Mallory have been a bit too quiet lately. Yet again, as much as I want to question, I shouldn't because now is not the time and place for that. Maybe once Veronica finishes her speech and we head back to our home, then I can ask Jax and possibly interrogate him as well—because I *need* to know.

We join the mass of people migrating to the headquarters, compiled of nothing except sleek panes of glass transpiring from the ground and stretching into the sky as a jagged needle. There are dozens of ERUSA vehicles parked in front of the entrance and planted by the very front and center of the head-quarters entrance is a searingly white podium with a jet-black **ERUSA** sign emblazoned across it. All the air is squeezed out of my lungs as I see the intensity of the confused crowd, ranging from men, women, and children of all shapes and sizes. We've been living in solitude for so long that I almost forgot there are tens of thousands of people residing here, even amongst Veronica's quasi-dictatorship.

When we settle in between the crowds—not too close and not too far from the podium—I release a shaky breath as Jax holds my hand, squeezing it. He gives me a wordless glance, nods once, and grasps my jaw as he kisses my forehead. I give in to his touch, forgetting my doubts about him for just this one moment.

However, when he releases from me, a snapping movement of heavy combat boots ensue from the front. I snap my eyes to where the commotion is occurring. Ten ERUSA soldiers are packed in a single-fine horizontal line like sardines, pressing their rifles to their chest and pointing them to the sky. They release out a strong colliding and cascading of grunts and pull back on the triggers. Immediately the bullets release out into the sky, followed shortly after by almost an artificial thunder-clap. Some children start wailing, grasping their ears and begging for their mothers.

The soldiers bring the tip of the rifle under their forearms and march outward, splitting in the middle and creating a gaping hole from where the podium is. The marching of their boots creates a cacophony, harsh claps and snaps of leather pounding against concrete. The men grunt once, twice, and thrice before stopping at the entrance.

Moments later, a pale-haired and frail woman walks up to the podium.

This is when I feel a dose of fear trail up my skin and raise my hairs because this speech can go in two different directions: either this goes smoothly and we all go back home safe and sound, or we enter a lifeless and endless pit of despair—something we've been desperate to avoid for the longest time.

I gulp as she positions herself by the microphone and, to my unfortunate avail, starts to speak.

PROSECUTE

JAX

"WELCOME TO THE DETROITIAN headquarters." Veronica's eerie voice climbs onto the speakers around us in a slow and tantalizing manner. "I am Veronica Reaves, Detroit's leader and the ERUSA's Lieutenant. I have a special statement to make, so I expect everyone's undivided attention. Before I begin though, there are some ground rules I'd like to lay down, besides the former: number one, there shall be no conversations amongst yourselves; number two, everyone must stand erect for the entirety of the speech; number three, there shall be no direct or indirect defamatory remarks toward me and my soldiers; and number four, no one is allowed to leave the premises early, even if you're clinging onto your last breath and you're about to die. When I call people for an essential statement, I expect everyone to be present both in physical and mental matters."

She pauses, her glassy eyes roaming around the crowd with her cracked lips tugged into the thinnest of lines. *I'd rather eat chalk than be in her line of sight.*

My hold on Blaire tightens, and whether that is from desired comfort or unfortunate fear, I have no idea. I know she's onto me, especially after the meeting Mallory and I had with Veronica. Veronica's words still trail into my mind, saying that she'll do something *worse* than killing Blaire. God knows what the hell she means by that, but I'm not taking any chances—which is why I've been clinging onto Blaire as if she's quite literally my other half.

And as much as I want to tell Blaire about my meetings with Veronica so far, I know that I *can't* because her life is still at risk —if not more since the she-devil herself decided to do something worse than blatantly murdering someone. I may hate Veronica a lot, but I hate myself more for keeping this from her. But I know this is all for her safety and nothing else because I have no other choice . . . even though I wish with all my heart that I did.

"Let me start off by saying that my reign here will continue on until my very last breath," Veronica continues. "I made quite an extensive effort to escape the ruins of D.C., form this companionship with multiple cities, and come here with the intentions to refine and rebuild this city according to my likings. I've enforced rules here too, which, unfortunately, not many of you are adhering to, such as not reciting the Pledge every morning, staying out before and after curfew, speaking behind your superiors' backs, and wearing raunchy clothing no matter the heat index. This is the society you're living in now, so you must follow the rules, otherwise you will meet the dire consequences." She pauses. "That is why I'm utterly disappointed to announce that, because of the lack of allegiance in Detroit, I must exemplify those consequences."

Waves of low murmurs and protests erupt in the crowd, for which Veronica raises her hand to immediately quieten the area. "As I said before, no direct or indirect defamatory remarks toward me or my soldiers. Be careful of your behavior, especially because I am not here to engage in jovial and colloquial approaches. I am here to enforce my ideals, which you must respond and adhere to."

I turn to my side, where the others currently stand, looking confused as well. *What could Veronica possibly want to tell us now? Hasn't she caused enough damage to begin with?*

Veronica's cracked lips close and part in erratic movements, as if she's hesitant to say whatever's going to come out of her mouth next; however, her eyes are anything but hesitant, raging with cold blue flames and speckled with rigid stalagmites.

Her gaze suddenly collides with where we stand. "Mallory Reaves and Jax Remington, please come up to the platform."

I immediately feel my throat dry and my hands clam up, my feet rooting and meshing to the ground. *What the hell?*

Everyone in the entire crowd, including my friends and my girlfriend, turn to Mallory and me in almost accusing glances. I shoot Mallory a desperate look, for which she frantically shakes her head. "Wh-why is she calling us up there?"

"I don't know," I whisper, turning to Blaire and the others. "I don't know why she is."

A thick cloud of air stuffs itself into my throat, making it hard for me to breathe. Meanwhile, Blaire glares at me with those searing green eyes of hers and says, "It's okay. Go up there. Let's see why exactly she's calling you guys up to the platform."

Knowing her, I am 100 percent certain she said that in a passive-aggressive tone.

I gulp, squeezing her hand. "All right." Then, I turn to Mallory, who looks like she's on the verge of tears. "Ready to go?"

She bites on her lip. "Yeah."

I take another look at Blaire, who nods twice slowly. *I am so sorry for what I've done. I shouldn't have lied to you. I should've told you before I came here. I should've let you in when all I did was shut you out.*

Reluctantly, I release her hand, feeling a weight slam down on my chest the moment that I do. I walk away from her, Vi, Nicolas, and Jeremiah as Mallory comes to me, wordless and trembling with fear.

When we meet, the crowd in front of us parts, making a visible path to the platform where Veronica stands. I truly wish they didn't, so I'd have an excuse to not go up there. For all I know, her "consequence" for Detroit could be killing off Mallory and me. But then again, why would she kill us? There is no visible reason why she would want to commit that.

The gravel beneath our feet cracks and crumbles with every hesitant step forward. Mallory walks side-by-side with me, unwilling to leave my side. That's exactly what I need, considering how her mother is staring at me with those icicles lodged into her eye sockets. God, Blaire should've stabbed Veronica in the eye instead of my father at this point. We could've been in a much better position right now.

When we reach the platform, I train my eyes to the ground and take one, two, three steps forward, the bottom of my shoes colliding with the marble flooring. Veronica, with one swift hand gesture, motions for us to stand in front of the podium, or rather in front of *her*. In any other situation, I would take the risk and refuse to adhere to her ideals, but both mine and Mallory's life is on the line, and I'd much rather obey than receive the flattened end of the deal. So, we stand in front of the podium now, the bone-rattling presence of the ghostly woman floating behind us.

Her voice screeches into the air again, and I gnaw on my back molars, the clashing of teeth and speech resounding into my ears. "I have in front of me my estranged daughter, Mallory Reaves, and the son of Tobias Remington, the deceased President of the United States, Jax Remington. I brought them up here for a reason that is in opposition to what you all are thinking. I will, in no way, bring harm to them. They are what I deem as Pure bloods because they were born into Rich households. I first called Mr. Remington into my office almost a month ago because I wanted him to spy on the Detroitian military for me, which he accepted. Later on, I called my daughter in and asked her to assist him in my request, which she accepted too. Since then, they have been in alliance with the ERUSA.

"Granted they had questionable morals and resided with tyrannical individuals, I believe that, deep down, they have more than enough potential to become true American leaders one day and bring pride to our country again. America, as purely evident, ran primarily on those with wealth and power, but the moment someone of the lower class questioned our authority was the moment our country fell into shambles. It is quite obvious their rebellion was idiotic because we are now considered a third-world country. So, in order to not deepen that wound and create even more of a fool out of ourselves, I now will be announcing the imperative proposition I mentioned during the announcement today."

No, I think to myself, refusing to look at the Blaire and the others. *No, no, no! Don't believe her. It's not what you think. I swear. I never wanted to be a part of this. I only wanted to protect the woman I love.*

The words that come out of her mouth next are enough to slice, puncture, and damage my lungs, my heart, my mind. I wish I didn't kill my father. I wish I just obeyed him and left the Subversives so I wouldn't be here. So Mallory wouldn't be here. So everyone else wouldn't be here. This is all my fault. *All my damn fault.*

My entire time here in Detroit has consisted of nothing but a fragment of my mind haunting me, and I've always despised it. But now I won't mind it so much because I deserve pain. I deserve the worst out of the *worst.*

But there's only one person in the world who deserves more pain than me.

"It is with great pleasure of mine to announce the future engagement of Mallory Reaves and Jax Remington and their initiative to lead a purging of all Poor and Impure individuals starting next week."

From where the crowd is parted, I meet eyes with Blaire, whose face has fallen.

41

SHATTERED

BLAIRE

I'VE ALWAYS THOUGHT THE anger I felt in D.C. was the most intense, but I was ultimately proven wrong.

My screams drown into the cold and dark room, and I feel my bones quivering with every delayed movement forward, attempting to sob, but no tear seems to want to come out. It seems as if I've used them all after the hell this world has put me through.

To an extent, I thought it wouldn't get worse than D.C., and even when Veronica took over Detroit, I *still* had the hope life would get better. But, of course, I was proven wrong. Again.

People bang at the door, desperate to ask if I'm okay or if I need someone, which is quite a stupid question to ask because *of course* I'm not okay and *of course* I want to be left alone. Why else would I lock myself in a dingy storage closet that almost has the looks of a nightmarish chamber?

I slump against the cool wall, the rough texture poking into my back the more and more I slide down, my heart now leapt out of my throat and pulsing at my hands, no longer feeling comfortable inside of me. I was so quick to give my heart to him when, in the end, it was stomped on and thrown to the side like a piece of trash. Even after he fed me his empty promises.

Now, I'd rather stay starving than be fed his bullshit.

When Veronica announced his and Mallory's little *engagement,* I couldn't believe my own ears. I, of course, sided with Jax at the start, but the more I saw his neutral features, especially when she stated their *companionship* together, the more I lost faith and trust in him. Even after everything we went through, I was still betrayed, and even worse, by the person I least expected. I at least could forgive Mallory because we had no connection that was close to the type Jax and I had, but I don't know if I have it in me to do the same for him. This was unforgivable, and I don't know what to do anymore.

I feel the cool peridot stone resting against my chest, and normally I would feel comforted by it, but all I feel now is restriction, as if it were stopping me from utter bliss and bringing me to my inevitable demise.

Suddenly, the door bursts open.

I gasp, clinging onto the wall behind me, immediately scurrying back as if I was a secretive creature unknown to the human world. All I see are people huddled around the door, familiar faces shown too—Vi, Nico, Jeremiah, AJ, and even Ren, who did not even hesitate to comfort me when we arrived at the bunker—but there's one that stands in the middle that stops all movement in my heart, lungs, and veins.

No. No, no, *no.*

As I yell out a protest, the door slams behind him, and he stands in front of me, his dark eyebrows drawn together. For a second, his soothing gray eyes draw me into peace and harmony and almost make me forget the horrid news announced barely an hour ago. For a second, I want to fall into his arms and stop time, stop the world, stop everything. For just a damn second, I want to forgive him just so I can love him one last time.

But that is only for that one second because all my sympathy has dissipated and transformed into *hate hate hate.* I hate those eyes of his, I hate that smile of his, I hate that body of his, that voice, that hair, that personality, that *everything.*

When I pull out a small knife from my pocket, his eyes widen as he rushes to stop me. But I could care less because right now, I just want to *kill him,* for this little moment I'm pushing my heart and all my feelings to the side.

I release a cry as I run to him, bringing my knife back and aiming for whatever flesh I can drag the blade into. He's weirdly calm, dodging my hits while avoiding hitting me. He brings his large hand forward and grabs my wrist so tight, I almost cry out in pain. I try to push and push and push against his force, but it's almost unbeatable. And I *hate* that.

"Are you sure you want to do this?" he says calmly, still holding onto my wrist. We're inches apart, his eyes drilling into mine. "Are you sure you're making the right decision here?"

"I don't care," I wheeze. "I want to *kill* you, Jax. I hate you. I hate you so damn much."

I push him against the nearest wall, feeling a new wave of energy and anger crash over me and as I slowly drive the blade near his neck. I don't know what I'm doing, or whether this will truly make me happy, but it will definitely appease my anger. And that's all I want to do right now. *Appease my anger.*

His hard muscles dig into my abdomen, flashbacks of our intimate night unraveling almost like a punch to my face. I don't want to be reminded of what's holding me back while I'm adamant to do *this.* I don't need sympathy or any other sort of feelings rushing through me.

Unfortunately, my faltering moment allows him to dip his head down, grasp my wrist even tighter, and push me back, making the knife clatter to the hard ground. He grabs both of my wrists now and brings me down to the floor, my chest rising in and out as his torso collides with mine. His fingers encircle through mine as he brings my hands above my head, his furious and disappointed gray eyes latched onto me. I feel his heart beating into mine, so close to me I almost forget what he's done.

Almost.

"Nice try, Blaire," he whispers oh-so softly, I almost feel his voice crawling down my throat.

"Shut the hell up," I gasp. "I don't want to talk to you ever again."

"And why is that?"

I scowl at him. "Don't act dumb with me. You know damn well why I'm upset with you."

He lets out a soft sigh. "Because of what Veronica said, right? Do you really think I would ever do that?"

"I don't know what to think anymore, so you tell me."

His hold on my hands loosens a bit, but not to the point where I can release from his wrath. "First let me explain to you everything. Once I do, you can think whatever you want about me. Okay?"

I grind on my molars. "Okay."

"But you have to promise that you won't attempt to kill me again." He gives me a half-smile. "Even though you look really hot when you're mad."

I instantly fight off a grin, not wanting to succumb to his antics. "Okay. I promise."

Immediately, he releases from me, and I let out a sigh as we stand up, inches away from each other. Jax looks down at me, his lips drawn into a frown as his Adam's Apple visibly bobs up and down.

And he tells me everything. By the time he finishes, I am speechless, my head running in multiple directions and not knowing of the words thrown at me. I am unable to comprehend anything, as it seems. It's like I'm walking in a gray cloud, blind, and completely vulnerable. Any step in any direction leads to the unknown, and frankly, I don't know where to go, or what to think anymore.

"Do you understand now?" he asks desperately. "Do you understand why I had to do what I had to do?"

I look up at him, looking into his gray eyes to see if there's even an ounce of sincerity residing in his pupils. "I still don't know what to think anymore, Jax."

His face visibly falls. "Do you not trust me?"

"I . . ." I sigh. "I can't answer that question because I don't know myself. I just don't understand . . . why lie to me? I know it was to protect me, but were you really listening to every word she said that blindly?"

"I wasn't *blind* to it. I was just doing whatever I could to protect you."

"I can protect myself, though."

"I know you can. But I want to protect you too."

"I don't need your protection."

"God, what don't you get?" he grumbles, smashing his lips to mine. My heart beats at my throat as his addicting taste dissolves into my mouth, more and more eager to intertwine myself with him. He releases briefly afterwards, breathless and his expression desperate. "I am *obsessed* with you, Blaire. I think about you every single waking moment of my life, even when you're gone. It killed me to meet with Veronica every night because I was betraying you, which I had no intention to do. *I did what I had to do.* Imagine if I said no to her, Blaire. That meant she would kill you on sight. You know how batshit crazy she is. I would have to live with constant regret, knowing you were killed because of me. You are the only person in my life who I can share every single fragment of my life with because you get me like no other. Not even Mallory, who I have zero feelings for. I only love you. My love only runs deep for you, and no one else."

At my unwavering expression, he releases a defeated sigh

and presses his lips together. "You can think whatever you want to think about me, beautiful. Just know that I love you, more than you'll ever know, and every decision I make always has to do with you. Just know that. Please."

Jax lets me go, nodding once right before he kisses me briefly on the lips. Finally, he walks away, opens the door, and closes it, leaving me with my overwhelming thoughts and emotions that I just want to rip away from me now.

Just like this damn necklace.

I grasp the pendant and tug on it, feeling the leather cord dig into the back of my neck. I grit my teeth, angry tears releasing from my eyes, wanting it off me now, now, *now*. Jax may have given this to me to bring me an eternity of luck, but all it seems to bring me now is an eternity of *misery*.

However, when I yank at it, my grip slowly loosens and I sigh, letting it rest against my chest still. For some reason, I can't take it off. It may be because of my heart, which is still holding onto Jax. I know he didn't do anything, but I can't bring my thoughts together, so I don't know what to think anymore. Maybe he's lying, maybe he's not. He did spend an entire month doing so, so I wouldn't be surprised if he lied to me just now either. Frankly, I don't know. I don't know, I don't know, *I don't know*.

All I can do is cry in this empty and dark room, left with nothing but my shattered heart, broken to such an extreme I don't know how to put the pieces back together.

42

CONFRONT

JAX

"THIS IS THE DEFENSE line up I expect you to be in when we march into Detroit shortly," Commander Thatcher says as she slowly walks back and forth, her arms slung behind her as she scrutinizes us, especially Vi. "Are there any questions?"

"Yes, I have one," Ren says, who is a couple of rows behind us. "How exactly will we be marching in? Isn't Detroit several miles away from here?"

"That's why we have jeeps, dumbass," Vi murmurs to herself.

"Language, Powers," Commander Thatcher snarls. "But anyway, Levine, we will be traveling to Detroit in jeeps and we will set our ranks right where the headquarters are. I expect Veronica will be notified of our venture there, especially since Reaves and Remington were involved with her too."

I gulp, ignoring everyone's eyes on both me and Mallory. It's been a week since everyone found out about our interactions with Veronica, and it's also been a week since Blaire and I stopped talking. Well, I make efforts to talk to her, but she does her absolute best to avoid me. I've kept on trying to get her attention somehow and someway, but she just doesn't seem to want anything to do with me anymore. I understand maybe it's because she's still stomaching the announcement of what *Veronica* wants Mallory and me to do, but I told her multiple times that we were both unaware of that. Also considering how she expects us to get engaged to each other, which won't happen in this universe, or in any other. I do love Mallory, but not like *that*. The only person who I love like *that* is Blaire, but she's ignoring me, and I don't know what to do anymore.

What I don't get, though, is why she's still upset with me when everyone else seems to have forgiven us. Of course, when we left the headquarters that day, the others were absolutely *enraged* at the announcement—especially Vi, who was about to physically attack us—but we explained to them everything as soon as we arrived at the bunker. Blaire had locked herself up in the room, so she wasn't there to hear it, but the moment we explained everything, they came to their senses and we quickly moved on from there—even Nicolas, who's held on-and-off opinions of me ever since I started dating his younger sister. The only person who's still struggling to understand everything is Blaire, and I have no idea why. Wasn't my explanation enough?

But now that everyone is aware of Veronica knowing our whereabouts, we have been careful lately, quite literally walking on boobytrapped grounds. One wrong step, and the entire universe will go up in flames. There haven't been any physical encounters with the ERUSA yet, which is concerning because that just indicates the she-devil has something even *worse* up her sleeve, so we decided to take the initiative first and make our mark before they do.

Once Commander Thatcher notices there are no other questions, she motions for us to move forward. Immediately, the sound of heavy armor thuds into the docking room as we climb into the dozens of jeeps stationed by the exit. Our first rank, who are basically us Subversives, climbs into the first jeep, and my breath hitches as I see Blaire in front of me. Her eyes meet mine, and she presses her lips together, her expression seeming to be unreadable. I want so badly to fall into her arms again because they feel just like home would feel. But I know she needs her space—her time to realize whatever she needs to realize. So I will grant that to her, no matter how much I want to damn all formalities and kiss her madly. God, I just miss her *so much.*

I notice Mallory purposefully sitting a few seats away from Blaire, and that is only because she wants to give her space too. She's been absolutely gutted by what her mother said too, and she's been doing whatever she can to at least bring me and Blaire on the same page again. I don't know how she feels about our execution that we are supposed to enact, according to Veronica's statement, *tomorrow,* or our falsified engagement too. We haven't met up with her since the night she said I should watch myself for the next few days, so I have no indication of what she meant by that.

Everyone else sits themselves as well, including Vi, who's sitting beside me. Her brown eyes latch on me, and she asks me, "Ready to take these sons of bitches down?"

No, I'm not ready at all. But I don't say that out loud. Instead, I brave a smile when all I want to do is scream until my lungs are aching, sore, and shriveled. "Ready as I'll ever be," I lie.

———

A storm seems to be brewing in the distance, the entirety of Detroit smothered in thick, angry gray clouds. The air is murky and hot, making me almost choke in my heavy gear. I wish we all showed up in shorts and tank tops instead. That would probably make the environment a little less . . . *humid.*

Commander Thatcher leads the line of jeeps speeding

toward Detroit, and in her vehicle are, of course, all the top soldiers—including AJ and Annie. I haven't spoken much with AJ lately, but I'm assuming that's because he's been too in his head about marching into Detroit and being almost just as good of a role model as Commander Thatcher is. But I don't care whether he talks to me or not—it's not like we're friends or anything.

I couldn't care *less* about him. Seriously.

I lean against the seat, clenching my jaw with anticipation as the city grows in both intensity and size. The air is bursting with humidity now, and lightning spreads across the sky, followed by a quick burst of thunder. The ground rumbles as a result, causing me to clench my jaw a bit more. While I am thankful it's going to storm because of the rumored water drought, I am also a bit terrified as well because it's been a while since I've seen a storm like this. There were storms in D.C. too, but they've never been as intense as the one I'm seeing right now.

Something tells me this day might go either really well . . . or really *bad*.

Once we cross the Ambassador Bridge, we are met with the entrance of Detroit. It looms in front of us like a threatening oasis, perched beneath a dark gray atmosphere emblazoned with streaks of lightning. Suddenly, heavy downpour initiates, rain pounding into the open-roofed jeep. The air is still humid, but the cool rain brings energy in me again, an energy I've kept hidden ever since I killed my father.

After six treacherous weeks, we can finally take the ERUSA down with peace and non-violence. No lives will be lost, and we will find a way to calm Veronica and persuade her to retreat. We have to. I'm sick and tired of being under her reign. I'm sick and tired of *her*.

Suddenly, Commander Thatcher's jeep in front of us rolls to a stop, and we do the same, including the many jeeps behind us.

A thick band of ERUSA soldiers is present at the entrance of Detroit, and they march up to us with cocked guns in their hands. She, alongside the other soldiers in her jeep, jump out of the vehicle and hold up their shields while stuffing their guns into their armor bands. We do the same, my breathing heavy as we climb down the bridge and make our way behind them. The soldiers behind us do the same too.

This is it. The moment we've all been waiting for. The moment we demand for the enemy to retreat so we can get our home *back*. Innocent people will stop dying, Detroit will stop suffering, Blaire will forgive me, and life will be back to normal. As if the past six weeks never happened.

"Lower your weapons!" Commander Thatcher yells to the ERUSA. "We just want to resolve our matters in mature ways. There is no need to quarrel at all."

"You're incorrect, Thatcher." A calm, slithery voice attached to a frail and lifeless woman who walks to us, a rifle wedged beneath her underarms. "There are many needs to quarrel when you're emphasizing your revenge, your unavoidable need to get justice for your loved ones. I'm sure you would know."

Her face visibly falls. "What are you talking about?"

Veronica lets out a cold laugh. "Are you forgetting that I have access to everyone's files whenever I'm in the headquarters? I know all about you, *Heidi*. I know all about your husband's suicide, your past alcoholic addiction, your multiple miscarriages, and your estranged children. Quite a sad past, I'd have to say. I'm sure you can relate with where I'm coming from then."

"Leave my life out of this," Commander Thatcher growls. "I am still offering to handle these issues in pragmatic terms. So I would like for you to zip your mouth shut, Reaves."

"You have no right to speak to me like that."

"I have every right to speak to you in whatever way I'd like. Be grateful I'm not attacking your troops right now, and I am instead willing to quite literally sign a peace treaty on this."

"A peace treaty will never appease my circumstances."

"Look, Veronica," Commander Thatcher says slowly, "I understand you're upset about your husband's death. Trust me, I really do understand. I was raging out of my mind the moment I found out he committed suicide. But I knew it would be unfair to others if I threw my anger on them, so I decided to channel all my emotions toward better things, such as being a part of an army that is fighting for equality for *all*. Your army is fighting for the death of innocent individuals. That's why I ask kindly of you to turn in your weapons to the true residents of Detroit and retreat to a different place. Do not do this to others, and especially yourself. Please, Veronica. I mean this as a widowed woman to another widowed woman, so please know I am speaking this from the bottom of my heart. Trust me."

It's quite strange to see Commander Thatcher speak this kindly to someone, but I know she's doing it to calm Veronica's anger and help her see eye-to-eye for once. Let her know that being angry and blaming others for her misery is not the way to absolve her mourning and despair. And, for just a brief moment, I think it is possible by the softening of Veronica's glassy eyes, swarming in bright blue flecks that just now seem to come to life. For just this brief moment, I am ecstatic, buzzing with an ounce of hope I've cast away for God knows how long.

Until her lips quickly curl into a deep frown.

"You must be idiotic to think I will agree to your proposition that easily. I am not a simple-minded woman, Heidi. I have goals I wish to accomplish, and no one is going to stop me. Not even you. Not even your mindless army. And not even the rebels that have wronged me and this country.

"This encounter does not mark your desired peace treaty," she spits out, marching up to Commander Thatcher until the front of their armors almost collide. Her long, pale hair flows behind her, embellishing her brutally white skin and ghost-like features. Heidi, on the other hand, is fuming red, but her eyes are almost emblazoned in an emotion I've never once thought she could have.

My knees almost give out from what Veronica says next.

"Instead . . . this encounter marks the beginning of a war."

43

INFLAME

BLAIRE

THE FIRST GUNSHOT IS fired.

And then another.

Another, another, *another.*

So many I start to lose count.

Bullets fly and spring around us, and I frantically hold onto my shield a bit tighter, my knuckles turning white. My nails dig into my palms, and I dig my right knee into the cemented ground, grinding my teeth in a slow and calculating matter. The soldiers start to march toward us, shooting bullets at us, but from our end we don't dare to fire back. It takes all my guts and willpower to not press the trigger because that is all I want to do. I want to channel all my fears and sorrows into a metal object packed with bullets that can send someone to their instant demise.

When the gunshots become louder and the oncoming stream of both soldiers and their bullets intensifies, I see our rank bounding forward and into the city. I follow behind them wordlessly, doing my best to reflect and defend myself, my heart pounding into my ears. Moments later, I am by their heels and panting loudly as we sprint past the soldiers and enter the heart of the metropolis. People in the city watch curiously at our violent encounter, but immediately retreat into their homes with piercing wails and cries.

I remember when Detroit used to be our desired residence of safety, when D.C. went up in flames. We were ecstatic to settle here, house our refugees, and begin a new life in a new place. There were several events and festivals held, the city was bustling with energy and inhabitants, and for the first time in my life, I was genuinely happy. But right after the Summer Solstice Festival, life took a one-eighty and we were back to square one again, fending for ourselves in a world that constantly spat on us. The bright and buzzing streets became dreary and desolate. Gunshots and cries of the wounded became normal to hear on a daily basis. Scorching flames in the distance sizzled throughout the city, destroying anyone or anything in its path. I hate to say it, but D.C. is heaven compared to the world we are living in now. At least back then people knew how to avoid the enemy's wrath; in a society like this, though, you can be merely roaming the streets and be killed for just being an odd one out in the crowd.

I try not to think of D.C. much, but as I run alongside my peers, my chest huffing with every abrupt movement, my mind falls back to its horrors. I constantly sought for a world better than the world I resided in the past, where there were Guards, and Tobias Remington was healthy and leading the city with an iron fist. That's why, when Veronica declared war on us, I felt a trickle of fear seep into my veins. It seems as if we are on a constant loop, each action leading to the beginning, and it repeats on and on until we come to the ultimate realization that this is our life now, and we have to live with it.

The only good that came out of my time in D.C. is convening with the Subversives and finally feeling as if I have people who care for me. Obviously I've had my family since the very beginning, but they're my home. At the end of the day, no matter who or what enters my life, I know that I will always have them. But, as I joined the Subversives, I felt as if I had *more* people I could eventually call my home too because, even though we had different upbringings, we all shared the same goal: serve justice and equality for all. To some extent, I'm grateful I met everyone, but, at the same time, I can't help but wonder if meeting them would be the origin of my eventual forfeiture.

The more and more people I love, the more and more I'm at risk for heartbreak. And I don't know if I can handle that.

As Commander Thatcher instructs some soldiers to advance to the city to defend the people, the rest of us fall back to the outskirts—or rather where the Summer Solstice Festival was held. I get a horrible realization that this is the place where life was seemingly going well until Ren's mother was assassinated by the ERUSA. This is the place where the leader revealed themself to be Veronica Reaves, Mallory's angry and frustrated mother. And this is especially the place where Jax and I confessed our feelings and began our relationship.

My heart heaves at the thought of Jax, and I look over to my side, seeing him running alongside Vi. His silver eyes are trained forward, working his jaw as he props the helmet on top of his messy dark hair. Rain coats his tan skin—or rather the only exposed skin on his face—and the breaths escaping his throat are ragged, heavy, and sharp.

Unfortunately, his head swivels to my side, his face slackening the more he studies me. I know I have been ignoring him for a while, but for what reason I have no idea. It's not to do with him; it's more to do with me and my inability to recognize my feelings. The terror and utter rage I felt coursing through my body when I learned of Mallory and Jax's engagement and notion to eradicate all Poors and Impures was enough to rip apart the entire city. Of course I had no idea it was all fabricated by Veronica, but even when Jax informed me of that, I still felt that terror and utter rage from before. Even when everyone else forgave Jax and Mallory, I still could not have the heart and guts in me to do that.

The more we look at each other, the more I become willing to forgive him and openly love him again. I miss him so much it physically hurts. I would do *anything* to fall in his arms again, feel his body against mine and his words soothing my ears. Maybe after all this we can start on a fresh slate. I can apologize to him, and we can move on. Act like nothing ever happened.

I rip my sight away from him, feeling a sudden wave of tears threatening to escape my eyes. I can't handle this right now. I must focus. When this is all over, I can talk to Jax and we can fix our situation. I *want* to fix our situation.

When we rush past the outskirts, I hear the water surrounding Detroit violently crashing onto the banks, splurges of water splashing onto us. It's not a lot to the point where we're drowning, but it's enough to seep into our armor and lose traction in our soles. We scamper past the drenched grounds, thunder rumbling in the distance. Normally, thunderstorms would soothe me, but today, I take it as a foreboding entity. And it physically sickens me.

As more bullets spring past us, almost slashing into our gear, Commander Thatcher leads us past the banks and onto the roads, jumping over the fences that separate the two. I frantically look around, moving my shield in sporadic directions and praying no bullets enter either me or anyone in this rank. The last thing I want is someone I care for to be killed by these bastards. In a situation such as that, I wouldn't adhere to Commander Thatcher's defensive plan.

Suddenly, Nico yells from the front, "We need to bring our families to safety! They can't stay in that home anymore!"

A gut-wrenching feeling settles in my stomach. He's right. If any one of these ERUSA soldiers make their way to the home, then consider my family and Jeremiah's killed. We can't risk that, especially since Veronica is well aware of our location.

Commander Thatcher quickly brings us to a stop, my legs feeling like a hundred pound weights, blood thrusting into my veins. "Nicolas is right. Some of us need to go there to bring the others to safety, and some of us stay here and defend as Reformers." Her brown eyes quickly peruse over us. "Blaire, Nicolas, Jeremiah, and I will go to the home, and the others will stay here. AJ, Annie, and Vienna will lead the Reformers. And . . ." She glances over at Vi. "You all may shoot back."

We all share confused looks with each other. *Commander Thatcher is finally letting us shoot back? What the hell?*

"Wait . . ." Nico furrows his brows at her. "Why all of a sudden—"

"Don't ask," she interjects. "Just do it already, for Christ's sake. Before I start to regret my decision." Commander Thatcher looks over at Vi, who seems to be fighting off a grin. "Also, you're right, Powers. Just because I'm a Commander, doesn't mean I have the right to act like a dictator. Your opinion matters. And I will listen to it.

"So, please, for the love of God and our country . . . fire back." She nods once. "Because our life depends on it. Got it?"

After a few moments, we all mutter in scattered responses, "Got it."

"Christ, what the hell was that? Where was the enthusiasm?"

"Got it!" we shout simultaneously.

"Good," she says. "Much better." And, with another nod, she starts to walk off in the other direction.

"Wait, Commander Thatcher," Annie says, "why are *you* going to the home?"

Heidi slowly looks over at me, her lips pressed together in thought and her eyebrows pushed up in determination. "Because I just have to."

44

HASTE

JAX

AS BLAIRE, JEREMIAH, NICOLAS, and Commander Thatcher depart, a wave of soldiers immediately pour in behind us. One of them in particular stands out from the rest, with their flowing red hair and widened green eyes masked between the helmet clearly engulfing their head. "Help! They're chasing me!" Ren shrieks, huddling within us and frantically holding up her shield.

"How the hell did you outrun them?" AJ asks as we hold up our shields, simultaneously shuffling backwards as fast as we can.

"I don't know," she stammers. "I just ran for my life."

"And you managed to do all that, while not getting shot too?" Vi asks unconvincingly.

"Okay, fine! I shot at them!"

When we settle behind an alleyway, still holding up our shields, we all look over at her in complete shock. *Renata Levine shot at the ERUSA soldiers? The same woman who burst out in tears when she accidentally stepped on an ant? There's no way in hell.*

"There's no way in hell," Vi voices out my thoughts.

"I know it may seem surprising," Ren says, "but I felt like I had no choice but to shoot at them. I escaped my other rank because the ERUSA was so close to us, and I felt so threatened. I gathered every bit of strength and knowledge in me then and shot at them like some sort of madman, even though we are not allowed to. What other choice did I have? And while it was a bit difficult because, of course, guns are just not my forte, it wasn't that hard at the same time either because I kept reminding myself that they were the same people that killed my mother. So that kept me motivated until I was able to outrun them . . . until I found you guys."

"Oh, my God," Vi says after a while. "Why would you shoot at them? You know we're not allowed to, right?"

"Vi, just tell her the tru—" Mal starts to say.

"No, I want to see her reaction," she whispers while fighting off a grin.

"I know." Ren frowns. "Please don't tell Commander Thatcher, okay? Gosh, that would be so embarrassing. I can't even imagine how bad that would be for me and my reputation. It took me *so long* to even be at the position I am at right now. Goodness gracious, what is wrong with me? Why would I shoot back? Why am I so—"

"You're allowed to fire back!" AJ blurts out.

Ren's face falls. "What?"

As he explains to her that Commander Thatcher finally said we are allowed to fire back, she gasps and pouts at Vi. "Why would you lie to me?"

"Because it's really funny." Vi shrugs.

"You—!" Ren harrumphs. "You're really mean."

As Vi is about to respond, a line of ERUSA soldiers peer into the alleyway and shoot at us, bullets twanging into our shields. After gathering our courage, we fire back at them, the feeling of finally being able to release strings of bullets at the enemy settling into my chest. *Thank God,* I think to myself in relief.

Once we manage to fend off the soldiers, we huddle in a circle and sit in silence for a bit, enjoying these few minutes of quietude before the soldiers in the back eventually catch up to us and we'd have to fight back.

"I can't believe Veronica declared war on us," I say after a while, picking at the rubbles and stones beneath me.

"Me neither," Annie says as she takes her helmet off her. We do the same. "I just hope we all make it out alive."

"We *will,*" AJ emphasizes. "As long as we fight back and stand our ground, we will be fine."

"I sure hope you're right about that," Mallory murmurs, "because I'm sick and tired of my mom torturing everyone like this." When she finishes speaking, I raise my eyebrows at her suggestively. Her cheeks redden as she says again, "Sorry. *Veronica.* Not my mom at all."

"You're not addressing her as your mom anymore?" Ren asks.

"Why would I? She's done everything but be a good mother. The last thing she deserves is being referred to as one. Thankfully Jax helped me realize that."

I nod at her, smiling slowly.

Moments later, Ren clears her throat. "So . . . speaking of you and Jax . . ." She fiddles with the tips of her long red hair. "Are you guys, like, actually engaged now? That doesn't make sense, though, because Jax is dating Blaire—but I doubt you guys are together because Blaire seems very mad at you—"

"Jesus, you just don't know how to shut up, don't you?" Vi grumbles at her.

"It is a genuine question I'm pretty sure all of us are wondering!"

"Yeah, I'm wondering that too"—AJ murmurs—"but I'm not asking that in the middle of a goddamn war."

"Language," Ren whispers.

Vi rolls her eyes. "Oh, please just *stop* with this *language* bull-shit already—"

"Mallory and I are not engaged!" I hiss. "I thought I already told you guys that Veronica made that up so we'd be forced to kill all the people she wants to kill—which isn't gonna happen either. Also, Blaire and I are still together and we're working on our relationship . . . in private." I steal an irritated glance toward Ren. "So, I'd appreciate it if you don't bring this up again, okay? Me and Mallory are, again, not engaged and never will be. We're just friends. That's it."

I release a pent-up sigh as I hug my knees, planting my chin on top of them. I still have not forgotten how Veronica mentioned those *completely* false propositions, especially in front of Blaire. I was going to let Blaire know about the entire situation soon anyway because, technically, Mallory and I were quasi-liberated from her. I hope we can come to a general consensus soon and life will, hopefully, go back to normal. I miss her aura, her touch, her smile, her taste. Time is ticking by, and it's only inevitable I'll go insane without her by my side.

Suddenly, Mallory clears her throat and clenches her jaw as she says, "Yeah. We're just friends." She audibly gulps, shakes her head once, twice, and gets up from her seat. "I'm gonna go stand over there for a bit. I just want to get some fresh air."

As she starts to depart, another round of distant gunshots resound into the air, and I unconsciously grab the hilt of my gun, grazing the trigger. *Shit, more ERUSA soldiers!* We get up from our seats, and Mallory reluctantly stands beside us, her hands shaking as she grabs her helmet and plants it on her head. We do the same, standing close together as we hide by the alley-way, constantly peering out into the clearing to see where the noises are originating from.

"What do we do?" Ren whines as she stands beside Vi—who, on the other hand, rolls her eyes at her and inches to me.

"We need to get out of here," AJ yells at us.

"No, let's fire back," Vi hisses.

"No way," Annie says. "It's too risky."

"I agree." AJ sighs. "Look at how many soldiers are advancing, let alone the speed they're coming at. We *need* to run."

"Where?" I ask. "And how?"

"I just got word that Reynolds and Brady are bringing a jeep to us and we will escape to the northern part of the city, near Dearborn. They, alongside the other soldiers, will be holding down the area here while we escape and hold down the other region." As AJ spews even more words at us, a rumbling of an engine nears us and appears in the crack of the alley. "There it is!" he yells, urging us to climb on there. "Let's go!"

Without a single thought, we make a run for the jeep with Reynolds and Brady climbing out of the front, the same soldiers that are known to be two of the most skilled in Detroit. "There are others coming," Brady says, "so you guys are good to go."

"Thank you so much," Annie gasps out as she climbs into the driver's seat. "C'mon, guys! It's either now or never!"

As AJ rides shotgun, the rest of us pile into the back. Mallory is next to me, and she gives me a wordless nod as she leers her eyes to the side of the jeep. *Why is she acting so weird with me all of a sudden?* On my other side is Ren, who struggles to compose herself, clutching her abdomen and murmuring, "I think I'm going to throw up."

"Please puke outside the vehicle." Vi scrunches her nose. "We don't need your remnants hanging out in the jeep with us."

As soon as Vi finishes speaking and the jeep rumbles to life, Ren lets out a loud gasp and seems to almost puke her *guts* out by the side of the jeep. When she finishes, she meekly clears her throat and says in a monotonous tone, "I'm finished. I think."

Immediately, Annie lurches the jeep forward, the tires screeching against the rough pavement as the body of the car trembles beneath us. I grind on my teeth, my heart seeming to almost burst out of my chest. We drive past the alley and out into the clearing, where the main road is filled with a couple of cars. The tires continue to screech, and the car lurches from left to right as we meander past the oncoming vehicles, horns honking at us and angry drivers hurling insults as well. We couldn't care less though, because—as I can see from my peripheral vision—a massive group of ERUSA soldiers is coming into view. They are lined up in several jeeps, shooting at us and gaining in speed.

"Annie, step on it!" Vi urges.

"I am!" she yells. The car is going at such a fast speed that I feel the wind and fat rain slapping my face, every ounce of contact irritating my skin.

As we continue to weave past oncoming traffic and manage to at least be a considerable distance away from the mound of ERUSA soldiers, I see railroad crossing gates almost several miles away from us slowly inch down to the ground, red lights flashing above them. A line of train tracks seems to be going down in the middle, and my eyes travel cautiously over to the far end of the tracks where a train seems to be speeding across it.

"Annie, the gates are going down for the railroad crossing ahead," I say frantically.

"I know," she responds, her foot still pushed onto the gas pedal.

"Did you not just hear him?" Ren shrieks. "There's a train coming ahead!"

"I *know!*" Annie hisses, seeming for it to be the first time I've actually witnessed her being annoyed. "Trust me, I know what I'm doing."

"Uh, are you sure about that?" AJ winces from the front, holding onto the edge of the jeep. "Because it seems as if you want to kill us."

"I'm not gonna kill you guys!"

"Why else are you speeding toward the railroad crossing while there's a damn train speeding across it?" Vi hisses. "Stop the goddamn car!"

"No cursing, Vienna!"

"I swear to God, redhead, if you say that one more time then I'm gonna—"

"Guys, enough!" AJ gasps. "We have bigger things to worry about right now!"

"Yeah, like your sister attempting to murder us!" Mallory yelps.

Suddenly, Annie's right hand grasps the gear stick wedged by the front-end of the vehicle and slams it all the way to the back, a bright white "S" instead of a "D" illuminated. Something beneath the jeep, presumably the engine, rumbles to life, and the car revs, meandering through the different cars, knocking into rails, trashcans, and streetlights, and getting closer and closer to the train tracks, the ground beneath it rising into a small hill.

I squeeze my hands into fists, my heart beating at my neck.

The front of the car suddenly nears the gates flashing red with the train nearing us, almost about to smash into the side. Suddenly, we crash into the gates, broken wooden splinters flying around us, and the tires squeal as the vehicle seems to almost lift from the ground.

I would say it happens in slow motion, but it doesn't. Instead, it all happens in one picture-perfect motion.

We are lifted above the ground, flying over the tracks with rain pelting inside our jeep. Meanwhile, the front of the train grazes the back of our vehicle, obliterating it into multiple pieces. Luckily it is the absolute rear, and not the part where Mallory, Ren, and I are seated. Otherwise we would've been crushed into smithereens. And the vehicle comes falling down, staggering to a stop as we crash into the nearest curb.

As I catch my breath, I hear the ERUSA vehicles crashing

into the side of the train, some even squealing their brakes loudly. *We did it. We managed to come out of this alive.*

I don't celebrate our survival too much, though, because I get the horrible feeling that this is just the beginning of the horrors that are about to happen.

45

TRANSIENT

BLAIRE

The jeep rumbles to a stop in front of the home. Lightning flashes and thunder rumbles as we climb out of the vehicle, my boots sloshing with the muddied grounds. Nico, Heidi, Jeremiah, and I trample over to the front door, and Jeremiah says, "I hope everyone's safe and sound."

"They better be," Heidi muses. "I don't see any reason for why or how the ERUSA got here."

"Well, let's not get too confident about that," Nico says as he pries the door open, "because this is Veronica Reaves we're talking about here."

The hinges creak, groaning in protest as we step inside. The clanking of our boots resound through the dim foyer, and I would probably be considering leaving the room if I weren't accompanied by others, simply because this place is too creepy to begin with. The floorboards beneath us moan with every step, and dust seems to be spreading amongst the crevices of the wall, tiny spiders residing in the dark corners. I never really noticed the details of the foyer until now, only because I come here just for peace and solitude after a tiring day at the compound.

We first knock on Jeremiah's room door, where Layla and Tamia should be. Jeremiah stands in front of the doorway as Layla opens the door. Her bright brown eyes widen as she gives him a limb-squeezing hug. "Baby, I'm so happy to see you're okay," she whispers into his broad shoulder.

"I'm so happy to see *you're* okay," he emphasizes, kissing her hair. "Where's our baby girl?"

"Right here, Daddy!" Tamia stands by the doorway, her tiny hands grasping his pant leg as she gleams with delight. *She reminds me of younger Em in so many ways.*

As he takes her into his arms, she gushes as he drowns her in kisses. "You're not causing Mommy any trouble, are you?" Tamia giggles mischievously, and she shrieks with laughter as he tickles the bottom of her feet. "Now you're gonna get it!" He laughs, kissing her cheek multiple times.

Once Jeremiah and his family reconvene, we climb up the stairs to our room. As Nico's about to knock on the door, Heidi says, "Wait!"

Nico turns around to look at her. "Yes, Commander Thatcher?"

She clears her throat. "I just want to let you know that I'll be standing downstairs when you guys reconcile."

As she starts to make her way down, I grab her arm and lure her back in. "Nope, you're staying here," I say, smiling at her.

She frowns and whispers, "I don't know if I can do it, Blaire. What if she wants nothing to do with me?"

"That's not true, Heidi. She misses you *so much.* You'll see when you meet her shortly."

She audibly gulps, nodding once and gesturing for Nico to continue.

He looks at us confused right before he knocks on the door thrice. "Hey, guys? It's Nicolas. Can you open the door?"

A couple of seconds later, my papa opens the door, holding a mug in his hands, furls of smoke lifting from the inside. "What are you guys doing here?" he asks, his dark green eyes perusing over us and raising his eyebrows in confusion at the short-haired woman beside me. "Who are you?"

"I'm . . ." She presses her lips together. "I'm Commander Thatcher. Commander *Heidi* Thatcher."

At that, my papa holds a hand up to his heart, shakes his head twice, and yells to the back, "Marianna! You have a visitor!"

Moments later, he makes way for my mama, confusion first drawn on her features. But when her soft brown eyes land on Heidi, she lets out a choked gasp, tears immediately streaming down her matured cheeks. "No . . . it can't be," she sobs. "Heidi? Are you my Heidi?"

She grins ear-to-ear, which almost takes me by surprise because Commander Thatcher *never* smiles. "Yes, it is me." Heidi walks forward, holding both of Mama's hands and squeezing them tightly. "Are you my Mari?"

"Yes," she sobs again, her lip trembling into a smile. "I can't believe it's you."

They immediately hug, my mama's cries drowning into Heidi's shoulder. Meanwhile, all Heidi does is smile, choked laughter escaping from her as she rubs her back. "I've been waiting for you my whole life, Mari. I'm sorry I had to leave D.C. and I couldn't keep in touch with you. You know how rough life was back then."

"Yes, I do know. I'm just glad we're together now. That's all that matters."

As Heidi and my mama have their moment, Em peeks out from the inside and squeals when she sees me and Nico. She gives us a tight hug and excitedly asks us, "Why are you guys here?"

The excitement is wiped from her features as Nico says, "We need to leave."

My mama slowly releases from her estranged best friend in terror. "Why?"

"Because Veronica just declared war on us," Heidi responds, "and it is not safe for you here anymore."

"Many refugees have died," Layla croaks out as she climbs into the back with Tamia curling into her arms. "Not a lot are left."

"What about the ones Heidi housed in the compound?" I ask as Em leans against my shoulder. "Are they safe?"

"Safe and without a damn scratch on them," Heidi says as she starts the engine. "That's why we're going to take all the remaining refugees and Detroitian citizens in need to the Detroitian compound, alongside your family and Jeremiah's."

"Actually, we don't have to take them there," Layla says.

"What do you mean, baby?" Jeremiah asks besides her.

"Well, I recently came in touch with the other remaining cities Veronica has not allied with yet. One of them is El Paso in Texas, and they are a safety regime tucked away and hidden from Veronica's eyes. I say we bring all of the surviving people, including our families, and any other soldiers that wish to leave as well." Layla directs her voice to Heidi. "You guys have aircraft carriers, right?"

"Plenty of them," she says, driving the vehicle forward.

"Perfect." Layla claps her hands. "As soon as we escape the city, we will board everyone on the planes and take them to El Paso. If some soldiers want to stay back and fight then that is more than fine, I just want everyone gone in the next two weeks because this place is clearly not safe anymore."

"Shouldn't Veronica be the one leaving and not us?" I grumble.

"I know," Layla says, "but we have no other choice, Blaire.

This is a matter of life or death over our dignity—and honestly, I just want to survive."

After a while, we sit in silence, tires quietly trailing against the fissured roads. When we approach the entrance of the city, I hear the loud rumbling of gunshots and startling cries of the wounded and killed. Nico, from the front, clenches his jaw and talks to Heidi about something I couldn't care less about right now. All I can focus on are the marred and deteriorating bodies around me, succumbed to human violence. Em whimpers into my shoulder, and I bring her closer to me, covering her eyes and ears so she doesn't have to hear or see the horrors of our world. A thirteen-year-old should never have to witness that.

As Tamia lets out a blood-curdling cry, Layla immediately does her best to silence her as Heidi begins to quickly drive down the road. Suddenly, the unlikely happens as the engine sputters to a stop, the vehicle lurching forward and back. "What's happening?" my papa asks from the back frantically. "Why are we stopping?"

"The engine seems to have died out on us." Nico slams the side of the car. "Goddammit!"

"We have to walk now," Heidi mutters as she climbs out of the car and urges everyone to get out.

"What about the ERUSA?" I ask frantically. "What if they see us?"

"We'll shoot at them," she responds after a while.

Once everyone escapes the broken-down vehicle in the middle of the road, we slowly meander past the objects seeping into the fissured roads, destroyed cars slung across the area and people wailing in the distance. Em clings onto my left leg behind me, and I turn off the safety for my rifle, my finger edging the trigger.

Heidi is in the very front, grasping her rifle as she scans the area frantically. "Be on the lookout for any of the ERUSA," she demands. "They can come from any direction, so be mindful of that."

"Got it," Jeremiah says as he clutches the butt of the rifle wedged in his underarm, Layla trailing behind him with a sniffling Tamia hoisted in her arms. She's managed to quieten her cries because if she hadn't, then we would all be in great danger right now.

Next to him is Nico, who is next to my papa. He's constantly scanning the area, his jaw clenched with determination as his long hair flows down his neck and rustles in the wind. As he continues his constant scanning, his jaw slackens as he hisses to us, "Incoming soldiers! Let's fall back over there."

Thankfully because of the heavy rain and the great hissing of the wind, our footsteps and strangled cries are drowned out. I feel the soldiers pounding at my heels, their figures like gray and amorphous entities amongst the smothering fog. I can't see anything more than a mile ahead of me, and the opposite direction we're heading in is unknown. For all I know, there could be *more* soldiers there.

"Everyone, stay together!" Jeremiah hisses as we trample further down the roads—but the rain is pelting at us, the fog choking and dissolving our surroundings.

Behind me Em seems to have let out a choked sob, and I turn around to see her sprawled on the ground, frantically pointing at her leg. "I tripped!" she cries. "It hurts so bad!"

"You're okay, Em!" I gasp out, pulling her up to her feet. "Can you walk?"

"Barely," she whimpers.

"It's okay," Nico says, coming over. "Climb on my back. I got you."

Wordlessly, she climbs on his back, grimacing to herself as we carry on forward. But we are all sprawled out now, heaving and dispersing in different directions because the fog is searingly white now, dissipating and pervasive. I can't even see my own feet in front of me at this point. I can feel their presence below me, but I can't *see* them. We have to stick together until we find another available jeep somewhere so we can get the hell out of here. There are soldiers somewhere near us, but we can't let our guard down that easily. We have to be wary—especially since we are drowning in vulnerability.

Soon enough, I don't feel anyone's presence around me.

It's the damn fog, the damn rain, the damn *wind* that's making me feel blind. I must be going crazy. Everyone's around me still. I swear.

"Where is everyone?" I shout, gripping my rifle so tight I lose all feeling in my arm.

"Over here!" I hear Jeremiah, Layla, and Tamia shout in the far distance, but nobody else.

"Where's my family?" I shout back.

"I don't know! I don't know where everyone else is!"

I grumble to myself, the rain smashing onto my skin like shards of glass. My boots crunch against the ground beneath me, and it's so painstakingly humid that I just want to tear this uniform off me. *Where the hell did my family go? How could I ever have been so stupid to wander off on my own and lose them?* I get a horrible feeling that something happened to them, that one of these soldiers caught them and killed them on sight. But no, that isn't possible. Nico is with them, and he's armed. He wouldn't let anyone get near our family.

Suddenly, I hear a gunshot and a strangled cry.

46

WOE

JAX

"STUPID PIECE OF SHIT!"

With one swift motion, Vi kicks at the mangled jeep door, unhinged from the vehicle. Steam rises from the engine and amalgamates with the drooping trees above us, and all I can hear in the background are the wailing ERUSA soldiers lodged into the neverending moving train behind us. Once we've all climbed out, AJ puts a hesitant hand on her shoulder and says, "Vienna, there's no way the jeep is gonna work because it crashed into the curb."

"Well, it should because it's not like it crashed into a goddamn *house,*" Vi grumbles. "This is the only way we can go about the city. If we're on foot then we're more vulnerable."

"Sorry, but that's the only choice we have," Annie says as she starts to walk away from the steamy and disheveled mess.

"This is all your fault, you know that, right?" Vi snarls. "If you hadn't run the car into the curb then we wouldn't have to deal with this situation."

"Excuse me? If I hadn't gone over the train tracks then we would've all been dead right now."

"Are they about to fight?" Ren whispers to me and Mallory. Mallory and I, on the other hand, share annoyed looks and slowly inch away from Ren.

"No one's about to fight," AJ drawls out. "We're instead going to leave this place before the train leaves and we're exposed to the other side. So I suggest we do that now, okay?"

After Vi finishes her death glare toward Annie, she harrumphs and starts to walk forward. We wordlessly follow behind her, clinging onto our guns with fear jabbing at our throat and veins.

As we continue to tread forward, constantly scanning the grounds for any signs of the enemy, the thick murky air begins to hug my exposed neck, sweat bathing underneath my uniform. "Can we take these things off already?"

"Sure, why not?" AJ says, stopping in his place to take his uniform off, revealing a loose cotton gray shirt and black pants. He immediately puts his bulletproof vest on "As long as you wear your protective gear on top, I don't see the problem."

So we all silently begin to peel off our layers of hell, inaudible breaths of relief escaping from us. Once I tear off my upper armor, revealing my black tank top with camo pants underneath, I lodge my bulletproof vest and protective pads on top. The only place I can even get shot is my head, but I don't have much to preserve there anyway—so I'm not too worried about that.

Once we've shed our uniforms, we drop them in the mangled jeep we left behind and resume our ambling, our boots clanking against the uneven roads. A constant cacophony of sirens, screams, and shots rattle into the air, and I grind on my molars, hoping and praying Blaire and the others are alive. Commander Thatcher hasn't contacted either Annie, AJ, or even Vi in a while, so I'm assuming she's caught up reconciling with Blaire's Mom. Whatever the reason is, *I just want them all to be okay.*

Behind me are Mallory and Ren, and Mallory is comforting a shaking and shivering Ren. I'm in the middle, grazing the trigger and imagining every possible way this exact moment in time can go wrong. *Better safe than sorry.* Meanwhile, in the front are Annie, AJ, and Vi, with Annie leading the group forward. We are entering the suburban part of Detroit, so it's not as raucous here as it is in the metropolitan area. That means we're going to have to be even more wary about our movements because we're more vulnerable to attacks here . . . since it is just us.

"Everyone stay close together," AJ whispers to us. "We are not splitting up in any sort of way, so I suggest we remain tight."

As our line tightens and intensifies, Mallory trailing very closely behind me, I press my lips together, furrowing my eyebrows at the very little, but also very many amorphous blobs and entities crowding in the distance.

"Am I going crazy, or are those ERUSA soldiers?" Ren whimpers out.

"I cannot believe I'm saying this," Vi murmurs, "but for once you're not going crazy because I see them too."

"What the hell do we do?" I ask frantically. "Should we run?"

"Where to?" AJ shoots me an indeterminable look. "We can't turn back because it is absolute chaos over there. We can't go left or right because there are nothing but houses and neighborhoods here, and we'd be disrupting them, so we have no other choice but to go forward."

"But what if they shoot at us?" Ren asks.

Mallory speaks moments later, her tone determined and unwavering. "I guess we're just gonna have to shoot back."

"Oh, no," she whimpers. "No, no, no, no, *no!* I'm going to die. Oh, no!"

"No one's gonna die," Annie rectifies. "So let's just relax here, all right? We've trained endlessly for this exact moment, we're geared to the bones, and there are many places to retreat to. Worst case scenario, I can just call over a couple of soldiers for back-up. As long as we stick together and keep our eyes peeled, then we will be okay."

I silently repeat Annie's words to myself, hoping to ease my anxiety. *We will be okay, we will be okay, we will be okay . . .*

I keep on thinking that until the first gunshot goes off.

Our paces quicken, my breathing too, and as we rush forward, the hilt of my rifle pointed at the unidentifiable entities that slowly morph into identifiable ones with jet-black armor, many and many of them appearing. There must be at least twenty at the moment. *Shit, shit, shit!* We're outnumbered tremendously. It'd be a miracle if all of us survived.

A bullet suddenly twangs into the streetlamp next to us, plunging into the light and shattering the bulb into pieces. A shard of glass grazes my shoulder, blood immediately seeping out of my flesh. I curse to myself, planting my hand on top of the wound mid-run, but it's too much that my hand begins to drown in my own crimson liquid.

Fortunately, Mallory hands me a rolled-up gauze—probably from the first-aid kit she always carries around. "Take this!" she yells.

"Thank you!" I gasp out, tearing the adhesive off with the front of my teeth and spitting the material out. I wrap it around my shoulder, blood still trailing down but I could honestly care less. Just like AJ said before, we have *much* bigger things to worry about.

The ERUSA soldiers are suddenly in eye's range, their guns pointed at us as they begin to shoot—this time, at *us.* I deflect the bullets thrown at me by ducking and making myself an unstable target. Standing in one place is never something one should do in battle. Meanwhile, I fire back at some ERUSA soldiers that have *dared* to fire at me, imagining myself hunting with my father and imagining the targets *were* my father.

My tactic seems to work because I fire rapidly, the uproarious gunshots leaving my gun so loud I feel it vibrate into my chest. I grit my teeth, standing beside AJ as he kneels to the ground, letting out a rapidfire line of bullets with not even his eyebrow twitching. His face is neutral, his almost-yellow eyes drilled onto his target. If only he wasn't attracted to Blaire, then I would *possibly* consider being his acquaintance. Just possibly.

"I don't know what to do!" Ren shrieks behind us. "I need help!"

"Who brought her here?" Vi grumbles from the front as she brings three bullets to an ERUSA soldier's head.

"Vi, go help her!" Annie yells from the front as she quarrels with two other soldiers. "Mallory can stay in the middle and AJ and Jax can come up with me!"

"Why do *I* have to help her?" Vi whines. "She's gonna hold me back!"

"She won't hold you back! All you have to do is stand in front of her and make sure she doesn't get shot!"

"Goddammit!" Vi roars out as she stomps on over to Ren, roughly grabbing her by the arm and planting Ren behind her. "Stay back there and if you get shot, then I *swear to God* I will kill you myself!"

As Vi and Ren stay in the back, with Mallory behind me, AJ and I rally up to the front, a cloud of dust and smoke suffocating my surroundings. Annie is currently shooting at a soldier while another claws at her hair.

"Get away from my sister!" AJ growls as he runs at the soldier top-speed, jumping onto the man and sending him to the ground. He rapidly punches at the man's face, and from where I stand, I notice his features are unrecognizable now, mashed and marred and pretty much bloodied. Meanwhile, I feel a rough pair of hands grab at my neck, and I yell in agony as the soldier brings me down to the ground, the rough sole of their boot digging into the back of my neck. My face is pushed into the road, pebbles and stones pressing into my flesh and scratching at my skin. I ground out a scream, bring my hand to the back of the man's leg and push it to the side, allowing him to plummet on my back. I turn around, while fumbling for my rifle, and I don't even wait to catch my breath when I send three consecutive bullets to the man's head. My mouth curls down in disgust as blood spills out of his head, cracking his skull open as he falls onto the ground next to me. Blood spreads out around his head, and I quickly get up, gagging to myself at the horrendous sight. *Jesus Christ, that's disgusting as hell.*

A good majority of the soldiers are dead now, and the only ones that remain are injured to the core, barely able to hold themselves upright. Vi's still reluctantly protecting Ren and shooting at the remaining ERUSA soldiers, Mallory is in front of her, chewing on her bottom lip as she frantically looks around for any other surprises, AJ is beating up another soldier, and Annie is . . .

Oh, no.

My blood runs cold at the injured soldier staggering up to his feet with a rifle wedged in his underarm, and he stands above Annie, who is getting up from her position, her back turned to him for that *exact moment.* Without even thinking, I spring up to my feet, run toward her, and yell at the top of my lungs, "Annie, *DUCK!*"

Unfortunately, my words don't travel fast enough amongst the earth-shattering gunshots as Annie looks at me confused, her lips forming to say something, but that is until a bullet lodges into her chest at an uninterpretable speed.

No, no, no, no, no.

As she falls to the ground, blood forming on her abdomen and staining her thin cotton shirt, AJ slowly turns around at her bloodied body. He lets out a choked gasp, trembling as he stumbles over to her, his hands shaking more than the core of this earth. Mallory, Ren, Vi, and I rush over there once all of the soldiers have fallen, and we all kneel beside her, speechless at what we see. *No, Annie cannot die. She's one of the best soldiers in the compound. She's basically made out of steel. There's no way a puny little bullet can kill her.*

Her eyes start to flutter close, a shaky breath leaving her mouth. AJ's jaw twitches, and he rapidly blinks, tears streaming down his cheeks. He doesn't scream, mourn, *nothing*. All he does is run his fingers through her hair, grief stricken on his trembling features. "Nothing happened to you, Annie," he whispers. "Get up, okay? You can't fool me. I'm not stupid."

She doesn't respond.

"Stop this, Aneesa!" he yells at the top of his lungs now. "Get up right now! Don't do this to me!"

"Ajay . . ." she suddenly whispers, her shaky tone as light as a feather.

Vi, Mallory, Ren, and I share confused looks, notating the way she pronounced his name differently. *Ajay? Aneesa? Are those their actual names?*

"Aneesa, *please*," he croaks out, his dark eyebrows pushed to his forehead as he sobs. "Get up, please. Please, please, please."

A single tear escapes from her eye, trailing down her cheek and curving around her chin. "You're an amazing little brother, Ajay. Thank you for being here for me, and I'm s-sorry I can't be with you anymore. I just want to let you know that I'm so proud of how much you've accomplished so far. I am sure you will accomplish even more in the future. Just . . . make sure to keep on making me and our parents proud, okay?"

"You're not going anywhere."

"I . . . I'm sorry. I'm so sorry."

"Stop, Aneesa!" he yells again.

I place a shaky hand on his shoulder. "AJ, I hate to tell you this but we *have* to let her go."

"Shut the hell up, Jax," he seethes. "Leave me alone."

"I'm sorry, but he's right." Mallory frowns as she inches next to him. "It seems as if the bullet went straight to her heart. I hate leaving her here too, but we have to move on."

"You guys don't get it." He rapidly shakes his head, his tears and his sister's blood staining his shirt. "I'm not going anywhere without her."

"Please go, Ajay." Annie's eyes are barely open now, and she brings a timid hand to her cheek, brushing tears away with an abrupt swipe of her thumb. "Please stop crying and leave me. You have a city to defend."

"Aneesa—"

"Go," she says nimbly. "There's no need to waste your time and energy on me. I'm begging you, go with everyone else and *make us proud.* Remember all the things I told you—what *Amma* and *Baba* told you. Keep on being and loving yourself. If you do just that, I promise that you will be fine, even without me by your side."

"But I don't want that," he urges. "You were the only one here for me when *Amma* and *Baba* were gone. How can I ever move on without you by my side?"

AJ waits for a response, but there is only silence.

It seems as if all air has left my lungs and flown out in the hot, heaving air because as I look down, I see Annie's eyes are closed, her entire torso drenched in blood. Mallory shakily checks her pulse—once, twice, thrice—but on the third time, she shakes her head at AJ, right before she rubs his shoulder and leans against him.

"No," he whispers. "This can't be happening."

"I'm sorry, AJ," I croak out, "but we have to go now. She isn't responding."

"What did I say, Jax?" he growls. "Shut. The. Hell. Up! You're the last person I want to hear speaking right now."

"Look, I get that you're upset, and you can say whatever the hell you want to me, but the least you can do for the others is let her go so we all can move forward. God knows when another round of soldiers are gonna come, so we have to keep on moving."

"I don't care, you guys can go on without me, but I'm staying here."

"I felt exactly how you felt my mom died in my own arms," Ren blurts out, her voice shaking. "I refused to leave her because she was the only person I had—the only person I could actually rely on. My bodyguards pried me out of her arms because I just didn't want to leave her. The reason I'm telling you this is because you're not alone in this . . . we've all lost loved ones too. I know it hurts. Really, I *do* know. But, sometimes, we have no choice but to move on when a big obstacle is thrown our way because we should not let the bad things get to us. Stay strong, AJ. We're all here for you."

"I can't believe I'm saying this," Vi breathes out, "but she's right. I've lost plenty of loved ones too, so I can assure you you're not the only one dealing with this. We're all here for you. But you have to leave her because . . . she's not breathing anymore. You have to let her go."

AJ dips his head down toward Annie, shaking his head multiple times before he breathes out in defeat. He abruptly wipes his tears away, his chest rising in and out as he cups Annie's cheeks and kisses her forehead, whispering to her, "I'll never forget about you, *Didi.* I promise."

He releases her, her face so calm, so majestic. I didn't know Annie as well as I'd hoped to, but I knew her well enough to assume she was a wonderful being inside and out. She was the complete opposite of AJ—kind, genuine, and calm-minded—and always had such a mature approach to everything. Her younger twin brother, on the other hand, is not kind, genuine, or calm-minded—well, to me, at least. But, even with their polar opposite personalities, they were still the dynamic duo that ruled the compound alongside Commander Thatcher, and without them, we wouldn't have been able to deal with her strict ruling. Annie, especially, played a significant role in that.

But she's gone now.

It's outrageous how this universe thinks it's so hilarious to take away the most beautiful human beings on earth. It's always the prettiest flowers in a bunch and the ripest of fruit that get picked first, and I guess we have no choice but to live with that decision for the rest of our lives.

As we finish consoling AJ, we help him to his feet because there is no doubt he couldn't care less about walking right now. We urge him forward while he constantly looks back at his sister, sprawled across the ground like a unique portrayal of nature. Amongst the other dead bodies, she stands out the most. And I have a feeling this particular loss will take forever to move on from.

Suddenly, he stops in his tracks and mutters to himself, his eyebrows pushed together in thought. I lean down to him and ask, "What happened?"

I expect him to snap back at me with a snarky remark, or even to just shake his head and murmur out a meek reply. But instead, he does the opposite. He works his jaw, a new sense of determination washing over his eyes that were once gleaming specks of sunlight, and he looks at Vi, who almost jumps back at his sudden movement.

"Tell Commander Thatcher to bring the cannons out," AJ asserts.

47

SUBDUED

BLAIRE

I GASP OUT A cry as I run over to where the sound occurred, ignoring the thick fog around me that suffocates my mind, my heart, my lungs, my vision. There is very little I can see, but I couldn't care less. I run in whatever direction my feet allow me, my limbs and muscles tightening with every fat droplet of water that crashes onto me. Lightning embellishes the sky above, and when thunder rumbles, shaking the grounds beneath me, is when the egregious gunshot occurs again.

And another one of those cries I've dreaded hearing again.

"No!" I screech out, my pace quickening, my speed so out of control I trip on a stray stone in the middle of the road and trample forward, bringing my hands forth as I fall so it doesn't impact my head. I let out heaving breaths, sprawled on all fours as the fog around me thickens, impeding on my line of sight. Very near me is a quivering breath followed after trembling cries—the same ones I've been searching for a while.

I crawl toward the noises, my body like tremors of the earth. I've never dreaded a moment such as now—the moment of pure fear unraveling through my bones. It's the rattling thought of knowing what's to see ahead that frightens me, the sight I'm about to uncover, the absolute *horror* I'm about to witness. It is my curiosity that gets the best of me—my determination to figure out the destination of the gunshot and the cry.

When the fog clears up in my line of sight, I notice a familiar pair of tennis shoes that lead up to tattered jeans and a shirt, parted cracked lips, dark green eyes peeled open . . .

And blood pooling from the back of their head.

My face slackens, and every nerve, movement, and system in my body ceases. I am frozen, rooted to the ground, with my heart crashing to the bottom of my stomach.

I let out a wheeze, crawling forward as my shaky hands tug at the hem of his shirt, tears uncontrollably falling down my cheeks and clinging onto my chin, indecisive whether or not they should let go. *No, no, no. This cannot be happening. I refuse to believe whatever I see in front of me is real. It's all just a trick played on me by my own mind. My mind is just messing with me. That's all.*

I lightly slap his cheek in hopes he'll awake. "Hey, please get up," I say in the most nimble tone.

No response.

"Enough with the jokes and just get up, okay? We need to get back to the others."

Still, no response.

"Please! Get up!"

Still. No. Response.

"GET UP!" I claw at his shirt, crashing down to the crook of his neck and sobbing into the side of his matured face—his kind smile, his kind eyes, his kind *everything.* He was the joker of the family, the one who kept us together when we were at each other's neck. The one who taught me how to enjoy, how to be happy, how to be *grateful.* The one who brought me a different perspective on life, something I'll forever cherish.

The one who fathered me. Bred me. *Worshiped* me.

I cup his cheeks, looking into his dark green eyes one last time. Even though I feel or hear little to no life from him, his eyes are still alive, bustling with energy. He won't be there when I marry, have children, and grow a family. He won't see me grow up into the woman he always aspired for me to be. He won't be a granddad to my children, inform and inspire them just like he did to me.

Because he's gone.

I sob again, my lip trembling as I croak out, "Papa, why didn't you stay with me? I could've protected you and stopped whoever did this to you. You should have stayed with me. Why did you leave?" My chest is heaving, burning, and on fire. "This is not fair to me. You can't do this to me. *YOU CAN'T!*"

A gasp followed by an elongated wail follows, and I clutch my chest with an enclosed fist, clawing at my uniform. I tear it off me, my throat hoarse with my screams and cries, followed by my camo pants. My vision is completely blurred with tears, so I fumble to fold them next to him, wrapping a recently torn off piece of fabric from the cuff of my pants around his bloodied head. And then, I cup his cheeks, pressing a shaky kiss to the cloth going around his forehead. There's so much I want to say to him, but I can't. It physically hurts me to speak, let alone breathe. I just want to spend my time here with him, holding on to the very little memories I have of him.

What are Nico, Em, and Mama going to think of this?

Another howl pierces through my lungs and escapes my throat, wishing so very badly it were me instead of him. *Anyone* except him. He never asked for this. He never asked for a bullet to his head. He never asked for a war. He never asked for dread and treachery all over again. *He never did.*

The only thing keeping me at bay is the notion of him leaving this hell just so God can have an angel by his side.

A lone tear pricks my eye and travels down my lip, already bathed in drool and snot. I wipe away everything with the back of my hand, not even caring an ounce about the mess I made. Then, I find the very little ounce of energy left in me and croak out to him, "Who did this to you, Papa? Who in the right mind would *ever* do this to you?" My grip on him tightens. "Once I find out who this person is, I will rip them limb from limb, bone from bone, and piece by piece. I will make sure nothing of them remains, not even their soul. *No one* lays a hand on anyone I love, and even if they do, I will make sure they regret it for the rest of their life."

As soon as those words escape from me like broken fragments of my being, I feel metal press against the back of my head.

My throat is dry—my mind empty yet the more chaotic—and I slowly turn, already regretting before I do.

The tip of the gun is planted between my eyebrows now, wedging itself into my skin, and I look up with parted lips, my heart beating at a million miles per hour.

I am met with glassy eyes, skin as pale as the lightning embellishing the sky, and long hair flowing behind them like a neverending cape. The curl to the lips the same color as their skin sends shivers down my spine, but also a tremulous wave right back up. I curl my fists tight, narrowing my eyes at the woman who's brought us nothing but stress, harm, and terror ever since summer's start.

Veronica Reaves.

48

TEMPEST

JAX

"Cannons?" I echo.

AJ lets out a trembling sigh. "The Detroitian military had them stored in the backroom since God knows when, and they were only planning to use them when time called for it. But obviously . . . now is the time." Instantly, he fishes in the crook of his arm for a slick black device and says into it, "Commander Thatcher, are you there?"

The receiving end is eerily silent.

"That's weird," Mallory says. "She always responds."

"I know." He pauses for a moment. "Something must've happened."

My jaw slackens, reminding myself Blaire is there too. "We need to help them."

"There's only so much we can do," he says. "We need to call in more reinforcements. Channel in most of the soldiers around the center of the city, where most of the ERUSA soldiers are. So, that way, we can see how Commander Thatcher and the others are doing."

"How are we going to do that, though?" Vi asks. "We don't even have a jeep. We can't possibly go all the way back to the center of the city on foot."

"I can ask Reynolds and Brady." He speaks into the device again. "Reynolds? Brady? Are any of you there?"

A voice speaks back seconds later. "Yes, Iyer. It's Reynolds."

"Hey," he breathes out in relief. "Do you guys have a jeep we can borrow? We're stranded by the northern area of Detroit and our jeep was destroyed while coming here."

"Of course. We'll bring one to you shortly by tracking your location."

"Thank you," he murmurs.

"No problem. Also, do you know where your sister is? I've been trying to reach out to her, but all I get is silence from her end."

AJ's chest sharply rises, his Adam's Apple visibly bobbing up and down. He looks over at a fallen Annie still sprawled across the bloodied grounds, the blood around her trailing away in a silent line of sorrow. He quickly looks away, dragging a hand across his face, and he rasps out, "She . . . she didn't make it."

The line crackles, almost as if it were sobbing. "Holy shit," Reynolds responds. "I'm so sorry, AJ."

"It's okay," he mumbles, wiping a sole tear away with the back of his hand. "But I'll talk to you later. Please make sure to bring a jeep here ASAP. I don't think I can stay here anymore."

"Will do. And I'm sorry, again. I know how close you guys were."

Immediately, he ends the line and falls to his knees, letting out a dragged groan. "I thought it was all a nightmare," he whispers. "But the moment I saw her again . . . it felt like a punch to my gut, knowing that this is all *real*, and not just a sick fucking joke this universe is playing on me. Why did this have to happen to *her*? She's a much better human being than I am. Shouldn't I have received the end of this universe's cruel punishment? Why *her?*" he bellows.

"Hey, AJ," Mallory soothes him by kneeling beside him. "Don't say those things about yourself. I know it seems unfair that she died instead of you—I know it does. But saying those things will not reverse time and bring her back to life. No amount of self-hate will bring Annie back, and I'm pretty sure she *herself* would not want to come back if her brother kept bringing himself down like this. Keep your chin up, AJ. Know that Annie is in a much better place now, where she doesn't have to deal with the perils of this world. She is free of harm, and not a single soul will hurt her ever again. Shouldn't that bring you peace, instead of pain?"

He contemplates to himself for a little, the muscles beneath his shirt loosening. "It should."

"*Exactly.* So I don't see why you're thinking or saying these things. Annie was a wonderful human being, and she lived her life to the fullest while she could. Now, you can carry on her legacy and live at peace, knowing that heaven has gained an angel now. Okay?" She gives him a half-smile.

AJ sighs, squeezing his eyes shut to allow another tear to roll down his cheek. His lip trembles, and he fists three, four, or maybe even five patches of grass and rips them from the ground, an uneasy breath leaving his mouth. "Okay," he murmurs, giving Mallory a slow look filled with appreciation. "And you're right. Annie would never like this sort of behavior from me . . . I just need some time to myself. I just want to spend as much time with her before the jeeps come. That's all I need right now."

We all nod, letting him be as we retreat away from him, but close enough where we can still keep our eye on him. We're seated by a lone lamppost, the memories from what just happened minutes ago jamming into my mind. I will never forget how frozen I felt seeing that single bullet lodge into her back, staining her entire abdomen as she fell like a lifeless, floating feather. The life in her eyes and being was all wiped out in a matter of seconds, and that scares the shit out of me. I don't think we acknowledge, as a society, just how terrifying that is.

What scared me the most was seeing AJ's face fall the moment he saw his sister in that condition—so limp, so fragile. I never felt sympathy for him before, but at that moment, all emotions and feelings I had hidden away were situated with him, regardless of my prior thoughts about him. He and Annie were like two peas in a pod, quite literal partners in crime. I don't know much about them, but I do know they've been through a lot. I don't know what exactly, but I do know it was a lot. That, in itself, requires the most energy and willingness to brave a scalding and scathing storm.

We don't speak much, while we're sitting together. I think we're still speechless from what happened, and seeing how vulnerable AJ looked and felt. It's just a constant reminder of how even the strongest of people can fall to their knees within seconds. Strength is fleeting, and it can all go away in just a snap of a finger whenever any sort of threat comes in hand.

From where I'm seated, I see AJ lean over Annie, bringing her frail and limp hand to his face, and his features scrunch up as he begins to sob again. Rain pours down on him, and the white, heavy fog engulfs his figure, emblazoning him as a spectacle from Mother Nature herself. It's almost a jab to the gut, seeing this emotional picture being painted in a matter of seconds. Each brushstroke is a reminder of what he lost, and each movement is a reminder of what it *feels* to lose something, or someone.

I count one-hundred-thirty-three seconds when a jeep comes rolling by. In the driver's seat is Reynolds, and next to her is Brady, who quickly waves us over. We get up from our seats and go over to AJ, who has still not left Annie. "Hey, AJ," Ren says, "they're here."

He looks up at us, his eyes as dull as ever as they travel over to Reynolds and Brady. He sighs, leaning over Annie to hug her, mumbling incoherent words. Finally, he releases, his cheeks stained with tears, and his eyebrows furrowed in despairing thought. AJ looks at us again, and we help him get up, his legs shaking as he brings himself up to his feet. Mallory slings an arm around him, and Ren goes around to the side as we trudge over to the jeep.

Once we've all climbed inside, it rumbles to a start and the tires screech as we escape the area, sleets of heavy rain pounding into the open-roofed car. I look back, a streak of lightning displayed against the dark blue clouds, and I notice Annie's frail figure slowly diminish, as if she were just a small atomic fragment in this large universe.

We stop at the pile of Reformers originating from the Ambassador Bridge—exactly where Veronica declared war on us. Once the jeep's engine shuts off, we march over to where everyone is. We huddle together with AJ in the center, who murmurs to himself still. We wait for him to say something, but he shakes his head and looks over at Vi. "Can you take over for me?" he stammers.

She widens his eyes at him. "Uh, sure. Of course."

He retreats back, pushing past us and standing by the railing of the bridge, his figure sulking and shaking with every sob.

Vi situates herself in the center, and she takes a deep breath in, her tattoos gleaming against the raindrops on her exposed skin. "I will be taking over for AJ Iyer because his sister, Annie, unfortunately died in battle." Trails of murmur and gasps erupt in the air. "I'd appreciate it if you hold back on your condolences and expressions of grief for AJ. He just wants to be left alone right now.

"Besides that, I would like to announce that he himself has stated he would like the cannons to be brought out. I was informed they were in the backroom and would only be used if the situation was dire enough—which it clearly is. I will assign fifteen of you to retreat back to the compound and bring the cannons out. I will have AJ's device with me, so if you have any questions, I will answer them to the best of my ability. As per now, do you have any questions or concerns?"

No one answers.

"Good." She clears her throat again. Once she's assigned fifteen soldiers, she says, "I expect everyone to be back here in exactly fifteen minutes, so I suggest you step on it while driving. When the cannons are brought over, I will initiate further instructions then. Got it?"

"Got it, Powers," the soldiers say simultaneously.

As they retreat to the jeeps and hurriedly drive off, she instructs the remaining soldiers to divide throughout the city and defend the citizens. "Shoot back if necessary," she demands. "Never hold back when your life or other lives are threatened."

Eventually, all the soldiers have left, and it is just us, catching our breath by the Ambassador Bridge. Jet-black waves crash onto the banks beneath us, monstrous beasts determined to be unleashed. The sky is even darker, a royal blue with a tinge of obsidian black. The sky's enlightened with lightning sporadically, intrinsic and unique designs drawn upon the canvas that are the storm clouds. The rain never stops, though; it's constant, harrowing, and dangerous, and I'm afraid if it were to strengthen, then it would cut through my skin and wound me forever. The wind howls, swaying us back and forth—but AJ's feet are grounded and rooted, as if a puny little storm could never outweigh the hell he just experienced. And the air is hot, flames that curl into my bones and reside there forever—like a parasite to its host.

A major storm is raging.

49

PERISH

BLAIRE

ALL I CAN THINK OF when I see Veronica's face are my papa's cries. They're lodged into my mind, running on an endless track with every repeat squeezing my heart and disposing of its bloody contents like a used dishrag. I can still feel my veins pounding against my flesh, ready to burst out and run for its life away from my inhabitable system. *I'll never forget that sad look in his eyes. Never.*

She's the reason behind that sad look in his eyes. She's the reason for all the harm and pain caused to my poor family, and I want to kill her at this very moment, but I'm on the verge of claiming defeat. The harm is done—she's taken one of the most important persons to me in just a snap of a finger, a damn blink of an eye. There isn't much I can do, besides beg for mercy and for her to let me go.

My throat is as deserted as my heart, which once held emotions and feelings. "Drop the gun, please," I manage to croak out. "I surrender. Just please leave me alone."

"And why would I do that?" She sneers.

Tears fall down my cheeks at a rapid pace. "Y-you killed him! Why would you do that? He never did anything to you."

"But his daughter and son hurt me plenty." She pushes the barrel of the gun into my head, and I begin to prepare for my eventual death. "Your brother is the one who started this rebellion organization in the first place. If it weren't for him, then not only would Tobias Remington be alive right now, but D.C. would remain as it was, and as it should be—*divided.* Your generation just does not know how to remain in one place, huh?"

"Don't blame this on him," I whisper.

"Then should I blame this on you instead? I mean, you are the one who last joined the Subversives. You are also the one who's brainwashed Jax into your idiotic ideals. He would've been a very put-together man if you hadn't stepped in."

I shake my head once, slowly succumbing to the pervasive darkness growing in my heart and mind. "Please, Veronica. Let this be. You already did your harm, and I accept my defeat. I'm just done and exhausted with everything. Please . . ." My voice trails off, and my throat aches as I begin to sob, each tear a different memory of my father. It's just me, Mama, Nico, and Em, and there is no more Papa. *He is gone.*

"No can do, darling." Veronica cocks her head at me. "You will not come in the middle of my mission, when I have just begun to proclaim my victory in this war. I will eradicate *each and every single one* of you animals who have ridden the earth with your disease-filled presences."

A clicking sound initiates from the gun, and my eyes widen as I shriek, "Don't do this! Let me go!" Without even thinking, I knee her in the abdomen, and she lets out a low moan, sending a bullet barely grazing the side of my ear. Suddenly, I feel cool liquid dribble down my ear, and I pick at the remnants, immediately reminded of my papa sprawled around me. I shiver, tears bursting through the windows that are my eyes, allowing my melancholy desires to escape.

I dust myself off, and as I attempt to run away from a staggering Veronica, she starts to shoot at me again, but the bullet twangs several feet away from me and she falls to the floor, crimson liquid smearing the back of her left thigh and drizzling down in a slow and taunting manner. I watch, speechless, as she falls to the ground, the gun inches away from her.

Behind her are three figures, which reveal themselves as Nico holding on to a shaking Mama, and Heidi next to them, who cocks the gun that just shot Veronica. She gives me a relieved glance, almost as if it were for me. But her eyes immediately travel down to the lifeless body beside me, and her face falls.

The wail that escapes out of my mama is enough to shatter the fragile world into pieces.

She crumbles to her knees, clawing at her chest and screaming at the top of her lungs. "David!" Mama shrieks, crawling to him hurriedly. She lifts his upper-body off the ground and shakes him frantically, sobbing into his shoulder. "David, no! Wake up! Don't do this right now!"

Nico is still frozen in place, and his face hasn't even twitched.

I sulk forward, squeezing my eyes shut as I take in my mother's cries, loud and heartbreaking. Tears leave my eyes again, but I don't sob. I just sit here, broken—inside and out.

I am a wilted flower, and not even sunlight can bring me to life anymore.

Heidi stands over a bleeding Veronica, who grits her teeth as she says, "Well, look who's here."

"Get out of here, you bitch," Heidi spits at her.

"Oh, looks like someone dropped their nice act already. Are you fed up with me that much?" She chuckles, but her lips barely move. The only part of her that's moving are her eyes, which trail over to the gun splayed on the ground inches away from her.

As I start to shout at her with whatever energy that's left of me, Heidi points the gun at Veronica simultaneously when she reaches for the weapon on the ground and points it at her. Two gunshots go off—one very near Veronica and the other very near Nico.

He exits out of his trance, his eyes darkening as his jaw hardens.

"Looks like you finally came back to life." She sneers at him. "Who do you want me to kill off next? Your sister, or your mother? The choice is yours."

His mouth twitches, his dark hair flying around him. "Stop. Talking," he enunciates, taking one deadly step toward her.

As Veronica slowly staggers to her feet, clutching the blood streaming down her flesh as if she was a corpse awoken from the grave, Heidi attempts to shoot at her again, but the gun clicks instead.

Veronica gives her a tight-lipped smile, waving the gun at her. "The odds are just not in your favor today, am I right?"

My mama's screams have converted into whimpers, and she rapidly kisses my papa's cheeks, murmuring that she loves him over and over and over again.

I push all my might into my feet as I get up, feeling like there are weights attached to my limbs. I just want this nightmare to be over. I want this *all* to be over.

I want Heidi to kill her already.

It's as if she's read my mind, though, because Heidi throws the empty gun to the side and garners all of her force and strength into this one swift movement. She lets out a bloodcurdling scream as she plants her large hands on Veronica's chest and sends her flying back, dust formulating around her as her back hits the ground. Simultaneously, the gun falls out of her hand and clatters to the ground.

Time slows down from here.

As Heidi's harsh features scrunch up into fury, her hand outstretched for the gun, Veronica grabs it instead, her long hair sprawled around her. Her finger rests against the trigger, and she aims it at Nico, who's staring at my papa.

I am in submerged water, and all I hear are drowned out voices and cries.

I push all my sorrows and tears away and channel it into the very little energy I can as I sprint toward Nico—or try to, at least. I try to run faster, but I can't. The water I'm drowning in won't let me.

I don't notice my mama running beside me, though.

And from there is when time goes fast. Fast, fast, fast. Too fast. Just like the bullet that escapes out of Veronica's gun and hurdles toward Nico. Just like my mama's cries when she jumps in front of him.

I squeeze my eyes shut.

I clamp my hands over my ears.

I don't want to hear this.

Or see this.

But even then, I still feel it in my bones.

I feel my mama falling to the ground. I feel that soft, cold blood growing around her like roots beneath a plant. I feel the vibrations of Heidi and Nico's screams explode around me.

Just like my heart that explodes into many, *many* different pieces.

And finally, I open my eyes.

I don't know why I do.

It's like a knife to my gut, whatever I'm seeing, hoping it's all just one giant nightmare.

It's a nightmare. That's all it is.

But the environment, the screams, the cries, the blood is just *all too real.*

My entire body is on fire at what I see. The amount of *red* I see.

All surrounded by my mama.

Nico grabs her face, screaming at her to wake up, *please* wake up, do something. But she doesn't fucking respond.

I want to cry, I really do. But I'm pretty sure all my emotions have left me, my mind too. I can't think. I can't speak. I can't do much.

The only thing I am, though, is just a giant figure of numbness. Numbness in my veins, *everywhere.* No blood pulsating into my heart. Nothing.

Nothing, nothing, nothing . . .

Except for a dose of anger I haven't tasted since D.C., and it fills me up like no other feeling.

No. Other. Feeling.

50

CRUSADE

JAX

IT'S BEEN ALMOST FIFTEEN minutes, and AJ has still not left from where he was standing before.

To make the sight even more concerning, even a single muscle in his body hasn't seemed to twitch or even jerk in any directions. His clothes are the only part of him moving due to the wind rustling the fabric. Even with the cold rain smearing at his skin, he has not moved an inch. I start to genuinely wonder whether this man is dead, or just simply has passed out from the stuffy air. Or maybe I'm just going insane because Vi, Mallory, and Ren—who I am sitting next to in a small circle—don't seem to be worried.

"Have you heard any word from Commander Thatcher and the others yet?" I ask Vi, just to distract myself from AJ's almost-lifeless figure.

"Nope," she says. "It's all been static from everyone's end."

"How the hell are we gonna know whether they are alive or not?"

"I don't know. I guess we just hope for the best."

I frown at her disappointedly. "Are you not the slightest bit worried about them?"

Vi shrugs. "Never said I wasn't. Besides, I'm pretty sure they can fend for themselves. For Christ's sake, Jeremiah, Nico, *and* Heidi are all together. I'm pretty sure not a damn thing will get to them."

"You better not jinx that." Mallory raises an accusing eyebrow at her.

Vi raises her hands at her in defense. "I won't." She leans back against the railing of the bridge and knocks on it thrice. "There."

Ren raises one thin eyebrow. "That's not even wood."

Vi shrugs. "Eh. Close enough." Silence falls between us, but she breaks it moments later by saying again, "I can't believe Commander Thatcher's name is Heidi."

"Me too," Mallory says. "And I never expected Commander Thatcher to have that much going on in her life. I feel really bad for her."

"Don't we all?" Ren sighs. "When my mother was alive, she used to visit her all the time. The Detroitian military wasn't established back then because, well, we didn't really need it, yet she was always uptight. Now I know why she is."

Mallory looks over at her. "Hey, speaking of your mother, how are you feeling about that? If you don't want to talk about her, then that's okay, but I just want to let you know that we are all here for you and are more than willing to listen to you."

I nod encouragingly while Vi scowls at Mallory, who just shoots a disappointed look at her.

"Really?" Ren smiles tight-lipped at us. "That means a lot to me. But yeah, um . . . in all honesty, I'm not over my mother yet. She was the one who gave me love and comfort when nobody or nothing else did. How can I ever move on from such an impactful woman like her? I had hoped to marry one day and give her grandchildren so she can cherish many mini-me's." She chuckles sadly. "She would've been the perfect grandmother.

"But, it seems as if this cruel universe had other plans for her because . . . she's not here anymore. And every moment without her is so painful, sometimes I can't even breathe." Her lip begins to tremble. "I haven't told anyone this, simply because I didn't want to. I don't want to be constantly reminded of my past and what haunts me. But at the same time, I want to move on from it and not let it define me anymore."

Mallory reassuringly rubs her back. "I think you should go with the latter, Ren. Your past should *never* define you, no matter how good or bad it is."

The fog around us tightens as she nods once. "I guess you're right." She takes a deep breath in and starts to speak again. "I lived in Russia until I was sixteen. My parents and my little sister died by the hands of the government when I was ten, and I was orphaned ever since then. It was just oh-so convenient that I was distracted by the beautiful craft displayed on the market shelves in the middle of Moscow while my family was getting reprimanded by the Russian military police and were eventually shot to death for God knows what or why. Just from hearing those gunshots I ran because I knew my family was on the receiving end.

"Then I was orphaned, living on the streets and fending for myself. Luckily, some American ambassadors were visiting Russia for an international relations meeting, and one of them was Charlotte. When she saw me on the streets of Moscow, she immediately talked to me—in Russian, of course—and I was just obsessed with her. Our relationship grew so much that she escaped some of her meetings just to talk to me.

"One day, when I had just turned sixteen, Charlotte told me that she always wanted a daughter, and she immediately asked me to go to America with her, and she wouldn't tell the Russian authorities. I was as desperate as ever for some mother figure and accepted. When Charlotte left for America days later, I somehow managed to escape with her in her private jet and flew all the way to Detroit, Michigan—situated in the lovely America I always dreamed about. The adoption papers were quickly signed, and my identity completely transitioned. For one, my last name changed from Astanova to Levine. I learned English and forgot about my Russian background. I know I still sort of have a Russian accent, but it was heavier in the past." She chuckles.

"Charlotte, my new mother, treated me well for as long as she could. My memory of her will never go away because she is just *that* unforgettable." Ren sighs, looking at us now. "I know I went on for a very long time, but there was no way I could've shortened that."

"It's okay, Ren," Mallory whispers. "Don't apologize for that. You are a very strong woman and I promise life will get better from here. Just keep your chin up and know that we are all here for you. All right?"

Ren grins at her. "All right."

Suddenly, I hear engines rumbling and nearing behind us.

If it weren't for the railing behind me, I would've fallen back into the waters by how much I jumped back in shock. Twelve jeeps drive across the bridge and stop where we are seated, and one soldier comes running out and spews to Vi, "The cannons weren't working."

She slowly gets up to her feet, her face falling. "What the hell do you mean by that?"

"They just aren't working, Powers. We tried everything, but they're extremely old, and it would just be treacherous to the lands."

"This is bullshit," she grumbles. "Are you sure you tried every single method out there?"

"Yes." The soldier nods.

"Jesus Christ, you've got to be kidding me. Okay, I guess

we're just gonna have to find some alternative to this, since apparently the number one weapon we need right now is barely sputtering to life."

"What do we do now?" I ponder aloud, standing next to Vi.

"We fight with our flesh and bones."

A very familiar deep voice rings into the air, louder than the rain thundering onto our skin. AJ appears behind Vi, and we look at him, bewildered. His tear-stained cheeks glisten against the moist air, and his dimmed eyes that were once gleaming are now cast upon us.

The soldier lightly shakes his head. "We can't take that risk, though, Iyer—"

"I don't care," he grumbles. "I'll do anything to take that bitch down. Even if I die in the process."

And with that, he leaves us again, going back to the other side of the bridge and leaning over the railing, his shoulders shaking with each silent sob.

Suddenly, we hear shouts and cries from the entrance of the city.

Vi rapidly waves her hand at me and says, "The rest of you go and take care of that. I will be here with the soldiers and we'll decide what to do."

I nod, and Mallory and Ren follow behind me, watching three blurry figures emerge from the midst of the fog that has engulfed Detroit. I finger the trigger of the gun, prepared to shoot whoever the soldiers are on sight, but I immediately lower my gun once I see Jeremiah and Layla running from the city, Tamia held in Layla's hands as she wails, and Em clinging to Layla's thigh, her eyes red from past tears. When they see us, they immediately approach us on the bridge, their skin glistening from sweat.

They reach us, and we hug them, grateful to see they're alive. But one worry nags at my mind, and as I release Jeremiah, I ask, "Where's Blaire and the others?"

He frowns, his exhausted brown eyes darkening with worry. "We have no idea. We were separated from the others a while ago, only because it was hard to see or hear each other with the fog and the gunshots. Layla and I just walked in whatever direction we could, and we found ourselves here."

"Have you communicated with Commander Thatcher?" Mallory asks. "Or anyone else that has a device?"

"Yes, but no one responded."

"Shit," I curse.

"We need to go and save them," Layla interjects, cradling Tamia in her hands. "Especially because we need to get out of this city."

Ren pushes past us and asks, "Why are we leaving?"

"We were hoping that once we all escaped the city, we would go to the compound and leave from there with the aircraft carriers to a safety regime in El Paso, Texas. I've been in contact with the leader there for a while, and they said they're more than willing to house us. But we can't go there without Commander Thatcher."

Leaving Detroit to go to El Paso? "We can't leave this place," I murmur. "This is our *home.*"

"I get that, Jax," she says. "But we have no other choice. Do you not see the condition of this place?"

"I don't care, we'll build it all back up if we have to."

"That is if we're even alive," Jeremiah hisses. "With every ERUSA soldier we kill, there are ten more to fight. We have to think realistically. There's no way we can win this battle."

"What about Veronica? If we leave then we're just feeding her massive ego."

"Jax, this is your *life* we're talking about here," Layla rasps. "We already lost Annie in battle, and God knows whether Heidi and the others are alive. Veronica's ego should be the least of your worries."

"Wait, where *is* Veronica to begin with?" Ren contemplates.

As Jeremiah begins to respond, a startling cry from the midst of the city erupts and explodes into the air, and the vibrations of the scream reverberates into my ear so much I almost stumble back.

Something terrible has happened.

51

DOOM

BLAIRE

NICO BRINGS MAMA'S LIMP body onto his lap, his figure shaking with every violent, silent sob. I've never seen him break down like this, even when seeing Papa. I guess seeing Mama was his breaking point.

As is mine.

Vibrations of energy emanate through my body, surging through my veins and pumping my blood. Oh, how badly I wish Heidi's gun was filled with ammo so I could've put bullets through Veronica's head. But even that won't make me feel better.

Nothing will make me feel better at this point.

I so badly want to comfort Nico and hold Mama too, but how can I when I'm barely able to stand on my own two feet? How can I serve others when I can barely serve myself? When I can barely *breathe?*

A major thunderstorm heaves and swirls around me, and my chest rises in and out slowly, another dwindling inside my bones. I've tried to suppress my anger when I held my bleeding

Papa, but now Mama is gone—and I can't make that same promise anymore. My determination to protect them has failed, and I have to live with that for the rest of my life. I have to live without *them* for the rest of my life.

I. Just. Want. Time. To. *Stop.*

I hear Heidi's breath twitch and waver as she wipes her tears away abruptly with the back of her hand. I can't imagine how she must be feeling either. She finally reunited with her long-lost best friend, and in just barely a day of meeting her, she watched her go away right in front of her own eyes. I almost thought Heidi had no emotions, but she does, as I watch her push her tears away. I wish I could cry, too. I don't want others to think I'm emotionless—that I don't care about Mama and Papa. I do care. I just have no energy in me, and frankly, all I want to do is die. Curl up in a box with no holes and let myself succumb to the darkness. Maybe I can reunite with my parents then.

As Veronica brings the gun to her hips, smoke amalgamating from the tip, I charge toward her—determined to annihilate her —but Heidi jumps in instead and tackles her to the ground. Both of their bodies land in a muddled heap, and Heidi easily dominates her by straddling her waist and punching her square in the jaw. Veronica lets out a strangled cry and claws at her face, long bruised lines etched on her tan skin.

Meanwhile, my shaky legs lead me to the gun, and as I bend down to pick it up, Veronica's hand stretches out to it and grabs it before I can. I let out string of curses and try to steal it from her, but she shoots at me instead, bullets flying haywire and barely missing me. Heidi growls and stomps on her hand, and Veronica's grasp on the gun loosens as she wails again. Her wails are unmatched compared to my papa and mama's, whose cries will forever be etched into my soul. I wish I could go back in time, so I could protect Papa and I could jump in front of Nico, not Mama. *It should've never been them to go. It should've been me. I've been nothing but a nuisance to others. There's no one who can possibly love me now.*

I'm a monster. A cold-blooded monster.

Veronica sneers at me and Heidi, her teeth stained a crimson red. "Just accept that I won and you lost this battle. Accept that you took not only my husband but my beautiful city away. *You* and these filthy scumbags are the real enemies. Not us."

Heidi sets her lips into a firm straight line, shaking her head rigidly. "No. *You are.* It's always been you that's been the real enemy. You are just blinded by your hunger for power. *You are the real enemy.*"

The blood has begun to stain her lips now. "Go to hell."

Her mouth twitches into a cold smirk. "I'll see you there."

Suddenly, something awakens in Veronica's glassy eyes, almost like flames dwindling. As Heidi goes to punch her again, she abruptly brings the watch on her wrist to her mouth and breathlessly says into it, "Bring all the soldiers here to the middle of the district and kill these rebels. *Now.*"

I freeze.

Heidi does too.

Veronica cackles, her mouth nothing but red. I'm surprised she hasn't choked on her own blood by now. "Now there is absolutely no way this battle can be won. You are all outnumbered to the max. What shall you do now?"

"We need to run," Heidi whispers to me. "We need to get the hell out of here."

She immediately gets up to her feet and grabs Nico, whose entire hands are stained from Mama's blood. I get up too, but I don't want to leave. Only because Mama and Papa will be left here.

Veronica sits herself up, throwing the gun to the side. "I won't be needing this," she says, "when I have my entire army coming here, I'd say, *very* soon. If you run you won't be able to make it very far."

We ignore her taunts as Heidi kneels beside Mama, kisses her forehead, and murmurs something to her. Then she brings herself up to her feet as Nico does the same. He's still crying, but not sobbing. He sniffles, and they both look at me simultaneously.

"C'mon, Blaire," she urges me.

I immediately shake my head. "No."

Nico furrows his eyebrows at me. "Bumble Bee, please don't do this."

"I'm not leaving them! I didn't even get to say goodbye to Mama!"

"Well, it's too late for that now, huh?" He scowls at me. "You had the perfect chance, but you were just standing there, watching her die."

"I couldn't move," I gasp out. "I wanted to, but I *couldn't.*"

"Now is not the time to argue," Heidi growls. "Get your shit together and let's get moving."

"I'm not leaving, Heidi." I give her a stern look. You guys can, but I'm not."

As I go over to Mama and start to take in her broken, frail, and bloodied body, Nico yanks my arm and pulls me up. "It's too late, Blaire," he whispers to me. "You need to come with us. We're not leaving you."

"We can't leave them!" I wail, the tears coming out now.

"They're *DEAD!*" he bellows, the intensity of his words making me flinch. "What don't you get?"

I shake my head rapidly, tears blurring my vision where all I can decipher Nico is just one frantic amorphous silhouette of frustration. "I'm. Not. Going. Anywhere."

Suddenly, we hear the distant marching of soldiers in the far distance.

That's when Nico steps closer to me and grumbles to me, "You've left me with no choice, Blaire."

The next minute is a blur.

I remember Nico slinging me over his shoulder, my entire upper body thumping against his back as he and Heidi run past a cackling Veronica, her mouth still smeared in blood. I remember my cries being so loud that it rattles into my bones, causing my throat to swell up and dry. I remember tears dampening the upper lining of my shirt, soaking into my collarbone and barely grazing the wretched peridot stone necklace. I remember gunshots from the ERUSA soldiers rapidly firing at us, bullets flying everywhere, yet not one hitting us because Heidi fires back at them—yet I wish every single one of them hit me.

And I remember my parents' lifeless figures slowly decreasing in both life and size as we escape Veronica, the gunshots, and this city that was once so beautiful, but is nothing but a despairing abandoned town. All of its liveliness is gone, and God knows how many people remain.

This isn't what I wanted. This isn't how I wanted my summer in Detroit to go.

My birthday is just two weeks away, yet I have no urge to celebrate. If anything, I want to disappear off the face of this earth.

My wails and screeching cries continue to echo across the city, leaving nothing but my aching lungs and shattered remnants of my heart shriveling and eventually disappearing altogether until there is no life left inside of me.

RIFT

JAX

THE CRY TRANSFORMS INTO multiple raging gunshots, and Vi and I look at each other, knowing exactly what to do.

"We need to go and help them," I murmur to Layla.

She shakes her head. "There are ERUSA soldiers advancing through the city, and it's only inevitable they will come here and shoot us all. We all need to *leave*."

"Everyone is there!" Vi hisses. "We can't leave them!"

"I understand that," Layla says calmly, "but Nico and Heidi are there, which means everyone is bound to stay safe. They will make it through. I promise."

"And what if they don't?" I challenge. "Then what?"

She presses her lips together, looks away from me, and brings Tamia closer to her. "Then I guess some of you can stay to fight back while the rest of us leave. I'll go because I know where the safety regime is, and I'll take Tamia and Emilia with me. Ren, you can come too if you want. Everything else is up to the rest of you guys."

"I'm staying," Vi blurts out immediately.

"Me too." I nod.

"I'll stay too," Jeremiah says. Layla whips her head back at him, but he hurriedly says, "I'll be safe, baby, I promise. But I need to fight because that's my job, and that's just who I am."

"Daddy, you're leaving?" Tamia pouts.

"I'm sorry, darling, but yes, I have to. Daddy will be back, though." He kisses her forehead, and then he kisses Layla on the lips. "Don't worry about me, Lay. I'll make it back."

"You promise?" She raises her eyebrows at him.

He nods, no word needed to be said.

And then they hug, Jeremiah resting his chin against Layla's head as she buries her face into his chest, tears streaming down her cheeks. I feel a hint of jealousy crawl into my veins, wishing that were me and Blaire instead. I wish I could start off on a clean slate with her and *forget* this altercation with Veronica everhappened. The desperation to have her back is too much to handle now, yet I don't know what to do anymore. I don't even know if she feels the same either.

I hope she does.

That's when I see figures emerging from the fog, but I immediately notice them as people on our side because they are not pointing guns at us; instead, they are staggering forward, their faces crumpled with tears and worries.

It's Blaire, Nicolas, and Heidi.

But David and Marianna are nowhere to be seen.

When they see us on the bridge, Heidi's jaw slackens and she rushes Blaire and Nicolas forward. Nicolas joins her stride and runs toward the bridge, but Blaire's steps have faltered, and she slows behind them, refusing to look at us.

As we start to drown her with questions, Heidi frantically waves her hand at us to dismiss our pleas. "The ERUSA soldiers are advancing through the city," she gasps out.

"That's why we're going to El Paso, Texas," Layla says. She looks at her confused, for which Layla carries on to explain. "I came in contact with the leader there and told them of our situation. They told me they are more than willing to house us. I was going to take everyone, but some people want to stay behind and fight with the other Reformers that have stationed themselves here. What do you say, Heidi?"

She nods. "That's a good idea, actually."

"Great. I was thinking of taking the children and Renata and everyone else can do as they please."

"All right," Heidi murmurs. She sees AJ still standing by the other side of the bridge, as he doesn't seem to acknowledge that they are here. "What happened to him?" she asks.

"Uh . . ." Vi clears her throat. "Annie died in battle, so he just wanted some time alone."

Her jaw immediately slackens. "No."

Vi nods. "She was shot."

Heidi frowns, rubbing her forehead with the back of her hand. "Annie was one of the best soldiers I had. She couldn't have gone."

"Well," Vi says, "she unfortunately did."

Silence settles in around us, and Emilia goes up to Heidi and taps her arm. "Where's Mama and Papa?" she asks.

Blaire's face crumples as she storms away, going over the bridge as her combat boots thump against the road. *I have to go to her.*

Heidi breathes out slowly, looking toward Layla. "Can you please cover her ears?"

Emilia's lip trembles. "What—"

As soon as Layla covers her ears, Heidi turns to us and says, "We lost David and M-Mari too. They were both killed by Veronica."

My blood runs cold at her words. *Blaire's parents . . . were killed?*

Everything turns to static around me as Heidi's words are now incomprehensible, and the look on Emilia's face physically *pains* me. I can't bear to look or hear this anymore. I *have* to go to Blaire.

Without even excusing myself, I run toward her, my heart thumping so hard against my chest I feel it throbbing at my throat. Her figure quickly grows in size, and I see her in the middle of the road at the peak of the bridge, falling to her knees and crumbling to the ground. I follow behind her and kneel beside her. "Hey, it's me," I whisper frantically. "I'm here for you, beautiful. I promise."

She slowly turns to me, and I expect her to fall into my arms —just like she always does when she's upset—but she instead glares at me, her eyes hard and rigid. "Leave me alone," she mumbles.

My mouth falls. "What?"

"I said *leave me alone,* Jax," she enunciates.

"What the hell are you talking about, Blaire?"

"Please don't make this harder than it needs to be. Just go. *Please.*"

"I don't understand what I did. I'm just trying to help you feel better—"

"Well, clearly it's not gonna work because my parents are *dead* and I'll never see them ever again," she hisses at me with narrowed eyes.

"I'm sorry," I whisper. "I'm sorry to hear that, I really am. But I don't see why *I'm* the enemy here. I know I screwed up in the past by not telling you about Veronica, but there's no need to be mad at me about that anymore because it's all in the *past,* and I'm never gonna do that ever again."

"You're hiding something else, aren't you?"

I freeze. "What?" *There's no way she knows about my cut and what happened on the train . . . right?*

"Don't act dumb with me. I *know* you, Jax. I know there's something you're hiding from me and I don't know why. So I suggest you spill. Before I get really mad."

I hesitate for a moment. God, how stupid could I be? Why did I even hide this from her in the first place? She's told me *everything*—including her own nightmares—yet I never had the courage to tell her mine? What the hell is wrong with me?

"I . . ." I take a deep breath in. *Don't think. Just do, Jax. Just* do. After a while, I clear my throat and say, "There have been a couple of things I've hidden from you. When . . . when I came back from the second meeting with Veronica, I was incredibly upset with myself and smashed the mirror in my bathroom with my fists. That's why they were bandaged. And . . ." *C'mon, Jax. Just say it already.* "When Jeremiah and I were alone, fighting together on the train, my father—he came to life, I guess, and I killed him. A second time."

"What?" Blaire says immediately. "What the hell do you mean by this? Why are you just telling me this?"

"I don't know," I stammer. "But *please*, Blaire. *Please* don't be mad. I never did this on purpose, I was—"

"Oh, bullshit. This is all just *bullshit*."

"No, don't—"

"I don't want to hear it anymore." She squeezes her eyes shut. "Please, Jax. I never . . . I never knew you hid *this* much from me. Did you never trust me? Was I never someone you felt comfortable with?"

"No, Blaire, please don't assume that. This is just an internal problem I have. I just—"

"Stop talking!" she yells. "Just . . . stop."

"No, I won't stop," I manage to say, my heart on fire. "I want to say sorry and move past this. I won't hide anything from you again, I promise."

"God, it's not about that anymore," she says exasperatedly. "What don't you get, Jax? Not only are you hiding shit from me, but I also don't have the heart in me to love someone anymore. I can't bring myself to do that."

"I get that, Blaire. I really do. But please don't push *me* away, when all I want to do is comfort you."

"I don't need your comfort, Jax. Just please leave me alone. I don't know what to feel or think or believe anymore. I just don't feel loved anymore. This world hates me. *Everyone* hates me."

"I don't hate you." I take a step toward her. "I love you, and you know that. Don't even try to deny it." As I take another step forward and start to wrap my arms around her, she pushes me square in the chest, and I stumble back, my heart starting to crumble into ashes.

"I said leave. Me. Alone." She snarls, inches from me. This is not the Blaire I know anymore. This is a version of her I'm genuinely terrified of, and I know it's only because she lost her parents, who she worshiped even more than herself. Now they are gone, and she feels like the entire half of her body has been ripped and shredded away from her. And, to add more, *I* am adding to her pain by hiding my life from her, after she was so open with me.

Suddenly, as if the day couldn't get any worse with Annie and Blaire's parents dying, she curls her fingers around the peridot stone and yanks the necklace, breaking the cord from where it connected into two. I see the hesitation in her eyes, quickly followed by another splurge of tears, and she throws it at my chest. It falls to my feet with a dull clank, just like my heart.

I rapidly shake my head. "Blaire, please don't do this."

"I want you to go," she says monotonously, with no trace of remorse in her tone or eyes. "Please, I can't handle you being so close to me. I can't handle being near someone who's brought me so much happiness but also pain at the same time. I just . . . I need some time to myself. Just go, Jax. Go before I say something that I know I will regret."

"I am *not* leaving you," I grumble. "I spent my entire time in Detroit obsessed with you, and now that I can finally call you mine, I'm not gonna throw it all away just because you can't *handle* me. You need to let me in, when all you're doing is shutting me out. I am your boyfriend, Blaire. Boyfriends are supposed to cherish and comfort you."

"You can't do that anymore," she says, "because I have no emotions inside of me. Everything around me feels so fake, yet so real at the same time. If I can barely keep myself together, then how can you do the same?" Blaire shakes her head. "Just go, Jax. *Now.*"

I shake my head one last time. "No!"

"Go, you asshole!" she yells at me. "Go and never talk to me ever again! I don't want to see your face! In fact, go to El Paso! I don't want you here at *ALL!*" I think it is over, until she speaks again, seemingly to herself. "You're just like him."

My jaw tightens as I lean into her. "What did you say?"

She shakes her head, regret finally smearing onto her features. "No."

"Say it."

"No, I'm not saying anything."

"Say it!"

"You're just like your father!"

The entire world around me slows down.

Her voice is trembling, tears continuously streaming down her cheeks, and her big green eyes are widened in regret, but I don't care anymore because she said what she had to say. I don't care whether she meant it or not, but I will respect her wishes and leave . . . since clearly she doesn't want me here anymore. I don't want to leave her, but I'll do it.

Just so she can be at peace.

"Okay." I nod. "I'll leave and go to El Paso immediately. I'll do whatever you want me to do, Blaire. But just know . . ." I take a hesitant step forward, our torsos colliding against each other as rain surrounds us, falls on us. "Just know that I still love you, even after what you've said. You can say whatever you want, but I'll *still* love you, if not even more. If that doesn't make you realize just how big of a mistake you're making, then I don't know what will.

"Goodbye, Blaire." The words are like melted steel seeping into my mouth—so wrong, and so repugnant. "I hope you feel better, I really do. I'll see you soon."

I turn around quickly, not able to take in Blaire's scrunched up features. It seems as if she was about to say sorry, or say *something,* but I can't bring myself to hear that anymore. I don't want to leave her, but if she wants me to, then I will. I don't want to make her even more upset. I would never do that to her.

I hope one day she heals and she comes back to me. Even as I'm walking away, rain pounding against my skin so hard it starts to hurt, I miss her unbearably. The moments we'll share together have now come to an end, but I don't want them to. I *don't.*

Every step I take away from Blaire is a continuous stab to my gut, and I've begun to cry so hard I can't even distinguish it from the rain thundering down on me.

We board on the large aircraft carrier shredding through the fissured runway beneath. The engines thrum in the back, and a pilot seems to bring us in by pushing the entrance doors open. Layla boards first with Tamia in her arms, and then it's Ren, shortly followed by me, Em, and Mallory. I never wanted to leave; I wanted to fight.

I left because she wanted me to.

There's not much space inside the carrier, but that's fine by me. At this point, I have no desire for a considerable life anymore. How can I ever live peacefully, knowing I bring pain to Blaire? But maybe it's not me that's the cause of her pain. Maybe it's because she witnessed her parents die in front of her own eyes, and she has no idea how to distinguish her emotions, and I am the only one who understands her best, so it's only reasonable that she throws them on me.

You are just like your father.

Once we are seated, I lean against the window that begins to rumble as the plane travels over the runway, the seats shaking beneath us. Mallory is sitting beside me, and once we are sprung up into the air, she nudges my shoulder and whispers to me, "I heard what happened with you and Blaire. I'm so sorry."

I squeeze my eyes shut, remembering just how difficult it was to leave Detroit behind and come to Windsor to board the plane. We suggested AJ come too, but he wordlessly shook his head and went back to his usual contemplating. It's just us, but I don't want to be here. I want to be with her, fighting to take our city back. I want to take back what's ours.

You. Are. Just. Like. Your. Father.

"Jax?"

I jump out of my thoughts. "What?"

"Is everything okay?" She immediately shakes her head, chuckling to herself. "All right, that was a dumb question. Of *course* you're not okay."

I attempt to smile, but there's no more happiness left in me anymore. "It's fine, Mallory."

She gives me a half-grin. "I'm here if you ever want to talk. You're my best friend for a reason."

I sigh, taking in her peaceful and comforting features. "Yeah. I know."

The rain pounding against the rattling windows brings me out of my trance and I look out to see clouds smothering the city and beyond, lightning embellishing the sky. God knows why we're flying out here in the first place, but I guess a little thunderstorm couldn't hurt us when there's a major war going on.

I lean against the square of the window, closing my eyes not to sleep, but to try to forget.

But how can I forget when I am constantly reminded of who I really am?

VIGOR

BLAIRE

I REMEMBER WHEN I *was eight years old, and my mama bought a lilac-colored dress for me from the markets. Nico had gotten a boxy radio set, and my unborn little sister got diapers for when she would come out into the world in two months. We couldn't afford it—we couldn't afford much, really—but my mama still bought it.*

Nico wasn't as ecstatic about his boxy radio set as I was for my lilac-colored dress. It hugged my tiny body perfectly, and I remember twirling in front of the cracked mirror, an ear-splitting grin glued onto my face. I remember my mama asking me if I liked it, and I told her that I didn't like it—I loved *it.*

Eventually, I had to take the dress off, and me, Nico, Mama, Papa, and my unborn little sister were seated around our rickety dining table. Mama got toasted sandwiches for us from the supermarket, and we all cut up our different portions on the footlong bread that was on the table. I remember laughing at Nico as a slimy piece of lettuce landed on his tattered shirt, and he scowled at me, flicking my forehead. I remember Papa yelling at Nico to not do that to his younger sister, for which he pouted and I made a funny face at him.

I remember that night, when we all curled up into the same bed as usual, Mama and Papa were telling us that they'll always be there for us, even if the world fell apart. I told them that there's no way they can be here for us if the world fell apart; that's impossible. I remember Mama chuckling, and then sighing as she pressed a kiss to my forehead. I remember my breathing slowing as I curled into her, and she said to me that I should always stay strong no matter what.

Stay strong no matter what.

I lean against the railing of the bridge, watching the jeeps that carry the people leaving from Detroit slowly disappear. ERUSA soldiers roar in the distance, and it's only inevitable they'll come out here, which means we're going to have to shoot at them.

The others have started to gear up—even AJ, who's left his side of the railing and has now joined us, yet he refuses to say more than three words to anyone. I don't blame him for that, though; he lost someone, just like I did. People are bound to detach from life and society when someone they cherish leaves them and this world.

I, on the other hand, haven't left this parameter ever since Jax and the others left for El Paso, which was about ten minutes ago. I don't want to think about him, or the things I said to him before I forced him to leave. I don't want to think about much, really. I just want to close my eyes, imagine me in my mama's arms as she soothes me of all my troubles. Just like she used to when we were all a family.

Were.

At this point, I don't even know if it's my parents leaving me that hurts me the most; it's me attempting to protect them from every single issue and nuisance in this world, just to have them die in front of me. This world is cruel, but I didn't expect it to be *that* cruel. I must have done something truly terrible to deserve something like this. And I do deserve something like this because I am a monster. I've brought nothing but pain for everyone, especially Jax. I couldn't bring it in me to love him anymore because I am emotionally scarred to my bones, and I hurt him. *I know I did.* A part of me wants him back, but the other part of me doesn't because I don't deserve him. He deserves better, someone who's capable of giving their heart to someone else.

I don't even have a heart in me to give anywhere because it was ripped and shredded into pieces the moment I saw my papa on the ground, and the moment I saw my mama *fall* to the ground.

It should've been me. Not her. Not Papa. *Me.*

I go to feel the peridot necklace wrapped around my neck, since I always touch it whenever I feel frustrated or agitated, but a knife twists into my gut the moment I realize it's gone, that I ripped it off me and left it on the ground, right where Jax stood. I loved that necklace, I really did, but I felt as if it were the origin of all my troubles, and I couldn't stand it anymore . . . also because it kept reminding me of Jax. And I didn't want him to be tied down to a woman who's lost all control of herself and her unattainable emotions.

The others have begun to trek into the entrance of the city, gear engulfing them and shouting to others on where to fall back. Meanwhile, I have remained glued to the side of the bridge, my heart heaving at my throat. I want to be down there, fighting for my parents who will never get to see me, Nico, and Em grow up. They won't be able to hold us anymore, and we won't be able to hold them.

They're gone. And there's nothing I can do about it.

The only thing I can do, though, is avenge them and the life they never got to live.

I may be a cold-blooded monster, but I am one with a newfound purpose. I may have no heart, but I do have a mind, and I will use it to my advantage. I may have let go of the only man I've ever loved and ever will love, but I will forever keep him in my heart as the person who's helped me realize who I truly am.

I want to shoot every single one of these damned soldiers, and that damned evil woman. I want to tear them apart with my bare hands, and I want to record their cries just so I can satisfyingly listen to them afterwards. I will not hold back now; I am *never* going to hold back. I want to release all this anguish out of me and kill every person in my way if I have to.

Nothing is holding me back now.

Not even the sliver of sympathy that remains in the tattered pieces of my heart.

So when we all line up at the battlefield, the rain thundering down on us, I gather all the rage burgeoning inside of me and prepare to unleash it on the enemy. I close my eyes, remember my mama's soft laugh and my papa's wise words and keep all the memories close to my heart. I remember who I am and what I came here to do.

As Heidi is about to signal for us to fire, I make eye contact with her. Her eyes soften for a moment—a rare sighting itself. *This is for them,* she mouths to me.

This is for them.

Moments later, Heidi finally gives us the green-light.

And I fire, screaming until there's nothing left inside of me.

END OF BOOK TWO

ACKNOWLEDGMENTS

If you were to tell fourteen-year-old Ruhi that not only would she publish her debut novel four years later, but she would also publish her *second* book eight months later, she would probably burst out in laughter and exclaim, "Are you crazy? How was I ever able to do that?" I would expect I had done it all on my own, when, in reality, I would never have been able to concoct and spit out two dystopian novels in the same year if it weren't for the several people that had helped me throughout this unpredictable yet exhilarating journey.

First, I would like to thank my two editors, Hannah Rossio and Casey Kaiser. Hannah was one of my amazing beta readers who volunteered to fully edit my novel, and Casey is an amazing editor I found from the vast universe known as the internet. I would like to thank both of these extremely helpful women for polishing the utter garbage that was my first draft. I am incredibly indebted to you.

Now that we're on the beta reader spectrum, I'd like to thank my four other beta readers—Alie Woods, Julia Green, Lexee Valy, and Sophia Collie—for taking time out of your day as well and providing helpful thoughts and opinions on my story. I appreciate all you guys have done for me.

I would like to thank my family as well for at least *trying* to understand the crazy process that is *publishing a freaking book* and also trying to understand why I have been up until four in the morning almost everyday. And no, it is not because I was doing homework (sorry, Mom).

Of course, life is always a little bit easier with friends. And while I do have lots of amazing friends (okay, honestly, I really have four friends but let's pretend I have more), there are two people that have supported me tremendously throughout my writing journey: Mahi Patel and Antra Patel. Mahi . . . I cannot possibly thank you enough for all you have done for me. You have read the most *vile* stories I have ever produced when I used to write on Wattpad and *still* continue to have faith in me and my stories. And Antra . . . I don't even know where to start with you. You know the ins and outs of my life, especially my writing life. You know how much writing truly means to me, and you help me realize my potential whenever I start to doubt myself. I love you both so much.

Perhaps my greatest supporters of all have to be my readers who would probably support me until the world probably ended. No, seriously, someone DM'd me the other day that they would endure a whole war if it meant they could read the third book in this series. That just goes to show how *die-hard* my readers are, and words cannot possibly explain how thankful I am for each and every one of you—whoever you are. If it weren't for you guys, and the 18,000 followers I have on my WriterTok account, I would never have faith in myself. So, thank you for pushing me and making me realize just how far I've come. I love you guys so much.

Okay, I know this is getting pretty long, but bear with me, please.

Lastly, I'd like to thank myself. And yes, I know what you're thinking: *Ruhi, you thanked yourself in the acknowledgments for* Subversion *too. Isn't that a bit self-righteous of you?* And while you may be very correct, I have to say this at the very least . . . writing this book was very hard. Not only did I stay up much longer than I wanted to some nights, I also went into a dark place, especially when I wrote the hardest parts of this book. *Subversion* may have been dark, but *Conversion* was even darker —and God knows how the third book's going to be. But I love this series, and I'm going to keep writing it because it has a special place in my heart. So, again, I'd like to thank me for all my hard work and pushing myself regardless of how much I didn't want to write somedays. If anything, my determination was well-worth it in the end.

Sorry. *Now* we're done.

All attempted humor aside, I'd like to wrap up by saying . . . *thank you* for reading this book. I promise you the third book is going to be twice the action and intensity in comparison to the first two books—if not more. And, in all honesty, you're probably going to need a box of tissues.

And in even more honesty . . . I might need it, too.

Love you guys. :)

Printed in Great Britain
by Amazon

16464514R00263